One Summer

Roisin Meaney

W F HOWES LTD

This large print edition published in 2013 by
W F Howes Ltd
Unit 4, Rearsby Business Park, Gaddesby Lane,
Rearsby, Leicester LE7 4YH

1 3 5 7 9 10 8 6 4 2

First published in Ireland in 2012
by Hachette Books Ireland

A CIP catalogue record for this book is available
from the British Library

ISBN 978 1 47124 437 7

Typeset by Palimpsest Book Production Limited,
Falkirk, Stirlingshire
Printed and bound by
www.printondemand-worldwide.com of Peterborough, England

Mixed Sources
Product group from well-managed
forests, and other controlled sources
www.fsc.org Cert no. TT-COC-002641
FSC © 1996 Forest Stewardship Council

PEFC Certified
This product is
from sustainably
managed forests
and controlled
sources
PEFC www.pefc.org
PEFC/16-33-415

This book is made entirely of chain-of-custody materials

For Gru, who left the party much too soon

If you leave Dublin in good time and drive in a south-westerly direction you will, after four hours or thereabouts, arrive at a small car-ferry terminal with a little slanting pier – the width, perhaps, of three vehicles – that sticks its toe into the Atlantic Ocean. If you park in the designated waiting area and get out to stretch your legs you'll be met, as you open the car door, by a wash of pure fresh salt air, by the heartbreaking call of seagulls, by the intermittent slap of water against stone.

If you stand at the edge of the pier and look out to sea you'll catch a glimpse, on a clear day, of a landmass sitting on the horizon, cradled between the two outermost edges of the bay on whose coastline you stand. If you drive on to the modest ferry when it arrives – every twenty minutes, with room for eight cars – you will cover at a leisurely pace the fourteen nautical miles that separate the mainland from the most westerly of Ireland's islands, barely seven miles long by four wide.

And if you disembark and drive through the little village, past its two pubs and single hair salon and three cafés and scatter of craft shops and art galleries, if you continue on past the graveyard and the creamery and the holy well, if you ignore signs for the lighthouse and the beaches and the prehistoric remains, and keep to the main artery as it winds upwards towards the highest of the island's cliffs, you'll come at last to the end of the road.

And there, two feet or more beyond the safety fence, stuck into the most outlying promontory and pointing straight out into the Atlantic, you will see a sign that looks like any other road sign you'll have passed along the way. The sign reads, *The Statue of Liberty: 3,000 miles*, and it has stood on that spot for as long as the oldest islander can remember.

And nobody – not the local county council or any of the island's three hundred and forty-seven year-round inhabitants – has the smallest idea where it came from.

Welcome to Roone.

DECEMBER:
THE PLAN

'Six weeks,' she said, tipping powder into the drawer of the washing-machine. 'That's all it would take.'

Silence.

She slid the drawer shut and turned to look at him. 'Honey? What do you think?'

Still no response. His back to her, leaning into the radiator as he looked out at the garden, or pretended to. Not much to see in the dark.

She pressed buttons and the washing-machine growled into life and got to work. 'Forty-two measly days, that's all,' she said. 'What's that in the grand scheme of things? Nothing.'

'Hardly nothing.'

She shouldn't have converted it to days: forty-two did sound like a lot. 'OK, it's not exactly nothing. But what's a few weeks when we've got the rest of our lives together?'

The words caused a lick of delight inside her. The rest of their lives: thousands of days ahead of them. She wiped down the draining-board and squeezed the dishcloth into the sink, smiling at the water that dribbled down the plughole. Smiling at everything, these days, she was. Happy as a pig in muck, she was.

They were getting married. In September he'd asked for her hand in marriage, down on bended knee on the beach, and she'd said yes – no, she'd shouted yes, pulling him up to waltz with him into the oncoming rush of water, laughing at his protests. And next December, on her thirty-fourth birthday, they were going to bind themselves to each other till death them did part.

Years and years ahead of them, barring any nasty accidents or diseases. Assuming that neither of them crossed paths with a crazed gunman or boarded a plane that was destined to have an encounter with a tall building.

'Promise me we'll always travel together,' she said, reaching behind to untie her apron. 'In planes, I mean.' If she was going to be flown into a skyscraper she wanted him right there next to her, squeezing her hand all the way to eternity.

He turned. 'What?'

She often puzzled him, poor love. She dropped the apron on the draining-board and regarded him happily. 'Oh, nothing,' she said. 'Just thinking out loud.'

Look at those cat-green eyes, that adorably full bottom lip, the silky muddy-blond hair that just begged to be tousled. Look how lucky she was, the luckiest girl on Roone.

They were different, oh, just about as different as two people could be. He was the cautious one, always planning for the future; she liked diving into days without a plan.

Her wardrobe was full of things that didn't go with any other things. He shopped for clothes once a year, with a list; he was lost without a list. She regularly ran out of phone credit. He had new toiletries waiting when the old ones were still a quarter full.

He frowned at her; she laughed at him. He didn't get the way her mind skipped ahead of itself sometimes, darting from one idea into another without waiting for anyone to catch up. He was more the one-logical-step-at-a-time kind of person – which meant, of course, that he was ideal for her. She needed somebody logical in her life, to grab her when she veered too far off course. They were the perfect match, polar opposites irresistibly drawn towards each other.

Tim, of course, had been scandalised when Nell told him she'd bought the first house she'd looked at, three years earlier at the ripe old age of thirty. It had belonged to Seánín Fionn, seventh son of a seventh son, and recently deceased after eighty-seven years of healing that no doctor could achieve, or explain.

The house was in need of much redecorating – Seánín Fionn's interests had lain beyond wallpapering and painting – but as soon as Nell had stepped through the peeling front door she had experienced the strangest rush of well-being, as if she was doing something exactly right. '*Oh –*' she'd said, causing the estate agent, who'd come all the way from Dingle, to ask if anything was wrong.

'No,' she'd told him, her hand pressed to her happily fluttering heart, 'nothing's wrong, nothing at all.'

And if she'd had any doubts after that that this was the house for her, they'd been banished by the black and white dog that was still hanging around the property, looking hungry and sad, it seemed to Nell.

'Is anyone feeding him?' she'd asked the estate agent. 'Are you trying to find him a home?'

The young man – whose name, he'd told her, was Brendan, and whose stiff new shirt collar was chafing his neck – was clearly doing nothing of the sort. 'I've had no instruction about the dog,' he'd said, ushering Nell through to the little sitting room, pushing a bent metal coat hanger out of the way with the shiny toe of his black shoe. 'He's not really our concern.'

Not their concern, shivering outside the window, looking in at him and Nell with an expression that said, 'Don't you care? Doesn't anyone care about me any more?'

On the spot she'd made an offer. She'd gone straight from the house to the supermarket for a plastic pouch of dog food, and brought it back to him. She'd torn it open and placed it on the lawn, and he'd gobbled its contents, licked it clean and looked hopefully up at her, tail wagging. A week later she'd signed the contract. Every day in between she'd returned to the garden with her dinner leftovers, and rashers stolen from her mother's fridge.

A month later, having kept up the daily feeds, she'd got the keys and moved in with a stack of books, a microwave and a camp bed. Her new neighbour, whom she already knew, of course, this being Roone – and who'd also, she discovered, been on dog-feeding duty – had told her that the animal was called John Silver, and Nell had been happy to leave that unchanged. It was perfect for him, with the black patch around his right eye. They'd taken to each other wonderfully.

And from the start, it was as if the house had accepted Nell too. She'd lain in her camp bed at night, deliciously drowsy, smelling the fresh paint and wood varnish that no amount of open windows would banish – it would leave when it was good and ready – and she'd felt safe and cherished, and truly at home. Maybe it was Seánín Fionn, sending gentle good wishes from whatever dimension he'd travelled to.

'I can't believe you bought the first house you saw,' Tim had said. 'You didn't even look at any others?'

'I loved it as soon as I walked in,' Nell had told him, 'and it loved me back. And this is Roone, remember; I could have been waiting ages for another to come up. And, anyway, this house had a dog going with it, and he needed me.'

Tim had opened his mouth again, no doubt to

put forward another argument. Nell had felt obliged to put an end to it by kissing him.

And now here she was, trying to plan ahead for once, like he was always telling her to do. You'd think he'd be delighted, but he wasn't showing an ounce of enthusiasm. Clearly, more work was needed, which didn't bother Nell at all. She had a history of getting her own way with him.

She brushed a scattering of crumbs from the tablecloth into her hand. 'Houses around here are getting four hundred euro a week in July and August,' she said. 'Two bedrooms, just like this one. In six weeks we'd make well over two thousand euro.'

'We don't need two thousand euro,' Tim said. 'You know I'll pay for the wedding, I've said I will. You know I can well afford it.'

'And you know I'm not going to let you,' she replied, 'because I'm stubborn and independent, and all those other things you love about me.'

'I don't love *everything* about you.'

She adored the huskiness a head cold gave to his voice. She walked over to him and slid an arm around his waist. 'Oh, yes,' she said softly, standing on tiptoe to kiss his chin, 'you do.'

He didn't care what kind of a wedding they had, or honeymoon. He'd get married in this kitchen if she'd let him, and book into a B&B in Ballybunion for a week afterwards – and lovely as Ballybunion was for a summer afternoon stroll along that magnificent beach, Nell was aiming a bit higher for her honeymoon. As high as Barbados, maybe, or Bali.

'Come on,' she said, burrowing into his neck. 'Say you'll think about it, at least.'

He sighed. 'Honestly, Nell, I'd rather not. For one thing – well, the main thing, really – where would we live if a bunch of strangers moved in here? Have you thought about that at all?'

'Oh, who cares?' she said. 'Anyway, that's only a minor detail for you – aren't you in Dublin most of the time?'

From Monday to Friday he worked in the capital, and lived in the apartment he'd bought several years earlier, right in the centre of the city. Nell had been to it twice, and had no particular wish to return. Their life was on Roone.

'I spend every weekend here,' he said. 'Are you suggesting we camp out on the beach for six weeks?'

She laughed. '*I* would, no problem – God, it would be fabulous – but I can't see you sleeping under the stars, even for one night.'

'Well, I'm glad we're agreed on that at least. As far as I can see, our only option would be to move in with your folks and, no offence, I'm not sure I'd fancy that.'

'No . . .'

She'd already decided that bringing Tim to live in her parents' house was out of the question. The smallest bedroom had been converted into her father's office for years, which left Nell's old room

– and she wouldn't ask them to let her and Tim sleep together in there, not when she knew they wouldn't be comfortable with it. What she did in her own house they accepted was her business, but under their roof she was happy for their standards to apply.

No need to point that out now, though, when Tim had already vetoed the idea of moving in with them.

'And James wouldn't have room for both of us,' he went on, 'not that I'd be rushing to stay there either.'

'I suppose not.' She'd ruled out James too: his house was small for two, let alone four, although he'd probably have been fine with it, bless him.

'So what do you suggest?' Tim asked. 'And, yes, it does matter to me where we live. It matters a lot.'

She was going to have to break it gently. 'Well,' she said, playing with a button of his flannel shirt, 'I was thinking of that room off the salon.'

He caught her hand. 'The room off the salon? You're not serious. It's tiny – and it's full of junk.'

'Actually, it's not junk, it's my supplies. But they could be cleared out, we could make it lovely and cosy.'

'Cosy is the word,' he said. 'Cosy enough not to be able to swing a cat.'

She let a beat pass. 'How long have you been living in this house?' she asked.

He looked down at her. 'About . . . eight months, isn't it? What's that got to do with anything?'

'In eight months,' she said, 'you have never once swung a cat. What makes you think you'd suddenly get the urge if we moved out?'

'Be serious.' He drew away from her and went to look out into the darkness again. She could feel the disapproval coming off him in waves. He plunged his hands into his pockets, and she heard coins clinking off one another. He always jingled his coins when he was thinking.

'You sound like Santa,' she said. 'Jingle bells.'

He turned to face her. 'The whole thing is daft,' he said. 'I've offered to pay for the wedding. You know I can easily afford it, but you insist on doing it your way and, frankly, your way just sounds plain daft.'

'It's not daft, it's . . . innovative,' she said, damping down a flick of irritation. 'Look, try to see the big picture. It's my wedding day, the only one I'm planning to have, and I'd really love to splash out with a clear conscience. If you were paying for the whole thing I'd feel like I had to watch what I spent, and just once in my life I want to go mad. Just this once.'

He shrugged. 'Still makes no sense to me,' he said. 'You could spend what you like, I wouldn't care. But this is your house, you're the boss.'

She resisted the urge to cross the room and slap him, hard. He could be like a two-year-old sometimes. As if she'd lay down the law because the house they shared had her name on the title deeds, as if she'd ever used her ownership of the house to her advantage in the eight months since he'd moved in.

At this stage, she considered it as much his house as hers. He paid half the mortgage and the entire electricity bill, and he'd bought the garden furniture and the bathroom cabinet and the rug in front of the sitting-room fireplace. It was their house in everything but name – and of course she'd change that when she got around to it.

And she wasn't trying to lay down the law here, for goodness' sake – she was just attempting to persuade him, in the gentlest way possible, to let her contribute to the expense of their wedding. Because there would be expense, a lot of it.

She thought of the dress she'd seen in a Killarney boutique, how it had slithered down over her bra and pants as if all its life it had been waiting for her to come along and lift it off the hanger. The perfect fit of it, the off-the-shoulder, handmade-silk-flower sexiness of it – not to mention the colour, which was the palest sea-green: how absolutely perfect was that? Who wanted boring white on their wedding day, especially if they were lucky enough to live in a place that was surrounded by the sea?

And the teeny triangular buttons tinker-tailoring down the bodice; triangular, not heart-shaped. Nothing sissy about that dress. That dress had serious attitude.

But attitude didn't come cheap. Attitude cost almost as much as Nell earned in a month cutting hair – and the bed she wanted them to begin married life in cost almost as much as the dress. And she was pretty sure that the two-week honeymoon she was planning would cost much, much more.

Two thousand euro certainly wouldn't cover everything – it wouldn't come close. Tim would still be footing most of the bill, and she had no qualms about that. His computer programmer's salary was ridiculously high, even during these tighten-your-belt times. He'd easily cover whatever was left after she'd spent the money they'd get from letting the house.

But she still had to sell the idea to him. She approached him again and leant into his back. 'I know it's daft,' she said, sliding her arms around his chest. 'I know it'll be a pain. But it'll make me happy, and it's the only thing I've asked you for since we met.'

'You asked me to stop wearing white socks,' he said.

She smiled. They were on the right track: he was lightening up. 'Yes, I did – but that was for your own good. I'd have had to leave you otherwise, and you would have been heartbroken.'

'You made me cut my hair.'

'Again, in your own interest.'

'And switch to boxers.'

'Oh, please – ask any woman which she prefers. I can't believe you got away with those other horrors for so long.'

He turned to face her at last. He cupped her chin in his hand. 'I wish I didn't love you,' he said. 'Life was so much easier before we met.'

She laughed. 'Come on, you don't expect me to believe that. I'm the best thing that ever happened to you.'

He pulled her into his chest. She took that as agreement. 'We're getting *married*,' she said, pressing against him and closing her eyes, hearing the gentle rattle of his breathing beneath the shirt and the thermal vest, smelling the comforting warmth of the eucalyptus-scented ointment she'd smeared earlier on his chest. 'It'll be worth it, I promise. We'll have the perfect wedding and honeymoon, and I'll never ask you for another thing.'

'Can I have that in writing?'

'You're joking, aren't you?' She stood on tiptoe and kissed his cheek. 'I'll show you the website I found. It's very safe. We can dictate all the conditions, say what's allowed and what's not. Pets or no pets, that kind of thing. And no smoking, obviously.'

'Smoking?' he asked sharply, drawing back. 'We could get *smokers* staying here?'

Damn. Three steps forward, two back.

'No, we couldn't. We'd make it clear that smoking in the house wasn't on. People are used to it now – everyone goes outside to smoke. That wouldn't be a problem at all.'

It was two days before Christmas. In just under

a year she would stop being Nell Mulcahy and start being Nell Baker. She loved the idea of taking his name and making it hers – and Mrs Baker sounded so cosy. Mrs Baker had rosy cheeks and wore a checked apron and made the best apple tarts in town. All the children loved Mrs Baker because she gave them homemade lemonade and chocolate-chip cookies when they called round.

'Do you think children prefer chocolate-chip cookies or cupcakes?' she asked.

'What?'

'Nothing.'

'So,' he said, 'you're proposing that we both squeeze into that tiny room at the weekends.'

'Well, if you really hate the thought of it you could ask James if you could stay with him. I'm sure he wouldn't mind.'

They weren't close, not the way Nell imagined two siblings should be. At forty, James was five years older than Tim. He lived with his son in a house that had been built as a holiday home, with small rooms and little storage space, but he and Andy seemed to manage fine. And they had three bedrooms, so there would be room for Tim.

'You could talk to James,' she said. 'Just put it to him and see how he reacts.' It wasn't as if they didn't get on, they were just very different. 'But I'd miss you.'

'Would you?'

'Course I would.'

Nell and James got on wonderfully well. He was

quieter than Tim, and creative where Tim was logical. He painted houses around the island and beyond, and occasionally he worked behind the bar in Fitz's. And when he wasn't painting walls he painted canvases, with considerable skill. His work was on sale in various locations around the country – including, of course, the island's two art galleries – and Nell had a small collection on display in her hair salon. When she and Tim had got engaged James had presented them with a view of the old harbour which was quite beautiful, and which hung above their bed.

'OK,' Tim said.

She drew back to look into his face. 'OK? OK what?'

'We can try the little room,' he said. 'We can give it a go.'

'Only if you're sure,' she said, trying not to look triumphant.

She'd won. She'd got what she wanted. They were on the way to the perfect wedding, followed by the bit where they got to live happily ever after. Mr and Mrs Baker and their large, cheerful family. She planned at least four children, as close in age as she could manage. More, if the humour took her. The biggest family on Roone they might have. 'I don't know how Mrs Baker does it,' everyone would say. 'All those children, and still managing that hair salon and baking all those apple tarts.'

Tim sighed deeply. 'I think,' he said, 'it's going to be a long summer.'

'Not at all,' the future Mrs Baker replied, smiling up at him. 'It'll fly by. Wait and see.'

Katy –
Big news: we're letting the house for the summer! Well, just for six weeks, which should net us over two grand, would you believe? Looks like I'll get the wedding of my dreams after all! Tim not bowled over with the idea but going along to keep me happy, bless him. So in January we'll register with a holiday-home letting website and see what happens – watch this space! Hope all's well, happy new year, let's hope it's a good one!
N xxx

Nell
Letting the house, great idea – maybe I'll book it myself and FINALLY get to meet you! Keep me posted – and on all the wedding plans, of course. I'm back at work already, no rest for the wicked, but there's a big company party planned for the 31st, so I'll be ringing in the new year with a splash . . . and hopefully not holding my head for too long afterwards! Happy new year to you and Tim,
K xxx

JANUARY

'They're asking for a security question,' Nell said. 'They want the name of my first best friend, or my mother's maiden name, or my favourite movie star.'

'I should choose my mother's maiden name,' Walter replied. 'The others are all subjective, whereas that one is a constant. You won't be trying to remember which person you decided was your best friend, and so on.'

'True.' She clicked on the mouse and began to type. 'Should I write Fitzpatrick with a capital "F"?'

'Oh, yes. Write it exactly how you always do, and that way you won't be wondering.'

She smiled at him. 'I knew you'd be the best person to help me with this.'

Walter wondered privately why she didn't regard her fiancé – who was, after all, far more au fait with computers than Walter – as the most suitable person to help her fill in a form that was located on a computer screen, but he held his tongue. No doubt she had her reasons.

'Right, property description – there's a checklist.

One bathroom, two bedrooms, zero en-suites, zero cots available for infants, number of seats in dining room—' She looked up. 'I don't have a dining room.'

'In that case, put in the number of seats in your kitchen,' Walter said. 'Wherever you eat, I should think.'

'Oh, right. We have only four kitchen chairs – but I could borrow one or two from Mam and Dad. Then again, the house only sleeps four.'

'Perhaps your couch could sleep a fifth?'

She looked doubtful. 'Well, we have had the odd pal spending the night on it, but only for a weekend, and they weren't paying. I'm not sure I'd fancy sleeping on it myself.'

'I should leave it at four then.'

'Yes, four is plenty, so four chairs will do.' She scrolled down. 'Maximum number of people accepted – four.' She stopped again. 'Does four sound too few, though? Am I limiting my chances of getting people?'

'Not at all. A couple, or a couple and two children, or a small group of friends. Plenty of scope, I should think.'

'OK, four it is then . . . Next is external features. What external features have I?'

'Patio with furniture,' Walter offered. 'Front and rear landscaped gardens.'

'Doesn't sound very exciting, does it? Maybe I could get a barbecue. Must ask James where he got his . . . Right, here's a box for additional information. What can we add?'

'Scenic island location. Adjacent to beautiful beach.'

'Is half a mile adjacent?'

'Absolutely. Walking distance to village with shops, pubs, cafés. Numerous walks, suitable for cyclists, tourist attractions such as lighthouse, prehistoric remains, holy well—'

'Slow down.' She tapped the keys rapidly. 'Right, holiday type, another checklist. Let's see . . . not city, not winter sun, not ski. Yes, beach, yes, relaxing, yes, walking holiday, yes, village, yes, waterfront, yes, seaside. That should do it.'

'Another sherry?' Walter asked, sneaking a look at the clock on the opposite wall.

Nell shook her head. 'Better not, thanks . . . Sports and activities, oh dear, no horse riding, no golf, no tennis, no skiing, no pony trekking – oh, thank goodness, fishing, cycling, surfing, walking. I thought I wasn't going to be able to tick any of the boxes.'

They made their way through arrival details, availability and rental rates, and then Walter decided the time had come to speak up. 'In fact,' he said apologetically, 'it's getting on for one o'clock, so perhaps we'd better—'

'Lord, it's not, is it?' Nell flipped the laptop closed. 'Sorry, Walter, I lost track. Come on, I'll grab my books and meet you outside.'

The mobile library visited Roone every Monday and parked on the main street for two hours from eleven till one. Nell and Walter rarely missed a visit, being equally greedy bookworms, even if Walter's literary tastes ran more towards gardening and biographies, and Nell favoured whodunits and historical romances.

Nell covered the mile to the village in her yellow Beetle far too quickly for Walter's heart, but thankfully, the night's sub-zero temperatures hadn't caused problems on the dry roads, and they made it safely with minutes to choose their new books. Walter opted to walk home afterwards, saying he needed one or two things in the supermarket.

'Oh, but I'll wait for you.'

'No need,' he assured her. 'The walk will do me good.'

'Well, let me take your books at least, I'll drop them over later – or will you come to dinner tonight? Oh, do, I'm trying out a beef casserole, with apricots. Come around seven.'

She was the best of neighbours, generous and reliable. He'd miss having her around for six weeks. Not that she'd be gone far, of course – nowhere was far on Roone. And it might be interesting to have new faces across the stone wall from him, just for a little while.

He walked along the village street, humming the first few bars of 'Three Little Maids From School Are We', and wondering what business apricots could possibly have in a beef casserole.

'Tim,' his boss said, 'how's the Dickinson job coming along?'

26

Tim clicked an icon on his screen and a new dialogue box popped up. 'Fine. Should have it for you by end of play on Thursday.'

'Any hope of a bit earlier? I've just had a call from Liam Heneghan at Slattery's – a few of them are coming in to talk to us first thing on Wednesday about overhauling their system, and you know they always want things done yesterday.'

Earlier than Thursday would mean late nights from now till he delivered. The price you paid for a fat salary. 'No problem.'

His boss vanished. Tim slid open his desk drawer and took out the sandwich he'd bought on his way to work. Crab and cucumber on rye, same as he always got. Routine soothed him the way the sea seemed to soothe Nell. He pressed the intercom button.

'Yes.' As usual, his secretary sounded as if he was an inconvenience to her day, but her superb organisational skills made him put up with her.

'I'll take a black coffee, please.'

She disconnected without a response. Tim opened the cardboard box that housed his sandwich, still studying the screen. Below his third-floor window cars passed in unending jittery lines. Horns blared constantly, drivers rushing to appointments, impatient with anyone who got in their way.

He loved it all. He thrived on the pressure, the fast-paced feel of it. He bit into his sandwich and tapped in rapid bursts at his keyboard. When his coffee arrived he barely looked up. Sorting out system glitches, devising new programs to ensure that companies ran smoothly, this was what he was good at, why they paid him a laughably high wage. Some days he didn't have time to think of Nell, so heavy was his workload. When she did cross his mind, when he pictured her in the hair salon, or rowing around the harbour in her little boat, it was with a sense of unreality, as if Roone existed only in his imagination. A wonderful fantasy undoubtedly, but a fantasy nonetheless.

And try as he might, he found it desperately hard to imagine what it would be like when he lived there all the time.

'I was thinking of a buffet.'

Henry Manning, third-generation proprietor, manager and general dogsbody of Manning's Hotel, peered at Nell over the top of his green-framed glasses. 'A buffet? At the end of December? Really, Nell?'

'Well, a hot one, of course.'

'Yes,' he said doubtfully. 'Hot.'

'It's just that you could fit in more people, couldn't you, with a buffet?'

The buttons on Henry's flowered waistcoat strained slightly in their buttonholes as his chest advanced in Nell's direction. 'Well, of course, our dining room can accommodate eighty-eight comfortably, and we can always manoeuvre things to squeeze in another table or two. How many guests were you actually thinking of inviting?'

Might as well come out with it. 'It could be about two hundred and fifty, Henry.'

To give the hotelier his due, the only indication that Nell's response had alarmed him in any way came from his pencil, whose point, resting against his clipboard, snapped. Henry waved away the graphite fragments and adjusted his glasses. 'I see. Two hundred and fifty.'

'I know it's a lot,' Nell said hurriedly, 'but there are so many I'd love to invite.'

She wanted them all there – she'd bring the whole of Roone to the wedding if she could. She wanted as many people as possible to share her happiness, to see how perfect a married couple she and Tim were going to be.

Henry regarded her over his glasses. She remembered him standing in the hotel lobby the day she'd made her first holy communion, presenting each child who entered with a silver balloon that said *Congratulations*.

'Of course we'll certainly do everything we can to make sure you have the day you want,' he said. 'If you need us to feed two hundred and fifty, it will be done.'

Poor man was probably having palpitations at the thought. Nell thanked him warmly, promising to come back as soon as she and Tim had final numbers. Tim's guests were few, which was just as well – his mother, James and Andy, and a small handful of cousins.

Outside the hotel the frosty air sliced into her

lungs. So calm the sea was today, as still as a mirror, reflecting the milk-white sky. She looked across at the mainland, imagined the miles and miles of tar and cement and whatever else that separated her from Tim. Dublin was another world.

She untied John Silver's leash from the bicycle rack and they set off for home.

'So, how's the new term going?'

Her father turned a page of his *Time* magazine. Thank goodness for Walter, or her customers, male and female, would be limited to *Hello!* and *Marie Claire*. 'Fine so far. Things don't generally start to drag till February.'

Nell bent to snip at the cat hairs on his neck. 'And then you have the mid-term, and St Patrick's Day not long after that.'

'True, won't feel it. Any bald patch back there yet?'

'No, you're lucky. Poor Jimmy Cullen has started, and he's not even thirty.'

'Jimmy Cullen . . . I don't think he ever came to school for a full week. He spent more time on the sea than in the classroom.'

She laughed. 'You're such a principal. And hasn't he done fine, with his little bait-and-tackle business now? Mind you, I've never once got a tip from him, so maybe he didn't learn all he needed.' She straightened. 'There, that's you done.'

As she swept off his cape and handed him a

clothes brush the salon door opened and her next customer came in.

'Look at that for timing,' Nell said, taking Denis's empty cup from the ledge under the mirror. 'Tea or coffee for you, Nora? I've a lovely cake today, apple cinnamon, made with Walter's magic apples.'

'Aren't you terrible, to be tempting us like that. I'll have tea, love, lots of milk, one sugar.' Nora lowered her supermarket bags to the floor and dropped her scarf on the back of the nearest chair. 'Isn't it a shocking cold day, Denis?'

'Desperate altogether,' he agreed, lifting his overcoat from its hook and opening his wallet as Nell returned.

'The house is up,' she said. 'Walter helped me.'

'That's good . . . How're things otherwise? Any news?'

'That's it? Have you nothing else to say about it?'

'What else is there to say? You've put the house on the website, end of story.'

'You could show a bit more interest. You could ask if anyone had viewed it.'

'Has anyone viewed it?'

'I don't know. There doesn't seem to be any facility for checking that. But you could have asked.'

She heard his deep intake of breath. She imagined the look on his face. 'I've gone ahead and booked the hotel,' she told him. 'Henry didn't quite faint when I said two hundred and fifty guests, but he looked like he wanted to.'

'Nell, are you quite sure you want that many?'

'Don't start – we've had this conversation. They're my friends, I want them there.'

'OK . . . Anything else?'

'Mam won a tenner on a scratchcard,' she told him. 'She bought five more cards with her winnings, all duds. Dad told her it's a mug's game, and she nearly killed him.'

He laughed. 'I miss you,' he said.

'Me too. You will get down at the weekend, won't you?'

'Should do, they're forecasting a thaw tomorrow.'

'Yes, I heard that. Drive carefully, take your time, last ferry's not till ten. Love you.'

'Me too.'

> *Katy –*
>
> *One step closer to the perfect wedding – house is gone up on the website this week. My lovely neighbour Walter went through the horrendously detailed form with me, I decided to spare Tim the ordeal! Fingers crossed that someone will actually want the house – better spruce it up a bit between now and July. And I booked the hotel for the reception, so that's sorted too. Hope all's well with you – isn't it freezing? Donegal looks fabulous on the news, but I suppose it's tough for the people living there. Tim hasn't been able to get down for the past two weekends, the roads are so bad.*
>
> *N xxx*

Nell –

Haven't been home myself in three weeks, simply can't get there. Dublin is relatively easy to get around, though, one of the many benefits of living in the big city, whatever you say about it! Great that the house is up on the site – are there photos? I must look it up and check it out! Keep me posted on bookings. Great news about the hotel being booked, brings it that bit closer. I look forward to getting my invite – imagine, we'll actually meet this year!

Keep warm on your little island,

K xxx

FEBRUARY

'Would you like a job?'

Her mother whisked briskly as she dripped oil into a bowl of vinegar, mustard and deep orange egg yolks. 'What do you mean, would I like a job? In case you haven't noticed, I already have a job.'

'I know, but this would be during the summer holidays, just a few hours once a week.'

Moira glanced up, still whisking. 'I assume this has got something to do with you letting the house.'

'Yes, it has.'

'I still don't know why you won't just let me and your father help out. Parents are supposed to pay for their daughter's wedding.'

'Not any more, not since couples can do it themselves. And I'm determined, so you can save your breath.'

Moira shook her head. 'You sound like me at your age. So what's this job then?'

'I was wondering if you'd like to manage the changeovers every Saturday. I'll be at work so I won't be able to. I was asking Hugh at lunchtime if he could think of anyone I could ask, and he suggested you.'

'Did he now.' The last of the oil trickled into the bowl. Moira went on whisking as her mix emulsified into a thick, creamy gloop. 'My little brother is sorting out holiday work for me.'

'Well, he knew you'd be perfect – and I'd pay, of course.'

'I should hope so. Get me those jars, would you? So what would this job involve?'

Nell passed across the three waiting jars and watched as her mother began to spoon in the mayonnaise. 'Well, cleaning the house when one group leaves, getting it ready for the next, meeting them when they arrive and settling them in. That's it, really.' She caught a dribble of mayonnaise as it slid down the side of a jar, and brought it to her mouth. 'Mm, hope one of those is for me.'

'It is, of course, and you can bring one to Walter and tell him his egg yolks are in it. So I'd be making beds, hoovering, washing floors.'

'That kind of thing, yes.'

Moira brought her empty bowl to the sink. 'And Saturday is the changeover day.'

'Well, that's what most of the other properties on the website were putting so I just went along with it. Mind you, as nobody has attempted to book the house yet, that may change – or it may never happen, I suppose.'

'Oh, I'm sure it will. It's early days, most people

38

don't think about summer holidays till Easter. And Roone is always popular in the summer.'

'Hope you're right.' Nell screwed lids on to the jars. 'And I've said they must be out by eleven, and the new ones can't come till two at the earliest, so you'd have time enough to get the place clean.'

'Three hours – yes, that should be plenty for your house, assuming nobody leaves it like a dump.' Moira took labels from the press and began writing. 'I wouldn't mind doing it, I suppose. You said six weeks you're letting it for.'

'Yes, no more than six. Tim is showing a distinct lack of interest in the proceedings.'

'Don't mind him, he's only here at weekends. But do you think you'll cope with living beside the salon? You know you could come here, and let Tim use the other at weekends.'

'Thanks, Mam, but I'm sure I'll be fine. Once I tidy up the room it'll be grand.'

'You'll have no shower, though.'

'No . . . I might come here, if that's OK, after work. And when Tim is around he can use James's shower.'

'Of course that's OK – and what about a bed? You could have your own from here.'

'I was hoping you'd say that.' Her old bed was a single, so weekends would be a bit of a squeeze, but no need to mention that now. And sharing a single bed with Tim wasn't something she could imagine objecting to. 'So you'll do it?'

'I will, why not? I'll be looking for something to do in the holidays.'

Moira worked five mornings a week as secretary in Roone's primary school, where her husband was principal. The arrangement had been in place for more than eight years, since the old secretary had left the island to get married, and Moira had taken over in the school office, with her husband as her boss – in name, at least. The arrangement, as far as Nell could see, suited both her parents.

'Now,' Moira went on, sticking labels to the jars, 'since the eggs are from Walter's hens this'll be fine for a fortnight, so that's the date I've put on it. Make sure you mention that to Walter, in case he doesn't notice.'

Nell took the two jars. 'He'll be delighted.'

'Will you stay to dinner? We're having lasagne.'

'I won't, thanks – I'm having James and Andy over, I've a chicken in the oven. But if you want to put my name in the pot for tomorrow night . . .'

She hated eating alone. Food was made for sharing, so she did her best to find someone to share it with. Walter from next door was a regular visitor – he repaid her with eggs and honey – and her uncle Hugh often came too, when he wasn't working behind his bar. Her house, she always felt, was happiest with company around, and so was she.

'Mind the roads,' her mother warned, as Nell wrapped her pale pink cashmere scarf – a Christmas

40

present from Tim – tightly around her. 'After all that rain they'll be tricky.'

They were lucky on the island. The sea helped to keep things mellow, stopped the roads icing over except on the bitterest of days, softened the rare snow they saw, melted the frost quickly. Just another reason to adore it, as Nell did.

She drove home carefully, avoiding the water-filled ditches, taking the bends gently. As she parked outside her house James's car appeared from the opposite direction. She stood waiting as he pulled up, hands dug into her pockets against the chill.

'I hope this doesn't mean you haven't started cooking our dinner,' he said, climbing out.

'Don't worry, there's a chicken in the oven. I had to run something by Mam.'

'That's OK then.' He hugged her briefly, and she caught the tang of white spirit.

'You've been painting.'

He rubbed a hand across his face as they drew apart. 'I had a shower – did I miss a bit?'

'No, all gone – I'm just psychic. Hi there,' she added to Andy, as he came around from the passenger side. No hug: fourteen-year-old boys didn't hug older women, even if they were going to be related to them by marriage soon.

'Hey,' he replied, hunched into his leather jacket, navy beanie pulled low on his forehead. She wondered if he only wore it when he knew he was going to meet her.

'Hungry?' she asked, and he nodded, giving her a quick smile.

'And frozen,' James said. 'Are you ever going to let us in?'

Nell turned towards the house. 'You're such a bully. I'm telling your brother when he comes.'

'Yeah, Tim got all the manners in the family.'

When she opened the front door he walked straight into the sitting room and picked up the scuttle to add coal to her simmering fire. Nell loved how familiar he was: it made her feel as if they were already brother and sister – for that's what they would be in less than a year. The thought made her grin with delight. Her very first brother, and a brand new nephew.

'Come on,' she said to Andy, who'd crouched to say hello to John Silver. 'You can help me make the gravy.'

Nell's mother was going to be cleaning Nell's house. He found the thought vaguely unsettling.

'It's as much your house as mine,' Nell kept assuring him. 'We're together, we're sharing every-thing, right? You've taken on half the expenses. So it's our house, not mine.'

But Tim still thought of it as more hers than his. Not that he didn't love it – who wouldn't love a quaint little cottage by the sea? It was just that she'd bought it and done it up, she'd put her mark on it, long before they'd become reacquainted, long before he'd decided that she was the one he wanted to spend the rest of his life with. Maybe in time he'd come to think of it as theirs, but—

There was a tap on the door and his secretary entered. 'Mr O'Connor would like to see you in his office.'

Tim looked up. 'Did he say what it's about?' His boss didn't normally ask to see him out of the blue.

'No.'

'I'll be right there.'

He saved what he was working on and put his computer into sleep mode, his mind travelling over recently completed jobs. Nothing amiss, all delivered on time.

The thought of Moira in their house, making their bed, cleaning their bath, going through the kitchen cabinets, didn't wholly appeal to him. Not that they didn't get on – he and Moira were fine, no problem there – and they'd be moving anything personal to the attic anyway.

He left his office and made his way down the corridor to Mr O'Connor's.

Moira wasn't really the problem, though, was she? The problem was having to move out of the house, handing it over to strangers for six weeks. Who was to say it wouldn't feel even less like his when he and Nell moved back in?

He straightened his tie and tapped on his boss's door.

Walter Thompson's hair was thinning a little on top,

but otherwise he was carrying his sixty-nine years well. All that healthy eating, his own best customer for the organic vegetables and fruit he grew commercially, for the beautiful big eggs his happy, feathery hens laid for him, and the sea lavender and apple-blossom honey his bees produced.

And when he wasn't reading or tending his business, Walter walked. There wasn't an inch of the island, a grassy hillock, a sandy dune, he hadn't explored. He'd tramped the lanes and pathways, crossed the beaches, scrambled over the rocks. The only thing Walter didn't do was swim. Nell had never known him even to paddle.

'Not my cup of tea,' he'd say, if anyone questioned him. 'Prefer to admire the sea from a distance.'

Walter's father had drowned. Like a lot of island families, including Nell's, the Thompsons had lost a member to the unpredictable tides that surrounded Roone. The waters of the harbour, facing the mainland, were generally safe, but the rest of the island's coastline was respected by the most seasoned fisherman – and the west side, looking towards America, could often be wild and forbidding.

'I hope the hens don't mind this cold winter,' Nell said, lathering shampoo into Walter's hair. 'Haven't seen them out and about much.'

'No, they're lying low – but laying as usual, thank goodness. Your mother's mayonnaise is quite delicious, by the way. I must drop in to thank her.'

'Isn't it lovely? Much nicer than shop-bought stuff. And it didn't take five minutes – I was there.' Nell rinsed away the shampoo and reached for the conditioner. 'She says she'll be my caretaker while the house is being let.'

'Excellent. Now all you need are some tenants.'

'That's right. Let's hope some turn up soon.' She wrapped a warm towel around his head and secured it with a peg. 'Now, we'll let that sink in while I make tea, and you'll have a slice of honey cake. I used that lavender honey you brought to dinner last week and it's given it a wonderful flowery flavour.'

'Sounds quite delicious.'

She hid a smile as she turned away. He still sounded like a country squire, but in the turban he reminded her of a slightly younger Gandhi.

'Hi there.'

'Hi – what's happening?'

'Not much, really. I had James and Andy over last evening for dinner. Andy must have eaten at least half the chicken.'

Tim laughed. 'He's a growing lad . . . Any bite on the house yet?'

She was pleased he'd asked, even if he was probably hoping nobody would want it. 'Not yet, early days. How's work?'

'Fine, busy . . . Actually, I have something to tell you.'

'What?'

45

'No, you have to wait till I get there. I have to do it in person.'

'Oh, come on, I can't wait two more days. Is it good or bad?'

'Good – and I'm not telling you any more, so you can stop asking.'

'You're such a tease.'

'I know, sorry.'

'By the way, did I mention that I'm stark naked right now?'

'. . . Are you?'

'I am indeed, just out of the bath, all warm and rosy.'

Silence.

'Still there?' she asked.

'Still here.'

'What are *you* wearing?'

'Actually, I'm naked too.'

'. . . Really? How interesting. Do tell me more.'

Breakfast was silent, as always. Andy crunched Rice Krispies, his eyes fixed on the cereal box. James decided he had to know it off by heart, so intently did he study it each breakfast time.

'Chilly one,' he said, topping up his coffee. He didn't need to get up so early, but he didn't like the thought of Andy eating alone – even if Andy would probably have preferred it. 'Anything on after school today?'

'Nah.'

'So you'll be home at four.'

'Yeah.'

A bus took the Roone secondary-school students across on the ferry each day and drove them to the school, which was about a mile from the pier. On stormy days when the ferry was grounded, the Roone teens were expected to study at home; one of the hazards – or benefits, depending on how you looked at it – of living on an island.

'I'm at Fitz's this afternoon,' James said, 'so I'll see you around half six.'

'OK.'

'Will you turn the oven to two hundred at six o'clock, and put the lasagne in at ten past?' Ready-made lasagne, bought yesterday in the super-market, but better, hopefully, than sausages or fish fingers.

'OK.'

Engaging Andy in conversation was a bit like talking to a robot, but something drove James on. Maybe it was the need to make some noise, to distract him from the questions he really wanted to ask: Why are you shutting me out? What have I done except try to get us both over the shit that happened? Why won't you let me in? Can't you see I'm all you've got?

The bus horn sounded outside. Andy dropped his spoon and took his bag off the floor. James had given up asking him to brush his teeth before the bus arrived.

''Bye.'

'Don't forget your coat. Have a good day.'

47

Another day, and a morning free to paint. James drank his coffee and listened to the bus pulling away, his mind already on reds and pinks and golds.

'I *am* pleased,' she said.

'You don't look it.'

'No, it's great, honestly it is. It's just . . .' She trailed off, searching his face.

'Just what?'

'Well, you're still leaving, aren't you? After we're married, I mean.'

'Course I am, don't be daft. It's only a promotion.'

'OK . . . because you know money doesn't bother me. I'd rather we were poor and together.'

He laughed. 'We won't be poor, my darling. I've no intention of being poor.'

'OK.' She began to undo the buttons of her blouse. 'But if you were poor, I'd still love you. Just remember that, in case you lose all your money some day in a . . . freak financial something or other.'

'Good to know.' He pushed her hands out of the way. 'Here,' he said, 'let me help you with that.'

Katy –
Latest development is Mam has agreed to manage the house lettings for me. I'm delighted, because she'll be brilliant. Still no bookings, but I'm trying not to worry. Tim got a promotion

at work so we went out to celebrate on Saturday night, ended up in Fitz's till all hours – one of the advantages of living a ferry ride from the nearest police station, and having an uncle with a pub! How's the big city? Any new romance yet?
N xxx

Nell
Congrats to Tim, sounds like a real high flier. Bet he loves getting away from it all to Roone, though. No new romance since Liam, sadly, but there's always hope . . . Great that your mother's on board for the house, everything's falling into place. I looked it up on the website, by the way – it's gorgeous, you never told me it was so quaint. That dinky little patio with the view of those hills out the back – and I LOVE the painting over your bed. Did you say Tim's brother did that? I just might have to meet him . . .
K xxx

MARCH

Nell flew down the stairs and burst into the pub. Two older fishermen seated at the far end of the bar halted their conversation to stare at her. She rushed to the counter, waving absently at them. 'I got one,' she said excitedly. 'I just checked my emails.'

'Hello to you too.' James finished topping up the pint of Guinness in front of him and set it before one of the men, who nodded placidly.

Nell almost jiggled with impatience. 'James, I got a *tenant*. Someone wants to stay in the house.'

He wiped his hands unhurriedly on a small towel that said 'Smithwicks'. 'You didn't.' He turned to his two customers. 'Did you hear that? She got a tenant.'

The men turned identical blank faces towards her. 'You're opening a B&B, Nell?' one enquired.

'No, I'm letting my house for the summer – and guess what,' she added, turning back to James, 'they want it for two weeks. Not one week, but *two*. Isn't that fantastic?'

'It is indeed fantastic.' He took a small bottle of pineapple juice from the shelf behind him. 'Here, this might calm you down.' He poured it into a glass and set it before her.

She ignored it. 'It's three adults – two women and one man.'

James frowned. 'Miss Mulcahy, I hope you're not bringing that kind of thing to Roone.'

She reached across to slap his arm. 'James Baker, take your mind out of the gutter – it sounds like a husband and wife, and a friend or a sister or something. Isn't it great, though? I was beginning to get worried.'

James sipped the juice. 'And when do they want it?'

'The last two weeks, July the thirtieth to August the thirteenth. Two weeks booked, only four to go.' She grabbed the glass from him and drained it. 'Right, I have to fly I left Maisie Kiely under the drier.'

When she'd gone, leaving behind a whiff of bleach mixed with coconut, the older of the fishermen lifted his new pint and drank deeply. His companion gazed silently into the middle distance, and life resumed its placid mid-afternoon pace in Fitz's public house.

'Marian and Vernon McCarthy, and Imelda O'Brien.'

'Vernon – that's not a name you hear at all now. I'm guessing he's a bit older.'

'Maybe. They're from Westport.'

'And you don't know if they're related, or what the connection is?'

'Well, it sounds like Marian and Vernon are married, doesn't it? But I haven't a clue who Imelda O'Brien is. A friend, maybe.'

Moira offered the plate of ginger biscuits and Nell took one.

'Isn't it great, though? My first booking.'

'Did they pay a deposit?'

'They sure did – it's gone straight into my wedding fund. We must go and look at that dress again.'

'If it's still there. I said you should have put a deposit on it.'

'I couldn't when I didn't know if I could afford it – but now I might just go ahead and chance it.' She regarded the half-eaten biscuit. 'Probably shouldn't be having too many of these, if I want to fit into it.'

'Will you stop – your figure is fine. And the wedding's not till December.'

'True. I can starve myself in November.' She dunked the remains in her coffee. 'How's Dad? Haven't seen him in a while.'

'Busy. Once the second term gets going it's always a bit hectic. He's off to some course tomorrow in Tralee for principals and vice principals.'

'Be a break from school for him anyway.' Nell finished her coffee and pushed back her chair. 'Right, I'd better be off – I'm going for a drink tonight with James.'

Her mother cradled her cup and watched as Nell

pulled on her raincoat. 'It's a wonder Tim doesn't get worried, with you and James so pally.'

'Not at all; he knows well we're just good friends.' She bent to kiss her mother's cheek. 'See you soon, don't get up.'

Walking the half-mile of coast road back to her house, watching the white caps on the waves, Nell marvelled once again at how she and Tim had ended up together. She'd barely known him in Dublin: he was just another customer in the alarmingly expensive salon where she'd worked. It wasn't until she was back living on Roone that they'd been properly introduced, four years after they'd last laid eyes on each other – and it had been Tim's brother who'd done the honours.

If James hadn't moved to Roone with Andy, Nell would never have known him, and would probably never have come face to face with Tim again. Strange how things worked out: strange and wonderful.

She quickened her pace as the rain began again.

It was happening. Someone had booked the house. It had taken an effort to sound positive on the phone, but Nell had been so delighted with her news that Tim had felt obliged to try.

'They're from Westport,' she'd told him, her voice bubbling with excitement. He could imagine her face, all lit up.

'And have they been to Roone before?'

'Nope, their first trip. Isn't it great?'

'Yeah, great.'

Tim yawned as he shut down his computer. Ten o'clock, his third late one this week. He could always work at home on his laptop, but he preferred to keep the two places as separate as possible.

His stomach growled as he walked towards the lift, trying to decide which takeaway to get. Chinese, maybe, or Thai; both were on his route. Or he could phone for an Indian when he got home – he'd have it in twenty minutes.

Roone had no takeaways. If you wanted to eat after ten o'clock, when the last of the cafés closed, you cooked your own food. No big deal as long as you were forewarned, but still. No cinema, no theatre, a library that arrived once a week in the back of a truck. Living there all the time would sure take some getting used to.

The lift arrived. He got in and pressed the button for the ground floor.

'I don't want anything posed,' she said. 'Nothing formal, no groups standing around looking polite.'

The photographer grinned. 'James warned me you had a mind of your own.'

'I'm glad to hear it. And it's my wedding day, so I get to choose, right?'

'Dead right. So – no poses, I just wander around and point the camera, is that it?'

'Well, yes, but in a totally artistic way, of course. And make sure you get everyone, especially the

57

older guests – they'd love copies.' She handed him a mug. 'James told *me* you're not too dear.'

He sipped the tea. 'I won't fleece you.'

Another artist pal of James's, living just outside Dingle, who took photos when he wasn't working behind the counter of a craft shop. Good photos, according to James. Bloody good, to quote him exactly.

'So when's the wedding?' he asked.

'December the twentieth,' she told him. 'My birthday.'

'Nice. You're getting organised early.'

'I know – it's not like me at all. But I'm enjoying this.'

She was having a ball. She was loving everything about this wedding. At night she lay in bed and pictured Tim standing at the altar in a suit, James beside him. Both of them watching as she walked up the aisle on her father's arm, the sea-green dress floating around her. All her friends and neighbours there, the people she'd grown up with, her mother standing in the front pew beside Hugh and Andy.

Tim waiting for her. Waiting to become her husband.

'Have some cake,' she said to the photographer. 'I'm practising for the big day.'

He took a slice. 'You're doing carrot cake for your wedding?'

'Maybe. I'm going to bake a different cake for each tier, but I haven't decided which ones yet.'

Fruit cake had never appealed to her – why would the most important cake of her life be one she didn't like? From now till December she was going to try out lots of different recipes and choose her four or five top ones. Give people a choice on the day.

'So,' the photographer said, his mouth full of cake, 'a December bride.'

'That's right. A winter wedding.'

'And the honeymoon?'

'Not decided yet either. But somewhere exotic and hot. More cake?'

After he'd left she took their plates and mugs to the sink. Outside, John Silver was nosing into the shrubs that were picking themselves up after the winter: the hypericum, the fuchsia, the sea lavender, the cotoneaster. Across the stone wall she could see Walter pottering in his greenhouse, planting his new lettuces and cucumbers, no doubt. Everything coming to life again, everything budding, greening up.

This time next year she'd be looking out the same window, but everything else would have changed. She might even be pregnant.

She turned up the radio and dried the cups, singing along as best she could with Beyoncé.

'You're quiet today.'

'Am I?'

'A bit. How was your principals' course last week? Mam was telling me about it.'

59

Her father drank tea. 'It was the usual old guff. How're the wedding preparations going?'

'Great. I suppose Mam told you I booked the photographer.'

'She did . . . That's good.'

He *was* quiet today. Just finished school for the afternoon, and probably tired. 'You and Mam should go away for Easter,' she said.

He studied her reflection in the mirror. 'Go away? Where did that come from?'

'Just thought you could do with a break. Get a bit of sun, maybe, head to the Canaries for a week.'

He smiled. 'Ah, no, I don't think I'd fancy that . . . but I might take up golf.' He raised his cup again.

Nell looked at him in surprise. 'Golf? There's no course here.'

'There's one this side of Dingle. I'd be there in less than an hour.'

'I suppose . . . Seems a long way to go, though, for a bit of relaxation.'

'I'm only thinking about it,' he said, 'now that the days are getting a bit longer.' Lifting the cup to his lips again as she cut into the hair that grew around his ear.

'So what's new?'

'The photographer's booked.'

'The guy James recommended?'

'Yes, he's lovely. I told him no formal poses.'

'Fine.'

A phone buzzed in the background. 'Is that yours?' she asked.

'Yeah, better take it. I'll call you later.'

''Bye,' she said – but he was already gone.

Katy –

Fantastic news – we've got our first booking, so it's going to happen! Three adults from Westport, and they want the house for TWO WEEKS. I'm so excited now – oh, and I booked the photographer, so another thing crossed off the list. By the way, what's your favourite cake? I'm doing a bit of research for the wedding. How are you?

N xxx

Nell

Your first booking, thrilling. The others will follow, don't worry – who wouldn't want to escape to a magical island for their holidays? And a photographer sorted, that's great. I hope you don't want any of those horrible posed shots. For my wedding, if it ever happens, I'm getting my cousin to walk around with her camera . . . My favourite cake is sour cream coffee walnut, no question. I'm attaching the recipe, it's Mum's speciality.

All well here, no scandal to report, sadly,

K xxx

APRIL

Nell emerged from the changing room. 'What do you think?'

It was her mother's first time to see the dress. 'Well,' she said, and stopped.

'That's it?' Nell asked – and then she began to smile. 'Mam, tell me you're not going to cry.'

'Of course I'm going to cry.' Moira pulled a tissue from her bag and pressed it to her eyes. 'It's practically mandatory for the mother of the bride.'

'You like it then.' Nell did a slow twirl. 'What about the back?'

'The back is just as magnificent as the front – or it would be, if you didn't have a black bra on.'

'I know . . . I forgot when I was getting dressed.' She stood in front of the full-length mirror and gazed at her reflection. 'This is the one, isn't it?'

'Yes.' Moira got up and gathered Nell's hair into her hands. 'What are you going to do with this?'

'I don't know. I'm a hairdresser and I haven't a clue what to do with my hair on my wedding day.'

Moira let it fall back on to Nell's shoulders. 'Plenty of time. We can try out a few styles beforehand.'

Nell turned to face her mother. 'Mam, I'm getting married.'

Moira's eyes filled with tears for the second time. She rummaged in her bag again. '*Now* look what you've made me do.'

'If you don't mind my saying,' Colette Baker remarked to her younger son, 'you're being a bit negative. I think it's sweet that Nell is trying to make some money for the wedding.'

Tim spooned horseradish on to his plate. 'You're supposed to be on my side.'

'*Your* side? Tim, you're getting married – if you and Nell aren't on the same side now, you never will be.'

He smiled. 'You know I'm joking. It's just the hassle of having to move everything out and stay in that poky little place for six weeks.'

'*Nell* will be in it for six weeks,' his mother corrected sternly. 'You'll only be in it for six weekends. Surely you can put up with it for two nights a week if she can do it for the entire time.'

He took her out to lunch about once a fortnight, to a little French restaurant a block from his workplace. He told her his troubles and she put them into perspective. It suited both of them perfectly.

'You're right,' he said. 'Six weeks is nothing. It'll fly by.'

He cut into his rare beef fillet. She drank her sparkling water.

'How's the book club?' he asked. 'Read anything good lately?'

And for the rest of the meal Roone, or the house letting, wasn't mentioned.

'Still no new bookings. I'm beginning to get worried again.'

It was too cold for *Jupiter* – foggy and still, with a sharp bite to the air – but they'd taken her out just the same. James rowed, his cheeks pink, his hands in the navy mittens Nell had knitted him for Christmas with leftover wool from Andy's beanie.

'Don't fret,' he said. 'They'll come. Plenty of time yet.' His words puffing out in little clouds.

Nell pushed her chin further into her scarf. The tip of her nose tingled with cold. 'Hope so . . . On a lighter note, I put a deposit on a wedding dress last week.'

'You did?'

'I did. Two hundred euro.'

'Two hundred euro? You mean it costs more than that?'

She grinned. 'Dear sweet innocent James.' She leant back, palms braced against the seat behind her, and looked up at the ghost-white sky. 'You do know that we're putting you into a top hat and tails on the day, don't you?'

He stopped rowing. 'That had better be a joke, or else.'

'Or else what?'

He pulled the oars. 'Or else you're going over the side.'

Nell laughed. 'You don't scare me, Baker. I'm the original water-baby, remember?'

'The original what?'

'Oh, come on, you've heard that story – you must have.'

'What story?'

'The one about me falling into the sea as a baby.'

He smiled. 'You fell into the sea? Please.'

She sat up. 'Honest to God. I can't believe Tim didn't tell you – it's practically a legend around here. We were out on a boat – not this one, a bigger one – my parents, grandparents, a few others. The boat belonged to some neighbour. Nobody knows how it happened, but they heard a splash – and I was gone in.'

He shook his head, still smiling. 'You're making this up.'

'I'm really not – ask my mother. Although don't – she still gets the shivers thinking about it. One minute I was lying on a blanket, next I was in the water.'

'How old were you?'

'Ten months, maybe a bit more. Mam says I was on the point of crawling, so they think I must have crawled to the side and somehow got over the ledge.'

'Couldn't happen,' he said. 'You couldn't possibly have done all that by yourself.'

'It's true,' she insisted. 'This is Roone, don't

forget. Things happen here, you know that. You've seen Walter's apple tree, the one that blossoms whenever it feels like it. You've got apples from him all year round, haven't you?'

'Well, that's—'

'And what about the mushrooms that grew out of the blue in Annie Byrne's garden last year and cured her arthritis practically overnight? She's perfect now – and they've never had another mushroom on that lawn.'

'Well, I suppose—'

'And the signpost on the cliffs – where did that come from? One day it was just there. And why does everyone smell chocolate at the cemetery?'

'I know, I know, weird and wonderful Roone. So you fell into the sea in your nappy – and then what?'

'Well, several people jumped in after me, of course – my mother included – but they said I was swimming away quite happily. And apparently I cried bitterly when they took me out.'

He shook his head. 'I'm still not convinced that this isn't another product of your very active imagination. Mind you, you *are* a damn fine swimmer.'

'Thank you.' Nell turned to look at the little pier behind them, the scatter of houses that led into the village just beyond. The sea that encircled Roone, dangerous and irresistible. She'd been swimming in it for as long as she could remember, all year round except on the very coldest days. *I'd die without the sea,* she thought. *I'd just shrivel up and die.*

And when it was too cold to swim in it, she had *Jupiter*. Named for one of his beloved planets, the little boat had belonged to her grandfather, lost at sea in the same sudden, vicious storm fifteen years earlier that had claimed the life of Walter's father. The two of them had been fishing from Maurice Thompson's trawler, which had been dashed to smithereens.

Remembering Grandpa Will now, the familiar loneliness flooded through Nell. He'd often taken her as a child to the beach at night. 'Look up,' he'd whisper. 'See the stars, millions and billions of them, more stars than grains of sand. Look, there's Sirius, the brightest one of all. And the Plough, just below the North Star – see its crooked handle. And look, over there is Sagittarius the archer, your special sign.'

'I can't see him,' Nell would say, searching the sparkly black sky. 'I can't see the archer' – and he'd lead her to the constellation, he'd guide her across the sky until she saw.

He'd taught her about the planets, showed her where to find the visible ones. 'Venus,' he'd say, pointing. 'The dazzler. Look how beautiful she is. And Mars, the red planet – go on, wave to the Martians. And see there, there's Jupiter, bright white, with all its Galilean moons. Lovely Jupiter.'

'I can't see the moons.'

'Me neither, my darling, but they're up there, believe me.'

She remembered Galileo, the kite they'd made

together, named after the astronomer because it, too, explored the heavens when Nell played out its string and allowed it to fly. And then one day the string had broken, and Galileo was pulled by the wind high into the sky – never, Nell assumed, to be seen again.

But six months later, when she'd all but forgotten it, a package had arrived for her, addressed to *Nell Mulcahy, Roone Island*, and she'd pulled out the tattered remains of her kite – the name and address she'd scribbled in the corner miraculously intact – along with a postcard. *I found your kite in a field*, ten-year-old Katy O'Donnell had written in green felt tip, *and my mother said I should send it back to you*. The postcard had a photo of a mountain on the front – *Errigal, Derryveagh Mountains, Donegal* – and Katy's address at the end of the message.

'You should write back and thank her,' Nell's mother had said, so Nell had bought a postcard of Roone's lighthouse and written, *Thank you very much for sending back my kite*, even though Galileo's trip to Donegal had ensured that his flying days were forever behind him, and his tattered remains now sat uselessly on Nell's dressing-table. *This is a picture of the lighthouse on the island where I live*, she'd added, before slipping the postcard into an envelope, so the postman in Donegal wouldn't be able to read it.

Three weeks later another postcard had arrived, also in an envelope. This time Katy had used an orange marker. *It's so cool that you live on an island.*

What age are you? I'm ten. I have one brother and one sister.

And on they'd gone over the following twenty years, a postcard travelling in both directions roughly once a month, through their transition to secondary school, music and boys, Nell's move to Dublin and return to Roone, Katy's arrival in Dublin, a few months after Nell had left, to take up a new PA job. *You should have waited,* Katy had written. *We could finally have come face to face.*

In all that time they'd never met – but in December Katy was coming to Roone for Nell's wedding.

'You've gone uncharacteristically quiet,' James said.

'Sorry – miles away.' Nell pulled a flask from her basket and unscrewed the top. 'Coffee with a teaspoon of brandy to keep the hypothermia away.'

'Brilliant.'

They drank the brandied coffee, then James replaced the oars in their cradles and rowed them home. When they reached the stone steps Nell lifted the mooring line and got out.

'Careful, they're slippery,' she said, climbing to the top and looping the end of the rope around an ice-cold pillar.

'You're the one who fell in, not me.' He hefted her basket and their bag of books on to his shoulder and they left the pier, and turned for the village. 'How're we doing for time?'

'Plenty – only gone twelve.'

The long white library van was parked in its usual position outside the supermarket. Nell and James mounted the steps as Walter Thompson approached on foot from the opposite direction, and Monday ambled along the way it generally did on Roone.

Tim lifted his glass. 'To the cook. Moira, another triumph. Don't tell my mother, but I think your lamb beats hers.'

Moira smiled. 'Aren't you nice? I hope she didn't mind us claiming you for Easter dinner.'

'She has James and Andy, she's fine.'

Their mother lived in Dublin, where Tim and James had grown up. Widowed for ten years, Colette Baker had remained in the house overlooking the sea in Dalkey that her husband had inherited from his parents.

Nell had visited it twice. The first occasion had been her future mother-in-law's birthday, the second just after she and Tim had got engaged. She'd been welcomed warmly both times, Colette showing her, on her first visit, around the large rear garden with its rockery and crazy paving and herbs that grew in an old cast-iron bath.

'I've been to Roone, you know,' she'd said, digging out mint and basil, easing the root balls into little pots of damp compost. 'I went there when James first bought the house.'

'He told me,' Nell said. 'What did you think of it?'

73

Colette misted water on the herbs. 'I got a feeling there,' she said slowly. 'I felt a wonderful energy on the island, a friendly, positive energy. I thought it was just what they both needed, after Karen. I think they'll be happier there.'

Nell nodded. 'I hope so. I'm always happiest on Roone.'

'You're lucky,' Colette told her. 'To have grown up there, to have been a child there, must have been amazing.' She handed the pots to Nell. 'You can see if they grow for you – but I feel sure they will.'

They had. Nell supplied anyone who wanted it with basil and mint. The herbs thrived on her patio, they flourished cheerfully in the pair of long ceramic planters she'd bought when they'd outgrown a series of pots.

'How's the work?' Denis asked Tim.

'Hectic, most of the time,' Tim held out his plate for more lamb as Moira carved, 'but I enjoy it – most of the time.'

'It'll be a change for you when you move down here,' Hugh put in. 'After the wedding, I mean.'

'A good change,' Nell said. 'No more trekking across the country all the time. Much less stress.'

Once they were married he was going to give up his job and switch to freelance computer programming. He was going to live on Roone with her, sleep under the same roof seven nights a week, or as many as they could manage.

There would be times, of course, when he'd have

to travel for a job, attend meetings that couldn't take place online, sort out problems and set up systems in person, but hopefully those times wouldn't happen too often.

Hugh pushed back his chair. 'Well, it's all right for some, but I have a pub to run.' Seamus Carmody, his back-up when James wasn't around, had opened up earlier, but Hugh would be needed to cope with the Easter holiday crowds in the evening.

'I'll make sandwiches,' Moira said, getting up. 'There's a pile of meat left. You'll have them for your supper.' At fifty-one he was still her little brother, with no wife to roast lamb for him or make sandwiches for his supper.

Tim and Nell walked the half-mile home afterwards. 'Come down to the beach,' she said, crossing the road to the laneway that led to the sea.

'It's freezing,' Tim said.

'Just for a minute.' After the warmth of her parents' house she needed to hear it, to smell it, to breathe it in. She crunched over the pebbles, listening for the dull thump of the waves on the sand. She reached the end of the lane and stood waiting for Tim, rubbing her arms.

The night was clear, the stars winking in the sky, the moon a curved sliver. She found Venus easily, and Sirius.

'Hey, Grandpa Will,' she whispered – and at that moment a star shot through the sky, trailing a shower of sparkles. 'A shooting star,' she said to Tim, coming up behind her – but he'd missed it.

'Short back and sides,' she said. 'Right?'

Andy smiled into the mirror, a polite smile for her repeated joke. 'Just a trim.'

'One day,' she warned, picking up her scissors, 'you'll ask me for short back and sides, and I won't say, "I told you so," when you see how gorgeous you look. So how was Dublin?'

'OK.'

'Granny in good form?'

'Yeah.'

Colette was his only grandparent in Ireland. A few months after Karen's death her parents had relocated to her mother's home place in Wales. Andy had met them once since then, when he and James had gone on a three-day visit last summer. Neither of them had said a lot about it afterwards, and Nell had been left with the distinct impression that it hadn't been a roaring success.

Poor Andy. Nobody apart from James to look after him, to make him feel wanted. Nell did her best with dinner invitations and the odd trip around the harbour in *Jupiter*, but she was a poor substitute for his mother.

She snipped half an inch off his hair, wishing he'd let her do more. He seemed determined to stay hidden behind the brown curtain that fell to his shoulders. She wondered how he wasn't sent home from school, told to tidy himself up.

Maybe schools weren't allowed to do that any more.

It was hard to know what Andy thought of Roone. He wasn't a talker, not even with his father. Least of all with his father, according to James.

'It's my own fault,' he'd said one evening over a bottle of red wine in Fitz's. 'I was glad he didn't want to talk about Karen after she died because I wasn't sure I could handle it.'

'Don't be too hard on yourself,' Nell had replied. 'It was horrible for both of you. Who knows how to cope with grief? I don't. And Andy was just ten, still such a child.'

'I should have tried talking about her, though, but I didn't – and later, when I felt able, and I brought her name up in conversation, he just switched off. He drifted away from me, and I haven't been able to get him back. I thought moving here might help, but it's been a year and I can't see any change in him.'

'He'll come round,' she'd said. 'Give him time. Let Roone work some more on him.'

But it was three years now, and Andy seemed as remote as ever. Getting the ferry to school each weekday morning, coming back and disappearing to his room, emerging only to eat, or to travel to Nell's house if that was where dinner was being served. Roaming the island at the weekends, mostly alone, or with John Silver if Nell happened to spot him passing the house. At least, she thought, he'd have some company – and John Silver never objected to a walk.

Nell liked him, though. There was a softness in him, a vulnerability that drew her to him. Lost soul, looking to be found, she was convinced, if they only knew how.

'You don't have to dry it,' he said, as he always did when she'd put away her scissors.

'Fair enough.' She'd given up arguing. She waited while he dug in his jeans pocket for the tenner James insisted on paying her, despite her attempts to charge less. In his own way, Tim's brother could be as stubborn as herself.

'Tell your father,' she said, putting the note into the till, 'that you're both coming to dinner tomorrow night. Seven o'clock.'

'OK,' he said, shrugging into the leather jacket he lived in, winter and summer.

'I'm doing chicken and bacon lasagne, just for you.'

'Cool.'

His favourite, three helpings he'd have at least. Nothing wrong with his appetite, although you wouldn't think it from his skinny frame. The miraculous metabolism of teenage boys – shame she couldn't bottle it.

He lifted a hand as he walked out, his damp hair straggling around his head. Great ad for her salon.

'See you,' he said.

'Be good.'

Nell flapped out the cape and hung it over the

chair. Hardly worth his while coming, really; maybe James had insisted, thinking Nell needed the money. She swept up the scant handful of hair she'd been allowed to take off and brought cups to the sink. A proper tidy-up could wait till the morning: she was tired now after a busy Friday. She switched off the lights and locked the door and went downstairs.

Her father sat at the bar, a half-finished beer in front of him. 'Mine's a cider,' she said, taking the neighbouring stool and lifting a hand to Hugh behind the counter. 'How's your golf coming along?'

He was playing most weekends now, at a course twenty miles from the pier on the mainland. Sometimes he went on Saturday and Sunday. She supposed he was making up for lost time.

'Fine,' he said, raising his glass. 'Not bad.'

Katy –
The dress is bought! Well, nearly – I have a deposit paid. Can't wait until it's mine. Mam cried when she saw it, and it takes a lot to make her cry. No more bookings for the house, but I'm determined not to worry, and trust that it'll happen soon. Dad has taken up golf at the age of sixty-one and is loving it. Tim was here for Easter, we went hiking up Brandon on Saturday and it was full of people. Did you get home?
N xxx

Nell
I didn't go home for Easter, I went to Paris!
Liam put in a reappearance and surprised me
with a trip, talk about romantic – and I know,
I know, don't bother saying it, but it was lovely,
and he's trying hard, really he is. He swears
it'll never happen again. We'll see . . . You're
right not to worry about the house, bookings
will come. Brilliant news about the dress, can't
wait to see you in it. Can't wait to see you,
full stop!
K xxx

MAY

'What about Paris?' he asked.

'Paris? No way, much too clichéd – and freezing. We have to go somewhere hot. And by the sea.'

'The Canaries then.'

'Bit classier,' she said. 'I was thinking Antigua.'

'Antigua? That's the other side of the States.'

'No, it's not, it's this side. It's in the Caribbean, and it's gorgeous. I've been looking at photos. Like the beach in the Bounty ad, remember that? With the palm trees, and coconuts.'

'I can see you,' he said, 'swinging in your hammock.'

'You'd be bringing me piña coladas. And Bounty bars. Or maybe Jamaica.'

'I'd be bringing you Jamaica?'

'No – maybe we'd go there. It's around the same area.'

'Nell,' he said, 'I told you I might only be able to take a week off. These places are a bit long haul.'

'But you'll be leaving the job, you'll be moving down here. Can't you time it so you finish up just before the wedding?'

A beat passed.

'Tim?'

'Nell, it might not be that straightforward. I've got more responsibility now. I can't just up and leave if I'm in the middle of a project.'

Nell stopped rearranging her brushes on the shelf in front of the mirror. 'So what are you saying? You mightn't be leaving Dublin in December?'

'I'm just saying I mightn't be able to time it exactly right. I might have to work a little bit into January. It all depends on what's happening then.'

'I see.'

The salon door opened and Nell's mother walked in. Nell gestured to her phone, and turned away to face the bales of clean white towels stacked in the wooden cabinet she'd painted pale blue. 'I have to go,' she said. 'I have a customer.'

'Don't be cross. I'm just trying to explain.'

'OK.'

'We'll work something out.'

'OK. Talk to you later.' She hung up without waiting for his response and turned back. 'Sorry about that.'

Moira was hanging up her jacket. 'Isn't it a beautiful day? Let's hope it's a good sign for summer. God knows we could do with a decent one.'

'Are you tea or coffee today?' Nell asked.

Helen looked doubtfully at her reflection. 'I'm not sure that violet is my colour, really.'

'No, it makes you too pale.' Nell ran a hand along the fabric of the dress she held in her lap,

84

a dove-grey three-quarter-length raw silk. 'I preferred this one.'

'I did too,' Helen said. 'The colour and the style. But of course it's up to you; it's your day.'

Helen Mulcahy was Nell's first cousin, the eldest daughter of Denis's brother. Con had emigrated to Scotland before Nell was born, but each summer he'd returned to Roone with his family, and Nell and Helen, a year apart in age, had roamed the island together.

Helen worked in London now, and she and Nell met infrequently, but when it had come to choosing a bridesmaid, her cousin had been Nell's first choice – better to keep it in the family than risk upsetting her many island friends by selecting one over another – and happily, Helen had agreed.

'Here,' Nell said, 'let's get you out of that and go to lunch.'

'I must say, you're very organised.' Helen pulled the dress over her head and reached for her jeans. 'At the rate you're going, you'll be able to put your feet up well before December.'

'Yes, I suppose I will.' Nell buttoned her coat.

Helen glanced at her. 'Nell, is everything OK?'

'It's fine, it's nothing, really.' She dug her hands into her pockets. 'Tim isn't sure when he'll be able to quit his job, that's all.'

Helen frowned. 'I thought he was finishing up when you got married.'

'So did I. Now he's saying he might have to stay on a bit longer, that he can't walk out if they're

85

in the middle of something. And he says we can only have a week of a honeymoon because he can't guarantee that he'll be able to take two.'

Helen pulled on socks and pushed her feet into shoes. 'That's a bit of a bummer. Are you talking weeks, or months, or what?'

Nell ran a hand through her hair. 'Oh, just a week or two into January, he says. It's no big deal, really – just that I was so looking forward to having him around all the time.' She slung her bag on to her shoulder. 'I'm just so *sick* of him disappearing every Sunday night.'

Helen finished dressing and tucked her arm into Nell's as they left the changing area. 'It's early days, it might never happen. And even if it does, what's another week or two when you've got the rest of your lives together?' She held the shop door open for Nell. 'You never know – six months into married life, you might wish he still worked two hundred miles away!'

'That's true.' Nell squeezed her arm as they walked down the street. 'I wish *you* didn't live so far away. We don't see half enough of each other these days.'

'Well, I'll be back again in early August, and I can try on a few more then. Keep an eye out in the meantime – whatever you like will be fine by me. Your own dress is so fabulous that there's no danger I'll outshine you, whatever I wear.'

Nell felt instantly cheerier. 'It *is* fabulous, isn't it?' As they made their way towards the restaurant she'd chosen for lunch, she decided to think positive. So what if Tim had to stay in Dublin a bit longer? It wouldn't kill her.

And a week of a honeymoon would be fine too, she mustn't be greedy. Wasn't she getting the wedding she wanted, and the husband she'd chosen? They could always get away again later.

They reached the restaurant and turned in.

'Come on,' she said, peeling off her top. 'Last one in's a rotten egg.' She wriggled out of her jeans and left them in a heap at the bottom of the boat. 'Come on,' she repeated, stepping on to the seat, bending her knees and raising her arms. 'You can do it.'

John Silver barked as she dived in, the movement causing *Jupiter* to rock gently. Nell rose to the surface, whooping at the cold. Despite the sunshine, the sea still held the chill of winter. 'Come on,' she called, treading water – and with another joyous bark John Silver leapt from the boat to land with a splash beside her.

'Good boy,' she laughed, 'let's go.' She cut swiftly through the deep water, moving in an arc around him, switching effortlessly from crawl to butterfly. They swam for ten minutes, and when the cold began to grab at her fingers and toes she hoisted herself back into the boat and dragged John Silver in after her.

As he shook himself dry Nell shrugged off her wet swimsuit and wrapped her towel around her. She tingled from head to toe, her heart thumping, her blood racing. Was there a better way to banish her cares, to push away her silly, niggling worries? She never came back from a swim without feeling uplifted. After a while she pulled on her clothes, the sun warm now on her skin, and combed out her hair before rowing them back to the pier.

As she moored the little boat she noted the number of new craft around the pier. The trickle of holidaymakers which had begun last month was steadily increasing now, every day bringing more new faces to the village street, more cars with unfamiliar number-plates meandering over the island's narrow, winding roads.

Everyone wanting to spend some time on Roone – but nobody, apart from her three original tenants, looking to stay in Nell's house. No booking since March, and now it was nearly the end of May, and less than six weeks before the second of July, when her letting period started.

What if nobody else made an enquiry? What if her single booking was it? Their rent wouldn't even cover the cost of the dress. She'd have to admit defeat and let Tim pay for the wedding. She'd feel obliged to cut corners, even if he said she didn't have to. So much for her wonderful plan.

At the end of the pier she turned left, away from the village. She passed her parents' house without making her usual visit – the swim had left her too hungry for dinner – and covered the further half-mile to her own house in less than ten minutes.

While her salmon cutlet was grilling she switched on her computer and opened the house-letting website. *Two new messages*, she read. Her heart skittered out of its usual rhythm. Two new messages since last evening, the first activity on her account in almost two months.

She clicked on the first. A request for her house for two weeks from July the second. She clicked on the next. A request for her house for two weeks from July the sixteenth. Both enquiries had already paid deposits.

No, that couldn't be right. It was far too good to be true, even for Roone. She reread both messages, and found them unchanged. She sat back, letting the implications slot one by one into her consciousness.

The house was let, fully booked for the entire six weeks. Her plan had worked. Her dream wedding was back on.

In a month and a half her house would be occupied by someone else, who considered it worth paying four hundred euro a week for the privilege of staying there.

She smelt burning and rushed to the kitchen to pull the salmon from under the grill. She took her phone from her bag and dialled a number. 'I've got two more bookings,' she said, 'just now, and guess what – they've each booked two weeks, and they're not clashing. They're fitting perfectly into the calendar, so the six weeks are fully booked as of now.'

'That's fantastic,' James replied. 'What did Tim say when he heard?'

Nell watched a grey cat crouching by a corner of her shed, body tensed, tail waving slowly, eyes fixed on a bird that was hopping along the stone wall. 'He was over the moon,' she said, rapping on the window.

Tim walked the twenty minutes from his office to his apartment. The familiar pavements were lined with the usual buskers and beggars, all looking for his money. A bus roared past, pushing water from last night's rain out of the way with its wheels, the spray narrowly missing him. A man holding a bouquet of flowers put out his hand for a taxi. A pair of females hurried by, leaving a drift of lavender.

As he approached his apartment building Tim's phone rang. He took it from his pocket and saw Nell's name.

'Hey, babe.'

'What are you up to?' she asked.

'Just getting home from work.'

'So late? It's nearly eight.'

'Believe it or not, this is an early one,' he replied, stepping into a segment of the rotating door, pushing it around. 'What's happening?'

'We've got two more bookings.'

'Oh?' He lifted a hand at the security man as he made for the lift. 'Hey, that's good. When for?'

'Well, here's the amazing bit. They both want two weeks, and they're not clashing with each other.'

He stepped into the waiting lift. 'So that means we're all booked up?'

'Yes – the six weeks are full. Isn't it brilliant? I'm just off for a drink with James to celebrate.'

A flash of resentment sliced through him. She'd told James first. He shoved it away quickly – for all he knew, James had met her before she'd had a chance to make a call. *Get over it, Baker.*

'Enjoy,' he said, stabbing the button for the fourth floor. 'Don't stay out too late. No leading James astray.'

When he got to his apartment he went straight to the fridge and pulled out a beer bottle. He'd celebrate as well. She kept telling him it was his house too.

'Well, things appear to be working out for you. I'm so glad.'

Nell brushed the stray hairs from the back of Walter's neck. 'You're not the only one. I was getting a bit worried that nobody else would want it. There, all done.'

She held up the hand mirror and Walter peered at the back of his head. 'Many thanks, my dear. A lovely job, as usual.' He got to his feet, and she brushed off his jacket. 'So, I shall expect my first new neighbours in a few weeks.'

'Neighbour,' Nell corrected. 'One man on his own for the first two weeks – isn't that strange?'

Walter considered this as he slid his wallet from his trouser pocket. 'Perhaps he's a writer of some sort, or an artist, and is looking for solitude.'

'Oh, that's better.' Nell took payment and made change. 'I was feeling very sorry for him, thinking he couldn't find anyone to come with him on holidays.'

'Well, I suppose that could also be a possibility.' Walter moved towards the door. 'Shall I order you a drink downstairs?'

'Do – a bottle of cider. I'll be right down.'

She hurried through the tidy-up, the rain pattering gently against the big salon window. So much for the sunny spell, which had lasted all of two days. Not to worry: the whole summer was still ahead of them – and anyway, with three lots of strangers about to come into her life, who cared about the weather? Much more interesting to see who'd chosen her house above any other, and how they'd get on for the two weeks they spent here. She willed the next few weeks to hurry by, so the first man could arrive and she could have a look at him, and try to figure out why he was alone. Maybe she could find him—

Stop. Don't interfere. The poor man hadn't set foot on the island and already she was matchmaking. She unplugged the kettle, and locked the door, and took the stairs two at a time, like she always did.

'I've asked James to paint the room next to the salon,' she said. 'We're bartering – he and Andy are getting six free haircuts each. I said a dozen but he beat me down to six.'

'Hmm – not sure either of you have grasped the

concept of bargaining. Is there much clearing out to do up there?'

'Not really, won't take long.'

'I'll give you a hand when I'm down at the weekend.'

'No need, honestly. I'd be better doing it on my own, so I know where everything is.'

But he was trying, he was making an effort, and she loved him for it.

'So,' he said, 'it's all sorted.'

'Sure is, we're all set.'

'OK . . . How's everything otherwise?'

'Fine. Business has been booming this week – lots of holidaymakers in for their washes and blow-dries. I had Walter and Hugh for dinner last night. Mam is thinking about changing the curtains in the sitting room. What else? Oh, yes, my husband-to-be is coming down from Dublin tomorrow.'

'That'll be nice for you. Isn't he great to make that journey every weekend all the same?'

'Ah, he knows it's worth his while.'

'Hmm. So what's on for the weekend?'

'Wouldn't mind a trip to Dingle on Saturday night,' she said. 'The new Robert Downey Jr film has arrived.'

'Oh, right. You want me to take you to the cinema so you can drool over another man.'

'Precisely. And afterwards I can pretend you're him, when we're playing doctors and nurses.' Smiling at John Silver, who was dozing at her feet.

'Fine – as long as I can pretend you're Keira Knightley.'

'Feel free, Doctor Robert.'

Life was good. She was so lucky.

Katy –

All sorted – would you believe I got two book-ings on the one day, and both of them wanted two weeks! So the house is fully booked, thank goodness, and now of course I'm beginning to panic at all the preparation I have to do. Tim's brother – the artist you want to meet – is going to paint the room we'll be living in for the six weeks, and Dad will help with moving of furniture, bless him. So roll on July when the fun begins! What's happening with you and Liam? Any holiday plans?

N xxx

Nell

House sorted, that's great. All well here, Liam busy at work so doesn't look like we'll be swan-ning off anywhere for the next while. My sister and family are taking a house in France for three weeks in July and I might join them for a bit of it. My nephew and niece are four and five, and I'm the doting aunt so they'd love to see me. Nothing much else happening here. Hope all the preparations go well (sounds like Tim is getting off lightly there!).

K xxx

JUNE

'What's this one?'

'Apricot and coconut. What do you think?'

Her mother eyed the cake dubiously. 'I preferred the one with rum and dates. This is a bit dry.'

'Duly noted. So what else do I need in the house?'

'Eggcups.'

'Really?'

'Of course. What if they want to boil an egg for breakfast?'

Eggcups would never have occurred to Nell. She never used them, preferring to eat her boiled egg chopped up in a bowl with lots of salt and a knob of butter, but she supposed she could hardly assume that all of her paying guests would share that preference. Paying guests: delicious ring to it.

'They could use Tim's eggcup,' she said, just to see the reaction it got.

Her mother brushed cake crumbs from her cardigan. 'I won't dignify that with an answer.'

Tim's eggcup wasn't an eggcup. It was roughly the

right size, but it was made of glass and had started life filled with a rose-scented candle. When the candle was gone Nell had washed and dried the little glass and sat it on the kitchen windowsill, along with all the other bric-à-brac she hadn't the heart to throw out – a cracked mug filled with biros of dubious working order, a lidless teapot that held elastic bands and paperclips, a stack of little plastic flowerpots – until Tim had moved in, and boiled an egg, and discovered her lack of eggcups.

He'd spotted the little glass on the sill. 'This'll do.'

'That's a candle-holder,' Nell had told him.

'Not any more.'

And it had done the job perfectly, until now. Nell wrote *eggcups* on her list, underneath *toilet brush* and *cooker-hood filters* and *cushion covers* and *facecloths* and *steak knives* and *tablecloth*. So much to think of, and she was such a novice.

'I'll wash Tim's eggcup and put it in with the glasses in the sitting room,' she said. 'Someone might fancy a tequila shot.'

Her mother raised her eyes to heaven.

'You missed a bit.'

James dipped his brush into the paint. 'Very funny. Are you here to tell me it's lunchtime?'

'Yes. What do you want to do?'

'Give me five minutes to finish up,' he said, 'and we'll get a sausage roll in Lelia's.'

'OK.' She crossed her arms and leant against

the door. 'It looks great, by the way. I'm so glad I didn't go with the white.'

'Listen to Uncle James and you'll never go wrong.' He'd persuaded her to choose a creamy yellow that washed the room in a soft glow.

'But I do want to keep the woodwork white.'

'So you tell me.'

'It's not too small, is it? This room, I mean. To live in for six weeks.'

James stroked paint in a long steady line just above the skirting-board. 'It's small, but you'll manage.'

She'd cleared it out, redistributing the clutter of hairdressing supplies between the salon and Hugh's shed behind the pub. She'd washed the walls and scrubbed the windowsill and door, in advance of James's arrival. There was an alcove with built-in shelves to the left of the window, perfect for the portable telly and microwave oven Hugh was lending her. She'd manage.

'Are you sure you don't mind taking John Silver?'

'No problem. Andy's delighted.'

She hated having to farm him out but he couldn't come here: it wouldn't be fair to keep him cooped up. She'd go to see him when she could, and on her two days off, Sunday and Monday, they'd have long walks together, and trips in *Jupiter*.

She crossed the room and stood at the wide open window, looking down at the village street. 'I love that I'll be right in the middle of everything when I'm living here. There's Maisie Kiely – what on earth is she wearing? Looks like she made a skirt out of someone's sitting-room curtains, like that one in *Gone With the Wind* . . . oh, here comes the sweetest little girl skipping along the path, her hair's just like Shirley Temple's – she's adorable . . . and there's Terence, you could set your watch by him, into Fitz's for his lunchtime pint. Hi, Terence,' she called, waving.

James painted on, her voice skimming over him as he finished the final corner. When it was done he squeezed what paint was left on the brush back into the can before getting to his feet. He wiped his hands on a cloth and turned to look at Nell Mulcahy, with whom he had been ridiculously in love for more than a year now, and who was marrying his little brother six months from now.

She wore a dress with tiny red and blue flowers scattered across a cream background. It had three-quarter sleeves and was gathered at the waist, the full skirt coming to just above her knees. Her chestnut hair was pulled today into a careless ponytail and tied with a blue ribbon. On her feet were the little white ballerina shoes she always wore in the salon.

James looked at her calves, pale golden and firm from all her swimming and walking. He allowed his gaze to wander up to her hands, braced against the sill. To the back of her neck. To the lobes of her ears, studded with silver. To all the precious parts of her.

'Done,' he said, to make her turn. Wanting to see her face, needing to have her look at him.

She swung around and smiled, making his heart somersault with happiness. 'Thank God for that,' she said. 'I could eat the side of a house.'

Tim added a chicken and mushroom pie to his basket and moved to the produce section, where he selected two mangoes, a pineapple and a punnet of black grapes. Shopping was way down the list of his favourite activities but it had to be done, far too often for his liking.

He'd tried getting his groceries online but he'd ended up with hideously green bananas, milk that was dangerously close to being out of date and the wrong brand of washing-up liquid. Like everything else, if you wanted it done right you had to do it yourself.

He walked along the breakfast-cereals aisle until he found the muesli he always ate. Routine, that was the thing. Routine comforted him: it held his busy days in place. Nell laughed at his habits, preferring her more slapdash, come-what-may attitude to life, and he had to concede that she was one of the happiest people he knew. Each to his own.

He added toothpaste and mouthwash to his basket and moved towards the checkout. He knew the face of the girl at the till but he had no idea what her name was, even though he shopped there at least once a week.

On Roone Nell knew every shopkeeper by name. Most of them came to the salon to get their hair cut, but she knew the ones who didn't too, and usually their parents and grandparents. Sometimes Roone felt like a giant family to him, one to which he was always warmly welcomed when he arrived but in which they managed equally well when he wasn't there.

James had been adopted by the Roone family. Getting the job in Fitz's had probably helped. Now he was part of them, they'd drawn him in and made a space for him. Andy's status, it seemed to Tim, was still that of a guest – but to be fair, that was probably down to the boy's own attitude. Andy belonged nowhere right now; hopefully, that would sort itself out when he'd got over his teens.

Tim took his change and walked towards the supermarket exit. And what about him? Would he be accepted once he and Nell were married? Would he become part of Roone, part of that quirky community where life moved at a radically different pace from his own?

He opened the boot of his car and loaded in his bags. Of course he'd be accepted. When he was married to Nell Mulcahy, whom everyone adored, they'd take him in like they'd taken in James. Like they'd take in Andy if he would only let them.

He got into the car and crawled home through the rush-hour traffic.

* * *

Nell Mulcahy's father drove off the ferry with his golf bag lying across the back seat, clearly visible so anyone he met would assume, wrongly, that he was off to play a game or returning from one. He'd bought the bag, complete with clubs, for forty euro in a charity shop in Dingle. He thought there were seven clubs inside, but he couldn't quite remember.

After a handful of miles he reached a T-junction. To his right was Dingle, and the golf course he'd driven to once, to check how far away it was. Denis turned left and arrived within fifteen minutes at a small crossroads, where he turned right on to a narrower road. He drove carefully, as always, keeping well within the speed limit and checking his rear-view mirror regularly, although the road was quiet and he usually encountered no other vehicles.

At length, thirty minutes or so after driving off the ferry, he turned into the car park of a small hotel that was located on the edge of a medium-sized village. He parked beside a red Renault, smiling as he observed the haphazard way it had been positioned, how it straddled the line that indicated where one space ended and another began.

He transferred his golf bag to the boot before walking to the hotel entrance and pushing open the big wooden door and making his way past the reception desk – unattended – to the bar.

He crossed the deep red patterned carpet to a table in the far corner, where a woman sat reading a newspaper. In front of her on the table were a cup and saucer, a milk jug, a sugar bowl. As Denis approached, she lowered the newspaper and smiled. 'There you are,' she said.

'What about the cuckoo clock?'

Nell's mother considered. 'I'd move it, I think. You'd hate anything to happen to it.'

The cuckoo clock had been her very first Christmas present from Tim, a few months after their paths had crossed for the second time. They'd been romantically involved for just six weeks, and the present had taken her by surprise – and filled her, already half in love with him, with delighted hope.

It was transferred, along with Walter's engagement present of Galway crystal wine glasses and Hugh's bog-oak sculpture of a sparrow, to the attic. They moved on to the main bedroom.

'What about James's painting?' Nell asked. 'Should I move it?'

'God, no,' Moira replied. 'Leave that there – it's the best thing about the room.'

'Exactly, an original oil painting. He gets hundreds for them.'

'I know he does, but they're hardly going to take it off the wall, not when you know where they live.'

'I suppose not.'

'But I'd put away the mirror,' her mother went on, pointing, 'just in case.'

Nell hesitated. 'Actually, I think I'll leave that where it is.'

Her grandfather's shaving mirror, hanging between the wardrobe and the dressing-table, was small and oval, the size of a two-dimensional rugby ball. The glass was spotted with age and the plain gilt frame tarnished in places, but the thought of trying to clean it had never occurred to Nell. It had aged along with him, and she wouldn't change it.

It belonged on the wall, it felt right there. Tim had complained that it was too small, and positioned too low for him to use, but it was the perfect height for Nell. When she looked into it she sensed Grandpa Will: she heard the scratch of the razor as he pulled it across his jaw, she smelt the bar of shaving soap he'd chosen over foam from a can.

'Come on,' she said, walking out to the hall. 'Two rooms to go, and then you get coffee.'

'Wait till you see the place. James has done a gorgeous job.'

It was Thursday of the week before their first tenant arrived. In nine days Gavin Connolly from Dublin was coming to stay on Roone for two weeks, all on his own in Nell Mulcahy's house.

'Can't wait,' Tim replied.

Nell ignored the sarcasm. 'Dad is going to bring my bed over this evening,' she said. 'And I told you Hugh is giving us a telly, didn't I? And a microwave. We'll be very cosy.' She heard the salon door opening. 'Better go, I have a customer.'

'See you tomorrow,' he said. 'Love you.'

'Me too.' She hung up and walked out.

Her uncle was unbuttoning his jacket. 'I'm not early, am I?'

'Not a bit,' Nell said. 'Come and see the room.'

Hugh Fitzpatrick hadn't exactly been the reason, six years previously, that Nell had returned to Roone – she would have found a way, so hungry was she for the island when she'd lived in Dublin – but her uncle had provided her with the perfect opportunity to come back when his bid on Considine's pub had been accepted.

'There's an upstairs to it that he says he's not going to use,' Moira had told her. 'It would be perfect for you, if you wanted to come home and open a salon.'

And Nell, closing her eyes and picturing Roone as she'd stood in the hallway of her rented accommodation, had felt a longing so strong it had made her eyes sting. 'I'll have a look at the weekend,' she'd said – because in those days she'd travelled from Dublin to Roone every Friday, just like Tim did now. Except that she hadn't been driving then, so she'd had to take the train to Tralee and have her father meet her at the station. Five and a half hours from door to door, on a good day.

The upstairs of Considine's – or Fitz's, as it had come to be known – had been in dire need of renovation. Jack Considine had used it as a dumping ground for furniture that had come to the end of its natural life in the pub below. Rickety tables and stools minus legs, ancient television sets and cracked toilet bowls were piled higgledy-piggledy throughout the two rooms.

But Nell had skirted the lot to stand at the cobwebby window and look down at Roone's village street, and she had known immediately that this was the place for her. She'd handed in her notice the following week and left Dublin a month later, with most of the clutter already cleared from the upstairs rooms by a few of Roone's more energetic teenage boys.

Within another month Hair Upstairs was open and she began her new life, back where she belonged. And if she occasionally remembered a certain man with muddy-blond hair and green eyes who'd made small-talk with her as she'd washed his hair or brought him a cappuccino, he never occupied her mind for too long, so busy and happy was she.

Hugh stood in the doorway that led to the smaller room and surveyed her future living quarters. 'Very nice. I thought you were going with white, though.'

'James persuaded me to make it a bit warmer, and I think he was right.' She rubbed a smear off the window with her sleeve. 'I'm going to put the bed by that wall, and the table here, by the window. And it gets the sun in the afternoon, which is great.'

Hugh grinned. 'You sound like a little girl playing house.'

'I feel a bit like that.' She ran a finger along the newly painted sill. 'It'll be an adventure, won't it? Just hope Tim feels the same.'

'Why wouldn't he?'

'Well, it was totally my idea to let the house. He wasn't that keen, really.' She turned to look out the window. 'Then again, he'll only be here at weekends.'

'I'll try to keep the noise down for him,' Hugh said, 'but I can't promise anything.'

'Pity about him – he can sleep all he wants in Dublin.' She turned from the window and crossed the room to him and led him back into the salon. 'Right, we're going with the purple streak today, are we?'

'In your dreams,' her uncle replied.

Katy –
Four days to go until my first tenant arrives, and I'm as jittery as a bowl of jelly. What if he doesn't like it? What if he leaves after two days and demands his money back because he doesn't have a power shower, or because the cold tap drips in the kitchen sink? Maybe the house is terribly shabby compared with what else is on offer. I need reassurance, please! Weather has been mild and not too showery lately, fine for walking, so hopefully he's into that. Everything well with you?
N xxx

Nell
Calm down, he's bound to love the place.
Who cares about power showers on holiday?
And he's hardly likely to walk out because of
a dripping tap. I'm more interested to see how
you get on living above the pub – will you get
a wink of sleep at the weekends? Do you care?
I suspect not! All well here. Liam and I went
to the new Brian Friel play last evening,
wonderful. I think the only thing I'd miss if
I lived on Roone would be a theatre. We'd just
have to start our own drama group!
K xxx

LETTING THE HOUSE:
THE FIRST TWO WEEKS

Nell's father shook off his shoes and left them on the step outside the back door. He pulled on his walking boots and laced them up. He took the blackthorn stick that rested against the wall. 'I'll be off then,' he said, through the open kitchen window.

'See you later,' his wife replied from within.

Nice balmy day, breeze as usual off the sea but no cold in it. For a change July was behaving itself so far. Denis took the ring road that led to the school. His stick, its rubber tip long since worn away, tapped out a rhythm on the tarred road surface. He loved walking, always had. Walked the twenty-five minutes to the school winter and summer, unless the weather was truly awful or he had a load to carry.

He passed the creamery, waved at Con Maher going out in the truck. Con's twins long since left the school, Paul gone to Canada on work experience, Fiona doing some kind of interior-design course, wasn't it? Virtually everyone on the island under the age of thirty had passed through Denis

Mulcahy's hands, and he tried to keep track of as many of them as he could.

A car came up behind him and he heard it slowing down. He stopped as it pulled in and waited for his brother-in-law to slide down the passenger window.

'You don't look like you want a lift, but I said I'd check.'

Denis rested his arms on the door frame. 'Just out for a walk. How're things?'

He and Hugh had always got on. Hugh had had it tough, but you'd never know it by him – maybe because he'd always been the way he was. He'd never been bullied at school, the way anyone different was usually bullied. Truth was, people who knew him didn't notice the disability, probably because Hugh never seemed to notice it himself, never looked for any kind of special treatment because of it.

'Will we see you tonight?' he asked Denis.

'You will, of course.'

He'd rarely missed a Friday night since Hugh had taken over Considine's. Moira seldom accompanied him – she'd never been a drinker and wasn't particularly at home in a pub, even if it belonged to her brother – but Denis enjoyed a weekly chat with the fishermen and farmers he'd grown up with.

After Hugh had driven away Denis walked on, passing the fields he'd passed as a young boy. Different cattle and sheep in them now, looking out at the sixty-one-year-old man he'd become. A husband and father, a respected member of the island community. Not that he felt like any of those things these days, the happiness bubbling up in him one minute, the frustration and guilt pushing it away the next.

He reached the school, silent and locked for the summer. The empty playground looked so much bigger than it did during term time. He saw it in his mind's eye full of running students. He heard the clamour and the chants, the swish of a skipping rope, the thwack of a basketball against the backboard. The bell that elicited such groans at the end of break. He'd hear that bell on his deathbed, so familiar a sound had it become to him.

'You've a great life,' his friends said. 'Short working day and off all summer.' Not a clue, any of them. Never a school day without a challenge, everyone pulling out of him, everyone expecting the principal to solve their problems.

And the hours he spent when all the others had gone home, filling in forms and reading circulars, writing reports and applying for grants. Lonely hours, sitting in his office in silence – but no less lonely when he locked up and went home to his wife.

A great life indeed. For years it had been as empty as a shucked-off snakeskin. Putting up a front because it was expected of him, because there wasn't an alternative that he could see. Going to work, coming home, putting in the minutes and the hours until bedtime. Doing his best, always trying his hardest, at home and at school, but the emptiness remained.

And then, out of nowhere, everything had changed, his world had tumbled upside down in the space of a single unforgettable day. Nothing the same now. Nothing could ever be the same again.

It was the most wonderful thing to happen to him, he couldn't regret it. But now he was living a lie, snatching happiness when he could, and battling the rest of the time with the guilt his actions caused him. What sort of existence was that? How long could it go on?

It couldn't go on. It had to go on. He sounded like something out of Beckett.

You've a great life. If only they knew. If a single one of them had the smallest clue.

He turned in at the school gates and let himself into the silent, chilly building. He punched buttons on the alarm pad, and its beeping shut off abruptly. He walked along the deserted corridor that smelt of wax crayons and books and floor polish, past the infant classrooms with their miniature furniture, past a store cupboard holding old photocopiers and black bags of recyclable books, box files and an overhead projector.

He unlocked his office and sat behind his desk and lifted the phone and dialled a number he knew by heart. He settled back in his leather chair and listened to the soft double burr of the other phone ringing.

'Hello?'

He swung his feet on to the desk and closed his eyes. 'It's me,' he said. 'Will I see you later?'

'More peas?'

'Thanks.' Nell held out her plate and James spooned peas on to it. Peas always reminded her of 'The Owl and the Pussycat'. 'Imagine sailing away for a year and a day with nothing but a jar of honey and a wad of money,' she said.

Tim peeled a potato and smiled across the table at Andy, a she's-a-bit-daft-but-we-love-her kind of smile. Nell was familiar with it.

'Imagine getting your wedding ring from a pig's nose, though,' James replied. 'Not very romantic.'

Nell cut into her pork chop. 'No, but they were in love so they didn't mind where it came from. And I'm sure the owl cleaned it well.'

'Dipped it in the sea.'

'Exactly, or wiped it on a bong leaf.'

'I don't know which of you is worse,' Tim said, putting a wedge of butter on his potato.

'She started it,' James told him.

It felt like the Last Supper to her, the four of them gathered around James's table, pretending it was just another dinner. But afterwards, because their bed had been made up with fresh sheets for the man who was going to be sleeping in it tomorrow night, she and Tim weren't going home.

Everything was ready for them in the room off the salon: the furniture, such as it was, in place, a vase of montbretia on the windowsill, Nell's slippers under the single bed. The television, the microwave, the few bits of crockery and cooking utensils she'd scrounged from wherever she could find them, all neatly arranged on the built-in shelves. Milk for their morning coffee sitting in the little salon fridge.

She'd miss her patio, miss sitting out there on fine mornings, sipping coffee and looking at the hills before she had to leave for work. She'd miss their bed, and her big old cast-iron bath, and the couch where she curled up with Tim on Saturday nights, watching DVDs. And she'd miss John Silver, dozing at their feet.

He sat under James's table now, head humped on his paws as if he knew she was leaving him. Her bare toes curled on his back. Not for long, she told him silently. Just for a little while. I still love you.

They had mini Magnums for dessert, and afterwards Andy disappeared to his room, and James and John Silver walked the mile or so back to the village with them. The night was clear and chilly, the stars bright in the sky. Tim put an arm loosely around Nell's waist as they walked. She looked for Sagittarius, as she always did, and found him.

'So tomorrow Moira will be the welcoming committee,' James said.

'Yes. The man is due between two and three.' Nell twined her fingers around Tim's to draw him closer. 'Hope he gets decent weather.'

'Forecast is fairly settled for the next few days.'
'That's good.'

The three of them walked in silence for a while, the sea across a field to their right, the water luminescent under the night sky. Nell breathed in deeply and tried to push away a melancholy that had been nudging at the edge of her consciousness all day.

Six weeks stretched ahead of her, alarmingly far ahead, all the way to the thirteenth of August. Until then strangers would be putting muddy feet on her couch, doing whatever they felt like in her bed, being careless with Grandpa Will's mirror, maybe, so it crashed to the floor. Oh, why hadn't she put it away?

And the grey cat – what would happen to it? Would any of her tenants feed it when it turned up on the patio looking half starved, as it did every now and again? It didn't seem to have an owner, nobody around the place had laid claim to it. Nell had tried to hang on to it when it had first shown up, even though John Silver had growled every time he'd spotted it.

'Oh come on,' Nell had told him, 'there's plenty of room for both of you.' But the cat hadn't seemed interested in moving in. It stayed around barely long enough to devour whatever food Nell left out, and didn't reappear for days.

Maybe it was the only food it got, though. Maybe nobody at all would feed it for the next six weeks. She couldn't very well ask her tenants to look out for a half-wild cat that might or might not show up. She'd just have to hope it survived without her.

She whistled softly and John Silver came trotting back to nuzzle into her free hand.

'He'll be fine,' James said. 'We'll spoil him rotten.'

Nell scratched the dog's warm neck. 'I know.'

It's only six weeks, she told herself. It's no length of time at all. It'll fly by, and everything will work out fine. It'll be a story for our children, how the house was handed over to strangers just so their silly old mother could help pay for the most wonderful wedding.

They approached the village and she dug into her pocket for the key to the salon.

Two hundred miles away, Gavin Connolly added a second pair of jeans to his suitcase. Socks, underwear, shirts, sweatshirts, walking boots, umbrella, rain jacket. What was he forgetting? His toilet bag was filled and ready, waiting for his toothbrush to be thrown in next morning.

His first proper holiday in more than four years, and he was wondering what had possessed him to book it. No, he knew exactly what had possessed him: that evening in May when he'd come home from work and opened the first of the two letters that were waiting for him.

The divorce certificate had been a bit of a disappointment. Short and to the point, no crinkly paper, no fancy script. They gave out better-looking certificates to kids who came second in the zoo's colouring competitions. It said what it had to say and not a word more. No longer joined in holy matrimony was the gist of it. Single again, after his two-year mistake.

But Aisling wasn't single. She was with Whatshisname, having the babies she'd told Gavin she didn't want. He had laid the certificate aside and studied the second envelope, the one with the Killorglin postmark, and his name and address typewritten on the front. Don't let it be points on his licence, caught speeding by a camera somewhere in Kerry.

It wasn't points on his licence. It was a leaflet with *You're a Winner!* on the front page, and the Prize Bonds logo at the top. He'd opened it and read *Congratulations, your winning cheque is enclosed*. He'd slid out the cheque and read his name and *one thousand euro*.

He'd gone into the bathroom and turned on the taps. He'd sat on the edge of the bath and read the cheque again, and it was still worth a thousand euro. He'd counted the noughts, just to make sure. He was officially single with a big cheque to spend.

He'd book a holiday. The idea had jumped into his head.

When the bath was full he'd turned off the taps and gone to his computer, and begun looking for a place to rent. After about forty minutes of hit-and-miss surfing he'd found a two-bedroom house on an island off the west coast that he'd never been to. It was available for the first two

121

weeks of July, which was the holiday period he'd been allocated by his boss.

He'd scrolled through the photos of the house. It wasn't the Ritz, but it looked comfortable enough, and walking was mentioned. He'd clicked *make a reservation* and gone through the subsequent steps. He'd surrendered his credit-card details so that two hundred euro could be taken out of his account and given to N. Mulcahy on the other side of the country.

When the booking had been made he'd shut down the computer, wandered into the kitchen and made a bacon and Brie sandwich. By the time he'd remembered his bath the water was stone cold.

He'd drained it and begun again. He'd just won a thousand euro: he could afford to be a bit spendthrift. As he'd peeled off his clothes in the bathroom, which was steaming up for the second time that evening, he'd begun to wonder if he'd been a bit hasty.

A holiday on his own, in a place where he didn't know a soul. A whole two weeks, fourteen days, with nobody to talk to. The win must have gone to his head, or the divorce. Or maybe it was a combination of both, snatching away his common sense for an hour or two.

And why had he chosen somewhere on the other side of the country? What was wrong with finding a little place on the east coast? Come to that, what was wrong with driving to Dollymount Strand from here in about twenty minutes, spending the day there and getting home in time for the *Six One News*?

Instead he'd blown most of his Prize Bond winnings for the privilege of moving into a stranger's house for two weeks, surrounded by more strangers. He lay in the bath, his mood deflating.

Over the following days the idea of holidaying alone had become more and more daunting. Probably rain every day, he'd be stuck inside with nothing to do. Or the weather would be OK and he'd go out, and everywhere he went he'd be surrounded by couples or families or groups of friends, all those happy units having fun together. He'd see them checking out the man on his own in the corner; he'd smell their pity.

Three days after he'd booked the house he'd received a handwritten letter from N. Mulcahy, who turned out to be a female called Nell. She thanked Gavin for the booking, enclosed a receipt for his deposit, and told him that she was looking forward to meeting him. She had addressed him as Gavin rather than Mr Connolly, which he liked, but he was still flooded with uncertainty about the whole venture.

By the end of May his mind was made up. He wouldn't go. He'd cancel the booking, forfeit whatever he had to forfeit. What did he care about the money, so easily come by? He still had eight hundred euro left. He'd email Nell Mulcahy and say something had come up, some emergency at work that meant he couldn't take the time off, sorry about that.

He logged on to his computer and found the holiday-homes website. He looked again at the photos of the house, backed by rolling hills. The sky was too blue to be true in the outdoor shots – it must be doctored. Or maybe the fact that the place was surrounded by the sea made the sky look bluer, some reflection of all that water.

Surrounded by the sea. He'd always fancied the idea of living on a small island, with the taste of the sea in the air wherever you went. That was what had drawn him to the little house in the first place.

If he got good weather for the fortnight he'd be laughing. He could sit on that patio under that blue sky and read all the books he wanted. He could bring his bike; he could go swimming. *Adjacent to beach*, the ad said. He might even go fishing – that was something he'd always wanted to try. There were surely lots of fishing opportunities on an island.

He clicked *check availability* and there were his two weeks blocked off. Reserved for him; nobody else allowed to take it. He switched off the computer. He'd think about it for another week or two.

June arrived, drier than normal and quite mild. Each day he sat on his back step with a bottle of beer when he got home from work and listened to the twittering swallows that came back every year to nest under the eaves of his shed. He watched the parent birds swooping across his sadly neglected garden, and listened to the constant stream of cars, and thought about the island house that was still waiting for him.

Should he go? Wouldn't it be good to be out of the city, away from the crowds and the traffic? Wasn't it time he did something with his summer weeks off, rather than hanging around the house reading, like he'd done in the years since Aisling had left? And surely at the age of thirty-eight he could handle a holiday on his own.

In the end he decided to take the house – and now, the evening before, all his old doubts had come hurtling back. He closed his suitcase and moved it to the chair by the window. Too late to cancel now; he'd go and make the best of it. He'd walk and swim, and go for a pint in the evening, and hopefully the natives would be friendly.

He began to undress.

'*Jesus.*'

Nell kept her eyes closed. Hopefully he'd think she was asleep.

'Nell? You awake?'

Damn. 'Nearly,' she murmured.

'This is ridiculous. How are we meant to sleep with that racket downstairs?'

She manoeuvred herself around to face him. Changing position when you shared a single bed was an operation requiring no small amount of care.

'It'll finish soon,' she whispered, sliding a thigh over his. 'They'll be going home in a while.'

'But they'll be back tomorrow night. Are we going to get this every weekend?'

'I'll have a word with Hugh in the morning,' she promised. 'Tell him no talking allowed after midnight.'

He turned away from her. 'It's not funny.'

But it *was* funny, when you thought about it. And in the grand scheme of things it was only a minor inconvenience. He was tired after his week's work and the journey down from Dublin. He'd sleep on in the morning, she'd tiptoe out to work and ask her customers to keep the noise down till he woke up.

And she'd find someone going to Dingle, ask them to pick up a pair of ear plugs. There were ways around everything, if you thought about it.

He'd get over it. They'd manage.

James Baker added a smudge of titanium white to the blob of Naples yellow on his palette and blended them with his brush. He loved early summer mornings here, the fresh new smell of them, the clean briny sharpness you could almost taste, the chirruping and calling of the birds that flitted brazenly across the hedges to peck at the nut feeder he'd hung from the edge of the clothes line.

He was painting the garden, such as it was – a pocket handkerchief of lawn, a tiny shed, a rotary clothes line, an optimistic shrubbery, planted with cuttings from Nell – and the sky above it, which this morning was cerulean blue striped with shades of rose pink and magenta, cadmium yellow, gunmetal grey and viridian green, and every colour was changing by the minute. James worked rapidly, his brush flying over the canvas that he'd wedged into the top of his stepladder. He had no patience with easels: one stiff breeze and over they toppled.

The briny sharpness in the air mingled with the strong oily scent of his paints. A mug sat on the patio table to his left, a milky skin forming on top of the pale brown liquid. He made coffee every morning and poured it away, stone cold and forgotten, forty-odd minutes later. He forgot everything when he painted. The canvas was the thing, his mission to cover its ridged white surface with colour. Everything else was incidental.

His watch still sat on the bedside table, but his internal clock told him that he had about a quarter of an hour left. Today he was putting a second coat of deep ochre on the outside of Flaherty's dormer-windowed farmhouse. His degree in fine arts had qualified him for a variety of creative careers, from design consultant to stonemason, but the few he'd tried – graphic artist, interior decorator, lithographer – hadn't appealed, and he'd finally decided to make art something he did outside work hours, and to use paint in a very different way to pay the bills.

He enjoyed painting houses. It didn't nourish

his soul, like covering canvases did, but its honest simplicity appealed to him. And when he'd first met Karen, he was charmed to discover that her situation mirrored his. Her job as receptionist in a driving school was simply a way to make ends meet, and it was what she did outside working hours – in her case, writing poetry – that mattered.

When James and Andy had moved to the island after her death, James quickly discovered that there weren't enough house-painting opportunities on the island for him to make ends meet. While he was casting around for something part-time to bridge the gap, he'd been fortunate enough to need a haircut.

'My uncle's looking for someone,' the extremely chatty stylist had told him. 'He owns the pub downstairs, and one of his regular barmen is moving to Cork in a week or so. Go down and tell him Nell sent you.'

And Hugh had taken him on, although James had never before stood behind a bar in his life. He was to learn that serendipity was a frequent visitor to Roone. If he hadn't decided to get his hair cut, if the barman had moved away a month earlier, if Nell hadn't been so interested in the stranger who'd moved to the island with his son – 'We're all curious about you' – James might never have mentioned that he was hunting for a job, and it might never have happened.

His schedule at Fitz's wasn't regular. He worked whenever Hugh needed him – day shifts only until

Andy insisted, at thirteen, that he'd be OK on his own in the evenings – and fitted his house-painting jobs around his bar hours. His commute to the pub was a twenty-minute walk along a coast road, and after a week behind the counter he'd met more locals than he had in the two months since he and Andy had arrived.

It didn't take long for Roone to work its magic on James. He loved the way the island buzzed with life in the summer, but he also relished the different drama of winter, the wind that put roses into cheeks and drove the sea mad. He piled on layers and tramped the roads, or sat on the beach, his back against a rock, and watched the wildness of the waves.

He loved the way the locals reclaimed the island in the winter, settling back into familiar routines of card nights and knitting circles, and evenings spent gossiping comfortably around big turf fires in the pubs.

And, of course, he continued to make art, with a lot more time in winter when nobody was asking him to paint their walls. His pictures continued to sell fairly consistently for gratifying amounts of money.

But even if nobody ever bought one again, James Baker would keep on making art, every chance he got. Since Karen's death, painting had become as essential to him as eating – more essential, if the light was fading and it was a choice between stopping for dinner or beating the darkness. The food would still be there when he eventually got to it.

This morning Andy was still in bed, which seemed to be par for the course if you were fourteen and on school holidays. Occasionally he didn't appear until noon, or close enough to it. He'd emerge from his room, rubbing at his tousled hair and yawning, pulling open kitchen presses languidly in search of a late breakfast. Answering James's remarks with as few grunts as he could get away with.

Which was normal teenage behaviour too, everyone knew that. Ignore your parents whenever possible, sleep as much as you can, avoid showing enthusiasm for anything. All to be expected when it came to adolescence.

Not that they hadn't both been damaged when Karen had died. For months it had taken all of James's will to leave his own bed each morning, to carry on with life, when all he wanted was to shut everything out, to close his eyes and leave them closed. How much more awful, how terrifying it must have been for a ten-year-old child.

And despite Nell's assurance that James hadn't anything to feel guilty about, he thought he had. He'd handled it all wrong, never mentioning Karen, never instigating a conversation where her name might come up. That had been a mistake, to blot her out as if she'd never been, as if he and his son had somehow come together without her.

He had tried, when he felt able, to redress the wrong. About seven months after Karen's death, he'd suggested counselling to Andy. 'Someone to talk to,' he'd said. 'Just to get things off your chest. Apparently it helps.'

But Andy had looked blankly at him. 'What things?'

'Mum's death,' James had replied, the words causing a lurch of pain inside him. 'Maybe you need to talk about it. We've never really . . . With someone professional, I mean, not with me – at least, not unless you want to.'

Such a stuttering, pathetic approach he'd made, so belated and lame. Little wonder Andy had rejected it. 'I don't need to talk to anyone,' he'd said shortly, turning back to the science book that lay open on the table in front of him, and that had been that. And shortly afterwards, the idea of moving away from Dublin had come to James.

Maybe if they changed their physical surroundings, Andy might somehow find a way to unlock his feelings. It was a drastic step, but James decided to take the chance that it wouldn't make things any worse, and might just improve them.

But so far, Roone hadn't been the answer for Andy. Despite his father's best efforts, he'd made few friends on the island. He'd joined the primary school in sixth class, when friendships had long been established. At the end of the year most of his classmates had transferred, like Andy, to the closest secondary school on the mainland, and taken their friends with them. At parent-teacher meetings, Andy's teachers gave James no bad news, but seemed to have nothing very positive to say either. Andy, apparently, was moving through the system without causing any particular ripples. He was passing tests and handing in homework and not causing trouble.

Reading between the lines, James was left with the impression of an average, unremarkable student – which, of course, was fine as long as Andy was happy. But was he?

James had quietly hoped that Andy might show some artistic flair – he had no doubt that his own painting had been therapeutic after Karen's death, had healed him as much as he was capable of being healed – but the art teacher just spread his hands and told James that, while his son seemed to enjoy the class as much as any of the other students, he didn't stand out.

In time, hopefully, Andy would start to move in a particular direction – and whatever that direction was, James would encourage and support him, maybe compensate in some way for his earlier inadequacies.

He set down his palette and began screwing caps on to tubes. Time to stop: he'd done enough to be able to finish the scene later without it being laid out before him. He packed the paints away and swirled the brushes in turps and wiped them clean. The familiar, loved routine soothed him, as it always did.

As he pulled off his paint-spattered top and jeans

in the bathroom, he thought ahead to the rest of the day. House painting for the most part, with a lunch break that he'd spend on the little shingle beach just down the road from Flaherty's, if the weather held. Dinner with Andy, the evening shift in Fitz's afterwards.

He stepped under the shower, welcoming the hot water on his skin after the early-morning cool of the patio. He washed his hair, wondering how the new tenant in Nell's house would get on. No doubt James would hear soon enough. Word travelled fast on Roone, especially if you worked behind a bar.

Coming to the island had been a good move. He'd chosen the right place for them. Given time, Andy would fall under the island's spell too – it happened to everyone sooner or later. He would be healed on Roone: James had to go on believing that.

And in time, maybe, James would learn to accept that Nell had chosen Tim. He turned off the shower and stepped out, and reached for the least damp towel.

'Nice cake.' Hugh brushed crumbs from his lap.

'It's sour cream coffee walnut.' Nell parted his hair and began to cut. 'My penfriend sent me the recipe. I'm trying to decide if it's good enough for the wedding cake. So far, all I've settled on is carrot for the bottom tier.'

'Well, this one gets my vote.'

'I'll bear that in mind.' She snipped in silence for a few minutes.

'Where's Tim this morning?'

'Still asleep.'

'Ah . . . noisy, was it?'

She smiled. 'Just a little. But James is getting me ear plugs this afternoon.'

'Sorry.'

'Don't be daft: it's unavoidable.'

'You're not regretting giving up the house?'

'Not a bit – looking forward to my first week living smack bang in the middle of the village.'

He wasn't totally convinced. He imagined her stuck in one poky room every evening, having to put up with the noise from the pub below, not even John Silver to keep her company. But being Nell, of course, she was putting a brave face on it. And she'd have Tim at the weekends, which would help.

He recalled her delight when they'd started going out, her certainty, before very long, that she'd found what she'd been looking for. 'I think he's the one,' she'd said to Hugh one quiet evening in the bar just a few weeks after she and Tim had officially become a couple. 'I feel I can stop looking now.'

Nice for her. He was happy for her. She deserved to be happy.

'More tea?' she asked, and Hugh held out his cup.

'I told you,' she said, coming back with fresh tea and more cake, 'that it's a man on his own for the first two weeks. In the house, I mean.'

'You did.'

'I can't help feeling a bit sorry for him.'

'Oh, I don't know. Maybe he's just after a bit of peace and quiet.'

'That's what Walter said.'

Hugh had gone away on his own once, to the matchmaking festival at Lisdoonvarna. There were one or two he could have asked to go along with him, but he didn't want to take a chance on seeing their pity at the thought of Hugh Fitzpatrick looking for romance.

He'd parked the car and walked the length of the main street, weaving through the knots of people, all of whom seemed to know each other. Nobody standing apart, nobody looking as if they'd come on their own like him. He'd bought a pint in a bustling pub and found space to sit on a bench outside, and tried not to look as conspicuous as he felt.

After a while he'd wandered back down the street to a dancehall. He'd stood outside and listened to the music, and he'd known he couldn't go in. He'd walked back to his car and driven home to Roone. He'd talked to nobody, and nobody had attempted to talk to him.

The inner door of the salon opened and Tim appeared, in crumpled jeans and a black T-shirt. Unshaven, hair dishevelled, running a hand over his chin.

'Morning,' Hugh said.

'Hi, Hugh.' Tim looked at Nell. 'What do I do for breakfast?'

'You cross the road to Lelia's,' she told him cheerfully. 'Best full Irish this side of the Atlantic.'

He retreated into the room again, closing the door. A beat passed.

'I should have brought him back something when I was out earlier,' Nell said. 'I never thought of it.'

'He'll be grand, he's well able to get his own grub.'

'And it's not forever, only six weeks.'

'That's all.'

'Once he gets the ear plugs—'

The door opened again, and they both shut up.

'You must be Gavin,' Nell's mother said. 'You're very welcome to Roone. I'm Moira Mulcahy.'

The height of him – and that bush of hair, and thin as a rake. The kind you wanted to bring home and fill up with food. She was glad she'd brought the few scones.

'Is it your first time here?' Leading the way down the hall to the main bedroom.

'It is. I just liked the sound of it,' he said, in a rich Dublin accent. 'Being an island and all.'

A face full of freckles, a real Irish face. And those big front teeth, like a child's. A friendly, open kind of a face – and yet she sensed a vulnerability in him, something he'd lost, maybe, that had weakened him.

Then again, she could be all wrong. 'You'll enjoy it here,' she told him, pushing open the bedroom door. 'Everyone is very welcoming, and there's lots to see and do. Are you a walker?'

'I am – I love to walk.'

'Well, you've come to the right place.'

He stood on the threshold, taking in the room as he lowered his suitcase. Hard to tell what he thought of it. Maybe he'd been expecting more luxury.

'The house belongs to my daughter, Nell,' she said, running a hand over the duvet for something to do. 'She transformed it when she bought it – it was very run-down. An old man owned it before her. She has a hair salon in the village, which is why she's not here now. She'll call round after work to say hello and make sure you have everything you need.'

'Fine.'

He walked to the window and looked out. She hoped he appreciated the view of the hills. Odd, very odd, to be showing a stranger around Nell's house. He didn't look like the type to abuse it though.

'And my brother has a pub in the village, Fitz's. Be sure and say hello if you're in, and tell him where you're staying.'

'Will do, thanks.'

'Let me show you the rest of the house,' she said, 'and I'll tell you what there is to see on the island while you're here.'

The hair. Wait till Nell saw the hair.

As soon as the owner's mother had left, Gavin took his suitcase from the main bedroom and transferred it to the smaller room. He didn't suppose there would be any objection to his changing rooms – he was still using just one bed, one set of sheets.

Of course she'd assumed he'd want the other room, with its double bed. Adults generally slept in a double bed, whether they were sharing it or not – but since Aisling had left him Gavin had felt too alone in their bed, too abandoned. A single was safer; there was just enough room for one. Nothing was missing when you slept in a single bed.

He chose the one by the window, glad the room was at the back of the house, with its uninterrupted view of those marvellous hills, with their purples and greens and browns. He'd leave the curtains open at night, so he'd wake to that view.

He put his book on the bedside locker, his pyjamas under the pillow, his toothbrush in the glass on the bathroom shelf. He stored his jeans and shirts in the small wardrobe, his underwear and sweatshirts in the drawers of the dressing-table. He propped his umbrella by the front door, next to his walking boots.

He returned to the twin room and looked for a mirror to use for shaving. Bathroom mirrors wouldn't do: too steamy. Had there been one in the other bedroom, hanging on the wall? He went back and took it down, and as he balanced it on the windowsill of the smaller room he caught a whiff of soap. Must be laundry day somewhere in the neighbourhood.

The house was quite a bit smaller than his own, but something about it appealed to him, something he couldn't put a finger on. Silly, really, a house was just bricks and mortar – and this one was nothing special, with its mediocre furniture and cheap towels – but it felt . . . friendly, that was it.

He pushed his empty suitcase under the bed. Listen to him – must be the sea air going to his head already, making him think that the house was pleased to see him. But he wasn't imagining the lack of noise: that was real, and quite wonderful. Virtually no traffic, no sirens, none of the non-stop backing track of the city he hadn't realised was so loud until it wasn't there any more.

Here the noisiest things were the seagulls – and he thought he could make out the distant rumble of the sea, but maybe he was imagining that too.

He left the bedroom and went into the kitchen to make a cup of tea and eat one of the interesting-looking scones that Moira Mulcahy had made for him.

Her smile was dimpled. Her eyes were brown. She wore a blue dress and flat white shoes, and she was much shorter than him. Her hair was caught up behind her head, auburn tendrils trailing. An old yellow Beetle was parked behind his in the driveway.

'Hello there,' she said, looking up at him and putting out her hand. 'I'm Nell, the owner. I just wanted to drop by and say welcome.'

'Thank you.' Gavin shook her hand. 'Please come in.'

'Oh, I don't want to bother you—'

'Kettle's boiled this minute,' he told her. 'I'm just in from a walk. I was about to make coffee.'

'Well, if you're sure . . .'

In the kitchen she sat at the table. Gavin lifted the kettle from its base and poured water slowly into the waiting cafetière.

'It's funny,' she said, 'having someone else doing stuff in my kitchen.'

He turned. 'Would you rather—'

'Oh, no,' she said quickly. 'I'm quite happy to be waited on.'

'I was delighted to see this,' he said. 'The cafetière, I mean. I had planned to bring mine, and forgot. I'm an addict.'

'Oh, me too . . . How's it going so far?'

He brought the coffee to the table. 'Great. You have a very nice house. I feel completely at home already.'

She beamed. 'That's good. Do you have every-thing you need?'

'Absolutely.' He took mugs from their hooks and milk from the fridge. 'I only have full fat, I'm afraid.' None of the girls he worked with would touch it.

'Full fat is mandatory in coffee.' She added a generous splash to her mug. 'Where did you go on your walk?'

'I checked out the lighthouse and the holy well.'

'And you're lucky with the weather, so far anyway. Did Mam tell you about Walter next door?'

'The man with the organic food for sale?'

'Yes – eggs, honey, vegetables, apples. He's lovely, in a kind of country-squire way. His family moved here from England, generations ago. He's real old school, tips his hat when he meets a woman, that kind of thing. Oh, and he has a sweet little donkey that often puts his head over the wall and looks into my back garden. Just to let you know, in case he appears.'

She was easy to talk to. Maybe it was the diamond ring on her left hand that relaxed him. Already promised to another man, so she wasn't sizing him up and finding him wanting. Too tall, too skinny, too freckly.

'You'll have to come to Fitz's,' she was saying, and Gavin tried to remember what he'd been told about that.

'You can't miss it, right in the middle of the village. There are only two pubs, but Fitz's is nicer. Not that I'm biased, or anything. I presume Mam told you it belongs to her brother.'

'She did. I'll certainly call. Now, would you care for one of your mother's excellent scones?'

'No, thanks – my fiancé's taking me out to dinner.'

Her fiancé. He felt like warning her about marriage, but maybe she wouldn't appreciate it. And maybe she'd be one of the lucky ones.

She left soon afterwards, having given him her mobile number – 'just in case' – and a wedge of dark chocolate cake wrapped in greaseproof paper that she lifted carefully from her basket – 'Let me know what you think: I'm trying to choose wedding cake tiers' – and having told him to look out for a grey cat hanging around – 'It's a stray, but I usually throw it a bit of food when I see it. It always looks so hungry, poor thing.'

He stood on the doorstep and waved as she drove off. Would she have laughed if he'd said her house was friendly? He didn't think so.

And hopefully the grey cat would appreciate chocolate cake, which Gavin couldn't abide.

'He's terribly nice – but you should see his hair.'

'What about it?'

'It's like a bird's nest on top of his head. He mustn't have been to a hairdresser in years.'

'Good job he met you so. Presume you mentioned the salon.'

'Oh no, I couldn't – but Mam did.' She ran a finger down the menu. 'I fancy the prawns tonight. I still think it's sad, though, coming on holidays on his own. Like Shrek.'

Tim looked at her. 'Like Shrek?'

'You know, all alone in his swamp.' She paused. 'Maybe he was married and she died, like James.'

'Or maybe he was never married. Or maybe he's divorced, or separated.' Tim lifted his glass. 'Let me know when you find out.'

'I will,' she said, smiling.

The waiter approached, and they ordered food.

When he'd gone, Nell put a little paper bag on the table.

'What's that?'

'Open it.'

He pulled out the ear plugs, still wrapped in their hard plastic shell. He looked up at her. 'For me?'

'For you.'

He reached for her hand and brought it to his lips. 'I don't deserve you.'

'Probably not – but you've got me.'

'Forever,' he said.

'And a day,' she replied. 'Just for luck.'

'We met at the zoo,' Gavin said, 'of all places. Well, not so surprising really, given that I work there. I was chuffed that she seemed interested – well, look at me.'

His eyes were too small and practically colourless, the grey of the irises so pale it was almost silver. His nose was long and pointed, and the end veered oddly to the left. His two front teeth were ridiculously large, giving him the appearance of a giant, gormless child. And there wasn't an inch of his face that wasn't covered with freckles.

'But at least I have a full head of hair, right? Not every man can claim that at thirty-eight. Although my mother keeps nagging me to cut it.'

His mother was probably right. He hadn't given much thought to his appearance in the last five years. He hadn't given much thought to anything really.

'She walked out five years ago, you see. My wife. My ex-wife.'

Aisling had brought her nephew to the zoo for a birthday treat. Some time during their visit she'd managed to lose her car keys, and Gavin had been drafted in to help with the search. When he'd found them, she'd insisted on him accompanying her and the child to the coffee shop.

He often thought about that afterwards: if he hadn't been the one to find the keys he'd probably never have spoken to her again, they'd never have got married, she'd never have had a chance to break his heart. The little hiccups of Fate, the quirks of circumstance that find us all at some stage.

'She didn't seem bothered by my lack of physical beauty. She said I was like Tarzan of the Jungle, surrounded by wild animals. So naturally I asked to see her again, and incredibly she said yes. We went to the cinema.'

She was older than him by two years, thirty-two to his thirty. 'Voluptuous' was the word that came to mind when he thought of her figure, the shiny material of her skirt straining over her wide hips, her breasts pleasingly large and round inside a sleeveless polka-dot top.

In the darkened cinema she took his arm and placed it around her shoulders. 'Get comfy,' she whispered, a white satiny strap sliding out from under her top and slipping off her shoulder as her hand drifted on to his knee, causing an erection

144

that lasted the entire film, not a second of whose plot Gavin remembered afterwards.

'The week after that we went out to dinner, and two evenings later she cooked roast chicken in her apartment and I stayed the night, and from then on we saw each other at least twice a week, and I moved my spare toothbrush into her bathroom.'

He'd remained amazed at her continuing interest in him. What was it that had attracted her exactly? He supposed his personality was fair to middling, but there were plenty of men with decent personalities and good looks to go with them.

In retrospect, of course, it was easy to see what exactly had sparked Aisling's interest in Gavin, what had encouraged her to walk up the aisle and pledge her eternal devotion to him. It wasn't him she wanted, it was his money. Much as he hated to admit it, the fact remained that they both disappeared around the same time.

After years of saving most of what he earned – not having anyone to spend it on – and investing a lot of it fairly prudently, Gavin had been what could be regarded as comfortably off. He'd had enough money to take Aisling on the cruises she adored, to pay for the conservatory, the new kitchen and the second bathroom she'd felt his house lacked, and to trade in her eight-year-old Nissan for a new Saab.

'I never refused her anything. Shame she didn't give me the one thing I wanted. Before we were married she told me she wasn't really into kids, she said one nephew was more than enough. But having found a woman willing to marry me, I wasn't about to be put off. I told myself she didn't mean it, that she'd change her mind when we were married. I was convinced that sooner or later she'd get broody.'

But Aisling had shown no sign of becoming broody, and the marriage wasn't blessed with children. Eighteen months after they'd become man and wife, Gavin's finances were showing signs of dwindling, and Aisling became notable by her absence from the family home.

All her excuses had been classic – working late, emergency meeting, filling in for someone sick. Gavin had swallowed them all, like the sap he was. He'd never checked up on her, never thought he needed to – despite her increasing lack of interest, when she eventually came home, in any sort of intimacy with her husband.

'And then her grandmother had a stroke, and I phoned Aisling at work to tell her, and she wasn't there – well, I think you can guess the rest. We were married for less than two years, but I had to wait another five for the divorce to come through. Got it two months ago, finally. She's still with the man she had the affair with, and they have two children now.

'Sorry,' he added, 'I'm probably going on a bit.'

His companion remained silent. That was one of the many things Gavin loved about donkeys: the way they never criticised.

*   *   *

It was just as beautiful as when she'd first seen it. The intricate handmade silk flowers, the tiny mother-of-pearl triangular buttons, the way it flowed from her shoulders in one continuous sexy line, the beautiful pale green colour – all this was good, all this was exactly as she'd remembered it, and the reason she'd put the deposit on it in April. Her mother had cried when she'd seen her in it, for goodness' sake.

And now it was hers, the final payment made, the bill settled at last, the dress packed carefully in tissue and brought home to the island. And it still fitted her, still disguised her far from perfect shape.

But.

She turned this way and that in front of the mirror in her old bedroom. She pushed her bra straps off her shoulders and out of sight, held her hair up, stood on tiptoe so the hem skimmed the floor. Yes, it was a wonderful dress, worth every penny she'd paid. The perfect dress for the perfect wedding.

She closed her eyes and did a slow twirl, imagining her and Tim on the dance floor, moving together to 'What Are You Doing The Rest Of Your Life?', the song they'd chosen – well, she'd chosen – for their first dance as husband and wife. Tim's arms around her, every eye in the room on them. Mr and Mrs Baker, starting out on the rest of their lives.

She stopped, opened her eyes. Of course it wasn't going to feel wonderful now, when she was all by herself in her old bedroom in the middle of a summer's day. Everything was wrong, from the black knickers underneath to the hair that needed a wash to the shadows below her eyes from a third broken night in a row. Living over a pub sure had its challenges, even with ear plugs.

Tonight should be fine, though – Mondays were quiet enough. She began to undo the tiny buttons. Every bride felt nervous: she wouldn't be human if she didn't get the jitters in the run-up to the most important day of her life. It was par for the course, the way she was feeling now.

She slipped out of the dress and folded it carefully back into its box. She'd head to James's house in a while and take John Silver for a long walk – too breezy for *Jupiter* today – and he'd help to banish this nonsense. She pulled on her clothes and made a brief phone call before bringing the box downstairs.

In the kitchen her mother was shelling peas.

'What are you bringing that down here for? Leave it upstairs, it'll be fine in your room.'

Nell set the box on a chair by the door. 'Actually, I'm going to put it up in my attic – I rang Gavin just now and he's there. I'd like to have it in my own house . . . You don't mind, do you?'

Moira looked at her in surprise. 'Of course not – but why on earth are you putting it into that dusty attic?'

'It's well wrapped up, it'll be fine.' She couldn't explain the need to bring her dress home, she just

148

felt it was the right place for it. 'I'd better go; I told him I'd be there in a few minutes.'

'Will you come back for lunch? We're having salmon.'

'Would you mind if I didn't? I want to take John Silver out walking – and I'm not that hungry.'

She *was* that hungry. Her poached-egg breakfast had been at eight, right after Lelia had opened up. But if she stayed for lunch her mother would sense her mood, and Nell couldn't explain it. She'd get a sandwich on her way to James's and eat it on the walk.

She drove the half-mile to her house and pulled into the driveway behind Gavin's red hatchback. As she was lifting the box from the back seat the front door opened and he appeared. 'Here,' he said, walking over, 'let me take that.'

'Thanks . . . Hope you don't mind my barging in like this.'

'Not at all, happy to help.'

He brought the box inside and Nell went ahead of him to pull down the attic stairs and flick on the light switch. He looked doubtfully at the opening. 'Are you sure you want to put a wedding dress up there?'

Nell laughed. 'You sound like my mother. It'll be fine in the box.' She climbed up and took it from him.

'Will I put the kettle on?' he called as she disappeared.

'No thanks, can't stay.'

She stood at the top of the stairs, smelling the musty, comforting scent, her eyes gradually growing accustomed to the dimmer lighting. There was the stuff she'd moved up just last week, tucked into the triangle formed by the chimney breast and the slope of the roof. Behind it was the water tank, propped on breeze-blocks. Beyond that, the gable wall of the house.

It was silent and still. No birdsong penetrated; no breeze moved the air about. Nell laid the box beside the rest of their belongings. It would be safe here, nothing would happen to it.

As she descended the stairs and folded them up. Gavin reappeared from the kitchen. 'All done?'

'All done, thanks again. I'm glad you're getting the weather. Have you everything you need?'

'Absolutely.'

'Any sign of that cat?'

'Not yet – but I met the donkey.'

'Oh good. Isn't he sweet?'

He was so tall, must be well over six feet. She tried to avoid looking at his hair. She had a sense of something lost about him, some sadness behind those rather colourless eyes. 'If you're doing nothing tonight,' she said, 'drop into Fitz's for a pint. I'm usually in there around eight on Mondays.'

There had been no reported sightings of him over the last two nights; maybe he was shy about going in on his own. 'It'll be quiet,' she said. 'Nice for a relaxing hour or two.' She'd introduce him to a few of the locals, get him chatting to Hugh.

'I'll do that,' he said. 'Thanks.'

She left him on the doorstep, waving as she drove

off towards the village, heading for James's house on the other side. Hopefully he was enjoying the holiday. No way of knowing, really.

Katy –
My first tenant arrived, and he's lovely. You should see his hair though – I'm itching to go at it with my scissors. It's like something from the seventies, does nothing for him. Oh, and I got the dress, finally! I put it up in my attic, just wanted to have it in the house. It'll be fine up there. All well with you? Seen any good plays?
N xxx

Nell
You got the dress? Thrilling. Was it as wonderful as you first thought, or better? Can't wait to see you sashaying down the aisle in it! Tenant sounds like the last hippie in Ireland – but as long as he pays his bills, and doesn't trash the place, he'll do. Isn't the weather lovely? No plays, too nice to sit in a theatre. I'd rather be out walking, or sipping a glass of something in a beer garden.
You didn't mention the new living arrangements – how are you and Tim coping?
K xxx

Most of the time nobody asked Hugh Fitzpatrick if he needed help. Nobody asked him because most of the time he was perfectly capable of doing things for himself. Fifty-one years was long enough to get one and a half arms to do whatever you needed them to do. And one and a half arms were enough, if that was all you'd ever had.

Hugh's mother had sailed through her first pregnancy and given birth to a healthy daughter, whom she had named Moira. Seven years later she'd gone to her doctor complaining of nausea. He'd congratulated her on her second pregnancy and given her a prescription for a new drug called thalidomide, which he said was showing wonderful results in counteracting morning sickness.

First-time visitors to Fitz's pub tried not to stare at the arm that ended at Hugh's elbow, but locals had long since stopped noticing it. He pulled a pint, filled a short and opened a bottle as ably as anyone else, and he cleared glasses from the tables at the end of the night faster than many others.

He wasn't working now though. Mondays he took it easy, putting one of his barmen behind the counter for the day and only coming on duty at six for the evening shift. Mondays were for the mobile library, followed by the beach, if the weather permitted. And today was breezy, but otherwise fine.

The beach he favoured was probably the island's least attractive one. It never saw the sun, nestled into the cliffs on the northern side. It was accessed via a narrow sloping track from the road, with not even a signpost to indicate its existence.

It was pebbly and difficult to negotiate, particularly if you had only one and a half arms to keep your balance as you crunched your way along its curve. It was a narrow strip of land wedged between the cliffs and the sea, and had nothing much going for it.

But it suited Hugh, maybe because of the water that surged in gentle waves on to the stones and rattled away again. If there was a more soothing sound, he had yet to discover it. Or maybe it was the peace this beach afforded, deserted as it often was, even in the middle of summer. He'd never been drawn to the more popular spots, where you couldn't flick a towel without getting sand into someone's eyes, where people nudged their companions when they saw him, and children stared openly.

Hugh didn't mind the pebbles. Cleaner than sand, and nothing that a wadded towel couldn't cope with. He didn't mind the scramble it took to get here, slithering as much as walking down the track from the road, or the climb back it necessitated afterwards. For him the beach was an oasis, and he came as often as he could.

Today he had the place to himself again. He settled on his towel and watched the sea approaching and retreating. He slipped his feet out of his shoes and pulled off his socks and rolled his trousers up to the knees. He lay back carefully and closed his eyes and listened to the softly repeated wash and rattle of the water.

153

Business was good, a steady increase in the pub takings since the beginning of the tourist season, like every year. Winters of course were quiet, but the summer months more than made up for that. He was putting by a decent sum, building up a solid nest egg. He had nothing to keep him awake at night, no debts he couldn't manage, no sick relatives to care for. No health worries himself, thank God.

And if he got lonesome from time to time, so be it. He couldn't expect everything to go the way he wanted. Not everybody found someone. There were lots of single people in the world, and he was one of them.

He breathed deeply, lulled by the music of the sea. He was grateful for what he had. Leave it at that.

The latest painting wasn't working. There was a heaviness, a dullness about it. Somewhere along the way its early-morning freshness had been lost – one misplaced stroke, that was all it took – and the harder James tried to salvage it the worse it became. It was frustrating. It made him want to throw it against the wall.

'What do you think?' he asked John Silver, but the dog was scrabbling at something in the shrubbery and ignored him. James cleaned his brushes and wiped his hands on the old T-shirt he used as a rag. Waste of time, waste of paint. He'd let it dry and paint over it, start again. The joys of being an artist.

He went through to the kitchen. The house was quiet, Andy out somewhere. James poured himself a glass of pineapple juice and drank it leaning against the fridge, trying to breathe away his irritation.

'Hello, you.'

He turned to look out of the window and saw Nell crouching on the patio, her arms around John Silver's neck. He watched her murmuring to him, running her hands through his coarse hair. He saw John Silver's tail swishing back and forth, heard the dog's grunts of pleasure.

Her top rode up a little at the back, exposing a couple of inches of pale skin. James set his glass in the sink and walked out.

'James, you're there.' She stood. 'I'm taking this fellow for a walk. Want to come with us?'

He glanced at his watch. 'I'm on duty in Fitz's in half an hour.'

'We could go that way.'

'Hang on then.'

He went inside and changed quickly into clothes that didn't smell of white spirit. When he reappeared she was studying the half-finished painting. 'It's a disaster,' he told her, sliding the patio door closed behind him. 'I've messed up.'

'Have you? Looks fine to me.'

Despite himself, he smiled. She lifted his spirits, always. 'Glad someone likes it.'

He didn't lock the door – nobody did on Roone. They left the way Nell had come in, by the side of the house, and turned in the direction of the village. The banks of montbretia on either side of the road danced in the breeze. In the distance the sea sparkled with sunlight. John Silver bounded ahead.

'I paid the balance on my wedding dress this morning,' Nell said, pulling a sandwich wrapped in clingfilm from her rucksack.

James glanced at her. 'Did you bring it home?'

'I did, in a giant box. Want some? It's Brie and cranberry.'

'No thanks . . . Bet you put it on and danced in front of the mirror.'

'I did not.' She laughed, biting into her sandwich.

Her top was pink, with short puffy sleeves that reminded him of someone in a nursery rhyme – Little Bo Peep, or maybe the one who'd brought a lamb to school. Her hair was scraped off her face into a ponytail. He preferred it loose, or tied up badly so half of it fell down again.

They walked in silence for a few minutes. The wind lifted James's shirt-tails, blew through his hair. The sky was patched with small cotton-wool clouds. At the crossroads they turned left, the village street a hundred yards ahead. Nell whistled and John Silver came racing back towards them.

'You won't feel it now,' James said, 'till the wedding.'

'No.' Her face in profile looked thoughtful. She finished the sandwich and dabbed at her mouth.

'Nerves kicking in?'

'Just a bit.'

He remembered his own wedding day. Sick with fright he'd been, no hope of keeping breakfast down, his mother pressing him to eat something. His palms damp as Karen walked up the aisle to him in a white dress that stopped above her ankles and unfamiliar shoes with pointed toes, and little white decorations in her hair that he realised as she drew nearer were real flowers.

'The guest list is coming out at two hundred and thirty-seven,' Nell said. 'That's as small as it's going to get.'

'Just an intimate affair so.'

'That's right.'

Immediate family and a dozen friends was all he and Karen had had. An uncle of Karen's had married them, and then everyone had walked the two blocks from the church to the restaurant they'd booked for dinner. Their wedding night had been spent in a horribly anonymous hotel near the airport, their flight to Venice leaving at eight the following morning.

'We've decided on Antigua for the honeymoon, just for a week.'

'Very nice.'

Venice had collared James. He'd fallen utterly in love with the narrow cobbled streets, the bridges, the gondolas, the squares – and the art, the art. He and Karen had taken hundreds of photos, stood in front of countless paintings and fountains and statues, sipped coffee and cognac overlooking the water, their feet entwined under café tables.

'I did dance in front of the mirror,' Nell said then. 'Just for a minute.'

'Thought so.'

On the outskirts of the village they passed hedges of dangling red and pink fuchsia and bushes of coconut-scented yellow furze. Birds wheeled in the pale blue sky. James pulled a stick from the brambly hedge and flung it back the way they'd come, as far as he could. John Silver bounded after it, barking with joy.

'I hope it's been good for you and Andy,' Nell said, 'moving here.'

The comment was unexpected, but Nell often said something that seemed unconnected with whatever had come before it. Another quirk that James, of course, found completely endearing.

'It was a good move for me,' he answered. 'I just hope Andy feels the same. I still worry about him.'

She was the only person he talked to about Andy, the only one he felt would understand.

'He's quiet,' she said, 'but he's also fourteen, and motherless. Maybe he's as good as he can be. And he has you, so he's not too badly off.'

He felt a wave of gratitude towards her. He wanted to pull her against him, wrap his arms around her, feel the warm curves of her body.

'Thanks,' he said instead. Out of bounds, promised to Tim.

'For what?' Her cheeks were pink, from the sun or the breeze, or both.

'For being nice to him. He mightn't show it, but I know he thinks you're cool.'

She smiled. 'Good to hear.'

Being with her tore him in two, but the thought of not seeing her regularly was far worse. They approached Fitz's, and the blue door that led to Hair Upstairs right beside it.

'How long are you working?' she asked.

'Just till six.'

'You have to come back later then. I've told Gavin to drop in around eight. I want to introduce him to a few of the locals, make him feel at home.'

James felt a stab of completely irrational jealousy. 'I'll call in for an hour,' he said, watching as she turned and left the village the way they'd come – bound, no doubt, for the beach. Drawn to the sea like the mermaid she was.

He pushed open the door of the pub, his heart pattering about in circles like a lost pup.

Walter Thompson removed his gardening gloves and boots and shoved his feet into the house slippers that waited on the step outside the back door. He hung the clippers on their hook in the scullery and washed his hands at the Belfast sink before continuing into the kitchen.

He filled a glass with water and drank it, then set about preparing his evening meal. He lit the gas under a saucepan of water and added a chopped carrot and three small new potatoes, and sprinkled salt in after them.

He may have been mistaken. Just because it appeared that his new neighbour was talking to George VI didn't make it so. The man was undoubtedly standing next to the donkey, and certainly appeared to be engaging with the animal, but the voice Walter thought he'd heard coming from across the field might simply have been the calling of the gulls. Or the wind, perhaps, quite strong today.

He melted butter in the frying-pan and cracked an egg on top of it. He cut two slices of the multi-seeded soda bread Mags O'Donovan gave him in exchange for half a dozen eggs each Monday and Thursday.

As he refilled his water glass he glanced out the window and saw the man again, this time setting off on foot in the direction of the village. Going for a drink, perhaps; not much else to do in the evenings around here.

He wondered suddenly if perhaps the fellow had a fondness for alcohol. Being under the influence could certainly cause one to behave a little oddly. A person so afflicted might easily strike up a conversation with a donkey – or, indeed, with any creature that happened to be in the vicinity.

Walter drained the vegetables and spooned them on to his plate and placed the egg carefully on top. Not that there was anything inherently wrong with talking to animals – in fact, as drunken behaviour went, it had a lot to recommend it. Far better than shouting and roaring and throwing one's fists about, like some unfortunate drinkers were wont to do.

And as long as talking to the donkey was as eccentric as his neighbour's behaviour got, Walter wasn't about to let it bother him. He ate his dinner and turned his thoughts to the evening ahead, to the comforts of pipe, armchair and brand new library book.

'Stay,' he said to John Silver, and the dog looked at him, tongue lolling, tail wagging. 'Sit,' Andy said, pushing down on the animal's hindquarters. John Silver took the hint and sat.

Andy walked into the supermarket. He crossed to the magazines and stood looking at the covers for a few minutes before going to the counter. 'A quarter of apple drops,' he said to the assistant, whose face he knew but whose name he didn't. When she turned to take the jar off the shelf behind her Andy reached silently for a Mars bar from the display in front of him and slipped it into his pocket.

The assistant weighed the sweets and tipped them into a small white paper bag. 'One thirty-five, please.'

Andy counted out the money and left the shop without another word.

He walked the half-mile or so to the beach, John Silver trotting at his side. It was crowded with people Andy didn't know, grabbing the sunny day while it lasted. He thought it was Tuesday, but he often lost track during the holidays.

He didn't like the beach in the summer. It was too full of happy families, reminding him of what he'd lost. He liked the sea – no, he loved the sea – but he preferred when he was alone on the beach with the crashing water. He threaded his way through the crowd, making eye contact with nobody, until he reached the end of the sand where the rocks began.

He hoisted himself up and clambered over them, John Silver beside him. When the noise from the beach had faded and he'd left the last of the holidaymakers behind he selected a smooth flat rock, just a few feet from the water's edge.

He sat on the rock and pulled his jumper over his head and bundled it into a pillow. He lay back and looked at white smudges in the blue sky as he tore the wrapping off the Mars bar. John Silver settled with a grunt beside him.

He closed his eyes and listened to the water lapping and sucking against the rock shelf. A drift of spray landed lightly on his face, and he put his tongue out to catch the salt.

He didn't remember his first time on Roone. 'You were just a baby,' his father had told him, the day they'd driven from Dublin to see the house for sale, eight months after Mum had died. Andy had sat hunched in his seat, refusing to look interested, still lost without her, still unable to think about her without wanting to cry.

The thought of leaving Dublin hadn't bothered him much – how could it, when the worst thing that could happen already had? What did it matter where he lived or what he did after that? Not that he was interested in going to look at new houses, least of all one on an island miles away from anywhere, but he was eleven years and three months old, and he didn't get to do what he wanted.

He knew he wouldn't miss his friends if he and his dad left Dublin. He'd already lost them along with Mum. Looking at him funny when he went back to school a few days after the funeral, as if they were waiting for him to start crying. Talking to him in the playground before the bell rang, but not in the way they used to, not like he was one of them any more. It was as if he'd turned into somebody else, someone they'd been told they had to be nice to.

The teacher putting an arm around him when Andy walked into the classroom, asking if he was OK in a soppy voice. Stupid question. Imagine if Andy had said, no, he wasn't OK – what would she have said then?

And his father wasn't there any more, or it felt like he wasn't. Oh, he was in the house when Andy got home from school, cooking sausages or fish fingers or chicken burgers for dinner, but you could see his mind was miles away. He never asked about homework like Mum used to do, never remembered that Wednesday was PE day, or that Andy hated tomatoes unless they were in a pizza.

And he never talked about Mum, not once after she died, not even when they visited her grave after Mass every Sunday. It was like she'd never been there, and all they were visiting was a slab of stone in front of a rectangle of earth. Andy would stand in front of the gravestone and look at her name and try not to think about her lying in a coffin below him, because it hurt too much.

And then, months later, his dad asking him if he wanted to see a shrink. Of course he hadn't said it like that, but that was what he'd meant. As if Andy had some sort of mental disease, just because his mother had died.

He found it hard to remember the way he and his dad had been while Mum was still there. Her death had settled between them, had forced them apart, and Andy didn't know how to get back to before.

And it hurt to remember the good times, the trips to the cinema and the seaside and the zoo, sometimes the three of them and sometimes just him and his dad. That was all gone now, nothing of it left, so why get upset remembering it? Better to just leave it behind and go on pretending that things were OK.

He finished the Mars bar and screwed up the wrapper and shoved it under his balled-up jumper. Mum had taught him not to throw litter when he'd been very small. He remembered her lifting him up so he could put his sweet papers and ice-lolly sticks into a bin.

She wouldn't think much of him taking a Mars bar without paying for it, but she wasn't there to see it happening. She wasn't anywhere now, Andy couldn't feel her, so it didn't matter that he'd been helping himself to Mars bars for quite some time.

Would his father care if he found out? Probably not. Oh, he'd have plenty to say about it, but it wouldn't matter to him, not seriously. His father had stopped caring about things since Mum died. They talked a bit – or, rather, his father talked, probably because he felt obliged, and Andy responded when he had to – but there was no real communication between them, not any more.

He opened the bag of apple drops and put one into his mouth and sucked. Nell might be bothered if she knew about the Mars bars. She might be the only person who'd be bothered. He liked Nell: she talked to you as if you actually mattered. She was the only person on Roone he looked forward to seeing.

But even Nell was no help on the bad days, when missing Mum took over and left room for nothing else. On those days he cycled to the cliffs and climbed over the safety fence to where there was nothing between him and the edge, and he imagined stepping off into nothingness. He thought about the feeling of hurtling through the air, he heard the whistle the wind would make as it rushed by him. He imagined the icy sharpness of the water as he plunged in, as it closed over him and stopped him being miserable.

He didn't think anyone would miss him for too long. His father would do a few paintings and forget about him. Nell might be upset for a bit, but she'd be too busy getting married to remember him much, and then she'd have her own kids to think about.

He opened his eyes and looked up at the blue in the sky. He turned his head and watched a woman way back on the beach leading a little toddler to the water's edge. Even from this distance he could hear the child squealing as the sea rushed over his bare feet, as the woman swept him up into her arms, laughing.

His own mother's face floated into his head, the way it had looked the last time he'd been allowed to see her. Dark hollows where her cheeks should have been, a cough rattling in her throat when she breathed, brown rings around her eyes. The breath coming out of her mouth smelling bad, as if she'd eaten something rotten.

A yellow and blue scarf wound around her head, her lips painted a horrible unfamiliar red that someone, some nurse, must have put on her. Making her look like a stranger to him, some horrible clown who'd taken the place of his mother. Her fingers cold and bony when she'd reached her hand towards him, whispered for him to take it.

'You're my star,' she'd told him. 'My precious star. Always remember.' His ear to her blood-red mouth so he'd hear the words as they struggled

166

out, feeling nothing but revulsion for the creature she'd become, for the smell that came out of her. Wanting more than anything to bolt from the too-warm hospital room, to drop her bony hand and escape.

He turned his head away from the beach and lifted it to rest it on John Silver's warm belly, and closed his eyes again.

'Hello,' the man said. 'Gavin Connolly, staying next door for a fortnight. I'm told you have produce for sale.'

Walter shook his hand, feeling decidedly short in comparison to his caller. 'Walter Thompson. You're most welcome to Roone; please come in.'

His neighbour didn't look as if he'd spent the night drinking. Not terribly well groomed, to be sure, in a black T-shirt that Walter would have relegated to the duster bag long since, and a pair of baggy beige trousers that only travelled as far as the middle of his calves, and horrendous blue (blue!) rubbery sandals on his feet, but looking perfectly fit and well rested all the same.

Walter led him through the house and into the scullery, which held his jars of neatly labelled honey and cardboard trays of eggs. The man asked for lavender honey and half a dozen eggs. 'And I'd like some vegetables too, please – I want to make some soup.'

'Certainly.' Walter took a basket from its hook and put the honey into it. 'We shall go to the garden and you may select from what I have.' He led the way out of the house.

'I met your donkey yesterday,' his neighbour said, as they walked through the herb garden and Walter's small orchard beyond it. 'We had quite a chat over the wall.'

'Did you?' Walter attempted nonchalance. The man seemed perfectly normal otherwise. 'You like animals then.'

But his companion had stopped listening. 'Those apples look ripe,' he said. 'And it's only the beginning of July. I thought apples didn't ripen till September.'

Walter nodded. 'Yes, they're rather early this year.' He'd learnt not to mention that the tree produced excellent fruit for ten months of the year. For some reason the knowledge tended to make non-residents of Roone a little nervous.

In the vegetable garden his visitor selected onions, carrots, potatoes and a turnip, which Walter duly assembled and stowed in the basket. As he straightened, he saw the man looking across the field to where George VI pulled grass from the ground.

'I take it you like animals,' Walter repeated.

'I do – although I normally associate with less domesticated ones. I'm a keeper in Dublin Zoo.'

'Ah . . . Would you care to see my beehives and henhouse?'

'Certainly.'

They skirted the two beehives and approached

the wired-off chicken run outside which a dark-haired man sat on the ground, bent over a sketch pad as he observed the scatter of hens that pecked and scratched as if nobody was watching.

'James Baker, local artist,' Walter explained as they drew near, and James got to his feet, brushing dust from the seat of his jeans. 'Gavin Connolly,' Walter told him, 'staying next door.'

'We met,' James said, 'last night in Fitz's. I come to annoy Walter's hens every now and again,' he explained.

Gavin regarded the drawing. 'That's good. You should come to the zoo next time you're in Dublin – I could get you up close and personal if you want some new subjects.'

'That'd be great – and I'll drop that life-jacket over to you later on.' James turned to Walter. 'Gavin's going out to sea tomorrow with Willie Buckley.'

'Good for you,' Walter said, although a few hours in Willie Buckley's vessel would have been his idea of Purgatory. Each to his own. They left James to his sketching and turned back to the house.

In the herb garden Walter paused to add a selection to the basket. 'For added flavour,' he explained.

'Very good . . . The soup is for the trip tomorrow,' the man told him. 'I've never been on a boat before – apart from the odd car ferry, of course. Must say, I'm quite looking forward to it.'

'Ah.' Walter snipped off a sprig of parsley. Each to his own, indeed.

*   *   *

Nell picked up her brush and switched on the drier. 'He's going out with Willie Buckley tomorrow.'

Her mother frowned. 'Willie Buckley? All that fellow does is pull up lobster pots.'

'I know, but it'll be a novelty for Gavin. He's never been on a proper boat, can you believe it?' Nell began twining hair around the little brush. 'Hope he gets the weather.'

'It's not promised great. Did you tell him to wrap up well? He could catch his death out there.'

Nell laughed. 'Mam, relax – he's not going to the Arctic Circle.'

'Still, though, if a wind comes up . . . I hope he's bringing something hot to drink.'

'I told him there was a flask under the sink. He promised to drop in on Thursday and tell me how he got on.'

'Oh, good – maybe he'll ask you for a haircut. Isn't it desperate?'

'Terrible, but he must like it.'

Her mother sighed. 'Lord, that man needs a woman to put him right.'

Nell reached for the hairspray. 'Don't they all?'

He loved the city at night, loved to stand at his apartment window and feel the energy that pulsed all around him. Traffic and voices and music and sirens, a myriad of separate sounds, gloriously colliding. Smells of food and diesel and perfume that rushed at him when he opened the window, lights flashing and winking and beaming at him.

He was comfortable here, the city where he'd been born and brought up. He thrived on the noise and the bustle and the drama. He'd have to come back to it after they were married. Nell would understand. He'd make regular trips to the city, bring his children here, show them that Roone wasn't the only place to live.

Strange that he could be surrounded by noise here and sleep soundly, and last Friday night he hadn't closed his eyes until the last of the drinkers in Fitz's had gone home. Maybe it was because he expected Roone to be quiet, maybe that was it.

And he had to admit that the peace of the island at night was a welcome novelty after the week of city sounds. He'd lie beside Nell and hear the lulling thunder of the sea, or the soft hoot of the owl that nobody had ever seen but that made its presence known every so often. Of course he enjoyed all that – who wouldn't, every now and again?

But the room beside the salon was quite another story. The two of them trying to fit into a single bed above a noisy pub had been a very different experience. The ear plugs had helped a little on Saturday night, but he suspected that trying to get a good night's sleep in their temporary accommodation would prove to be an ongoing challenge.

He checked the clock on the wall above his entertainment system. Ten past eleven on Tuesday night. Nell would probably be in bed, curled up with a book. Or maybe she was having a nightcap downstairs with Hugh, now that the pub was on her doorstep.

The pub was where Tim and Nell had met, more than two years ago, when Tim had brought his girlfriend Amy to Roone. It was his first visit to the island, despite the fact that James and Andy had been living there for well over a year. It wasn't that he had any objection to seeing the place, but the long trek from Dublin had always put him off.

Ironic, when you thought about it.

So when he and Amy had been trying to decide where to go, Tim had suggested Roone, thinking it was high time he made the trip – and on their first night they'd dropped into Fitz's while James was working behind the bar.

Nell had been sitting on a stool at the counter, and James had made the introductions. Tim and Nell had regarded each other.

'I know you,' he'd said.

'We've met somewhere,' she'd agreed – and it had taken them all of half a minute to work out that he'd been a customer at the Hair Studio while she was working there.

And it hadn't taken Tim much longer to decide that he wanted to see her again. Travelling back to Dublin with Amy he was rehearsing his goodbye speech to her.

The following weekend he was back on the island, chatting Nell up in Fitz's, using every ounce of the charm he knew he possessed. It had worked.

Within a month they were an item – and the following spring he had stopped sleeping on James's couch every weekend and moved into Nell's house. And now the rest of his life was all mapped out, and he and Nell were going to spend it together.

On Roone.

He left the living room and went to bed.

At half past six the morning was full of promise, all pale blue sky streaked with pink, the air cool and crisp. Gavin wore three sweatshirts and an anorak under his borrowed life-jacket. Probably be peeling the layers off later when the sun got going.

He couldn't help feeling rather smug as he covered the twenty minutes or so from Nell's house to the pier. How many people went off to sea with a flask full of homemade soup made from organic vegetables? He'd packed an extra mug for Willie, who would surely want some when he smelt it. He'd also had the foresight to bring his book, in case Willie preferred quiet meditation as he sat with his fishing rod.

Gavin wondered how many fish he'd catch. Not that it mattered – the act of holding a rod would be novelty enough, the feeling that he was hunting for his supper. On the other hand, if he was lucky and ended up with a good haul, he'd offer a fish to Walter as a neighbourly gesture. And, of course, one to Nell, who'd organised the trip.

He whistled softly as he passed the quiet houses that flanked the coast road. Nobody else about at this hour, curtains pulled across every window. Nobody up but Gavin and the other fishermen.

Willie's boat was easy enough to find, Willie himself being very much in evidence, dressed in yellow oilskin dungarees and serious-looking foot-wear. He was coiling ropes and stacking empty crates on the small boat's deck as Gavin approached. Two empty white plastic barrels sat off to his left, a large box half filled with water beside them. No sign of seating. Fold-up chairs, probably, in the tiny cabin.

'Hop on,' Willie said, and Gavin hopped on to his very first proper boat – and promptly lost his footing and landed with a painful thwack on his backside, the rucksack thumping down behind him. He scrambled to his feet – 'I'm fine, I'm grand' – and attempted to recover his dignity as he made his precarious way across the deck.

It didn't take him long to discover that the surface was lethal unless your shoes were like Willie's and had tread like tractor tyres. He stood at the side of the boat and clung on tightly to the guard rail, his left buttock throbbing insistently from the fall. He hoped that the fold-up chairs, whenever they appeared, would be stable.

'Can I do anything to help?' he asked, hoping Willie wouldn't suggest a job that required him to move in any direction.

'You're grand, be heading out in a minute,' Willie

replied, tinkering with some sort of pulley system to the left of the cabin.

Gavin looked around. There was no sign of any fishing rods. He peered into the cabin and saw no fold-up chairs. He began to suspect that his idea of a fishing trip might not exactly coincide with Willie's.

He tried to remember what had been said in the pub on Monday night. He'd admitted to Nell and James that he'd never been on a boat, and Nell had immediately said, 'Oh, Willie's one of our fishermen, he'll take you out,' or words to that effect. Willie, sitting at the bar, had been duly introduced, and Gavin had been instructed to present himself at the pier before seven o'clock on Wednesday morning.

The more he thought about it, the less certain he became that 'fishing rods' had been part of the conversation. And what did the stacked crates have to do with anything, or the pulley? His unease grew, but he decided to say nothing and see what transpired.

'We're staying in the harbour,' Willie called over his shoulder, as he turned on the engine and steered the little boat away from the pier. 'All you have to do is keep out of my way when the pots come up.'

'Pots?'

'Lobster pots,' Willie said, glancing at Gavin, still clinging to the rail. 'Fifteen of 'em.' Jerking a thumb at the stacked crates. 'Fresh ones, ready to go down.'

Not crates, lobster pots. Fifteen of them. Gavin's heart sank. Had lobsters been mentioned in the pub? He had no recollection of it. No fishing, then, no leisurely catching of his dinner. Just Willie hauling fifteen lobster pots up from wherever they were hiding and replacing them with empty ones. And Gavin keeping out of his way.

He turned to look back as the pier drifted off behind them, and he felt the whip of the wind on his face. Grey-white patches were beginning to spread themselves across the blue sky. Might not be that fine a day after all.

Operation Lobster Pots began. Willie hauled them one by one to the surface with the pulley, whose diesel motor belched smoke directly into Gavin's face. Most of the pots contained no lobsters, but were full of crabs, starfish, sea urchins and lots of seaweed.

Willie put what few lobsters he pulled from the pots into the water-filled box. He snapped off the crab claws and tossed them into the white barrels, then flung the de-clawed creatures, along with everything else, back into the sea.

At one stage he caught Gavin watching as he removed the claws, and winked. 'Doesn't hurt 'em,' he said. 'Grow again.'

It sounded unlikely to Gavin. He suspected the truth was being manipulated in an effort to spare his sensibilities, but he didn't question it, too concerned at this stage with avoiding hypothermia to offer the crabs much sympathy.

It had grown steadily chillier the further into the harbour they'd travelled, with a lethal edge to the breeze and the sea spattering over the side of the boat every so often. Gavin was frozen, colder than he ever remembered being, even in the middle of the last harsh winter. His gloveless fingers were numb from hanging on to the rail. His teeth were clamped together in an attempt to keep them from chattering. He had long since lost the feeling in his toes.

Finally he could bear it no longer. 'I think I'll go into the cabin for a while,' he managed to push out through lips that almost refused to move.

Willie, seemingly unaffected by the cold, nodded as he hauled the latest pot over the side and thumped it on to the deck. 'Bit warmer inside,' he offered.

Gavin negotiated the deck inch by inch, skirting the pulley whose twining ropes threatened to snatch his jacket if he got too close. He thought longingly of the soup: a mug of that and he'd soon thaw out. Might settle his stomach too, which felt decidedly queasy from a combination of trying to keep his balance on a lurching boat and standing downwind of diesel fumes for an hour.

The cabin was marginally less cold. It took him a while to undo the straps of his rucksack, to coax his frozen fingers to perform the necessary mano-euvres. Finally he lifted out the flask and unscrewed the top, savouring the appetising smell that wafted up, anticipating the glorious warmth of the soup,

177

grateful that he'd taken the trouble to make it from scratch.

He set the flask's cup on a bundle of old magazines and began to pour – and a decidedly lumpy liquid slopped out. Hadn't he mashed everything to a fine pulp with Nell's potato masher? He stopped and peered into the flask – and realised, to his horror, that its inner section had smashed to smithereens, presumably when his rucksack had thumped on to the deck as he'd fallen.

He poured the soup and metal mixture back into the flask and replaced the lid. He returned it to his rucksack and took out a cheese sandwich. He offered half to Willie, who refused it. For the remainder of the time he huddled in the cabin, blowing feebly on his hands, too dispirited to take out his book. His whole body shivered. No part of him felt remotely warm.

He fantasised about the mug of coffee and the long soak in Nell's gloriously big bath he was planning when he got back. Later, when he was feeling human again, a bowl of stew somewhere, or a nice fat steak. Something hot anyway, and not in the least fishy.

An eternity later, they drew up at the pier. Gavin shook hands with his host. 'Many thanks,' he said. 'It was an experience.'

Nicely noncommittal. He was relieved not to be offered any crab claws from the almost-full containers. He thought he might never eat crab again. Or lobster.

He stepped on to the side of the boat and placed one foot on the steps that climbed to the pier – just as the little craft caught a wave and dipped away. For a terrifying second Gavin teetered above the gap, arms flailing, before tumbling down and hitting the water with a splash.

In fairness, Willie was extremely apologetic. He offered Gavin his fishy-smelling jacket and a lift home, if Gavin could wait while he unloaded the boat. Gavin took the jacket and declined the lift – almost four hours of hanging around was more than enough for one day.

He squelched the mile back to Nell's house, ignoring the stares and nudges of the people he passed. In the house he put the kettle on to boil as the bath was filling. He peeled off his drenched clothes and made a large pot of coffee. Just before he climbed wearily into the bath he wiped a circle of steam from the bathroom mirror and regarded himself.

His lips were dark blue. The end of his nose was a deep red, the rest of his face greyish-white. His hair stood on end. He looked like a terminally ill scarecrow. No wonder they'd stared.

He turned his back on the mirror and looked over his shoulder and peered at the reflection of his left buttock, the one he'd come down hard on in the boat. It was purplish pink, and felt tender. He didn't think anything was broken – was there anything to break in your backside? – but sitting might be painful for a while.

He hauled himself gingerly into the bath with his mug of coffee, deeply regretting that he hadn't packed a bottle of brandy in his suitcase. He lay back and closed his eyes. He rested his mug on his chest and gradually began to thaw out.

The story would be all around the village by teatime. He was the tourist who'd fallen on his backside getting into the boat and fallen into the sea getting out.

He grinned. When you thought about it, it was quite funny. And he was still in one piece, just about.

He'd take the ferry to the mainland in a while, find a place to get an early dinner, follow it with a couple of pints somewhere quiet, catch the ferry back and climb into bed with his book. Tomorrow he'd replace Nell's flask and call to the salon to fill her in, if she hadn't already heard. In the evening he'd drop Willie's jacket back to Fitz's like he'd promised, and endure the slagging he suspected was coming his way.

But tonight he'd take it easy.

'He fell into the sea.'

'What – in the middle of the harbour?'

'No, as he was getting out at the pier. He was halfway out and a wave caught the boat and he—' She broke off. 'Are you *laughing*?'

'Oh come on, it's funny.'

'It is *not* funny. He could have drowned.'

'What – at the pier, in full view of Willie?'

'Well, he could have banged his head or something. As it is, he's smothered in a cold – he must have sneezed a dozen times in the salon.'

'He was in the salon? For a haircut?'

'No, to tell me how the trip went. And he broke my flask, poor thing, when he was getting in.'

'Getting *in*? I thought you said he fell getting out.'

'Well, he fell getting in too – he fell into the boat, slipped on the deck . . .' She broke off, trying to stifle a giggle.

'Are *you* laughing now? You are, aren't you?'

'I am,' she admitted. 'It *is* funny. Poor Gavin, though. He's coming to the pub tonight, we'll make a fuss of him.'

'I'm sure you will. He'll remember his trip to Roone.'

She giggled again. 'He certainly will. So I'll see you tomorrow night, around seven.'

'Might be a bit later. I can't leave till I get something finished.'

'OK, do your best.'

She looked out the salon window and saw James on the opposite path. She rapped on the window and beckoned him up. She watched him cross the road and disappear through the blue door directly below her.

'I have to go,' she said. 'See you tomorrow. Hugs and kisses.'

The salon door opened as she hung up.

'You won't believe what happened to Gavin,' she said.

'Way ahead of you,' James replied. 'This is Roone, remember?'

Gavin pulled the front door closed and got into his car, setting his rucksack on the passenger seat. As promised by last evening's forecaster, the day was warm and sunny, with no sign of rain. He drove a mile and three-quarters away from the village, to a point where the road split and ran off in two directions.

'Don't turn for the beach,' Nell had said, so he took the right fork and made his way slowly along a much narrower road that climbed steeply upwards, his car brushing against the straggly hedges that bordered it.

The road became a grassy-middled lane that eventually lost interest and petered out beside a turnstile. Gavin parked and proceeded on foot, through the turnstile and into a field. He picked his way along the edge, avoiding cowpats and rabbit burrows and the odd darting dragonfly, until he reached a second turnstile.

This led, as Nell had promised, into a small wooded area through which he continued along an earthy, winding, sun-dappled path for about ten minutes until the trees came to an end and the path opened out into a grassy area about the size of a squash court.

Gavin walked to the safety fence at the edge of the space and slowly lowered his rucksack. On the other side of the fence, perched on the last foot of land, a signpost that read *The Statue of Liberty: 3,000 miles* pointed straight out to sea. According to Nell, the spot was known locally as Jackson's Lookout – although, in what Gavin was coming to recognise as typical Roone style, nobody knew who Jackson had been.

Because of its remoteness, the place was generally deserted. 'You'll probably have it to yourself,' Nell had told him, and so he had. He stood for a few minutes, drinking in the view.

Projecting out far below him was the headland on which the lighthouse stood, where he'd walked on his first day. Beyond it the sea, white and green and turquoise, rushed in to throw foam on to shiny black rocky slabs before slithering away again.

He saw the coloured dots of sailboats on the flashing, sparkling water, and the blue-grey of the horizon shimmering in the distance. Across the sea to his left was the mainland, a patchwork of greens and yellows and browns dotted with isolated white farmhouses and scattered villages.

In the far distance to his right, barely visible, was a darker strip that he thought might be the Connemara coastline. Above him the wide, wide sky, faded blue today and streaked with pure white, and cradling the fuzzy lemon yellow of the sun.

Gavin pulled Nell's blue and white throw from his rucksack and spread it on the grass and lowered himself carefully on to it, favouring his bruised buttock. He lay back, hands behind his head, realising he'd forgotten to bring sun cream. No matter, he wouldn't stay too long.

The head cold that had developed after his unscheduled dip in the sea was on the wane. He was still coughing but his throat wasn't as scratchy today, and he'd all but stopped sneezing. His head still felt a little light but his temperature, he was pretty sure, was back to normal after a night of burning face and shivering limbs.

He'd got off lightly. A dose of pneumonia, after his ordeal on the boat, wouldn't have surprised him. Today the sun would warm his bones and banish the last of his cold. He closed his eyes and listened to the gulls calling above him, and the crash of the waves far below, and he thought it was high time he began to live again.

Five years of nothingness since Aisling had walked out. Going to work each day, putting in the time until he clocked off and went home. Alive but not living – and now, for some reason, it had suddenly become impossible to carry on like that.

Maybe it was the divorce coming through at last – maybe that closure was nudging him to get going again. But the divorce had been more than two months ago, and it was only in the last week, since arriving on the island, that he'd been feeling an increasing urge to pull himself out of his five-year rut.

He had to change. He *would* change. He opened his eyes and sat up. He pulled his phone from his rucksack and found Nell's number and made an appointment.

'A haircut,' he said. That should make her day.

He'd seen his hair – really seen it – when he'd been shaving earlier in front of the little oval mirror that he'd propped on the windowsill of his room. As he'd run the electric razor over his chin his gaze had wandered upwards – and for the first time he realised how truly awful it was. Why hadn't he noticed it before? Why hadn't his mother nagged harder? Why had it taken a battered old mirror to show him what five years of neglect had done to his head?

He returned his phone to the rucksack and lay back again, resolution flooding through him. He'd turn things around, get out more. He'd find things to do that brought him into contact with other people.

He closed his eyes, weary after his broken night – and within a minute he was snoring gently as the sun continued to beam down.

'There was a busload of Americans here today,' Moira said, reaching across the table for a slice of bread. 'They invaded Lelia's for lunch. She was run off her feet.'

Denis spooned egg mayonnaise on to his plate. 'I'm sure she coped.'

'She did, of course. I'm just saying.'

A beat passed, during which Felix, standing by his bowl, mewed loudly and pointedly. Moira got

185

to her feet and scooped little brown pellets from a ceramic jar on the worktop into the bowl.

'You spoil that cat.'

'I know – but he's all I have to spoil since Nell is gone.'

Denis made no response.

'You heard about the tenant, what happened to him,' she said, resuming her seat.

'I did – he must be a bit of a clown.'

'Ah no, he was just unfortunate. Nell said he got a terrible cold after it. He was in the pub last night drinking hot whiskies, in this weather.'

'It's warm today,' Denis said. 'Wonder will it last.'

Moira refilled both their cups from the teapot. 'Are you golfing tomorrow?'

He added milk to his tea and stirred. 'I will, I think.' He looked at her. 'You don't mind, do you?'

She helped herself to more egg mayonnaise. 'Why should I mind? It's good exercise, and you seem to enjoy it.'

He sipped his tea and wondered how long he could go on.

Nell's mouth dropped open. 'Oh my God – what happened?' But it was obvious what had happened.

'Fell asleep,' Gavin said, shrugging off his jacket, 'at Jackson's Lookout. Forgot the sun cream. But it looks worse than it is.'

'It's not painful?'

'Well, it is a bit, but I'll live.'

'Natural yogurt,' she said. 'Get a couple of big

tubs in the supermarket. Keep it in the fridge, and keep slathering it on. It'll be messy but it works.'

'Right.'

'Are you still OK for a haircut today, or do you want to leave it till next week?'

'No, no, go ahead.' Gavin regarded the chair. 'But, er, you wouldn't have a cushion, would you?'

She grinned. 'Sorry – I forgot your other little problem. Hang on.'

She vanished into the next room. Gavin looked at his bright red face in the big mirror. Coming to Roone might have filled him with resolve to put his life back together, but the island wasn't without its hazards.

Nell returned with a pillow that she folded on to the chair by the sink. 'Now – that should keep you well padded. Still feels tender?'

'Yeah, just a bit.'

'Poor you.' She draped a towel around his shoulders. 'At the rate you're going, it'll be a miracle if you make it home to Dublin in one piece. I hope you're not sorry you chose Roone for your holiday.'

'Not at all,' he said. 'Not in the least. I think it's the best decision I've made in five years.'

'Good to hear that. As far as I'm concerned, it's the only place to live. Now, what kind of a cut do you want – just a trim, or a bit more?'

Gavin looked up at her. 'I'll leave that in your hands,' he said.

⋆　　⋆　　⋆

Andy lay on his bed and listened to Kurt Cobain. He hated soppy love songs, everyone happy, nobody dying. At least Cobain had sung about the world as it really was.

John Silver lay on the floor beside the bed, head resting on his paws. Andy's father didn't like the dog being allowed beyond the living room, but he was out, and what he didn't know wouldn't hurt him.

The net curtain billowed gently in the small breeze that slid in through the open bedroom window. It was a perfect day, all blue sky and sun, anyone could see that. Andy lifted his arm to check the time: ten past four. So far today he'd stayed in bed till after eleven, eaten a bowl of cereal and two slices of toast, taken John Silver for a walk and played a couple of games of poker on his laptop.

He'd talked to nobody. His father had left the house before Andy was up, and he hadn't met anyone he knew on the walk. He'd nodded at faces he recognised, but that had been it. Not once had he opened his mouth to speak all day.

In an hour or so his father would be home, calling him to help with dinner. They'd cook and eat, and then wash up, like they did every evening. His father would talk, and Andy would respond. After that Andy would probably take John Silver for another walk, then watch telly or surf the Net till it was time to go to bed.

He turned on his side and closed his eyes and let Nirvana's mournful lyrics wash over him.

Is this it? he thought. *Is this all there is? Is this how it's always going to be?*

The idea was unbearable.

Walter approached the stone wall that divided his property from Nell's, having spotted her tenant sitting in the shade of the patio umbrella, head bent over a book. 'I beg your pardon.'

The tenant looked up – and Walter promptly forgot what he had been about to say. His neighbour's face and neck appeared to be covered in some sort of awful white goo. Walter's hand travelled instinctively to his own face. He attempted, for the sake of politeness, not to show his horror. 'Er . . . you seem to, er, your face . . .' He trailed off, unable to articulate what he saw.

'Ah . . . yes, sorry.' The man laid aside his book and got to his feet. 'It's yogurt,' he explained, crossing the patio, 'recommended by Nell for the sunburn. I'm afraid I got a bad dose yesterday.'

'Oh dear.' Walter was vastly relieved to discover that the man hadn't contracted some mysterious, and possibly contagious, disease. 'I do hope it's not too painful.'

'Well, it did sting a bit, but the yogurt has cooled it down a lot.'

'I'm very glad to hear it.' Walter decided to make no mention of the boating mishap that Moira Mulcahy had told him about in the supermarket the previous day. The man was obviously accident prone. 'I was wondering if perhaps I might borrow

189

Nell's pruning shears, as I appear to have temporarily mislaid my own.'

'Yeah, no problem, if I can find them.'

'The shed, perhaps,' Walter suggested – being accustomed to forgetting where he'd set down his various gardening tools, and aware that all of Nell's, regularly borrowed, were kept there.

The shears were located – and Walter, about to depart with them, was stopped short for the second time in a matter of minutes. He stared at the other man's head, and blinked in astonishment. 'I've just realised,' he said, 'you've cut your hair.'

His neighbour smiled. 'Well, Nell did, actually.'

James Baker moved his bishop. 'Check.'

'Bloody hell,' his younger brother said, hand hovering over the few remaining white pieces on the board. Chess had never been Tim's game. He was more of a card player, but James didn't possess a pack.

Growing up, they hadn't played much of anything together. Five years was quite a gap when you were eight, or ten, or fifteen. By the time they were both in their twenties they might have found some common ground, but by then James had met Karen, and what little free time he didn't spend in her company was taken up with painting, so the two men had seen each other infrequently, usually at their mother's house.

They'd always got on, but they didn't seek each other out. Their lives were different. *They* were different. James knew that Tim was here today only because he was at a loose end, with Nell working in the salon and their house out of bounds.

'Think I'll admit defeat,' Tim said.

'Think you might as well.' James gathered the pieces together and slid them into their box. 'Looks like we're in for a shower.'

'Bloody hell.' Tim stood and crossed to the window, stretching his arms above his head. 'Always rains more in the west.'

'Actually, the sun splits the rocks here during the week.'

'Ha ha.'

James stowed the chess box on the shelf under the TV. 'Coffee?'

'Go on then.'

'So,' he said, spooning coffee into mugs in the kitchen, 'how's it going so far? Living above the pub, I mean.'

'Nightmare,' Tim replied. 'Worst move ever. After two when I got to sleep last night.'

James could think of worse things than lying awake next to Nell. He decided it might be wise to hold his peace on that topic. 'Have you met the man who's taken the house?'

'No.'

Gavin had been living in Tim and Nell's place for more than a week, and Tim hadn't laid eyes on him. Granted his brother was only here at weekends, but in Tim's position James was fairly sure he'd want to see whoever was renting his place.

They were different, no doubt about that.

'She got the dress,' Tim said.

'She told me.'

James didn't want to talk about anything to do with the wedding. Already he was dreading his role as best man, having to pretend that he was happy for his little brother, smiling for the cameras while his heart broke quietly.

The rain began as the kettle boiled. James filled their mugs as it tapped untidily against the kitchen window.

If you were quite short-sighted – and perhaps a little drunk – you might, on a particularly foggy night, be forgiven for momentarily mistaking Gavin Connolly, Dublin zookeeper, for Sean Penn, Hollywood actor.

Gavin studied his yogurt-free face in the little oval mirror. There was definitely a similarity from certain angles, if he kept his mouth closed so you didn't see the big front teeth. The nose, he thought, and the bone structure were pure Penn.

Amazing he'd never noticed it before. Amazing what a difference a haircut could make.

'You're sure about this?' Nell had asked. 'You're happy to leave it up to me?' When Gavin had said yes, she'd washed his hair, transferred him and his pillow to the cutting chair, and swung him around so his back was to the mirror.

'Better,' she said, 'if you don't see it as I go along. Better if you wait till it's done. Trust me.'

Hair began to accumulate on the floor all around him. Gavin watched and marvelled at the quantity. He wondered belatedly if she knew what she was doing. He had no idea what kind of a hairdresser she was. He tried to remember the haircuts of the men he'd met on the island, and failed. He decided this was a good sign. If they'd been shockingly bad he'd probably have noticed. He'd trust her, like she'd said. Not that he had any other choice at this stage.

And when she'd finally laid down her scissors and turned him back to face the mirror, he'd hardly recognised himself. His hair was shorter than he ever remembered having it, but even with his sunburn – and a stripe of white on his forehead that had been hidden up to now – it was plain to see that the improvement she'd wrought was miraculous.

He'd met her eyes in the mirror.

'Like it?'

'Love it.'

'Oh good – I can't *tell* you how much I was dying to do that.'

Her candour had amused him. 'It was bad, was it?'

'Horrendous. The worst hair I've seen in a long time.' She'd stopped. 'Sorry – am I being too honest?'

'Not at all.'

He didn't mind. How could he? She'd transformed him. He'd attempted to pay her, but she'd refused to accept a cent. 'I enjoyed that so much I feel I should be giving *you* money. And anyway, it's the least I can do, when you've paid for most of my wedding dress.'

She was wonderful. Gavin suspected that he was far from the only man on Roone who deeply, deeply regretted that she was promised to another.

He looked again into the mirror. His sunburnt skin, remarkably, had all but recovered. The bright redness of just a few hours ago had faded to a much more sedate pink, and the stinging pinch had completely vanished. If Gavin believed in magic he'd have put it down to that – but of course it was the yogurt, soaking like a balm into his burnt skin, moisturising and soothing.

His cold was gone completely too, not a single sneeze all day, no more scratchy throat, no rattling cough.

All things considered, he was looking and feeling a hell of a lot better than he had been a week ago, when he'd driven on to the little ferry and crossed the sea to Roone, with no clue about what was ahead of him. He remembered how he'd regretted his impulse to book the holiday, how close he'd come to cancelling the whole thing.

One week left, and already he knew he didn't want it to be over. He looked forward to whatever else the island had in store for him, as long as it didn't involve too much physical trauma.

★　　★　　★

'Wait till you see him. If I say so myself, it's a triumph. I should have taken before and after photos and made up an ad.'

'You don't need to advertise,' Tim pointed out. 'You have a captive audience – you're the only hairdresser on Roone.'

Nell lowered her wine glass and looked at him. 'My customers come to me, darling, because I'm good at what I do, not because there's nobody else.'

'Oh, leave him alone,' her mother said, pouring gravy. 'He was paying you a compliment.'

'He implied that my customers have no choice.'

'Well, they haven't, not the older ones anyway – but that's not Tim's fault.'

Tim smirked at Nell. Nell slapped his arm. Her mother sighed.

'You're like two children. I don't know how you'll manage when you have some of your own. Can I have the salt, Denis?'

Nell watched her father passing the salt cellar across the table, her smile fading. Had he lost weight? Was he sick? Was that what had been preoccupying him of late? Because something was on his mind, something had changed in him, she felt sure.

'How's the golf going?' Tim asked him.

Denis lifted a shoulder. 'Well, I'm no Darren Clarke but I enjoy it. How're things at work with you? They keeping you busy?'

She hadn't said anything to her mother, who gave no sign that she was concerned about him.

195

And if his wife, who lived with him all the time, had noticed nothing, then there was surely nothing to notice.

'So you're pleased with Gavin's hair,' her mother said.

'Delighted. You'll see it when he's leaving, if you don't bump into him before then.'

'Lelia told me he got an awful roasting at Jackson's Lookout.'

'Oh, he did, terrible. He was like a lobster, poor thing. I told him to get natural yogurt.'

Her mother tutted. 'You'd think in this day and age, with all the sun creams you can buy, that people would have more sense.'

'He fell asleep.'

'Is there more gravy in that jug?' her father asked, and Tim passed it over.

There might be nothing wrong with him. Nell might be imagining things. He was tired, that was all. Overdoing the golf, maybe. Two and three times a week, off to the ferry with his clubs. Still, he must be enjoying it. Nobody was forcing him to go.

Let her be mistaken. Let there be nothing wrong.

'Drive carefully.'

He put an arm around her shoulders. 'Always do, darling.'

'Wish you weren't going,' she said, pushing her face into his shoulder.

He planted a kiss on her head. 'You always say that.'

'Well, I always wish it. I can't wait till we're

married, and you're here all the time.' She drew back so she could see his face. 'It's OK, isn't it? The room, I mean. I know it's not ideal, but we're coping, aren't we?'

'So far so good.' He put a finger to her cheek. 'But you owe me, big-time.'

'I know.' She kissed his finger, reached up and kissed his mouth. 'Love you.'

'Me too.' He opened the car door. 'Call you later. Take care, see you Friday.'

She waved as he drove off. She pulled out her phone and selected his number and texted, *Miss you, love you, call me when you land xxx*

Think of the beautiful green dress, and the honeymoon in Antigua, and the new bed, and being back home where they belonged. She turned and walked back into her parents' house to get her jacket.

Gavin's phone rang as he was finishing his second breakfast egg. He laid down his toast soldier. 'Hello?'

'It's Nell – just wondering if you're free today.'

'Hang on – I'll check my diary.'

Her laughter bubbled down the line. 'Please tell me that's a joke. I'd be very worried if you were scheduling your holiday activities.'

'It's a joke.' He refilled his coffee cup. 'I'm free.'

'Oh good. It's my day off, and I'm going to take my boat out in a while.'

His smile faded. He laid down the cafetière. 'Boat?'

'No, no,' she said, the words rushing into his ear, 'don't be alarmed, *Jupiter* is a little rowboat. All I do is bring her out a bit into the harbour. And it's such a nice day – I just thought you needed a good boat experience to banish the other one.'

He was tempted. The sun was shining, the sea would be calm, and a little rowboat sounded very different from Willie's diesel monster.

'And,' she added, 'I'll bring a fishing rod for you.'

That did it. 'Count me in,' he said. He'd fill the new flask with coffee, just to be on the safe side. And watch his step at all times.

'Great – will we say one o'clock at the pier? Oh, do you mind my dog coming along? He loves the boat.'

'Not at all.'

'Bring your togs if you want – I'll be going for a swim. Oh, and one more thing.'

'Yes?'

'Don't forget the sun cream.' A smothered giggle.

'Very funny. See you at one.'

He hung up. It was just after eleven. Enough time to get in a five- or six-mile walk, cover the corner of the island he'd neglected up to now, the bit with the dinosaur-footprint fossils everyone kept reminding him to see.

Or he could sit on the patio with his book and check out the fossils tomorrow.

Or he could walk to the village for a newspaper,

198

drop into Walter on his way home, pick up another lot of eggs – he couldn't get enough of them – and a few jars of honey to bring back to his fellow zookeepers.

He went to the bathroom to brush his teeth and decide. The beauty of solo holidays, he thought – no, one of the beauties – was that you got to do whatever you pleased, every minute of every day. Another was that it forced you to talk to people.

Nell, of course, had made that part very easy for him. She'd introduced him to half the pub the first night he'd been in, and she'd engineered the trip with Willie. She'd made Gavin feel entirely welcome. And she'd helped him to look better than he'd done in years.

He pushed a hand through his new hair. He wondered if she'd see the Sean Penn resemblance, now that the colour of his face had returned more or less to normal.

'Dad – hang on.'

Denis turned.

Nell closed the salon door and walked up the street towards him. She carried a fishing rod and her red basket. 'Saw you from the window. Where are you headed?'

'Nowhere really, just out for a stroll.'

'I'll be with you as far as the pier. I'm on my way to take Gavin out in *Jupiter* for an hour or two.'

Denis took the rod from her. 'That'll be nice – you've a fine day for it.'

'We have. He's been pretty lucky with the weather.'

They passed the smaller of the art galleries and the craft shop that adjoined it. A couple of cars drove by, one with a British number-plate. The sun disappeared behind a cloud and slid into view again seconds later. Somewhere a dog barked repeatedly.

'So you're managing the new digs alright,' her father said. 'Not finding it too awkward.'

'No, I love being in the middle of the village . . . although of course it'll be nice to get back home.'

They passed Jimmy Cullen's bait-and-tackle shop and the other art gallery and the church, and Father William's little house beyond it. At the end of the street they turned left on to the coast road.

Nell glanced at her father. 'Dad.'

'Hmm?'

'I'm just wondering if everything's OK. You've been a bit quiet lately, and I'm hoping nothing's wrong.'

His expression didn't change. 'Everything is fine,' he said. 'What would be wrong?'

'Well . . . I thought you might be sick.'

'No, I'm not sick.'

But he wasn't looking at her, and he showed no surprise at her questions. He wasn't surprised that she thought something was wrong because something *was* wrong, but he wasn't going to tell her. Nell had no evidence to back up this knowledge, but it was there all the same. It was there.

'OK,' she said. 'I just wondered, that's all.'

What else was there to say?

James stood at the kitchen sink and scrubbed his nails with a brush dipped in turpentine, trying to remove the traces of stubborn paint that had lodged underneath. Through the open door that led to the sitting room he could see Andy hunched on the couch, eyes glued to the screen of the laptop he'd asked for, and received, on his fourteenth birthday in March. It had cost far more than James had intended to spend, but he didn't resent the expense.

Andy had been ten when he'd lost his mother to a horribly cruel death. Eighteen months after that, his father had dragged him a hundred and fifty miles from his home in Dublin to live on an island where neither of them knew a soul. He'd earned his laptop.

James had wondered plenty of times since then if he'd done the right thing in taking such a drastic step, in cutting his Dublin ties and taking Andy away from everything familiar. A fresh start for both of them, it had been meant to be. A new beginning, with the past and its heartbreak left behind. As ideas went, it hadn't seemed like the worst one at the time.

To this day, James couldn't say what had drawn him to the island. He and Karen had spent a single day there, years before she was diagnosed with the malignant melanoma that was to kill her. They'd driven from Dingle, where they'd been spending an uncharacteristically fine bank-holiday weekend. They'd crossed on the ferry in bright sunshine, parked the car by the sea and strolled for more than an hour along the coast road, finding a pub with toasted sandwiches for lunch before heading back to the beach for the rest of the afternoon.

Andy was there too, their tiny six-month-old son who'd slept through most of the walk, curled into a sling that had rested on James's chest. Afterwards he had lain kicking podgy legs under a beach umbrella as his parents read and swam and snoozed.

The day had lodged somewhere in James's subconscious, never thought of until almost a year after Karen's death, when propelled by misery and anger and an unnamed yearning, he'd begun checking estate agents' websites – and a house on the island had popped up.

And the minute he'd got out of the car at the pier on Roone, as soon as he'd set foot on the island, he'd felt an overwhelming conviction that he was in the right place. He still felt that; he couldn't imagine leaving the island now. But what of his silent son? What was Roone doing for him? Impossible to know when Andy never opened up, when he shied away from anything approaching the personal.

James rinsed his hands under the tap. The last few yellow paint specks had defeated him and would have to stay. 'So,' he said, turning off the water and reaching for the towel, 'fish and chips or shepherd's pie for dinner?'

'Whatever,' Andy replied, not looking up.

In the scullery Walter shook off his house slippers and pulled on a pair of green wellingtons. He picked up his egg basket and opened the back door. Cleared up nicely after last night's rain. Another fine week on the way by the look of it, although maybe without the heat of the last few days.

He skirted the herb garden and walked through the orchard, touching the damp, gnarled trunks of the apple trees as he passed them. He'd forgotten his cap; water dripped from the branches on to his balding head. He avoided the windfalls that sat in the longish grass, pecked to pieces by the birds or feasted on by the woodlice.

He remembered the apple jelly Geraldine had made from the windfalls, the house full of the smells of cloves and apple and lemon, the muslin bag of pulp suspended from the upturned legs of a kitchen chair, dripping all night into the basin below. And then the glorious rich red gleam of the apple jelly in the jars, the wonderful sweet-spicy tang of it on your buttered toast or scone in the morning.

He opened the little wooden gate that led from the orchard to the field that wrapped itself around two sides of the house. He made his way past the straight rows of onions and lettuces, cabbages and carrots, new potatoes and broad beans, turnips and cauliflowers, bending occasionally to pull a weed that caught his eye, or to pinch off a withered leaf.

He'd tried to make apple jelly once, almost a year after Geraldine had died. Sick with loneliness for her, trying to conjure her back with the familiar scents. He'd followed the recipe in her rounded writing as best he could, but it had been a disaster. The jelly hadn't set, had run off the knife when he'd tried to lift it up. In the end he'd simply used it as a sauce, poured it over a bowl of ice-cream or a slice of cake.

No woman in the house since Geraldine; no hairspray lingering in the bathroom or headscarves draped over chair backs, no female laughter or flowers on the table for Sunday dinner.

No Sunday dinner to speak of, not proper Sunday dinner. No roasting beef or chicken, no golden Yorkshire puddings, no gravy rich with meat juices. Walter was fair to middling in the kitchen, but his simple meals paled in comparison to the ones he remembered. No point in making a fuss for one.

He ate what he grew though, which was immensely satisfying. He pulled up a carrot and laid it in his basket. A couple of new potatoes to go with it, and he'd get a bit of fish at the pier when he went to the library in a while.

He reached the chicken run and lifted the hinge on the metal gate. Geraldine used to love collecting the eggs; when she'd moved into the house it had become one of her jobs, along with gathering the windfalls and tending the herbs.

He remembered the nerve it had taken to ask her out, after wanting to for so long. He remembered the long swallow he'd had of his mother's cooking sherry – the only alcohol in the house – before brushing his teeth twice and heading to Considine's pub, where Geraldine could generally be found behind the counter in the evenings.

The cinema, he'd suggested halfway through his pint of beer shandy, or perhaps dinner at Manning's Hotel. The sherry sitting nice and warm inside him, giving him the courage he needed. Twenty-seven he'd been then, and never romantically associated with any woman.

Geraldine's hair was red, the real Irish red that was generally partnered with pale freckled skin. Her lips were pale too, but wide and full. A small stye at the corner of her left eye hadn't bothered him in the least. Women were always getting styes then. Funny how you hardly ever saw them now.

Geraldine's eyes had been the green-grey of the sea on a chilly day, her lashes and eyebrows thick and dark above them. They'd grown up within two miles of one another, and Walter had loved her quietly for far too long.

They'd gone to see *Ryan's Daughter*, with Sarah Miles and Robert Mitchum. Walter hadn't much cared for it – he'd have preferred a western, or perhaps a musical – but he was content to sit in the warm darkness with Geraldine's thigh inches from his own, her flowery scent wafting towards him each time she brought a Black Magic chocolate to her pink-lipsticked mouth.

In his father's car on the way back to the island – she'd declined his offer of a drink after the cinema – Walter had struggled to keep the conversation going. Twenty-five minutes had never seemed so long. Geraldine didn't seem to mind the silences, her gaze turned out of the window into the darkness, her fingers absently folding and refolding the hem of her coat.

Yes, she had said, in answer to his question, her sister Noirin was doing fine in Washington, had found a job in a bookshop that also sold coffee and doughnuts, of all things. Yes, her grandmother's arthritis was much the same; they were thinking about a new hip for her. Yes, there was definitely a lengthening in the days. No, she wasn't too warm, she was fine.

When he had parked the car outside the Considine house there was silence, except for the ticking of the cooling engine. There was light behind the curtains in one of the upstairs windows, but downstairs was in darkness.

Walter wondered if he might dare claim a good-night kiss – had she given a sign, at any time during the evening, that such a gesture would not be welcome? As he turned towards her, deciding to take his chances, she had looked at him and smiled. 'Walter Thompson,' she had said quietly, 'I do believe you're going to kiss me.'

He had drawn back, shy suddenly – but she had touched his arm and leant across and placed her lips gently on his cheek. 'Thank you for a lovely evening,' she whispered, reaching for the door handle.

Walter had got out quickly and come around to open it. She'd stepped out and smiled at him again. They were almost exactly the same height.

'May I see you again?' he asked.

'Of course,' she replied, and in that instant he had known that his heart – already hers, completely hers – would be perfectly safe.

They married a month before her twenty-ninth birthday, shortly after Walter's thirtieth. Three years later, to their profound joy, she had become pregnant – and nine months after that he had lost both of them on a stormy, hellish night.

Thirty-six years on, the pain still had the power to make him want to howl. But life had gone on, of course. The obscenity of life going on, when the most precious part of his had been snatched away.

He collected the eggs and walked back towards the house, aware as always of the distant rumbling music of the sea.

'Come on in, it's gorgeous,' she said. 'Go for it.'

Gavin leapt from the boat, acutely aware of his lack of finesse, of his gangly frame, as he hit the water with a gigantic splash. The cold shock of it made him yelp. '*Freezing!*'

She laughed, treading water off to his left. 'Give it a minute, you'll be fine.'

She was like a fish, cutting smoothly through the water, adapting naturally to its ebb and flow. Gavin's clumsy homemade breaststroke was laughable in comparison, but she didn't appear to notice.

His body gradually adjusted to the temperature of the sea. He turned to float on his back, feeling supremely happy for the first time in ages. This was the way to live, bobbing on salt water, the sun on your face, the air so pure it went to your head. This was living.

Back on the boat, twenty minutes later, he towelled himself dry and reached for the factor fifty.

'You remind me of someone,' she said, pulling a T-shirt over her swimsuit. 'Since I cut your hair. Let me think.'

He waited for her to say Sean Penn.

She snapped her fingers. 'A young Harvey Keitel.'

Harvey Keitel. Not exactly the face that had launched a thousand ships. Still, she could have said Winston Churchill, or Liberace.

'Coffee?' He pulled the flask from his rucksack.

'Oh, you brought coffee, wonderful.' She watched as he poured carefully. 'Do you mind,' she said, 'if I ask you a question?'

Gavin passed her a mug and the 7-Up bottle he'd filled with milk. 'Fire away.'

'Have you ever been married?' She saw his

expression and added, 'Tell me to mind my own business if you want. I know I'm a nosy cow.'

'No, it's fine.' He poured the second cup and screwed the flask top back on. It wasn't a secret. He had no reason to resent the question. It was just that nobody had asked it up to now. 'I was married,' he said, lifting the cup to his lips. After the swim, its warmth and rich taste were even more welcome than usual. 'We got divorced. It came through a few months ago.'

'I'm so sorry. I hope you didn't mind my asking.'

'No.' He realised it was a relief to say it out loud. He drank more coffee. 'She left me for someone else,' he said. 'They have two kids now.' He looked into his cup. 'She'd always told me she didn't want kids. Looks like it was just mine she didn't want.'

'Oh.' Nell reached across the seat that separated them to press his hand briefly. 'For what it's worth, she must have been a very foolish woman.'

He looked up and smiled. 'Thanks,' he said. 'I'm fine now.' He realised it was true. Since coming to Roone a lot of things had become clear. 'I'm over her. It took a while, I sort of hibernated after it happened – for a long time – but now it's in the past.'

'Really?'

'Really.'

'That's good.'

They sat in silence, the boat rocking gently. John Silver, having shaken himself enthusiastically after his swim, was lying in the bottom of the boat, his coat damply ruffled. Gavin sat back contentedly with the remainder of his coffee.

And just then his rod, which they'd propped at the end of the boat before the swim, and which he'd totally forgotten about, gave a sudden twitch.

'He caught a flounder,' Nell said. 'You should have seen him – he was like a little boy who'd just been to visit Santa.'

'Ah, that's nice. Will he be able to prepare it?'

'We got Paudie Connor to gut it at the pier. Gavin invited me to dinner but I told him I was going to James and Andy's. I suggested he ask Walter, he loves flounder.'

Her mother eased up the long root of a dandelion. 'And you said he's divorced.'

'He is. She left him for another man.' Nell dropped her trowel and sat back on her heels. 'I'd love to find someone for him. I've been thinking about it since he told me. What about Paula Geraghty?'

Her mother stared at her. 'Paula Geraghty? She must be ten years older than him. And she'd drive him mad, never stops talking.'

'Well, what about Trish Muldoon then?'

'Ah no, she's too quiet for him. And her mother would be lost if she went off to Dublin.'

Nell stuck her trowel under another weed. 'No, no, Gavin would move here. He suits this place.'

Moira smiled. 'Does he? Have you asked him?'

'Well, not directly, but it's obvious he's a good fit for the island. It's making him happier. I can see it.'

'Maybe so, and if that's true I'm pleased for him . . . but if you're in the mood for matchmaking, I would have thought it would be more in your line to find someone for James.'

Nell stopped digging. 'James? He's not looking for anyone.'

'Well, he may not be looking, but wouldn't it be nice if he had someone all the same? He's been on his own for long enough.'

James finding somebody new. James with a girl-friend. James falling in love again. Nell turned the notion over in her head.

Her mother was right: of course he should have someone. Nell wanted him to be happy. Everyone deserved that, didn't they? 'I don't know that he's ready though,' she said.

'Of course he's ready. Four years is more than enough mourning for anyone. And Andy could do with a woman to look after him.'

'Andy has me,' Nell said. 'I look after him.'

'Ah, you know what I mean. Someone he can get close to, someone to make him feel he's part of a family again.'

Nell poked at a trail of bindweed. 'I'm sure James doesn't need my help to find anyone. He meets plenty of women in the pub.'

'Still, no harm if you gave him a little nudge in the right direction.'

'Mm.' She pushed back her sleeve and looked at her watch. 'I'd better get going, it's nearly six.'

'Right, love. You might put a match under the potatoes when you go in – and tell James and Andy I said hello.'

Walking the few minutes back to the village, where she had to change out of her gardening clothes and pick up a bottle of wine from Hugh, Nell felt oddly prickly. The heat, probably – although that didn't normally bother her. She was tired after her swim, that was it. Nothing that a night's sleep wouldn't cure.

As she entered the village her thoughts returned to the conversation in the garden. What did her mother know anyway? When James was ready to meet someone new, he would. There was no rush: he was only forty.

She opened the salon door and hurried up the stairs, trying to reclaim her earlier good humour.

'I think I may have a natural aptitude for it,' Gavin said. 'This was my very first attempt, remember. The fish practically jumped on to the hook.'

Walter's donkey tossed his head, which, as far as Gavin was concerned, was the next best thing to a round of applause.

'I've never tasted flounder, but apparently it's got a mild flavour. Nell said bake it in wine, so I've just put it in the oven.' He sipped from the glass he'd poured after giving the fish its share. 'Something about catching your own dinner, isn't there? Suppose it's in all of us, that ancient hunter-gatherer thing.'

For the first time in his life, he'd got what could be charitably called a tan. He worked out of doors in Dublin, of course, but it never seemed to do much for his pale freckly complexion. Here the sun and the sea breeze – not to mention his recent roasting – had combined to wash his features with a pleasing ruddy brown colour. At least he wasn't going back to Dublin looking like he'd spent the fortnight in a cave.

He heard a sound behind him and turned to see that the grey cat had discovered the flounder innards he'd brought back from the pier and left on a plate by the shed.

Nature was in charge here. People lived in harmony with it, moved in rhythm with the sea, grew or caught their food, abided by the ancient laws that had prevailed before a single human footprint was set down. Maybe that was the secret of Roone.

He took another sip of the wine he'd bought in the supermarket on the way home from the boat ride. It was cold and dry, and had been squeezed from Italian grapes. He could just as easily have booked a holiday in Italy, with its churches and fountains and ice-cream. What had made him choose Roone over Rome? What serendipitous impulse had led him here?

The doorbell rang, pulling him back to the moment. 'That'll be Walter,' he told the donkey. 'We'll have to continue our chat later.'

He picked up his glass and returned to the house. As he made his way through the kitchen a delicate savoury smell wafted from the oven.

'Hi.'

'Hi there. What's up?'

She slashed with her stick at the hedge as she strode along. 'Nothing's up. Does there have to be something up for me to ring you?'

'Hey,' he said, 'calm down.'

She took a breath. 'Sorry – long day. What's going on with you?'

'The usual. Still at work, another hour or so.'

'I hope you're getting overtime.'

He laughed softly. 'I think I am, darling. Remember all those noughts at the end of my salary?'

'I suppose . . . but you need a life too.'

'So what are you up to?'

'I'm on the way to dinner at James and Andy's. I brought Gavin out in *Jupiter* earlier, thought he needed a positive boating experience.'

'And was it?'

'Yeah, he enjoyed it. We went swimming and he caught a flounder.'

'While he was swimming?'

'Very funny. I think he's invited Walter around to share it.' She slashed the hedge again. Something satisfying about letting fly like that.

Pause. They never used to have pauses. Pauses were a new development. Let him say something: she was tired.

'So,' he said, 'it's pissing down here.'

'Dry here,' she said. Had she really phoned him so they could talk about the weather? She'd never been to his office, but she could imagine him sitting at his desk. Shirt and tie, making money all day, and half the night. One of those businessmen's toys, silver balls hanging on strings, clacking away in front of him. And he had his own secretary. She knew that because he'd told her. 'Ms Donohue,' he'd said. 'Never seen her smile. Can't remember her first name. Maybe I never heard it.' What a way to live, not even knowing the Christian name of someone you worked with every day.

Ahead of her she saw the red roof of James's house. 'Better go. I've arrived.'

'OK, sweetheart. Miss you. Enjoy your dinner.'

'Talk to you tomorrow.' She hung up and slid her phone into her pocket. A glass of wine: that was what she needed to shake off this crankiness.

'How many more sleeps?' From the top bunk.

Since she'd told them about the holiday they'd asked every night. Two pairs of blue eyes watched intently as she counted on her fingers. 'Tuesday, Wednesday, Thursday, Friday – how many is that?'

Long pause. 'Four.'

'That's right.'

'An' can I sleep in the top bed when we get there?' the resident of the bottom bunk enquired.

'The house doesn't have bunks,' she told them.

215

'You'll be sleeping in twin beds, which are made especially for twins.'

Wonderful how they accepted utterly everything she said. Couldn't last for much longer. Scepticism would set in around the time they realised that she didn't, in fact, have all the answers – which wouldn't be for a terribly long time, hopefully.

'Will you do the giraffe song?'

She'd been singing them to sleep since they were born. Stories left them wide awake, songs took about five minutes to send them off. She got her guitar and sang about Gerry Giraffe who forgot how to laugh till Bertie Bunny was awfully funny.

She made up songs for them all the time; they popped into her head as she dried dishes and stirred porridge, as she tied laces and blew noses. Ben's favourite was 'Say Cheese, Smile Please'. Seamus loved 'The Granny In The Moon'.

When they were asleep she tiptoed from the room and went downstairs. On her father's old computer she called up the holiday rental website and located Nell Mulcahy's house. She gazed at the photo – impossibly blue sky, had to have been doctored – and thought about driving there after four more sleeps.

She imagined them leaving Dublin and travelling the width of the country. Taking a ferry across the sea, getting off at the other side, turning left at the pier. Driving along by the coast for most of a mile, passing the sign for the holy well and looking

216

out for the first house after that with a red front door.

She'd memorised the directions, so often had she read them. She knew she didn't need them, not really. She'd find the house. She'd already found it – or rather, it had found her.

She knew how silly that sounded. She wasn't superstitious, she'd never believed in signs – but since she'd booked the holiday she hadn't been able to shake the conviction that they were meant to go to that island, to stay in that house. She'd entered the information – last two weeks in July, three people, two bedrooms, by the sea. She'd left the location open, not minding where they went, as long as they got out of the city – and immediately property 858 had popped up on the screen.

Just one house, out of the 1,053 that were on the website. A single house was being offered to them. Laura had looked at the photos and read *Patio with furniture, front and rear landscaped gardens, adjacent to beautiful beach, walking distance to village shops, pubs, cafés. Numerous walks, suitable for cyclists, tourist attractions such as lighthouse, prehistoric remains, holy well.*

She'd discovered that it was located on a small island off the west coast that was only accessible by ferry. She saw that it had two bedrooms, one double, one twin.

A small island. She'd always wanted to live on a small island where the sea was never far from you.

It was perfect. She hadn't known what she was

looking for, but she suddenly knew she'd found it. She didn't bother viewing any other properties. Within minutes she'd made the booking, paid her deposit online by credit card and received an automated acknowledgement.

Three days later a typed receipt had arrived in the post, accompanied by a cheery handwritten note that began *Dear Laura* and finished *Nell Mulcahy*, who apparently was looking forward to meeting them in July.

Four more sleeps. Their first proper holiday, unless you counted five days in a caravan in Wexford in the rain when the boys were two, which had so traumatised the three of them that it had taken until now for her to risk doing it again.

This time would be different. This time they were staying in a house with a red door on a small island. This time she knew it would be good.

Four more sleeps. She was as impatient as her five-year-old twins.

'Did you get your early night on Monday?'

Nell towelled James's hair. 'I did – at least, I went to bed just after ten, but I found it hard enough to sleep.'

'Noisy pub?'

'No, not particularly. That doesn't bother me anyway, I seem to be able to tune it out.' She threw the damp towel into the hamper and brought him over to the mirror. 'I don't know . . . maybe it's just not being in my own bed.'

James smiled. 'I thought you *were* in your own bed.'

'True – I spent the first twenty years of my life in it. It seems so long ago now.' She picked up a comb and began to guide it through his hair.

'How's Andy these days?' she asked. 'I know I see him all the time, but how is he generally, with you, I mean?'

James met her eyes in the mirror. 'He's about the same, doesn't tell me much. I don't know what's going on in his head. He loves having a dog around the place, though. I think I'll have to get him his own when you take John Silver back.'

'That might be good for him.' She picked up her scissors. 'What about a holiday job? D'you think he might be interested?'

'A job? He might take some persuading, but I know I'd love it. Had you something in mind?'

'Well, when I couldn't sleep the other night I was thinking about it, and I remember Walter saying a while back that he was considering getting someone to clear out his attic. I'm just wondering if that kind of thing would appeal to Andy.'

She tilted his head slightly to the left, her face close to his as she bent to shape the hair around his ear. James attempted to ignore her proximity – she smelt of roses – as he considered the idea.

'I'm sure he'd be glad of a few bob – he's always saying he gets much less pocket money than his pals at school, which is probably true.'

'Let me run it by Walter. If he has no objection, you could say it to Andy.'

Looking after them, following the instinct that led her, always, to help people. Was it any wonder James had tumbled into love with her, after being convinced that he'd never feel that way about a woman again?

'Thanks,' he said, as he'd said so many times to her. Thanks for finding me a job on Roone, thanks for being nice to my son, thanks for having us to dinner every so often. Thanks for helping me to feel again, even if what I feel is hopeless and tragic and doomed.

'We'll have to get Gavin down to the pub on Friday,' she said, running her scissors lightly up the back of James's head. 'His last night.'

'OK.'

'I think he's enjoying his time here – apart from falling into the sea, of course.'

James grinned. 'That was probably not his high point.'

'Wonder what the next lot of tenants will be like. A woman and her two small kiddies. Hope they don't wreck the house.'

'Ah, no, they'll be too busy robbing Walter's apples.'

'Lord – do you think so? I'd better warn him.'

The time passed. They moved from the salon to the pub, James being her last customer of the day. He walked home afterwards, pleasantly light-headed from two pints on an empty stomach.

What if he just told her? What if he confessed how he felt, and begged her not to marry Tim?

Maybe she felt the same without realising it. Maybe all she needed was a word from him.

He shook his head, impatient with his wishful thinking. She didn't love him, not like that. She loved Tim; she was going to marry Tim. He needed to get over it. Meet someone else, maybe. Move on.

He reached the crossroads and took the road for home.

Standing at his bedroom window Nell's father watched the sun go down, and thought about how he had ended up in the wrong life. It had been easily done, and he had nobody to blame but himself. Allowing himself to be flattered when pretty Moira Fitzpatrick had made it plain that she was interested in him. Letting his friends persuade him that he'd be a fool not to ask her out.

'You're lucky,' they'd said. 'She's mad for you.'

Of course he'd been pleased – why wouldn't he? Moira wasn't just good-looking, she was smart and kind and capable, the sort of woman any man would have been proud to have on his arm. The sort of woman who would make the perfect wife.

His parents had approved of his relationship with Moira, his mother in particular taking to her. 'Don't let her get away,' she'd urged Denis. 'She won't wait around forever. You'll regret it if you let her go.'

So Denis had proposed and Moira had accepted, and they were married in the church where they'd both been baptised, with their parents looking on approvingly.

How hard he had tried to love her, how he'd done his best to convince himself that he did. *I love you*, he'd told her over the years, willing it to be true, wanting so much to believe it.

And the early years had been happy ones, he didn't deny that. Nell had been born and Moira was a wonderful mother, like he'd known she would be. And when no other babies had come along he'd accepted it, because he already had everything he wanted, didn't he?

And as the years went by, through Nell's childhood and the deaths of his and Moira's parents, through his promotion to headmaster and Nell's departure to Dublin and eventual return, and Moira coming to work in the school, Denis Mulcahy experienced periods of bleakness, which he did his best to ignore.

I have a daughter I adore, he told himself. *I have a wife who loves me, and whom I admire and respect. I have so much more than a lot of others. I have no right to be unhappy.* And his life went on, and he acted the part he'd been given. The husband, the father, the responsible member of the community.

But the loneliness was never far away; the emptiness never really left him. He would lie beside his sleeping wife at night and imagine how differently things might have gone if he'd broken it off with Moira and held out for true, romantic love.

And then in March he'd gone to a one-day course for school principals and vice principals that was held in the conference room of a Tralee hotel. He'd listened to a talk on new regulations governing capitation grants and a proposed reduction in the number of special-needs assistants, and then a break had been called and they'd all trooped out to the lobby for coffee.

And at the table where the crockery was laid out he'd reached for the same cup as someone else, and she'd said, 'Oh, I'm terribly sorry,' and he'd looked into a pair of blue eyes.

And just like that, everything had been turned on its head.

'Denis,' he'd said, extending his hand.

'Claire,' she'd replied, her smile lighting him up.

And at sixty-one years of age Denis Mulcahy finally understood the terrifying and wonderful thing it was to fall truly in love.

Claire was fifty-four and vice principal of a big school in Killarney. She was married with three children, and her husband was a recovering alcoholic who had succeeded in destroying their relationship long before he'd finally climbed on the wagon seven years earlier. Claire had short brown hair and a small, oval face with a mole at the side of her mouth. She rubbed her forehead when she was thinking. She loved spinach and hated shellfish and was allergic to oranges.

She bit her nails and painted them amateurishly with pale pink polish. There was a small wart on the underside of her left hand's fourth finger. She was fond of gardening and adored peas and detested jazz, and her nose went red when she cried. She trembled when Denis held her. His name, when she whispered it, sounded musical.

When she kissed him she made his heart flood.

They saw one another when they could. Denis packed up his golf clubs and took the ferry to the mainland, and they met in the bar of a little country hotel where nobody knew them. They talked and drank tea, and afterwards, if she didn't have to rush away, they went upstairs to one of the rooms.

'Leave him,' Denis begged each time. 'Come away with me.'

'I can't leave,' she told him. 'There's Joe.'

Joe was her middle child. He was thirteen years old, and he had Down's syndrome, and Claire wanted him to have both his parents around him.

'I understand,' Denis said, but he didn't understand why someone who'd longed for love all his life should be shown it, and then have it pulled out of reach. How could anyone understand that? What kind of a God did that to you?

'I'm leaving Moira,' he told Claire. 'Whether you come with me or not, I'm leaving her.'

He couldn't stay. He couldn't continue with this dishonesty. He hadn't gone looking for anyone else but he'd found her, and even if he and Claire couldn't be together, his life with Moira was a mockery now.

Last month he'd applied for the principalship of a school in Tralee. He'd told nobody except Claire. He'd handed in his notice at Roone National School, asking the board of management to keep it to themselves for now. They'd agreed, no doubt thinking he had professional rather than personal reasons for asking.

Whether he got the other job or not, he had to leave the school in Roone, because he had to leave Roone. The island was simply too small for a separated couple to share. If he got the job in Tralee he'd find a place to live in the area. If not, he'd have to think again.

In the meantime he had to find a way to tell Moira he was leaving. He had to find the right words to say, and he had to do it soon. And he also had to tell Nell. Both prospects were horrendous.

'Dinner's ready.' Moira's voice floated up to him. Denis left the room, closing the door softly.

'There you are,' Nell said. 'I was on my way to see you – I just need a word with Walter.'

Gavin held up a bulging paper bag. 'I was stocking up on provisions to bring home.'

'Oh, it's just too bad you're leaving tomorrow. Will you miss us?'

'I will,' he said, in a way that let her know he meant it. 'I've had a great time.'

'You'll come back,' she said, 'now that you know where we are. You can sleep in the spare room when Tim and I are back in the house, and I promise I won't charge.'

He smiled. He had a lovely smile, all warm and toothy – and a wonderful haircut, if she said so herself. And his sunburn had faded to a reddish brown that was quite healthy and outdoorsy. Too thin, of course, but she'd fatten him up in a week if she had him to feed.

'Were you coming to see me for any particular reason?' he asked.

'I was. You have to come to the pub later since it's your last night, and I won't see you in the morning because I'll be working.'

'I'll drop in,' he promised. 'I was planning to anyway, figured you'd be there.'

'Great – see you around nine.'

When he'd gone Nell walked around the side of Walter's house. Chances were he was still in the garden on this fine day. She found him harvesting salad vegetables for his morning deliveries to the village cafés.

'Walter,' she said, rubbing the long ears of his little donkey, which had trotted across to meet her, 'I have a proposition for you.'

'Nell, how nice to see you.' He dropped onions into his box and straightened up, pulling off his gloves. 'Come along – I was just about to take some apple juice.'

'Lovely.'

Walter infused his cloudy apple juice with cinnamon and sweetened it with lavender honey, and topped it up with a little pure cold water drawn from the well his father had sunk at the rear of the property. The juice was believed by many of the locals to improve the humour of the drinker, and was in demand whenever Walter bottled a batch for the cafés.

'I was just wondering,' Nell said as they made their way towards the house, 'if you were still thinking of getting someone to clear out your attic.'

Walter held the little wooden gate open for her. 'Yes, indeed. It's high time it was done.'

'What about Andy?' she asked, walking ahead of him into the house. 'James's son. He's on holidays, probably bored stiff. He might be glad of a job.'

Walter took a jug from the fridge and stirred its contents with a long-handled spoon. He looked a little doubtfully at her. 'Really? You don't think he's rather young? There's quite a lot of clutter up there. I was thinking of asking the Hughes brothers, who moved my books up last year, after the woodworm.'

'Well, whatever you think, but Andy is available and . . .' she hesitated '. . . to be honest, Walter, James is worried about him. He's very quiet – oh, he's a good boy, and very trustworthy, but he keeps things to himself, you know. James says he's been like this since his mother's death, sort of closed off a bit. I just wondered if a job of some kind might help at all. Give him a purpose, you know? Buck him up a bit.'

Walter poured juice into the glasses. 'In that case, I shall be happy to offer it to him.'

'Oh, would you, Walter? You don't feel obliged?'

'Not at all – but if he does a good job, I shall certainly feel obliged to you.'

Walter's little joke. Nell laughed. 'Well, I hope he wants it now. Will I mention it to James? I'll be seeing him in the pub later.' Best not to admit that she'd already run the idea by James.

'By all means,' Walter said. 'If the lad is interested, ask him to give me a call or drop by.'

'Will do.' She sipped the ice-cold juice. 'I met Gavin just now, as I was coming in. Shame he's leaving tomorrow.'

'Yes, indeed. He seemed to enjoy his stay.'

'I think so. I just hope I'm as lucky with my other tenants.'

Driving the short distance back to the village, Nell passed her parents' house. She hadn't met her father since their last conversation, but he was on her mind most days. Hopefully, whatever was amiss would sort itself out.

She drove up the village street, her thoughts turning to Tim, due in less than an hour. Making his way towards her, coming home to Roone.

Gavin shook the pan and the sausages sizzled and danced about in the hot fat. He opened the fridge door and attempted to lift out a brown egg that had a little feather attached, but it slipped from his grasp and cracked open on the tiles.

'Oops—' He crouched carefully and tried to pick it up, but the yolk kept slithering between his fingers – such a lovely deep orange yolk, from one of Walter's comically fat hens – and in the end he had to leave it where it was. As he stood up he veered sideways. He caught at the edge of the table to steady himself and knocked over the salt cellar, which scattered an arc of white across the wooden surface. He scooped what he could into his hand and dumped it in the sink.

He managed to take another egg from the fridge without mishap and cracked it into the pan, fishing out as much shell as he could. He smelt burning and discovered that the end of his sleeve was on fire from the gas flame of the hotplate. He held it under the tap until it went out.

As he took a dinner plate down from the press he caught sight of a man's reflection in the kitchen window. He started, almost dropping the plate – and then he realised it was himself.

He loved Nell. Nell was wonderful. She'd made him look like Sean Penn. Sean Penn was wonderful too. Brilliant actor, brilliant. Divorced too, just like Gavin.

'Just goes to show,' he told the man in the window, squeezing water from his sleeve. 'Great minds think alike.'

He loaded his plate with sausages and fried egg and dumped the pan in the sink. He belched loudly and tasted beer. Beer always gave you an appetite – the more you drank, the hungrier you got. Gavin couldn't remember how much beer he'd had in the pub, but he was starving now.

As he reached for ketchup some movement outside the window, a quick flash, caught his eye. He peered out, hanging on to the sink. Another flash. It was the grey cat's eyes, reflecting the light from the kitchen. It was on the windowsill, looking in at him.

He took a raw sausage from the fridge and opened the back door and stumbled out. 'Here, puss, puss.' The cat leapt from the sill and streaked past him. He flung the sausage in the same general direction and returned to the kitchen.

He took his plate to the table, and on the way he stepped into the broken egg. He skidded across the tiles, managing by some miracle to remain upright but causing one of his sausages to slide off the plate and under the table. He bent and retrieved it, and brushed it clean with the sleeve that wasn't burnt.

He ate his supper contentedly. He loved Roone. It was the best place in the world. He was so happy he'd chosen it for his holiday. He was thrilled that he'd decided to sell his house in Dublin and move here and open a zoo.

He couldn't think why the idea hadn't occurred to him till tonight. Everyone in the pub had thought it was brilliant.

'You should have a tank of scorpions,' someone said.

'And a Yeti.'

'And a few wolves.'

'And eagles.'

Everyone was full of suggestions for his zoo, and they were all great. It was going to be the best zoo in Ireland, and people were going to come from all over the world to see it.

Nell liked the zoo idea too. Gavin wished Nell wasn't engaged because he really, really loved her. She was beautiful and kind and she'd make an incredible wife, even though he was never getting married again. He wished he could tell her he loved her, but he couldn't because her fiancé had been in the pub, telling Gavin about some holiday he'd had in Africa – or was it Hugh who'd been to Africa? Or maybe it was America.

Lots of people had heard about Gavin falling into the sea, people he hadn't even met until this evening. Lots of them wanted to buy him a drink. No wonder he was a small bit tipsy now.

Someone had walked home with him. Gavin vaguely remembered a conversation about chimpanzees as they'd negotiated the dark road together. He had a feeling one of them had sung 'The Fields Of Athenry', and he was fairly sure he'd toppled into the ditch at one stage. Maybe they both had.

He put his empty plate on the draining-board, yawning. He walked as steadily as he could into the sitting room to get his book, couldn't get to sleep without reading. He took it from the coffee-table and dropped on to the couch. He pushed his shoes off and lifted up his legs and stretched out – just for a minute. Within seconds he was snoring loudly.

'Missed you.' His mouth in the hollow of her neck, his words tickling, his fingers stroking.

'Me too.' Pulling him closer, breathing in his scent, running her hands over his warm bare skin.

They were on the floor, more room for manoeuvring. Bed was for later, when all they wanted was sleep. Now, with the buzz of the pub still below them, there wasn't much chance of sleep.

But the floor was hard, despite the duvet they'd spread on it. It dug into Nell's hip bones when she turned on her side, it pushed painfully against her coccyx if she lay on her back. For the first time since she and Tim had got together, she found it difficult to keep her mind on the task in hand.

He could have been a bit friendlier to Gavin this evening – the man was paying a lot of money to stay in their house, for goodness' sake. Tim had virtually ignored him, left most of the conversation to Nell and Hugh.

She hoped Gavin had made it home in one piece, none too sober by the time he'd left the pub. She'd asked Sean Ryan, who lived half a mile further on, to walk with him. Sean had had a fair few drinks himself, but he'd found his way home for years without any major mishaps, so she'd figured she was leaving Gavin in relatively safe hands.

Poor Gavin, recently divorced from a woman who'd left him for someone else. And poor James, another man with no romantic partner in his life. She didn't want James to be lonely, but there was nobody she could think of who'd be good enough for him.

Tim stopped and drew back. 'What's up?'

'Nothing,' she said. 'I'm just not very comfortable here, sorry.'

They moved to the bed and it was softer, at least – although for some reason, Nell still found it difficult to get involved with the whole business. She wasn't in the mood tonight, that was all.

LETTING THE HOUSE:
THE SECOND TWO WEEKS

'What happened to your jumper?' Moira asked.

Gavin inspected the sleeve's frayed and blackened end. 'Would you look at that.'

His face was pale, his eyes bloodshot. He'd clearly slept in his clothes. He didn't seem to know how his sleeve had got burnt. And what on earth was that congealed mess on the kitchen tiles?

Must have been a late night in Fitz's.

She returned his deposit. At least he hadn't burnt the place down. 'I hope you enjoyed your stay.' Poor man, looked like he was in dire need of a long shower and a cooked breakfast. Shame she had to see him off the premises.

She walked out to his car with him, hoping he wasn't still under the influence. The morning was fresh, a stiff breeze blowing in from the sea, the sky patched with clouds. 'Seems like you got the best of the weather.'

'It does.'

He shook hands and got into the car. Moira

stood waving until he drove off, her mind already on sheets, towels, mop, polish.

'So, what do you think?'

'Dunno . . . maybe.'

Andy knew Mr Thompson slightly. Soon after he and his dad had moved to Roone his dad had taken him to see Mr Thompson's hens, but they never did anything much except scratch the ground, and Andy had soon lost interest.

He and Mr Thompson had met again briefly at Nell and Tim's engagement evening, last year some time. Their conversation had been short, and very polite. Mr Thompson had asked if Andy was settling in to Roone, which was what everyone asked him, and Andy had said yes, because he knew it was what everyone wanted to hear.

Mr Thompson didn't talk like the other people around here. His accent was posh, so you thought he must be rich, but the paint was peeling from the walls of his house, and his car was ancient, and he always seemed to wear the same clothes.

He probably didn't remember who Andy was. When they passed each other on the road Mr Thompson would smile and touch the side of his hat, but he did that whenever he met anyone – and if it was a woman, he'd lift the hat a bit.

And now he wanted his attic cleared out, and he was wondering if Andy would like to do it. Andy suspected that his dad had had something to do with it – why would Mr Thompson offer a job to someone he hardly knew? – but he said nothing because, actually, it was kind of interesting.

Not the idea of clearing out an attic – that would probably be as exciting as watching grass grow, or one of his dad's paintings dry. But it was a job, and it would be paid, and Andy could do with a bit of money. The tenner he was given every week was gone long before the week was out, even though he hardly bought anything.

And he was sort of curious about attics, because he'd often seen them in films but never in reality. He couldn't remember if their house in Dublin had had one, but if it had, Andy was pretty sure he hadn't been up there. And the house they lived in now didn't have a proper attic, just a trapdoor in the bathroom ceiling that led to a small cubbyhole where the water tank was. His father had gone up there in January when the pipes had frozen, but such a poky space hadn't interested Andy.

Mr Thompson's house looked super-old – it could be the oldest one on Roone. It probably had a proper attic, like the ones in the films, with a useless light bulb that you turned on with a string, and cobwebs and stuff all over the place. Could be cool.

Andy could see his father really wanted him to take the job.

'Word will spread,' his dad said. 'You'll probably get lots of work if you take this. People are always looking for someone to do odd jobs.'

Maybe *he* was looking for an excuse to stop

handing out pocket money. Andy wondered how much Mr Thompson was thinking of paying for his odd job.

'Let him know soon, will you? Don't keep him waiting.'

'Yeah, OK.'

He'd call round to Mr Thompson, have a look at the attic, see how much was to be done. If he didn't like what he saw he'd think of an excuse – he'd say he was allergic to dust or something. He was pretty sure Mr Thompson would be easy enough to fool.

He'd go and check it out. He had nothing to lose.

> *Katy –*
> *Scribbling this in a rare break in my Saturday morning. Gavin is going home today, probably gone by now. We'll miss him, he was nice. Would you believe he let me cut his hair? Hurrah! Wonder what the new people will be like, a mum and two boys. I'll call over later to say hello. Tim is well, working hard as usual. He finds the new living arrangements challenging, even though he only has to suffer them at weekends – men! Any news yourself?*
> *N xxx*
>
> *Nell*
> *You cut his hair – well done! Pity I missed the transformation. Liam's working all hours, I'm*

tired of telling him to look for another job. I suppose he has a point when he says he's lucky to have this one, but it would be nice to see a bit more of him. Looks like our heatwave is over – didn't last half long enough. Keep me posted on the new tenants.
K xxx

There was a man with a jackhammer in his head. He'd been going at it full throttle when Gavin had woken on the couch at three o'clock, stiff and chilled and dying of thirst. He'd drunk three glasses of Nell's metallic-tasting water and dragged himself to bed in his clothes. The next time he'd opened his eyes his watch had said twenty-five to eleven and the man with the jackhammer was still busy.

His nose was blocked and he was parched again. All he wanted to do was drink more water, turn over and go back to sleep for about three days, but he had to get up because he was supposed to be out by eleven and he hadn't packed.

No time to shower. He filled the bathroom sink and ducked his head in it and brushed his teeth twice and ran his fingers through his wet hair. He tumbled everything into his suitcase and rammed it shut. In the kitchen, while the kettle was boiling, he stood at the sink and drank more cold water. There was no sign of next door's donkey. When Nell's mother arrived just before eleven he was gulping down his second mug of scalding coffee.

He yawned as he approached the pier. No sign of the ferry, couple of cars waiting. He pulled in behind them and slid down his window, and the delicious salty morning air rushed in at him. He'd stop in Killarney and fill himself with as many breakfast carbohydrates as he could manage, and then he'd have a snooze in the car before going on. He was in no rush to get back to Dublin. Nobody was waiting for him.

In the two weeks he'd been on the island he'd made the acquaintance of more people than he'd met in Dublin in years, even if he couldn't remember half of their names now. He'd fallen into the sea and got his hair cut and caught his first fish and nearly set himself on fire after getting very drunk indeed. He was bringing home a hangover and a fortnight of memories and the resolve to stop living in the shadow of his failed marriage.

The ferry arrived and he drove on. He stood at the railing as he crossed a sea that this morning looked more green than blue. He breathed in as much of the wonderful fresh air as his lungs could hold, and he wished he didn't have to go home.

As she was stripping the sheets from the small bed – why on earth had he slept in a single when he'd had the option of a double? – Moira heard a car pulling up outside. A minute later a female voice called, 'Hello? Anyone home?'

Someone looking for directions, having spotted the open front door. Moira walked out to the hall.

A woman in her twenties stood on the doorstep. Her blonde hair was piled haphazardly on her head, held in place by numerous clips and ornaments. She wore a bright green wide-skirted sundress, whose fitted top revealed what Moira considered to be a dangerous amount of cleavage, and gold sandals with straps that climbed halfway up her calves. Little green gems flashed in her ear lobes.

'Don't panic,' she said quickly, as soon as Moira appeared. 'I know we're way too early, but we're not staying, honest, we're just dropping the car and going away again, I just wanted to check I had the right house – although I must say your directions were spot on, you couldn't really go wrong. This is the right house, isn't it, Nell Mulcahy's? The thing is, we were all up at cock-crow – the boys were dying to come, they woke me after five, it was like Christmas morning – and I thought well, now that we're all awake, what are we hanging around here for when we could be on the road, so we just loaded everything up and headed off – and it was great, actually, because we missed all the traffic, we literally sailed down, although we did stop for breakfast in Tralee because we were all starving by then, and now we're going to get out of your way and head off to explore, we brought our bikes and we're planning to use them for the week, because you mentioned cycling in the description, and I looked up the island and it is quite flat, isn't it? Apart from the two hills in the middle, obviously. And you must be Nell.'

She smiled widely, and Moira jumped into the silence. 'I'm her mother, actually, Moira Mulcahy. You're very welcome to Roone, and to Nell's house.'

The blonde woman pumped her hand. 'Laura Dolittle, thanks so much, it's *wonderful* to finally be here. I've been looking forward to this for ages, and so have the boys. This is our very first time on Roone.'

Her almost childish enthusiasm was charming to see. 'Well, I'm sure you'll enjoy it,' Moira told her. 'It's perfect for cycling, and the beaches on this side of the island are all very calm and safe for children.'

'Fantastic – we can't wait to start exploring.'

'I'm sorry I can't let you in yet.' Moira glanced at her watch. 'The last tenant only left half an—'

'Of *course*, we're going to leave you alone this minute, and we'll see you later. Check-in is after two, right? So we'll be back here on the dot, to let you get off.'

'That sounds—'

'Or, better still, should I give you my mobile number and you can ring me when you finish up, so you won't be hanging around?'

'Yes, why don't—'

From the driveway there was a sudden enormous crash. The woman sighed, not looking unduly alarmed. 'Lord, what now?' She walked outside and Moira followed.

A pair of little red-headed boys, four or five years old, were standing on the bonnet of a small dark blue hatchback, on whose roof two bicycles were piled. A third lay on the ground, wheels spinning. Moira wondered how on earth they'd managed to climb on to the car, let alone dislodge the bicycle.

'He did it,' one of the boys said immediately, pointing to his companion.

'Did not – *you* did. You pulled the wheel.'

'Did *not*, I was only trying to get it down, and you pulled it off me and made it fall.'

'Did *not*.'

'Did *so*.'

'Stop it.' Laura marched across and righted the fallen bicycle. 'Get down from there this minute.'

They slid to the ground and stood glowering at each other as Laura examined the bicycle. 'I *told* you two I'd get them down,' she said, 'didn't I? Serve you right if there's any damage done.'

'Don't care,' one of the boys muttered. 'It's his bike anyway.'

'Shut up, you.' Reaching over and giving him a shove.

'*Stop*,' Laura repeated. 'Behave yourselves or it's straight back to Dublin. This is Mrs Mulcahy, who does *not* allow that kind of behaviour in her house.'

They regarded Moira, who thought it best to look mildly disappointed.

'My twins,' Laura told her, 'Seamus and Ben. They're usually good, I promise.'

Moira smiled. 'I'm delighted to hear it. Hello,

245

boys. I'm just getting the house all nice and clean for you.'

No response.

Laura began lifting down the other two bikes. 'What do you say to Mrs Mulcahy for cleaning up this lovely house for us?'

'Thank you,' they chorused, looking towards the lovely house.

'Is there a telly?' one of them asked.

'There is.'

'Does it have Nickelodeon on it?'

'Er, I'm not sure.' Moira had never heard of Nickelodeon.

'Don't worry,' Laura told her, wheeling the two small bikes towards the gate, 'we brought plenty of DVDs. Come on, you two – you can check out the telly when we get back. Say goodbye to Mrs Mulcahy.'

She'd forgotten about leaving her mobile number, but Moira said nothing. She looked young to be their mother, and no sign of a father. Still, she seemed happy enough, and the boys looked sturdy. And she was teaching them to say thank you, and bringing them on holidays.

When they were safely out of sight Moira peered in through the car windows. The back seat was a jumble of toys and clothes and shoes; the front was completely hidden under a mountain of super-market bags. Where on earth had the boys fitted? Had they lain across the luggage? And had their mother never heard of a suitcase?

She turned and went back into the house. They hadn't appreciated Gavin half enough.

Coming out of his gate at five minutes to two precisely, humming the opening bars of 'Surrey With The Fringe On Top', Walter Thompson had a near miss.

Something whizzed past him on the road, so close he felt the sharp wind of it, so fast it was gone before he could take it in. And even as he dropped his shopping bag with the fright, even as his arms flew up to regain his balance, a second something whooshed by, just as fast, and even closer than the first.

'*Oof*—' Further thrown, Walter staggered backwards into the left gatepost, which mercifully kept him upright.

'Oh! Oh, my *God*—' and here came a woman, all breathless, clambering off a bicycle that she flung into the ditch as she ran towards him. 'Oh, *Lord*, are you all right? Oh, I'm so sorry,' patting frantically at Walter's arms and shoulders, as if she was checking that none of him had disappeared. 'I'm so *dreadfully* sorry. Are you hurt?'

Walter caught his breath and did his own rapid check and decided that this shock was not the one that would carry him off. 'Yes, I believe I'm fine,' he murmured, heart still palpitating at a rate far above its usual sedate trot. 'I just got rather a turn.'

'I'm *so* sorry,' she repeated, stooping to retrieve his shopping bag, causing Walter to avert his eyes hastily from the rather generous view of her bosom the pose afforded. He looked down the road and observed the cause of his fright – two small crestfallen pink-cheeked boys on the road ahead, straddling identical bicycles. Orange-red hair with precisely the same cow-lick on each forehead, a pair of similar knobbly knees beneath the little blue shorts they wore.

'You gave this poor man a *terrible* fright,' the woman went on, in an altogether different tone. 'You nearly knocked him down. I *told* you not to go so fast, didn't I? I just *hope* you're sorry now.'

They regarded the man they'd almost knocked down, their ragged breathing clearly audible.

'Have you anything you want to say to him?'

'Sorry.'

'No harm done,' Walter told them. 'As you can see, I'm still in one piece. Perhaps you should watch out, though, when you cycle past gates in future.'

No response.

'Thank you for being so nice about it,' the woman said. 'We're actually staying next door for the next two weeks, so it looks like we'll be neighbours. We arrived early so we went for a cycle, and we're just on our way back now. I'm Laura –' extending a hand towards Walter '– and these are my boys, Ben and Seamus.'

Her hair was the colour of old gold, falling delightfully from its myriad clips to tumble about her shoulders. She smelt of cinnamon, and her figure was pleasingly full, if rather enthusiastically displayed.

Walter took her hand. 'Walter Thompson,' he told her. 'Delighted to make your acquaintance.'

'Well, I'm delighted too – and you can rest assured the boys will be more careful from now on. Won't you?' she demanded, and two small heads nodded.

Walter peered at them benignly. Typical little boys, mischief their middle names, he shouldn't wonder. He recalled playing knock-a-dolly around the neighbourhood with Cathal O'Dwyer at their age, ringing doorbells and scarpering. The fright Josie Tiernan had given them once when she'd rushed out and caught them, threatened to call the police and have them both carted off to jail there and then. Cathal, he recalled, had wet his trousers with the terror.

Walter's hand went to his hat, which miraculously had remained on his head throughout the drama, and raised it his customary two inches. 'We shall probably run into one another again over the course of your holiday.'

'Not literally, I hope,' she said, her laughter bubbling out richly.

Walter found himself looking forward to the fortnight ahead. Nice for a chap to have a pretty face to admire every now and again. Perhaps she would find herself in need of some of his vegetable offerings during their stay. No doubt Moira would mention his little enterprise.

He bade them good day and moved on in the direction of the village and his monthly haircut.

'So Mum got off OK?'

'She did.'

Their mother had gone to Italy for a long weekend with a few book-club friends. The destination had been inspired by their recent reading of *A Room with a View*, followed by an evening with the DVD adaptation.

'Everything else OK in Dublin?'

'Everything fine.' Tim watched a yellow and brown bird perched on the side of the feeder, pecking in little jerks at the peanuts. 'I'm busy, but that's the way I like it.'

They sat on the patio, the sun playing hide and seek but the rain, so far, staying away. They drank coffee and ate the remains of the cherry almond cake Nell had brought when she'd come to dinner earlier in the week. Baked in her mother's kitchen, she'd told James, due to her own being out of bounds.

Andy appeared in jeans and a rumpled T-shirt, looking half asleep even though it was well into the afternoon. John Silver, dozing at Tim's feet, rose immediately and went to him.

'Morning,' James said. 'Want the last of the cake?'

'Nah.' Andy scratched the dog's head. 'Have we any pineapple juice?'

'Not unless it's in the fridge. Write it on the list.'

He turned back into the house, John Silver at his heels.

'What about Mr Thompson?' James called after him.

'I'll go and see him tomorrow.'

Tim looked at his brother. 'What's he seeing Walter about?'

James outlined Nell's idea.

'There she goes again,' Tim said, 'sorting people out.'

His voice was impassive, but it sounded like a criticism to James. 'She likes to help,' he said. 'She was a big help to us when we first moved down.'

'I know.' Tim indicated the painting James had begun earlier in the day, wedged as ever between the sides of the stepladder. 'Does she know you're doing that?'

'Not yet.'

Tim made no further comment. James ate more cake. In the kitchen the radio came on abruptly, snatches of words and music drifting out to them as Andy shifted the dial between James's station preference and his.

'So you think you'll ever come back to Dublin?' Tim asked eventually, sweeping crumbs from the table on to his plate.

James looked at him. 'To live, you mean?'

'Yeah.'

'Can't see it.' He paused. 'It'll depend on Andy.'

'But you're happy here.'

'I am.' James thought about living in the city

again, and the idea didn't appeal. On the rare occasions he and Andy went to visit his mother, the novelty of it wore off after a day or two, and he faced the road back to Roone with relief. 'I think I've become an islander,' he said, smiling. 'It kind of sucks you in after a while.'

Tim looked at the new painting again and made no response.

'Funny, isn't it?' James went on. 'The two of us ending up here. You and me, I mean.'

'Yeah,' Tim replied, his eyes still on the painting. 'Funny.'

The kitchen door burst open and Ben skidded in. 'Mum, quick! Come out and look!'

Laura went on with what she was doing, which was covering slices of buttered white bread with cheese and onion crisps. 'I'm busy. What is it?'

Ben grabbed her arm. 'No, you have to come out!'

And from the garden, an echoing shout: 'Hurry up!'

Laura dropped the crisp packet and allowed herself to be dragged outside, where she saw two of the patio chairs over by the dry-stone wall that ran between the garden and the neighbouring property. Seamus stood on the wall, wobbling precariously as he watched something on the other side.

Laura raced across and lifted him down. 'What are you doing, climbing up there? Are you trying to get yourself killed?'

'Where's he gone?' Ben demanded, clambering on to a chair to look into the field.

'Where's who gone?'

'The horse. He ran over there.'

Laura scanned the field – greenhouse, vegetable plot, some kind of shed inside a wire fence up at the back – and made out a small grey animal standing near a huddle of trees to the rear of Walter Thompson's big old house. 'Oh, he's a sweet thing. But he's a donkey, not a horse.'

'He ran away when I got up on the wall,' Seamus told her.

'Well, that's probably because you scared him half to death.'

'Will he come back?'

'He might, if you're very quiet and don't make a sound. And if anyone tries to climb up on that wall again we're going straight back to Dublin. I'll call you when tea is ready.'

Back in the kitchen she took a stemmed glass from the press and half filled it from the open bottle in the fridge. She laid more slices of bread on top of the crisps and cut the sandwiches carefully into quarters and arranged them on a dinner plate.

She sipped cold white wine standing at the window, watching her two sons, who hadn't budged. Balancing on tiptoe, bodies pressed against the wall, two pairs of eyes trained across the field.

The first day of their holiday was drawing to a close, and she'd been right about the island.

She'd felt it as she'd driven off the ferry, as they'd travelled the road she'd travelled so often in her head, as the boys pressed their faces to the car window, on the lookout for a house with a red door.

She'd done right. She'd brought them to the right place.

She raised her glass again. With any luck she had ten minutes of peace. When you were the mother of five-year-old twins you grabbed what you could.

'We nearly killed your neighbour – did Moira tell you?'

'She did.' Nell turned away from the window, deciding to ignore the little boys, who were doing their best to clamber on to the stone wall. Hopefully the worst that would happen was a scraped knee.

Laura swept a bundle of comics from a chair, seemingly oblivious to the goings-on outside. 'Have a seat. He seems really sweet – Mr Thompson, I mean. He wasn't a bit cross.'

'Yes, Walter's a pet. I'm lucky to have him as a neighbour. I presume Mam told you about the stuff he has for sale.'

She saw a plate of white-bread sandwiches cut into triangles on the worktop, an opened crisp packet nearby. Nell couldn't swear to it, but the sandwiches appeared to be filled with crisps.

'Look at those two,' Laura said, crossing to the window and rapping sharply on the glass. 'I told them to stay off that wall. They saw a donkey a while ago and they're dying for him to come back. Hang on a sec till I bring them out their tea, and then we can chat properly.' She swept up the plate of sandwiches and disappeared.

Nell surveyed the kitchen her mother would have left pristine a few hours before. Half-emptied plastic bags strewn across every worktop, shoes scattered across the tiles, mountains of rumpled clothes piled on chairs, jigsaw boxes stacked in a higgledy-piggledy heap on the table.

She imagined Tim's horror if he saw it – she couldn't leave keys down for five minutes without him finding a hook for them. How could her new tenants have achieved such disorder in so short a time? And what was it going to be like after two weeks?

But it was only clutter; they weren't exactly trashing the place. And their rent would cover the honeymoon flights, pretty much.

The back door opened and Laura reappeared. 'That should keep them quiet for a few minutes. Don't worry about the mess, by the way; when I went to pack I couldn't find the suitcases – couldn't remember where I'd put them after our last holiday, it was so long ago – so we just flung everything into the car. I'll sort it out in the morning.'

She took a half-full wine bottle from the fridge and poured Nell a glass before topping up the one that already sat by the sink, talking all the time so Nell couldn't protest. 'There you go – I hope you like white, can't stand red myself. I just poured a glass five minutes before you arrived, in case you think I've been tippling away all afternoon. We were out for most of the day, we had a cycle this morning and went to the beach after lunch – we're only home about half an hour. It's beautiful, isn't it, the beach, I mean? And no big waves so it's very safe. We must try a different one tomorrow. I know there are loads, you're so lucky, and is this weather set to last, I wonder? Wouldn't it be great? Anyway, cheers – here's to a wonderful holiday.'

She clinked her glass against Nell's and drank. Tim would be waiting in Fitz's, having a pint with James before he and Nell went across the road to Lelia's for dinner. A quiet evening, after Gavin's unruly send-off the night before. Nell sipped the wine – she'd be late, but where could he go? – and found it to be deliciously gooseberryish.

'So,' Laura said, 'I take it you're getting married. I just spotted your beautiful ring.'

Nell smiled. 'December.'

'Oh, I love a winter wedding. I could come and sing – I have a weekly gig in my local pub at home.'

'You do? You're a singer?'

'Well, not a professional one, but I'm not bad. My day job is a crèche, six little tots, from five months to two years. I started it when the lads were one – decided I'd rather look after them myself than hand them over to some stranger, so I made it my paying job by taking in a few more.'

'And you sing at weekends.'

'Yeah, every Friday night. I play guitar as well.

I do Joni Mitchell, Adele, Norah Jones, that kind of thing. I get paid in wine, which suits me fine. The owner's a real buff, so it's not plonk.'

'Sounds good.'

'So where's your fiancé? Will I be meeting him?'

Nell hesitated. 'He's only here at weekends – he works in Dublin, so I'm not sure . . .'

Tim never mentioned the tenants, didn't seem in the least interested in making their acquaintance. He and Laura might well never come face to face.

'And what happens after the wedding?' Laura enquired. 'Are you moving to Dublin?'

'No, other way around. Tim is going to give up his job and go freelance, and base himself here on the island.'

'Lucky thing – bet he can't wait to leave the rat race behind.'

Nell smiled. 'Actually, he loves Dublin, he's always lived there. It'll be a big change for him moving down here, but I hope he'll grow to love it too.'

'I'm sure he will. So is this where you normally live? Have I put you out of your house?'

'You have – I hope you feel guilty. I'm living in a little room off my salon, just for six weeks.'

'Your salon? What do you do?'

'I'm a hairdresser. I have a salon in the village.'

Her face lit up. 'Really? That's great – I meant to bring the boys for a cut before we came here and I never got around to it. Could I book them in, and would you give me a trim while you're at it?'

'I sure will. Monday's my day off, so how about Tuesday?'

'Tuesday's perfect, any time in the afternoon. And now tell me what we should see while we're here, besides the inside of your salon.'

In the end Nell was half an hour late for Tim, and barely in time for the last dinner sitting at Lelia's.

'She's lovely. She runs a crèche in her house and plays guitar and makes up songs for the boys. Oh, and she's going to sing in Fitz's at the weekend – she does it in her own local in Dublin so she must be OK. I told her Mam would babysit.'

Tim sprinkled black pepper on his salmon cutlet. 'Didn't take you long to organise all that.'

'Well, I haven't asked Mam yet – or Hugh – but I'm sure they won't mind. And they're all coming to me on Tuesday for haircuts, the three of them.'

'Which I suppose they'll get for free.' He shook his head. 'You're the worst businesswoman I know.'

'Oh come on – I could hardly charge her twenty-five euro when she's paying me eight hundred for the house.'

He looked at her in disbelief. 'Twenty-five euro for three haircuts – do you know how much I pay for mine?'

'Of course I do – didn't I work there? I can't think why you won't let me cut it. Anyway, this is Roone: you can hardly compare it to Dublin.'

'Even so, I can't understand how you stay solvent.'

She took more broccoli from the little dish between them. 'Listen, one hard-nosed capitalist is enough in any relationship. Maybe I don't earn all that much, but it's plenty to live on. You know how unimportant money is to me.'

'I certainly do. You and James are both disgustingly non-materialistic – except, of course, when you insist on throwing us both out on to the street because you want to spend a bomb on one day.' He laughed lightly.

Nell stopped eating. She laid her cutlery down carefully. 'One day? You mean our wedding day. You're talking about the most important day in every woman's life. The only day that I want to be completely perfect, which unfortunately involves spending quite a bit of money.'

'Hey,' he said, still smiling, 'keep your hair on. I'm kidding, you know I am.'

'You're not, though, are you? From the start you've been against this whole thing, even when you knew how much paying for some of the wedding means to me. And we're hardly on the street – *Jesus*.'

'Not quite.' The smile fading now. 'We're just squeezed into a tiny bed in a poky room above a noisy pub. We've got no shower and virtually no cooking facilities.'

Nell felt her anger rising. 'If you're that unhappy, why don't you move into James's spare room for the rest of the time? It's only for another few weekends. I'm sure he wouldn't mind.'

She waited for him to protest, but he didn't. He'd thought of it already, she realised. It wasn't a new idea to him.

'Ah no,' he said, far too late. 'No, I'll stay. I'll manage. Like you say, it's only for another few weekends.'

I'll manage – as if it was a supreme sacrifice he was making for her. She picked up her fork and stabbed at the fish she suddenly didn't want. If he was so worried about his precious night's sleep, she sure as hell wasn't going to stand in his way. 'Actually,' she said, keeping her voice as light as she could, 'the more I think about it, the more sense it makes. You *should* move to James's. You should have done it from the start. We don't have to be together all the time, for goodness' sake.'

'You think?' He looked at her, his face full of doubt.

He wanted her to keep on saying what a good idea it was. She felt like flinging her wine across the table at him, but Lelia probably wouldn't appreciate that. Instead she drained her glass and held it out for a refill. 'Why don't you phone James now?' she asked as he poured. 'Wouldn't take you half an hour to move your stuff from such a poky little room.'

'You're cross,' he said.

'Not at all.' She forced a smile, the blood speeding through her veins. Maybe she could accidentally tip her water glass into his dinner.

'Look,' he said, 'just forget it. I'll stay with you.'

She opened her bag and took out her phone.
'What are you doing?'

'I'm calling James, since you won't do it.'

He said nothing. He wanted her to call. She drummed her fingers on Lelia's tablecloth as she listened to James's phone ringing.

'Hi – what's up?'

He sounded so normal. 'A favour,' she said, willing her voice not to tremble. 'Just wondering if Tim could move into your spare room.'

Pause. 'Course he can . . . You OK?'

'It's just for the next few weekends,' she said, her eyes on Tim, who was prodding at his food. 'We've decided the other is really a bit poky for two.'

'Nell, are you OK?' James asked again.

'That's great – thanks a lot,' she replied. 'He'll be over in a while, say an hour or so.'

'I'll call you later,' he said quickly.

She hung up. 'All sorted,' she said brightly. 'Just like that.'

'You don't mind?' he asked. 'Honestly?'

'Of course I don't. We're not joined at the hip.'

They were doing the sensible thing. It was only for a few weeks. It was no big deal.

Except that he'd chosen to leave her. And even though he was only going down the road, he might as well be two hundred miles away in Dublin.

'Nothing happened,' Tim repeated. 'There was no row.' Placing his toilet bag on the bathroom shelf,

261

slipping his toothbrush into the glass that already held two. 'It just makes more sense. That room is far too small, and neither of us was getting a proper night's sleep, crammed into a single bed over the pub. The noise didn't seem to bother Nell, but it bothered me.'

James made no reply, afraid that whatever he said might not come out the way it should.

'Thanks for taking me in,' Tim went on.

'No problem . . . You want a beer?'

'Go on then.'

They sat up for an hour, and Nell's name wasn't mentioned once. They talked about Ireland's chances in the World Cup and the latest political scandal and a documentary they had both seen recently. Tim gave an account of a project at work that had netted them two new clients, and James talked about preparations for the annual Roone beach barbecue, held each year on the last Friday in July, two weeks from now.

When Tim had gone yawning to bed in the smallest room, James took out his phone. He wouldn't ring: she might be asleep. He opened a text box.

> *Sorry didn't get back sooner. All OK? Will talk during the week, or call me now if you want, will be up for another while – J*

He was restless, wide awake. He made tea and sat in the kitchen, looking at the same page in the newspaper. He stayed up till two in the morning. His phone didn't ring; his text went unanswered.

Her phone beeped. She reached out in the darkness and took it from the chair by the bed. She read James's message, her eyes stinging with dried salt. 'Call me now if you want,' he said.

What would she say if she rang? What could she say to him, when she hardly knew what was in her head? Was it silly to let this upset her so much? It was only for a few weekends, they'd both sleep better. They were less than a mile apart, she'd see him first thing in the morning.

But they were apart all week: they only had two nights together out of seven. Surely he could have put up with a bit of discomfort for her sake. She'd have put up with much more for him.

She thumped her pillow and turned over. Oh, this was useless, it was getting her nowhere. All it was doing was making her unsure of him, and how ridiculous was that? She'd never been more sure of anyone. This was a tiny blip, that was all. He wasn't perfect – who was?

He loved her, she loved him. They were getting married. End of story. She closed her eyes and waited for sleep. It took an awfully long time to come.

As Laura refilled her coffee cup the back door opened and the boys burst in.

'We found loads of ants!'

'Millions and trillions!'

She regarded them calmly. 'Where?'

'C'mon, we'll show you—' They raced out again, and she lowered the coffee pot and followed.

A line of ants trooped from under the stone wall to some small object that was sitting in the grass by the side of the shed. It was completely covered with the creatures.

'What is it?' Ben asked.

'I don't know.' Laura found a stick and prodded it cautiously. It was soft and yielding – a mouse, a bird, some other little creature? She turned it over and discovered it to be an uncooked sausage.

A sausage? She turned back to the boys. 'Who put a sausage out here?'

'Not me.'

'Not me.'

And she believed them, mostly because they loved sausages far too much to share them with the ants. Easily proven anyway, with four sausages taken from the pound earlier. Easy to count the rest.

She impaled the sausage on the stick and moved it to the end of the garden, dragging it along the ground. She had no idea if ants could follow a scent, but if they were hungry enough they'd surely find it. May as well let someone eat it.

She left the boys monitoring the ant activity and returned to her coffee.

His rather colourless hair was far too long, and obscured a large percentage of his face. Walter was surprised his school allowed it, remembering the ubiquitous short back and sides of his day.

There was a cartoon of a gun on the front of the lad's red T-shirt. His trousers looked at least a couple of sizes too large, and hung precariously on his not very substantial hips. Walter doubted that his shoes had ever come face to face with a tin of polish.

On the whole, James's son – whose name, Walter realised, he had momentarily forgotten – had rather a lot to learn in the area of personal grooming. And surely he wasn't strong enough to haul boxes and bags down two flights of stairs. Walter wondered if Nell's innate desire to help had coloured her judgement somewhat.

Still, he was here, and Walter was nothing if not scrupulously polite. 'You've come about the attic,' he said.

'Yeah, my dad told me,' the boy said, in the peculiar mumble that seemed to be the prerogative of teenagers everywhere.

Walter reminded himself that good diction wasn't a prerequisite for the job. 'Yes, indeed. It's quite a large undertaking, so I'd better show you what's involved, and if you feel it's too much, then I shall be happy to look elsewhere.'

'OK.'

The lad didn't look unduly put out. Perhaps he also doubted his own ability for the task in hand, perhaps he was here only because he'd felt obliged to respond to the initial enquiry. Walter led the way upstairs, wondering how his house would appear to young eyes. Impossibly antiquated probably, given that it must be twenty years since it had seen a fresh can of paint or a new roll of wallpaper.

'Your father's,' he said, pointing to the little painting of hens on the landing. The boy glanced at it and made no comment. Well used to his father's work, of course. Not unduly impressed when he came across it.

The closer they got to their destination, the more certain Walter became that this had been a mistake. He opened the door at the bottom of the narrow attic stairs and began to ascend, conscious of the musty smell that wafted down to meet them. At the top he felt along the bare concrete wall for the light cord and tugged it sharply. The faint glow that the bulb emitted hardly made a difference.

Lord, he'd forgotten how cluttered the place was, so long since he'd been up here. As his eyes grew more accustomed to the half-darkness he made out the familiar stacks of boxes, the jumble of discarded furnishings, the paintings stacked against the walls, the old chests filled with mildewed linen and moth-eaten garments, the wicker baskets and the suitcases and the canvas sacks, all filled with the past.

So many mementoes of his parents' lives were packed away in this attic. Their clothes, their hats, their shoes. His father's sheet music and playing cards, his mother's magazines and hairbrushes and button jars. Their spirits were here, among the dust and cobwebs and discarded furniture.

And Walter's childhood was here too, his old tin soldiers and tennis racquets and stamp collections and plimsolls and fishing rods and exercise books and school uniforms, with his name hand-stitched by Mother to every shirt collar, every trouser waistband. There were letters he'd received from his parents – mostly from Mother – while he'd been at boarding school. He'd never thrown them out; they'd be here somewhere, tied with a rubber band and stored in a shoebox.

So many memories, so many things that had been dear to him once. But lately he'd felt a desire to tidy up, to leave the place clear for whoever would come next. Not that Walter was planning to vacate his house any time soon, but shouldn't he take some action now while he had the energy and enthusiasm, instead of waiting until it was too late and leaving the task to someone else?

But not this boy, standing silently beside him. Although he was taller than Walter by a good six inches at least, he was too young, too unformed for an undertaking of this size. Nell would be disappointed, and James too, probably, but really, it was out of the question.

He turned to his companion, 'I'm afraid I've been . . .' he began.

'When d'you want me to start?' the boy asked, at precisely the same moment.

*   *   *

It was weird. The second he'd stepped into the attic, as Mr Thompson pulled the string – he'd known there'd be a string for the light! – Andy had felt something he couldn't explain. Not warmth, because the place was chillier than downstairs, but something – oh, he had no idea what it was: all he knew was that it felt right up there, it felt like somewhere he wanted to be.

It smelt wonderful, old and leathery and musty and woody. And the peace was absolute. As Andy stood beside Mr Thompson in the semi-darkness he felt a silence so profound it made him aware of an infinitesimal buzz in his ears that was probably always there. Not even the hum of the sea – part of the background, always, on Roone – could be heard up here. It was a total silence he'd never known before.

And he loved its semi-darkness, even now in the middle of the day. The glass in the attic's only window, high up in the roof, was filmed with dust, allowing in virtually no daylight, and the single bare light bulb did little more than cast shadows. Andy had always liked the dark; it had never held any fear for him. He found himself wanting to poke into the dim corners of the attic, feel his way around all its nooks and crannies, send spiders scuttling into even darker cracks.

'When d'you want me to start?' he asked, his voice sounding far too loud in the silence, colliding with something Mr Thompson had started to say.

'Are you quite sure?' Mr Thompson sounded

doubtful. 'I was wondering if perhaps I was expecting too much from you.'

'It's not too much,' Andy said – wanting the job badly, now that it seemed he might not get it. 'I'm stronger than I look. I could start tomorrow. We could see how it went, just for a day.'

'Very well,' Mr Thompson said slowly. 'We shall give it a try. But you must promise not to carry anything too heavy.'

'OK.' Already he was impatient to begin. He should have said he could start right away, but it might sound silly to say it now.

'That's settled then.' Mr Thompson reached for the light cord. 'Shall we move downstairs and make arrangements?'

The attic stairs – proper stairs, not a ladder – were narrower than the ones in the main part of the house, and uncarpeted. Andy wondered if there had been servants in the house years ago, maybe when Mr Thompson had been a boy, and if they'd slept in the attic. He wouldn't mind going to bed up there in the silence. He thought he'd sleep wonderfully well.

In the hall Mr Thompson looked uncomfortable. 'Er, on the subject of remuneration, would, er, ten euro an hour be acceptable?'

Andy had forgotten about money. He had no idea what to say. Ten euro an hour sounded like a small fortune to him. His father gave him ten euro a week. 'Fine,' he managed, feeling the heat in his face, trying not to show his delight.

Trying not to look as if he was doing sums in his head.

'So,' Mr Thompson said, 'what time would you like to begin tomorrow?'

Again he was taken by surprise. He'd expected to be told what time to start, not asked. He thought quickly. He guessed Mr Thompson got up early.

'I could be here at half past nine,' he said. His father would drop dead when he saw him up at nine in the holidays.

'Perfect. I shall expect you then. And shall we say three hours?'

Three hours. Thirty euro. Again he struggled to remain impassive. 'OK.'

As Mr Thompson reached for the front-door latch the bell sounded, startling both of them.

'Oh – hello,' she said. 'That was quick – you must have been waiting for me.'

Her laugh was the rich, full gurgle that Walter remembered. She was flanked by her sons, one small hand in each of hers. She wore a red top and white shorts. Her sturdy legs were pale brown. Her top, like yesterday's dress, revealed rather more chest than a gentleman could feel comfortable with. She looked at James's son – whose name, to Walter's dismay, remained forgotten.

Thankfully, she didn't stand on ceremony. 'I'm Laura,' she said, when no introduction was forthcoming, 'and these boys are Ben and Seamus.

We're staying next door to poor Mr Thompson for a couple of weeks.'

'Andy,' the boy replied, his cheeks turning a little pinker. Walter filed the name firmly into his crumbling memory.

'You live on the island?' Laura asked.

'Yeah, about a mile away.'

'Lucky you, it's beautiful here. My boys love it, don't you?'

The twins stared at Andy – who in turn stared at their mother's abundant cleavage. She seemed not to notice. Maybe she'd got used to every male gaze being drawn to it. Walter, on the other hand, was mortified.

'I shall see you tomorrow,' he said to Andy, and thankfully the lad moved towards his bicycle and began to wheel it down the path.

'Nice boy,' Laura remarked, as he cycled off. 'So obvious when they're not brought up in the city.'

Walter decided not to mention that Andy had spent the first ten years of his life in Dublin.

'I was hoping to buy some of your eggs and honey,' Laura went on, 'if you don't mind doing business on a Sunday, that is.'

'Not at all,' Walter replied, turning and leading the way through to the kitchen. 'We shall—'

'Is your donkey a he or a she?' one of the little boys asked.

Walter was thrown temporarily off course. 'Er, a he.' They followed him into the scullery.

'What's he's name?'

'George the Sixth,' Walter replied, lifting his basket from its hook and opening the back door. 'He's called after a real king – King George the Sixth of England.'

'Has he a crown?' the second boy asked.

Walter looked at him. 'The donkey?'

'No, the king.'

'Er, yes, I believe he had a very nice gold one.' They walked past the apple trees. 'He also had a stutter,' Walter added.

'A what?'

'A stutter. It means he couldn't talk properly.'

The boys digested this solemnly. 'You can't be a king if you can't talk properly,' one of them pronounced.

Walter opened the gate that led to the field. 'In fact, you can. But poor George wasn't supposed to be king at all. His brother Edward was the proper king, you see, King Edward the Eighth – only he decided to, er, pass on his crown to George because, well, because he met a lady—'

'There he is!'

Walter broke off, relieved at the interruption. Ben was pointing excitedly towards George VI, who lifted his head from the far side of the field to regard the small party warily.

Little boys and donkeys, Walter decided, made a very pleasing combination. 'Would you like a ride on his back?' he asked, and two pairs of eyes lit up before swinging automatically towards their mother, who was smiling fondly at Walter.

'You're a dear man,' she said, and Walter's heart melted happily.

When Nell returned to the kitchen after seeing Tim off, her father had moved into the sitting room with the last section of the Sunday paper. Moira turned from the sink. 'You were quiet during dinner,' she said. 'Everything alright?'

'Everything's fine,' Nell replied, picking up the tea-towel.

She didn't look fine. She didn't sound fine. Her mother decided to dig a little deeper. 'Did you have a row with Tim, is that it?'

Nell shook her head. 'Not a row exactly.' She lifted a plate from the draining-board and began to dry it. Moira waited, scrubbing the roasting tin.

'Oh, you might as well know,' Nell said. 'He moved into James's house last night. He decided he'd prefer it to sharing the little room beside the salon with me.'

'Ah.' Her mother ran the tap over the roasting tin. 'Leave the rest of those, they'll dry themselves.'

But Nell took up another plate. 'I don't mind doing it.'

Moira cleared the salt and pepper from the table and returned the butter dish and milk jug to the fridge. 'I suppose it makes sense – that room is very small for two.'

'I know.' She took a cup from the draining-board, her back to Moira. 'It's just . . . I would have thought he'd put up with a bit of . . .' She trailed off.

'He does work hard during the week,' Moira pointed out gently. 'And then that long drive on Friday . . . and I suppose it's not that quiet above the pub, is it?'

'No.' She put down the cup and bent her head into the tea-towel.

'Ah, Nell.' Moira crossed and put an arm around her shoulders. 'Ah, don't let it upset you, love.'

'It does though.' Nell wept, her face buried in the blue and white check. 'I can't help it, I just feel . . . rejected.'

'Well, you shouldn't feel that at all.' Moira led her to the table and sat her down. 'Tim just wants to get a good night's sleep. You shouldn't make a big thing of it. He works hard all week, he needs his rest at the weekend. That's all there is to it.'

'I suppose so.'

Neither of them spoke for some time. Nell wiped her eyes and sat hunched in the chair.

'Nell,' her mother said quietly, 'there isn't anything else, is there?'

Nell looked up. Her face was blotchy, the skin damp around her eyes.

'I mean,' Moira went on, 'you and Tim are happy otherwise, aren't you?'

'Yes, we're fine.'

'You're absolutely sure?'

Nell frowned. 'Yes, of course I am – why wouldn't we be?'

'It's just that marriage is such a huge step . . . I'm just saying that if you had any doubts, it wouldn't be too late to change your mind. Nobody would think any less of you, that's all.'

Nell's mouth dropped open.

'I'm just saying,' Moira repeated. 'I want you to be sure.'

'Of *course* I'm sure,' Nell said. 'How can you even ask that?'

Moira remained silent.

'Why would you even think it?' Nell demanded. 'You said yourself he needs his sleep, that I shouldn't be making a big thing of it.'

'Nor should you.' Moira reached for her hand. 'I'm sorry, love. I suppose I'm a bit nervous myself, my only child getting married – I worry, that's all. I just want to be sure you're doing the right thing. Take no notice of me.'

'There's no need to worry. Tim and I are fine.' Nell stood, her hand sliding from her mother's. 'I'd better be getting back – I have Josie Murphy coming to me first thing for a perm.'

Moira saw her to the front door and hugged her. 'Don't mind me; it's just your old mother trying to look after you.'

Nell smiled weakly. 'I know. I don't mind. But honestly, you needn't worry. We're fine.'

Moira stood in the doorway as Nell climbed into her car. She waved as the little yellow Beetle turned on to the road and drove off. She wasn't psychic, she'd never before had a sense that she could tell what was coming, so she couldn't for the life of her work out why she'd felt such foreboding lately.

Maybe it was pre-wedding nerves, like she'd said to Nell – although up to recently she'd been quite looking forward to being the mother of the bride, the only chance she'd have. And Nell had seemed genuinely shocked at the notion that she would even think she might be having doubts about marrying Tim.

But what was it then? Where was this creeping sense of dread coming from? What had Moira in the kitchen at dawn most mornings, making tea she didn't want just for something to do?

She went inside and closed the door, wondering how long it would take her to fall asleep that evening.

Walter stood in the gathering dusk, his hand resting lightly on the gravestone. He always visited the cemetery when the light was fading. It was quieter then, and the half-dark seemed to suit the place.

He thought about the two little red-headed boys, their delight when he'd lifted them on to George's back. Their enthusiasm as they'd hunted for eggs in the hen run afterwards, darting around, quick as monkeys, shouting each time they found one, causing the startled hens to skitter out of their way.

Walter had almost been a father. He could still remember the feeling of the tiny body in his arms, the perfectly formed, beautiful face, the lashes so dark and long over the eyes that had never opened. Never looked at him.

A little girl he could have dressed in frilly clothes and sung to sleep at night. Dolls tucked into prams, miniature teacups she'd fill with water for him from a tiny matching teapot. Tottering across the floor in her mother's high heels. A tennis racquet under the stairs, sheet music, ballet shoes. A kitten, surely, at some stage. A pony, perhaps, later on.

And later still, boyfriends calling in shirts and ties. A wedding eventually, Walter in a morning suit making his way up the aisle with the bride on his arm, feeling the mixture of sadness and pride that all fathers of the bride must feel.

He'd called her Pamela after her grandmother, as he and Geraldine had planned. He'd baptised her himself on that nightmarish night: he'd bent and whispered the words into her ear, the midwife weeping softly beside him, the body of his wife covered with a sheet.

Dr Guiney had been on his annual holiday, and the storm was too wild to allow the coastguard to journey out from the mainland with another doctor, or to take Geraldine to a hospital. Too wild for a helicopter, too wild for any kind of help, other than that of Mrs O'Dea from the village, who had brought so many babies into the world and who had done her best for Geraldine and Pamela that night, and who had failed to save them.

Walter rested his hand on the gravestone and watched the sun sinking towards the horizon. Geraldine, if she had lived, would be celebrating her sixty-eighth birthday today. The two of them would be getting ready to go out to dinner at this time. She would wear the bracelet, perhaps, that he would have given her earlier.

Pamela would join them, maybe, with her husband and children. Or they might have called earlier with presents, yes, that would be better. He and Geraldine would enjoy a quiet dinner together, just the two of them.

A second cousin, English born and bred, was named in Walter's will to inherit the house and land. They'd met exactly twice, at family funerals, and Walter had an idea the man had moved to Newfoundland some years ago. He might well have no interest in a rather shabby old farmhouse stuck on a little island off the Irish coast, but there was nobody else, nobody at all.

He made the sign of the cross and turned towards the road, the scent of the sea in his nostrils.

By half past ten, an hour after Andy's arrival, his eyebrows and hair were filmed with cobwebs. His clothes were grey with dust, his shoes covered in it. He'd already brought down a considerable amount of bric-à-brac, careful to keep each load light so Mr Thompson wouldn't get worried he was doing too much.

Going up and down the stairs made him tired, but it was a good tired, like you got after a soccer match or a long cycle. And the attic hadn't lost its attraction. Each time he entered the space he felt its incredible peacefulness, and had to stop for a minute to let it soak into him. The dust didn't bother him in the least, or the cobwebs he kept bumping into. It would all come off in the wash.

He hadn't noticed the first hour passing. He was amazed when Mr Thompson told him it was time for a break. 'I have apple juice. Or tea, if you would prefer.'

They drank juice in companionable silence. Thankfully Mr Thompson didn't feel the need to make conversation all the time, unlike his dad. Just because two people were together didn't mean they had to talk, and Mr Thompson seemed to understand that.

This morning his dad had been painting on the patio when Andy had got up, which meant no conversation. It was like his dad went somewhere else when he painted, like he blocked everything out except what he was doing.

Andy had never felt the urge to paint, never been attracted to the idea of putting colour on paper, couldn't draw to save his life. Whatever he might have inherited from his father, it wasn't his artistic ability.

Most of what Andy brought downstairs was only fit for throwing out, broken bits of furniture, cracked lamp bases, bags of old shoes. Mr Thompson was loading up the little yellow skip that was parked outside the house. Andy wondered how long it would take to fill it, how many hours at ten euro an hour.

He finished his juice and got to his feet, already looking forward to being up there again.

'Where are you?'

Nell shielded her eyes from the sun. 'I'm out in *Jupiter*.'

'Come to lunch,' he said. 'John Silver's been asking for you.'

She smiled. She'd have taken John Silver out in the boat, but it would have meant calling to James's house, and she hadn't wanted to face James, after Tim's defection from the room beside the salon. She was afraid he might pity her, and she didn't want to see that.

'You don't have to talk, you just have to eat – oh, and you have to bring food. There's nothing here.'

She trailed a hand in the water, loving him for trying to cheer her up.

'Andy's out,' he said. 'He's gone to work at Walter's, would you believe? And I have wine, so if you'd rather not eat you can just drink.'

'I'll bring food,' she said. 'What time is it?'

'Twelve.'

'I'll see you at one.'

'Good.'

'Thank you,' she said.

'You're welcome. Hurry up, I'm starving.'

She hung up and slid the oars into their brackets and started rowing towards the shore, her library books in a bag at her feet.

★   ★   ★

'What you got for fifty cents?'

The girl behind the counter crossed her arms and regarded the small red-headed boy. 'Small Cadbury bar.'

He looked at the rows of confectionery displayed before him. 'Where is it?'

She pointed. He shook his head. 'Nah. What else have you?'

She sighed loudly. 'Sherbet dip. Or toffee lolly.'

'Nah. Have you lucky bags?'

'Lucky bags are two euro.'

'Have you gobstoppers?'

The girl, whose name was Hilary Dunne and who'd had a row with her boyfriend the night before, whisked the jar of gobstoppers off a shelf behind her. As she unscrewed the lid he said, 'Nah, not those ones. I want blue ones.'

She glared at him. 'I don't have blue ones,' she said. 'Just these.'

'Have you milk teeth?'

She banged the gobstopper jar on to the counter, causing him to jump. 'Milk teeth are sold by the quarter pound,' she hissed, 'and they cost more than fifty cents. Now, are you going to buy something or stand there wasting my time?'

He blinked. The supermarket door opened and a woman Hilary didn't know stuck her head in. 'Are you ready?' she asked the boy. 'Sorry,' she added to Hilary, 'he likes to take his time choosing.'

'I've told him everything I have,' Hilary said crossly. 'He can't make up his mind.'

A few moments passed. The woman pushed the door wider and walked in. She had the kind of breasts Hilary was saving up for. She scanned the empty supermarket. 'You're not exactly busy,' she said. 'He's a customer, he has money to spend.'

'He doesn't know what he wants,' Hilary said sulkily.

'I'll have one of them bars,' the boy said then, pointing to the small Cadbury he'd originally been offered.

'One of *those* bars,' the blonde woman said. 'And say please to the lady.'

'Please.'

Hilary handed over the bar and took his money silently.

'Thank you so much,' the woman said, walking with the boy towards the door. 'See?' she said to him. 'It's easy to say "please" and "thank you", isn't it?'

'*She* didn't,' he said, darting a glance back at Hilary.

'No,' the woman replied clearly. 'Some people forget how easy it is.' The door closed behind them, and Hilary took her mobile phone from her pocket to check again for a text.

'What can I do?' James asked.

'You can open the wine and pour lots into my glass.'

She put eggs on to boil and began to grate cheese. Their lunch was uncomplicated: she'd brought seeded baps and things to put into them

– ham, eggs, cheese, tomatoes – but as he uncorked the wine James was reminded of his late wife, in another kitchen.

He'd been clueless about cooking when he'd met Karen, could just about open a tin of something and scramble an egg to go with it. When she cooked for him, he would sit in the kitchen of the apartment she shared with two friends and watch as she chopped and grated and stirred and sautéed. He would sip red wine and marvel that she was his.

'Cheers,' Nell said. 'And thanks again. This is just what I needed.'

He and Karen had met at a writers' and artists' retreat, their week-long visits overlapping by two days. She was writing poetry, and had had a few of her poems published in various anthologies. He was working towards his second exhibition in a tiny art gallery in Dublin.

He'd sat across the table from her on his first night and watched her talking and laughing with the man on her left. The following night the man had disappeared, and James managed to grab the seat next to her. He'd sat tongue-tied all through dinner, eating food he couldn't taste while she'd carried on a conversation with the woman on her other side.

When the meal ended, a few diners rose and began clearing the table. James had reached for her empty dessert bowl. 'Excuse me.'

She'd turned. 'Hi.' Her eyes as green as a cat's.

'I'll take your bowl,' he'd said.

'Thanks.'

When he'd returned to the table, having shoved a few bowls into the dishwasher, she'd vanished. He cursed his slow-footedness – 'I'll take your bowl': what a killer chat-up line *that* was – and made his way from the dining room, planning an early night with his book.

'Hi again,' she'd said, pulling on a waxed jacket by the back door. 'Fancy a walk before it gets too dark?'

'Sure.' Attempting nonchalance as he got into his own jacket.

They strolled along a country lane in the gathering dusk. She smelt of ice-cream. She told him about her poetry, and asked about his painting. The top of her head barely reached his shoulder. She had a habit of touching the side of her face as she spoke.

'I'm going home tomorrow,' she told him, on the way back to the house.

His heart fell. 'Where's home?'

'Dublin.'

'Me too,' he replied, his heart picking itself up again.

'I'll keep an eye out for you so,' she said, smiling.

They'd parted at the back door. 'I'm just going to take another few minutes under the stars,' she'd told him. 'See you at breakfast.'

'Let's sit on the patio,' Nell said, 'while the eggs boil.'

He and Karen hadn't met at breakfast. James had lingered over toast and elderberry jam as long as he could, and everyone else had shown up except her. He'd gone to his studio and spent the day putting colours dispiritedly on canvas. He didn't even know her second name.

As he was leaving the dining room that evening, a woman he knew only by sight approached him. 'Are you James?'

'Yes.'

She handed him a folded slip of paper. 'Karen couldn't find you when she was leaving today. She asked me to pass this on to you.'

He unfolded the paper and saw a mobile-phone number, and underneath: *In case you'd like to keep in touch – K*

She'd left him her number. For the rest of the week it was all he could do not to use it. He added it to his phone contacts, and an hour later he wrote it inside the cover of his sketch pad in case his phone was stolen and he lost her slip of paper. The following day he wrote it again on an A4 page he took from the communal printer and stowed in his suitcase, in case he lost his phone, his sketch pad and her slip of paper.

'This is James Baker,' he said, when he finally used it, two hours after returning home. Terrified in case she'd forgotten him, or was regretting her impulse.

'When are you taking me out?' she'd asked, and their relationship had begun.

'You never told me you were doing this.' Nell stood in front of his latest work in progress.

James sat on one of the patio chairs and tossed his memories aside. 'He kept asking, I got tired of saying no. What do you think?'

'It's wonderful. What are you planning to do with it?'

'I was going to give it to someone as a wedding present,' he said, watching the smile taking over her face.

She came over to him and bent to kiss his cheek. 'You're lovely,' she said. 'We'd love it.'

'Wrong answer,' he told her. 'You're supposed to tell me you're not marrying Tim because you've realised that I'm the brother you love.'

Only, of course, he didn't say that. He tipped his chair back, the feel of her lips still on his skin. He sipped his wine and tried to ignore the sudden piercing melancholy.

'I'm a bit drunk,' she said. 'I was at James's for lunch and we polished off a bottle of wine.' She giggled. 'I'm spinning a bit.'

'So that's what you get up to when I'm not around.'

'Yup.'

'Hey,' he said, 'I really missed you on Saturday night.'

'So you told me all day Sunday.' But he wasn't saying he wanted to move back.

'Let's go to dinner at the Clipper on Friday,' he said. 'I'll book.'

'Lovely,' she said, her head buzzing gently. The Clipper was on the mainland, her favourite seafood restaurant. He was trying.

'What are you doing now?'

'I'm out walking with John Silver, trying to sober up. I'm going to Mam and Dad's in a while to bake a cake.'

'Wish I was there.'

'Me too . . . Hey, did you know James is painting John Silver?'

'Yeah,' he said. 'I saw it.'

'Isn't it wonderful? Did you know he's giving it to us as a wedding present?'

'No, I didn't . . . Look, I'd better go. I'll call you this evening. Miss you, sweetheart.'

'OK, talk to you later.'

She hung up and whistled for John Silver as she turned towards the village.

Not an inch of the kitchen table's surface could be seen. It was hidden under splayed books, scattered crayons, sketch pads, comics, toy cars, a jumble of Lego, a single canvas shoe, a hairbrush, a towel, crumpled T-shirts and plates with the remains of various food offerings on them.

The worktops on either side of the sink held an assortment of brown paper bags, a collection of bottles and jars, cereal boxes with gaping flaps, soup packets, an opened loaf of sliced white bread, half a head of lettuce, a box of teabags and a multi-pack of crisps.

Nell's grandfather's antique oval mirror, removed from its hook on Nell's bedroom wall, sat on top of the fridge, next to a lipstick, a mascara, a pot of blusher, an eye-liner pencil and a tube of tinted moisturiser.

Two red-headed boys in shorts and T-shirts and well-worn canvas shoes kicked a ball around the small back garden, occasionally thumping it into the wall of the house or the side of the shed.

The boys' mother stood at the sink, rinsing salt and sand from two small blue swimsuits. She wore a white short-sleeved dress and her feet were bare, revealing toenails that were painted green. Her hair was pulled on to the top of her head and held with a blue scarf, knotted carelessly. She squeezed water from the swimsuits and brought them out to the garden where she hung them on Nell's clothes line, narrowly avoiding a collision with the ball as she did so.

On re-entering the kitchen she glanced at her watch and saw that it was just past five o'clock. She dried her hands on the skirt of her dress and crossed to the fridge and lifted out a new bottle of wine. She listened to the happy shrieks of her sons as she filled a glass, and thought, *Aaron would have been mad about them.*

Aaron had never seen his sons; he hadn't waited for their arrival. A week before they were born he had left the bed he shared with Laura in the middle of the night and gone to the park behind their council flat and tied a rope around his neck and hanged himself from an oak tree. Depression finally claiming him, showing Laura once and for all that she was no match for it.

He left no note, no goodbye for twenty-year-old Laura and his soon-to-be-born babies. Nothing for her to do but move back home to a father who'd disowned her when she'd married an unemployed bricklayer at nineteen and who spent all day painting in his studio at the top of the house. He looked at his daughter across the dinner table as if she was someone he met occasionally but couldn't quite place. He never bothered with his grandsons, except to frown in their direction if they made too much noise or spilt something on the ceramic tiles.

Thank God for Susan, ten years older than Laura, who didn't seem to understand that she was the wicked stepmother. Susan who'd shared the night feeds and the nappy changes and the singing to sleep, who'd taken the babies out walking when Laura was curled in bed, unable to move with grief, and who'd persuaded Laura's father, the famous artist, to set up a monthly payment into his daughter's bank account until she found a way to support herself and her children.

As the months passed, with Susan's help Laura had slowly clawed her way back to life. On the boys' first birthday she'd signed a six-month lease on a small house and begun distributing leaflets door to door advertising the crèche she'd decided to open. A month later she got her first enquiry, and within three months she had five little customers whose parents paid her bills.

The early days had been hell. What madness had possessed her, what was she thinking of, signing up to spend her days with seven children under the age of two, hardly a minute without someone crying or puking or needing a nappy changed or spilling a drink or knocking over a bowl of apple purée or pinching someone else from nine in the morning till two in the afternoon? She was worn out at the end of each day, barely able, after her own two had mercifully nodded off, to open a bottle of wine or throw a frozen box of something into the microwave.

And then one day, brought almost to tears herself by the constant demands for attention by her brood, Laura had reached for her guitar and begun singing 'Old MacDonald Had A Farm'. Before the first verse was over the crying had stopped – and, somehow, the mess and the chaos didn't matter a bit.

She'd found her feet. She learnt what worked and what didn't. She marshalled the older ones to do what they could to help. She managed to get them all to sleep each day after lunch with a few verses of 'Sammy Sleepyhead' or 'Sail Away To The Land of Nod', two of her own compositions.

And then a father of one of her charges heard her singing to the kids one morning as he dropped his son into the crèche. He asked if she did any grown-up stuff, and when Laura told him she did, he suggested she come along and play in his pub some time. Susan had insisted on babysitting when Laura told her, and the single gig had turned into every Friday. Laura's life had begun to take shape again, and she couldn't have said she was unhappy. Lonely sometimes, maybe – often lonely, if the truth be told – but not unhappy, not with the boys.

She sipped wine. Here on the island she was truly happy. The longer they stayed, the more she could feel it working its way under her skin. It was a place of great charm, an island she could grow to love very easily. Already loved, if that didn't sound too silly. And this house . . . there was something about it that was comforting and welcoming and reassuring. Don't worry, this house said, everything is going to be fine, you'll see.

And look at sweet old Walter next door – you couldn't order a more ideal neighbour. Already the boys were nagging her to let them go back and feed the chickens and hunt for eggs and ride on the donkey. Poor Walter – but how lucky he was to live all year round on the island. At least he only had to put up with them as his neighbours for a couple of weeks.

She'd invite him to dinner, she decided suddenly. She'd invite him and Nell, and anyone else they met in the next day or two. She'd have a dinner party – how long since she'd cooked for anyone except the boys? – and she'd wear her favourite green dress. Good job she'd thought to bring the emerald earrings her father had given her for her twenty-first.

Susan had bought them, of course, paid with his credit card. Packaged them up and got him to sign the card. *Best wishes from Luke*, it had said. No mention of love, no x after his name. Luke he'd always been, never Dad. No hugs or kisses from Luke, who loved painting more than he loved his daughter.

She took another sip from her glass. She'd cook her chicken and lemon dish for the dinner party, the only recipe she could be reasonably sure of not ruining. She'd need to get a few bottles of red wine: some people might prefer it.

She took three of Walter's eggs from the fridge and cracked them into a bowl. She beat them with a fork and hunted in brown bags till she found tomatoes. She chopped two and added them to the eggs, and scattered in salt and pepper. No cheese: Ben couldn't stand it.

When the omelette was cooked she topped up her glass and called the boys in. 'Wash your hands,' she ordered, taking plates from the press, and they pulled a chair to the sink and clambered on.

'When can we go back to the donkey?' Seamus demanded.

'Tomorrow, after breakfast. We'll have to ask Mr Thompson first. Don't push him off, Ben.'

Tomorrow afternoon they were going to Nell's salon. The boys didn't need haircuts really, she'd got them done less than a month ago, but it was a chance to meet a few more locals, and Nell was nice.

She handed a towel to Seamus as he hopped down from the chair. 'We might invite some visitors for dinner while we're here – that'd be nice, wouldn't it?'

'Who?'

'Well, maybe Mr Thompson – and Nell, the lady who owns this house.'

'Can we have pancakes?'

'We'll see.' She sat them down and served up the omelette, wondering about a dessert. Pancakes, maybe, with ice-cream, and some of next door's wonderful honey drizzled over.

'Cocoa? In a fruit cake?'

'It's a chocolate fruit cake,' Nell replied, stirring the cocoa into the gently bubbling mix. 'No harm trying something new.'

'And you're cooking it in a saucepan.'

'It'll go into the oven eventually. This is just the preparation.'

'Ah, listen.' Moira raised the volume as 'Over The Rainbow' came on the radio. 'I love this song – who's that singing it?'

'Eva Cassidy.' Nell went on stirring, trying to ignore a faint but insistent thumping in her head. Served her right for drinking at lunchtime.

'I was just thinking,' her mother said, when the song had ended.

'What?'

'That Laura, in your house. She might suit James.'

Nell looked at her. 'What?'

'Well, remember we were saying it would be nice if he met someone?'

'*You* were saying.' Nell added cherries to the mix. 'Would you chop those walnuts?'

Moira reached for a knife. 'Well, I was thinking Laura might suit him. She has kids already, and presumably she's not with their father. And Andy would have two little brothers – I think that'd be good for him, might bring him out of himself a bit.'

'So you think she'd move down here, uproot the kids, just like that?'

'Well, maybe James and Andy would move back to Dublin. I mean, there's nothing really keeping them here, is there?'

'James loves the island – and I'm sure Andy does too.'

'Well, they probably loved Dublin when they lived there. It doesn't really matter where you live if you're with the one you want.'

'I'd never move back to Dublin, you know that.'

'Ah, it's different with you. You were born and bred here. But if for some reason Tim had to stay there, you'd move up, wouldn't you?'

'Tim isn't staying in Dublin, he's moving down here. You know that.'

'No need to get cross,' Moira said, chopping walnuts.

Nell added grated nutmeg to the mix. 'I'm not cross. Why would I be cross? Are those walnuts ready?'

'They are. What did you think of her anyway?'

'Who?'

'Laura.'

Nell shrugged. 'She's nice. Very messy – the kitchen was like a bomb had hit it. But she's friendly.'

She suddenly remembered Friday night. She opened her mouth to ask her mother if she was free to babysit – and closed it again. Maybe it wasn't such a good idea. Laura was on her holidays: she should be relaxing, not singing at Fitz's. Nell wouldn't mention it again. Laura might have forgotten all about it.

She took the saucepan off the hob. 'This has to cool for half an hour before it goes in the oven – is it OK if I grab a shower?'

'Of course it is – but I was just going to make tea.'

'Not for me, thanks.'

Nell left the kitchen and stomped up the stairs. Five minutes under a hot shower would banish her headache and make her feel less frazzled.

And so what if she was cross anyway? Everyone was entitled to be, now and again.

Walter pulled on wellingtons and let himself out the back door. He enjoyed a few early-morning turns around the field while the dew was still on the grass and most of the island was asleep.

Another fine morning, the mist with its promise of sunshine already beginning to lift. They were getting a nice run of it, good for the holidaymakers. Good for his neighbours, the little boys able to be out and about like children should.

He walked past the herb garden and the apple trees and emerged into the field, where he observed George VI several yards off to his left. In the still morning air it was possible to hear the soft tearing noise the little donkey made as he ripped grass from the ground. At the sound of Walter's approach he lifted his head.

Walter frowned. Some red object – a hat? a scarf? – appeared to have attached itself to the donkey. As recognition dawned, Walter's mouth dropped open, the colour flooding into his face.

Someone had placed a scarlet brassiere on George VI. There it perched, straps looped over his ears, cups dangling on his forehead.

It would have to be removed, of course, mortifying in the extreme as the prospect was. As he drew closer the donkey shook its head and took a few steps away. Walter followed grimly.

When he got within reach he grabbed the garment and yanked it off and plunged it deep into his trouser pocket. After a few seconds he pulled it out again and thrust it under his sweater.

What was to be done now? The thought of handing it back to its rightful owner – and Walter had little doubt of her identity – was out of the question. It would have to be returned anonymously.

He regarded the stone wall that divided his and Nell's properties. He would deposit the wretched thing there right now and have done with it. As he walked towards it he heard a smothered giggle, closely followed by a hissed 'Sssh!'

He moved closer, making as much noise as he could. There was a scurrying and a clattering before the two boys came into view, racing away from the other side of the wall. They sped into the house and banged the door behind them.

Walter took in the two upturned patio chairs before drawing the brassiere from under his jumper and depositing it quickly on the wall. He rushed off, back across the field and through the trees, past the herb garden and into the scullery.

He closed the door and leant against it, panting. They must have engineered it somehow from the other side of the wall. Tempted George over with an apple, perhaps. Little rascals. He pictured Laura finding the article later, and his colour rose again.

It was some time before he felt sufficiently composed to put his breakfast egg on to boil.

He turned over and read '7:10' on his clock radio. He reached out and disabled the alarm he hadn't needed for the past two mornings. Awake since well before seven, when he normally slept soundly till he was beeped awake at half past.

Sleep, or lack of it, was becoming an issue. Not surprisingly, given his current circumstances.

Roone, of course, had its own problems – first

the disastrous move to the village, and now James's spare bed, with its cheap mattress and knobbly sheets – but the real reason he was awake now had nothing to do with the fact that he and Nell were temporarily homeless, and everything to do with the news he'd been sitting on for the past ten days.

He had to tell her: she had every right to know. Not yet though, not until they were back in their own house, sleeping in the same bed at the weekends. They'd talk properly then, and sort it out. Nell would understand, he was sure. She'd have to.

He pushed back the duvet and got out of bed.

Laura walked into the kitchen to see Ben pouring Rice Krispies in the general direction of a bowl. She took the box from him and scooped the spilt cereal back into it. 'How long have you two been up?'

'Twenty hours,' Seamus said, ladling marmalade on to a slice of white bread.

'You should have called me.' She brought the kettle to the sink. As she held it under the tap she glanced out the window.

'Oh dear, it's raining. Let's hope it—' She broke off. She turned to look at the boys. They were both eating determinedly.

She dropped the kettle on to the draining-board and went out. Her red bra was damp from the rain. She scanned the neighbouring field and saw nothing but the little grey donkey, munching placidly near the hedge that bordered the road.

Back inside she held the bra in front of the boys. 'What's going on? How did this get out on that wall?'

Two innocent faces turned up to her.

'Dunno.'

'Dunno.'

Laura planted her palms on the table and leant in. 'Tell me how it got out there right now,' she said, 'or we're going straight back to Dublin.'

Silence.

'Right.' Laura opened the door that led into the hall. 'Come on.'

'Where?' Seamus asked.

'To pack. We're going home.'

The boys exchanged looks.

'Come on,' she repeated. 'Back to Dublin.'

'But we want to stay here,' Ben said.

'Me too, but unless you tell me how my bra ended up on that wall, we're going to be leaving in half an hour. Come on, hurry up, we have lots of packing to do.'

She tucked the bra under her arm and took her phone from her pocket.

'Who are you ringing?' Seamus asked.

'Nell – I have to tell her we're going. She'll be so disappointed.' She pressed keys and held the phone to her ear. 'It's ringing,' she told them.

'No,' Ben said hurriedly, darting a glance at his brother. 'We'll tell.'

She lowered the phone. 'Well?'

'We put it on the donkey,' he mumbled.

'You *what*? You put it *where*?'

'Only for a joke,' Seamus said. 'We didn't hurt him, we jus' put it on his head.'

'You put my bra on Mr Thompson's *donkey*?'

'But he didn't mind, he jus' flapped his ears a bit.'

'Hang on,' she said, slipping her phone back into her pocket. 'When did you do this?'

'When we got up.'

'And how exactly did you do it?'

'We went on the chairs an' then we called him over an' we gave him one of Mr Thompson's carrots that you got—'

'Yeah, an' while he was eatin' Ben put it on.'

Laura closed her eyes briefly. 'And who took it *off* the donkey and left it on the wall?'

'Mr Thompson did,' Ben mumbled. 'We runned away when he came.'

'Oh, dear God.'

She pictured their well-spoken, terribly correct neighbour making the awful discovery. She imagined Walter removing her bra from the donkey and depositing it on the wall, and she felt a powerful urge to laugh. She covered her face with her hands and groaned theatrically.

'I'm *so* disappointed,' she told them, her voice muffled. 'I can't believe you did that to a poor old man.'

'But Mum, we didn't do it to him – we jus' did it to the donkey.'

'Yeah – jus' for a joke.'

She turned towards the window, biting the inside of her cheek, trying to banish the image of Walter with her bra in his hands. 'We'll have to go to his house,' she said. 'You'll have to tell him you're very, very sorry and you'll never do it again.'

'But Muuuuuum—'

'Don't but Mum me. Finish your breakfast,' she ordered. 'We'll go straight after you've brushed your teeth.'

She brought the bra to the bathroom, where she gave it a thorough wash in the basin, leaving both taps running to drown the sound of her merriment. Poor Walter. There probably wasn't a hope of him coming to dinner now. But maybe she'd still ask, just in case.

'Here,' he said, 'let me do that.'

They'd said hello a few minutes earlier, as James was entering the supermarket and Moira leaving it. When he emerged with his newspaper she was still there, struggling to open her umbrella. Her eyes were the same dark brown as Nell's. They both had the same heart-shaped face. He knew Moira well by sight, of course, but they'd met properly only a handful of times, and always in the company of others.

'Thank you,' she said. 'I hope this is just a shower.'

'That's all, it's promised fine.' He passed her the opened umbrella. 'Actually, I'm going your way, I'm calling to Walter for vegetables.' He reached for her blue shopping bag. 'Let me take that for you.'

'Oh, there's nothing much in it.' But she handed

it over and he shoved his newspaper down the side of it.

They set off. 'How are things?' James asked. 'Enjoying the holidays?'

'Oh, I am, especially with the nice weather we've been having.' She tucked her hair behind an ear. Nell did that too. 'And you're keeping busy yourself?'

'Good enough. A few painting jobs, and the pub in between.'

'And Andy's well?'

'He is, very well. Doing a bit of work at the moment for Walter, clearing out his attic.'

'Yes, Nell mentioned. Isn't that nice for him?'

They reached the end of the village street and turned on to the coast road.

'James,' she said.

'Yes?'

She took another few steps without speaking. 'Oh,' she said then, giving a short laugh, 'you'll probably take me for a silly old fool, but I wonder if I could ask you something . . . in confidence.'

He glanced at her. 'Sure,' he said, wondering what was coming.

'I just wanted to ask you,' she went on, 'if you've noticed anything. With Nell, I mean. Well, with Nell and Tim really.'

'With Nell and Tim?' It was completely unexpected.

'Oh, it's probably my imagination, it's probably nothing at all. *She* says things are fine, but I just have this feeling, I don't know . . .'

James was at a loss. Had Nell told her about Tim moving out of the little room? Was that what this was about? But he couldn't mention it, in case Nell hadn't said anything.

'I can't say I've—'

'Nell told me,' she broke in, 'that Tim moved into your house – and I can understand the reason, really I can. I said from the start that that little room was far too poky for two, even for Nell staying there on her own . . . but it's just, I feel she's not herself lately, she's a bit . . . distracted, you know?'

Again James searched for a response. Had Tim seemed a little off at the weekend?

'I get the feeling,' Moira went on, 'that there's . . . a bit of a strain between them.' She turned to search his face. 'You haven't picked up on anything yourself? With Tim, maybe?'

James chose his words carefully. 'You probably know that Tim never really approved of Nell letting the house.' That was no secret, surely.

'Oh, indeed I do. Nell said it often enough.'

'That's probably all there is to it,' James said. 'They're both a bit . . . thrown by being out of the house.'

'Yes, you're probably right,' Moira said then. 'That's probably all there is to it.' Another little laugh. 'Don't mind me, James. I'm just being a typical mother of the bride.' She laid a hand briefly on his arm. 'You won't say anything, will you, to Tim or to Nell? They'd think I was daft.'

'No, of course not.'

The conversation turned to the upcoming beach barbecue, less than a fortnight away. But for the rest of their short walk to Moira's house James felt troubled. The last thing he wanted to do was discuss his brother's relationship with Nell – feeling about her as he did probably made him the worst possible confidant for her mother.

And it wasn't until he was pushing open Walter's gate, ten minutes after saying goodbye to Moira, that he remembered his newspaper, tucked down the side of her blue bag.

He knew as soon as he saw the envelope, even before he turned it over and looked at his name on the front, below the Tralee postmark. He closed the door and punched in the alarm code and the school was silent once more. He brought the letter into his office, along with the scatter of other post that had been waiting.

Dear Mr Mulcahy, the letter from Tralee began, *We are pleased to offer you* –

He laid it down. He'd got the job. He was leaving Roone.

He had to tell Moira and Nell.

He read the letter to the end, the page trembling in his hand. When he had finished he lifted the desk phone's receiver and dialled Claire's number. It wasn't his usual time to ring but he needed to hear her voice, even if it was only for a second or two.

'I got the job,' he said when she answered, his voice cracking slightly on the last word. 'I'm moving to Tralee.'

'Again, I'm so sorry,' Laura said. 'I don't know what you must think of us. You're probably counting the days until we go back to Dublin.'

She'd managed to avoid using the word 'bra', which she knew instinctively would mortify the living daylights out of Walter Thompson. She thought it best to avoid all mention of underwear-related words, so she called it 'the incident with the donkey' and left it at that.

Mercifully, Walter didn't seem angry. Embarrassed, certainly – his cheeks had deepened in colour when he'd opened the door to them – but otherwise not too put out. He was brushing aside her apology now, telling her that boys would be boys. As if she needed reminding.

She decided to chance issuing the invitation. 'We were wondering,' she said, 'if you'd like to come to dinner some evening. By way of an apology.'

'No, no,' he said, looking mildly shocked at the notion. 'I assure you there's no need, no need at all.'

'Well, I was thinking about it anyway,' she told him, 'before all this, and I was going to invite Nell too, to say thanks for lending us the house. We'll be seeing her this afternoon – we're going to get haircuts. Oh, do say you'll come.'

'Er, well, if you're quite sure . . .'

'Great – any night suit you more than another?

I was thinking maybe tomorrow. Not that I'm any kind of a cook, but I can do a chicken dish that usually works.'

'That sounds delightful,' he told her, 'and tomorrow night would be ideal – or indeed any night. Many thanks, I shall look forward to it. And now –' he turned his attention to the twins, standing demurely beside her, momentarily on their best behaviour '– shall we see if George would like to take a little trip around the field?'

Such a sweet man, a gentleman to the tips of his fingers. Laura bet he opened doors for women and stood to offer his seat to them on a bus. If he had a cloak he'd surely throw it over a puddle for her.

Shame he wasn't forty years younger – although she suspected she'd probably still be a bit of a handful for the poor man.

After his shower Andy dressed in a clean pair of jeans and a T-shirt and brought his second lot of dusty clothes to the kitchen. He stuffed them into the drum of the washing-machine where yesterday's were still sitting. He added powder and switched it on.

He opened the fridge and saw a half-full bottle of white wine. He took it out and pulled off the cork and sniffed. Horrible, like vinegar. He didn't know what they saw in it. He replaced the cork and took out the carton of juice.

He filled a cup and made a tomato sandwich. In his bedroom he laid his lunch on the locker and settled himself on the bed and reached into his rucksack for the book he'd taken from Mr Thompson's attic.

Today's three hours had flown even faster than yesterday's. He'd brought down lots more broken furniture – hadn't they ever thrown anything out? – and countless bundles of papers, and more bags of shoes, and several dark old paintings.

And just before his last trip upstairs Mr Thompson had said, 'I notice you haven't brought any of the books down yet.'

'What books?'

'They're stacked in boxes behind the door. They were moved up when I discovered a case of wood-worm, over a year ago now, in the bookshelves in the drawing room. I'm afraid I never got around to taking them back down when the shelves were replaced.'

Andy *had* noticed the boxes, twenty or thirty of them, but hadn't bothered to investigate. He loved the smell of old books. A few months ago his English teacher had brought a few age-spotted volumes of Dickens into the classroom; Andy had pressed one to his face and inhaled.

Maybe it was the scent of the books that was drawing him to the attic. He'd heard that smell was the most powerful of the five senses. He resolved to open one of the boxes when he went back up, just to have a look.

'Feel free to borrow some,' Mr Thompson went on, 'if you see anything you fancy.'

'Thanks.'

He didn't imagine the books would appeal to him. Just because he liked the way they smelt didn't mean their contents would interest him. Their teacher had read a few passages from the Dickens books, and Andy had nearly fallen asleep.

But when he returned to the attic he opened the top box and lifted out a book. He pressed it to his face and sniffed – and simply because the smell was so intoxicating, he decided to bring it home. He didn't even look at the cover until he showed it to Mr Thompson as he was leaving.

'OK if I borrow this one?' he asked – and only then did he spot the words on the cover.

'Of course,' Mr Thompson replied. 'One of my favourite poets.'

The Collected Poems of Emily Dickinson. The title would have put him off if he'd seen it. Poetry didn't appeal to him, he usually found it boring and long-winded, full of bits he didn't understand. Why couldn't poems be written the way people talked?

He liked the look of the book, though. The dark blue cover felt crinkly, like leather, and the title had originally been written in fancy gold lettering. Quite a bit of the gold had rubbed off, but the words had been stamped into the cover so you could still make them out.

Andy had never heard of Emily Dickinson, but he did like the sound of her name. He imagined her with curly blonde hair and blue eyes. He pictured her with her head bent over a piece of thick paper, an ink-tipped feather in her hand as she wrote her poems.

Mum had written poetry. Andy hadn't been much interested in it, but he dimly remembered her reading some out loud to him when he was very small, as he played with his toy cars or splashed in the bath. She'd stopped when he got older – he'd probably made it plain that it didn't interest him. His dad probably had her stuff somewhere, but Andy had never asked him about it. The thought of reading her words now was far too painful.

He opened the book and saw *Maurice Thompson, 1938* written in fancy brown handwriting in the top corner of the title page. He flicked through the spotted, wafery pages. He pressed the book to his face and drew its thick scent deeply into his lungs again.

He came to the first poem and began to read, his lips moving. He'd try a few, wouldn't kill him.

'Hang on,' Laura said, getting to her feet and crossing to the opposite side of the salon. 'These paintings.'

Nell snipped Ben's fringe.

'You have one above your bed. It's the same artist, isn't it?' Laura peered at the signature. 'Jack, is that his name? Jack something?'

'James,' Nell said. 'James Baker. He's my future brother-in-law. Keep your eyes closed, lovey,' she said to Ben, 'or you'll get hair in them.'

'He's very good,' Laura said, moving on to another painting. 'Does he sell them?'

'Yes – those are all for sale.'

She was bound to meet him, staying on Roone for a fortnight. A wonder she hadn't bumped into him already. Amazing Nell's mother hadn't invited them both to dinner.

'My father's an artist,' Laura said, her eyes still on James's beach at twilight. 'You might have heard of him.' She said his name.

Nell stopped and looked at her. 'He's your father?'

'Certainly is.'

'Wow.' Nell went back to Ben's fringe. 'Your granddad's really famous,' she told him. He looked unimpressed.

'So this James Baker,' Laura went on, 'he's a professional artist too.'

'Well, not really. He did a fine arts degree, but it's more of a hobby for him now.'

'And where's he based?'

'He lives here on the island.' Nell laid down her scissors and took the cape off Ben. 'There you go, all done. Let me brush you down.'

'He lives here?'

'Yup.' *And my mother thinks you'd be ideal for him.* 'Is he a local man?'

'No, he's from Dublin. He moved here a few years ago, after his wife died.' The last bit was out before she could stop it. Not that it was a secret, of course. Just that James mightn't like his private life discussed.

310

Laura leant against the mirror and watched as Nell brushed hair from Ben's shoulders. 'So what does he do when he's not painting?'

'All done.' Nell dropped the clothes brush on the shelf and straightened up. 'He paints houses, and he works part-time in the pub downstairs.'

'You mean your uncle's pub, where I'm playing on Friday?'

She hadn't forgotten. 'Are you sure you want to go ahead with that?' Nell asked. 'I was thinking after, maybe you'd prefer to relax when you're on holidays.'

'Not at all, I'd love it. If your mum is happy to babysit, that is.'

'To be honest, I haven't asked her yet, but I'm sure she will.'

She and James were bound to meet, sooner or later. And maybe Nell's mother was right, maybe they were suited. Laura was certainly attractive, with the Betty Boop figure that men normally went for. A bit in-your-face, maybe, with the low-cut tops, but very pleasant. Good company.

It would be nice for James to meet someone. A little fling maybe. Nell didn't see any harm in that. Not that they'd be able to get up to much, with the two boys in tow. And then Laura would go back to Dublin, back to her crèche, and that would be that.

'Almost forgot,' Laura said. 'You're cordially invited to dinner tomorrow night. Walter is already coming so please say yes, or he'll think I'm trying to seduce him.'

Nell smiled, picturing Walter shrinking in alarm from that bosom. 'I'd love to come,' she said. 'What time?'

'Is it alright for me to bring them in?' she asked. 'We're parched.'

'Fine,' James replied. 'No problem by day.' That was some cleavage. He kept his eyes on her face, which was lightly tanned and smiling. She ordered. He opened two bottles of Coke and stuck straws into them. He poured white wine into a glass.

'Don't tell anyone,' she said. 'I think the sun isn't quite over the yard arm.'

'My lips are sealed. You here on holidays?' He knew she was there on holidays. He knew she was staying in Nell's house. A woman with red-headed twin boys wasn't hard to identify. But you had to make conversation.

'We sure are,' she said, lifting the boys on to high stools. 'We're staying in Nell Mulcahy's house, and we have the nicest neighbour, Walter Thompson – but of course you must know him. He lets the boys ride on his donkey.'

'He's name is George,' one of the little boys told James. 'It's the name from a king.'

'Is that so?'

'An' there's chickens too,' the other boy said. 'We brang the eggs in.'

'Good for you.'

'I'm guessing,' their mother said, shifting the

strap of her yellow dress, 'that you're the future brother-in-law.'

James put out his hand. 'Guilty as charged. James Baker.'

'Laura Dolittle.' Her skin was warm and dry. 'And Ben and Seamus. We've just come from upstairs. I like your work.'

'Thanks.'

'My father paints too,' she went on, catching a drip of condensation on the side of her glass. 'I daresay you've heard of him.'

At the mention of his name James's eyes widened. 'Are you kidding? He's your father? He's probably the closest thing I have to an idol.'

Her laugh was a rich, fat chuckle. 'He seems to have that effect on people.'

The time passed. At just after four in the afternoon the place was quiet, a couple of tables occupied, three locals on stools at the far end of the counter. Laura asked James about the island and told him about Nell's suggestion that she sing in the pub on Friday night.

'Sounds good,' he said. 'Has she said anything to Hugh?'

'Haven't a clue.'

Presently a man at one of the tables signalled to James, and he took the order and brought it across. By the time he got back the other three were on the point of leaving.

'If you're doing nothing tomorrow night,' she said, lifting the second little boy down from his stool, 'Nell and Walter are coming to dinner, and as long as I'm poisoning two . . .'

James hesitated. 'Thanks very much,' he said, 'but I have a son at home.' He made a point of eating dinner with Andy each evening, had negotiated with Hugh to be on duty behind the bar either before or afterwards. Particularly during the school holidays, dinnertime was often their only definite point of contact during the day, and James hung on to it.

'Bring him,' she said immediately. 'The more the merrier. If you want to come, that is. No pressure.'

'Sure? You won't have too many?'

'Not at all.'

He'd be in Nell's company for a few hours – which, pathetically, was enough reason on its own for him to accept. And he was off tomorrow evening.

'Fine,' he said. 'Count us in, thanks very much.'

'Lovely. Around half seven?'

It wasn't a date, it was nothing like a date. It was dinner in the company of others. She'd be a good hostess – you could tell she liked being around people. Andy mightn't be all that enthusiastic, but he'd go if the alternative was a cheese and tomato sandwich at home.

After they'd left, James cleared the counter. The dark pink imprint of her lips was on the rim of her glass. She was nice-looking, with the kind of figure that was generally considered overweight in this day of stick-thin models, but as far as James was concerned, anything that reminded you of Marilyn Monroe couldn't be bad.

He found himself looking forward to the night.

Something was up with him. He'd always been quiet, but this was a different quiet. Moira added peas to the vegetable soup she was making for lunch and observed her husband putting chicken leftovers into a bowl on the step outside for Felix. He preferred the cat to eat out of doors.

Maybe it was Nell; maybe it was the thought of her getting married. Not that it would make the smallest difference to him – weren't Nell and Tim already living together, much to her parents' tacit disapproval? Nothing would change after the wedding, except that Tim would be around more, once he moved down from Dublin.

But maybe it was just the idea of his only child becoming a married woman, changing her status from daughter to wife. Maybe it was Denis having to hand her over officially to another man, even one as nice and steady as Tim.

Moira wouldn't ask him, he mightn't like it. He'd tell her in his own time, if he wanted. After thirty-six years of marriage they'd learnt to respect one another's privacy. Until he said anything she'd hold her tongue.

And, hopefully, whatever it turned out to be would be nothing too life-altering. At fifty-eight she didn't think she'd fancy having her life altered.

★　　★　　★

Because she could not stop for Death, He kindly stopped for her.

She felt a Funeral, in her brain.

She dared not meet the daffodils.

She lost a world the other day.

Andy didn't understand everything she wrote, far from it, but her voice rang true for him, and her bursts of words, her dark imagery, pleased him for the most part. He went slowly through the poems, rereading lines, reciting some aloud, for about half an hour.

Her picture, opposite the title page, was very disappointing. She looked like a woman who'd never married and who'd chased the neighbourhood children with a stick and smelt of cats. Andy had never actually met a woman who fitted that description, but if he did, he was pretty sure she'd look like Emily Dickinson. Still, her poems weren't bad.

He closed the book and tossed it on to the bed. He got to his feet, stretching the stiffness from his muscles, and examined himself in the full-length mirror that was stuck to the inside of his narrow wardrobe.

He wasn't handsome. There was nothing about him to make girls give him a second look. And he was much too skinny: he needed a few muscles. Maybe he'd buy some weights with the money Mr Thompson was going to give him.

He ran a hand through his hair. His father was always at him to get it cut. Bet Mr Thompson, with his short back and sides, thought it was far too long as well. He pushed it away from his forehead and studied the result. Did he look better or worse? He swept hair back from the sides of his face. He thought it made him look a bit older.

He remembered the first guy who'd stayed in Nell's house. He'd seen him around the village, before and after Nell had cut his hair. The difference had been startling. He'd looked like someone else.

Might be nice to look like someone else.

He checked the time and saw that he had an hour before the frozen pizza needed to go into the oven. He went outside and whistled for John Silver and they set off down the road together.

He'd get his hair cut. He'd ask Nell. It was time.

Hugh Fitzpatrick sliced lemons, using a little wooden platform he'd constructed to accommodate his shorter arm. 'Business OK?'

Nell nodded, her mouth full. Since moving into the little room upstairs she'd taken to bringing a sandwich into the bar in the evenings. 'I can't eat my dinner up there,' she'd told Hugh. 'It's like I'm in a bedsit.'

'Feel free,' he'd replied, glad of any excuse that brought her in. Full of chat whenever you met her, always seeing the positive side of things.

Apart from now. Bit subdued this evening.

'John Silver getting on all right with James?' he asked.

She drank some of her cider. 'Yeah, he's fine. Andy has taken him over, apparently. James is going to look for a pup for him when I take John Silver back.'

'The Clarkes' dog is expecting pups. Johnny was saying the other day.'

'Good. Tell James.'

Hugh swept the lemon slices into a bowl and nodded at her glass. 'Another of those?'

'Go on then.' She picked a piece of turkey from her sandwich.

Hugh remembered how thrilled she'd been when she and Tim had become an item. 'He's the one, Hugh,' she'd told him happily. 'My search is over.' When they'd got engaged she'd called to Hugh's house the following day to show him the ring, the delight flowing out of her. 'I don't know how we're going to manage it,' she'd said, 'with him in Dublin and me down here, but we'll find a way. There's always a way, isn't there?'

'Of course there is,' Hugh had told her – and sure enough, she'd announced not long afterwards that Tim would be moving to Roone once they were married.

'He'll go freelance, or do contract jobs or something,' she'd said. 'He'll be based here anyway. He'll be here much more than he is now.'

And all had seemed well. Hugh had been kept up to date with developments: he'd heard about the dress and the honeymoon plans; he'd sampled

318

all of Nell's test cakes. He'd particularly liked the coffee one with the walnuts.

And if Tim wasn't the only Baker brother in love with her, that was nobody's fault. James's dilemma was, he thought, not obvious to anyone else, but Hugh had been long aware of it. He had no idea how the knowledge had come to him, but one day it was there, lodged firmly in his head.

Some kind of sixth sense, maybe. Compensation for his missing lower arm, perhaps. Fair enough exchange, he supposed.

The subject had never come up between the two men. James, he was sure, had no idea that Hugh knew of his feelings for Nell. He imagined how tough it must be to fall in love with someone who was about to marry someone else, particularly if that someone else was your own brother.

Particularly if you'd been friendly with her first, if you'd been the one to introduce them. Poor old James.

Nell poured cider from the new bottle into her glass. 'I was wondering,' she said, 'if you'd like a singer for Friday night.'

Hugh finished off a pint of Guinness and set it in front of Willie Buckley, three stools away. 'Who's that then?'

'My tenant,' Nell replied. 'Laura Dolittle. She plays a regular gig in her local in Dublin, singing and guitar. I suggested that I ask you if she could play here, and she seemed keen.'

'What's she like?'

'If you mean her personality, she's nice, she's friendly. I haven't heard her on the guitar, but I presume she must be good if she does it every week in Dublin.'

'Fine. I'll expect her on Friday then.'

A couple of locals came in and greeted Nell. Her answering smile was a dim version of its usual self. Definitely subdued this evening. 'You OK?' Hugh asked.

'Course.'

Too quick. Hopping off her stool now, putting money on the counter, leaving half her drink behind, wrapping up the remains of her sandwich. Going to finish it off upstairs, where nobody could ask her if she was OK.

'I'm having an early night,' she told him. 'I'm bushed.'

'Right you are.'

His sixth sense might not be able to work out what precisely was up, but his common sense was quite sure that all was not well.

Tim was the man she'd been waiting for. She loved him, and he loved her. This was a rough patch, their first, really. And what exactly was wrong, apart from the fact that they were both a bit unsettled, with the house out of bounds?

She dialled his number, needing to hear his voice. She listened to it ringing until his voicemail message came on. Sorry he couldn't get to the phone, please leave a message and he'd call her right back.

'It's me,' she said. 'Just ringing to say hi. Hope you're having fun, whatever you're up to. I'm having an early night myself.'

She hung up and went to the window. She stood looking down at the village street. Lelia was closing up across the road and a few were heading into Fitz's, just below her. A car drove slowly down the street, foreign registration, driver on the wrong side.

A few teenagers were sitting on the wall outside the art gallery, watching as a man walked past them wheeling a buggy. Trying to get the baby to sleep, like her parents had done with her.

'The only thing that would send you off,' her mother had often told her. 'Five minutes in the buggy and you were out like a light.'

She turned from the window and opened the remains of her sandwich.

As Tim came out of the cinema he switched his phone back on and saw a missed call from Nell. *One new voice message*, he read. He listened to her message and checked his watch. Ten past eleven: she'd be asleep by now.

He slipped his phone into his pocket and ran to catch up with his friends.

Andy took jeans from the clothes line and brought them into the house. He and his father were eating in Nell's house tonight. The woman he'd met at Mr Thompson's with the two small boys had invited them, and Nell and Mr Thompson would be there too.

Andy didn't particularly relish the prospect. Nell and Mr Thompson on their own were fine, but a crowd was different. He felt embarrassed in crowds – he hated everyone looking at him. And Nell wouldn't be doing the cooking in her own house – that was going to be weird.

He took his jeans into the bedroom and changed into them. They felt a bit cold, but he thought they were dry. He hadn't another clean pair anyway, so he had no choice. He brushed his teeth and washed his face and pulled on a blue T-shirt before taking the second of Mr Thompson's books out to the patio while he waited for his dad to come home. 'I think you may like it,' Mr Thompson had said, lifting it from the box Andy had carried downstairs. 'It was a great favourite of mine when I was your age.'

It was hard to imagine Mr Thompson at fourteen – or hard to think that Andy would be as old as him one day, if he didn't die of some disease or accident in the meantime. Or if he didn't choose to die, like Kurt Cobain.

Mr Thompson didn't seem to Andy like someone who'd kill himself, even after what had happened to his wife and baby. Nell had told Andy and his dad about it soon after they'd got to know her. She'd been telling them about Mr Thompson selling stuff, and she'd told them the other thing too.

Mr Thompson knew what it was like to lose someone, just like Andy. He'd lost two people – and even though one of them was a baby he'd never met, Andy thought it must have been pretty horrible all the same.

He definitely liked Mr Thompson. He felt he was the kind of person you could tell stuff to if you wanted. He wouldn't laugh, or look at you as if he thought you were mad, or treat you like a kid. Mr Thompson was OK.

On the patio Andy stood before the finished painting, still stuck between the sides of the stepladder. His father had got John Silver spot on: it was as good as a photo. No, it was better than a photo. The colours, thickly applied, gave the picture a 3D feel that made it more alive, more real than any image from a camera. Looking at it, you could feel the warmth of the sun, you could smell John Silver's rough doggy smell, hear his rapid, shallow breaths. His dad had picked out spiky blades of grass in the lawn – you knew exactly how they'd feel under your bare feet.

He was a good artist, Andy could see that. He remembered the two of them going to the National Gallery lots of times, and some of the smaller Dublin galleries too. Andy remembered sitting on benches beside his dad and looking at paintings by Rembrandt or Brueghel or Osborne as his dad talked about them. Funny how their names had stuck with him.

'What do you think of your portrait?' he asked John Silver – but the dog was snuffling into his food bowl and ignored him. Andy sat on a patio chair and smelt the dusty cover of *Under Milk Wood*. He'd never heard of it, and the name didn't fill him with anticipation.

He opened the book and began to read, as John Silver left the empty food bowl and came to flop at Andy's feet with a huge sigh.

'Does he eat sweets?'

'Oh no,' Walter replied. 'Donkeys don't like sweets.'

'Why not?'

'They prefer grass and carrots and apples.'

'Ben hates carrots.'

'Yeah, well, *you* hate celery.'

'Do not.'

'Do so.'

'Shut up.'

'*You* shut up.'

'Who'd like another jelly baby?' Walter asked.

'Me. Can I have a yellow one?'

'Can I have a red one?'

They sucked in silence while Walter continued to lead George VI slowly around the field.

'Why hasn't he got no horns?' Ben asked eventually.

'Well, donkeys don't really need horns. They

don't have to fight with other animals, or defend their property.'

'Cows got horns an' they don't fight.'

'Well, yes, that's true . . .'

'Chickens don't got no horns.'

'No, they don't.'

'Can we get the eggs after?'

'Yes, we can.'

'Their father died,' Laura had told him, 'just before they were born. I moved back home for a couple of years – I didn't know what else to do – and my stepmother helped me to bring them up. We had our work cut out for us, I can tell you. Seamus didn't sleep through the night until he was almost one.'

Walter wondered what had befallen her birth mother, and why her father wasn't mentioned. She'd had a considerable share of heartache by the sound of it, yet she struck him as an exceptionally positive and happy individual. He heard no evidence of self-pity or resentment in her tale.

'Leave them with me,' he'd told her, 'if you want to have some time to yourself.' How often did she get a break from two extremely energetic five-year-olds?

She'd looked at him gratefully. 'You're sure? You'll give them back the minute they begin to annoy you?'

He could hear her now, strumming a guitar on the other side of the stone wall, singing a song he didn't recognise. Practising for Friday night, no doubt.

'I'll probably clear the place,' she'd told Walter, laughing.

Hearing her now, he didn't think so. Her voice was very pleasant. He imagined she would be a hit at Fitz's. Walter, not a big fan of evenings out, might be tempted to venture there himself. Just for an hour or so.

Shame he wasn't thirty years younger.

'Babysitting? It's a while since I was asked to do that.'

'Doesn't matter if you don't want to,' Nell said. 'I can ask someone in the village.'

'Not at all. I don't mind doing it.' Moira brushed crumbs from the table into her hand. 'What time does she want me?'

'Around eight. Are you sure?'

'I am – and wasn't it nice of her to ask you to dinner this evening?'

'Well, I'd say I was just invited to make Walter feel comfortable.'

'Oh, I wouldn't think so. I'm sure she's delighted to have someone her own age to pal around with.'

Nell took a lipstick from her bag. 'She's only in her mid-twenties.'

'Lord, and those two little kiddies to look after on her own. She hasn't said anything about the father?'

'Not to me.'

'What time are you to be there?'

'She said half seven. No rush. Say it to Dad about Friday – I presume he'll be in as usual.' Her father never missed a Friday night in Fitz's. 'Where is he, anyway?'

'Upstairs, on the computer.'

He hadn't had it long, it was one they'd been replacing at the school. She couldn't remember him ever being particularly interested in computers. But then, he'd only taken up golf a few months ago too. Maybe it was a mid-life crisis; maybe that was all there was to it. If he came home with a sports car one of these days she'd know for sure, or if he left her mother for a young blonde. She smiled at the thought.

'What?'

'Nothing.' Nell put away her lipstick and got to her feet. 'I'd better get going. Thanks for Friday. I'll let Laura know.'

As she made her way on foot the half-mile or so to her own house Nell realised she hadn't spoken to Tim all day. Better give him a ring now, rather than risk him interrupting the dinner.

'Hi,' he said. 'Meant to call you earlier, but I was up to my eyes.'

'That's OK – are you still at work?'

'Yeah. Not for much longer, though.'

'I called you last night.'

'I know. I was at the cinema with a few of the gang – too late to call you back.'

He had a whole other life in Dublin, a whole

other set of friends. His weeks were so different from his weekends. She'd met some of his friends on her last visit to Dublin, just after she and Tim had got engaged. They'd had dinner in an Indian restaurant and gone to a nightclub afterwards, and if Nell had felt like an outsider all evening she was sure that was down to her, not them.

'I'm on my way back to our house,' she told him. 'Laura invited me and Walter to dinner.'

'Nice. Say hi to Walter.'

'I won't keep you,' she said, 'you need to get out of there.'

He sounded preoccupied. He worked too hard. How many times had she told him that? And every time he'd tell her he loved it.

Her house came into view. A car that looked like James's was parked outside.

'I'll call you tomorrow,' Tim said.

It *was* his car. James had been invited to dinner? 'Nell?'

When had they met? Laura hadn't even heard of him yesterday in the salon.

'Nell, are you still there?'

'Sorry,' she said, 'what?'

'I said I'll call you tomorrow. Are you OK?'

'Yes,' she said. 'Talk tomorrow.' She hung up and turned into the driveway.

'I play every Friday night in my local,' Laura said. 'They pay me in wine, which suits me fine. I do weddings and funerals too, usually with a friend

328

who plays the cello, and I used to do singing telegrams, but I met a few weirdos so I gave it up.

'I run a crèche in my house. I opened it when the boys were one, because I didn't fancy leaving them with a stranger. At the moment I have one baby, four toddlers and a three-year-old. The three-year-old is my right-hand woman – don't know how I'd manage without her. My house is childproofed to within an inch of its life.

'My parents split up when I was twelve. My mother moved to Australia with her voice coach – she's a professional opera singer – and I've met her five times since then. She's seen the boys once, when they were babies. My father married again when I was eighteen, and Susan is ten years older than me. I was fully prepared to hate her, but it didn't work out that way. She's my best friend by a mile.

'I can't cook to save my life: this is the only meal I can prepare with any hope of success. It's a wonder the boys don't have rickets or scurvy or something. Once a week they get a decent meal, when we visit my father's house. Susan is a fabulous cook.

'I started writing songs for children a few years ago, when the boys were toddlers. The first was called "Gummy Gary", about a boy who never brushed his teeth. Ben was a reluctant tooth-brusher. It did the trick.

'You're all so incredibly lucky to live on this island. Anyone know an empty house we could squat in? We'd move down tomorrow – wouldn't we, boys? They love it too. I could open up a crèche – is there one here already? And I could sing in Fitz's at the weekends.'

Nell had to admit that she was the perfect hostess. She'd transformed the kitchen with candles, and there was no sign of the clutter Nell had seen on her previous visit. She'd managed to seat everyone around the table, with a mix of patio and kitchen chairs, and was attentive to each of her guests throughout the meal.

She wore the green dress Nell had seen on her first day, and earrings that flashed green in the candlelight. Her feet were bare, her toenails sparkling with silver polish. Her fresh, citrus scent wafted around the table as she spoke.

She made no mention of the boys' father, and nobody asked.

Throughout the meal Ben and Seamus regarded Andy with unconcealed interest, and largely ignored the four adults. Andy seemed oblivious to their attention as he disposed of two large helpings of chicken with lemon, and spoke only when he was addressed.

Walter had brought a dusty bottle of dessert wine, a jar of his own apple sauce and a box of Turkish Delight. He wore the dark grey suit Nell saw every time she invited him to dinner, and a maroon bow tie. He accepted a second scoop of the strawberry ice-cream Laura served for dessert, and appeared to be enjoying himself.

James was in jeans, as ever, and a blue shirt that Nell hadn't seen before. He'd brought a bottle of wine, and colouring books for the twins. He'd also scrubbed his nails; no trace of the paint that usually lived under there.

Over the course of the meal it emerged that Laura and James had met in the bar, directly after she and the boys had left Nell's. 'I wanted to see the artist,' Laura said, flashing a smile in his direction. 'I was curious.'

And James, with his scrubbed nails, didn't look as if he had any objection.

It also turned out that Laura had met Andy at Walter's house, when she'd gone with the boys to buy honey and eggs the day after they'd arrived on Roone. It seemed the Fates were conspiring to connect her with James.

After dinner the little boys, protesting mildly, were bundled off to bed. Laura moved everyone else into the sitting room, along with the candles. 'Talk among yourselves,' she told them. 'I won't be long.'

Within ten minutes she was back with her guitar. 'Time for the entertainment,' she told them – and sang, quite unselfconsciously, two songs by Willie Nelson. Her voice was pleasant, Nell decided, but nothing remarkable. Towards the end of the second song she forgot the words – not surprisingly, since her own wine glass had been scrupulously topped up all evening – but nobody minded.

Just before midnight, the evening broke up.

'Thanks so much, everyone,' Laura said, standing on the doorstep in her green dress and bare feet. 'You've all made us feel so welcome here. See you on Friday night – Walter, you will come, won't you?'

And Walter, instead of demurring like the rest of them expected him to, replied, 'Yes, indeed.'

'We'll drop you home,' James said to Nell, as the four of them walked down the path. 'Give me a minute to see Walter to his door.'

She sat into the front seat and Andy climbed into the back. 'How's the work going?' she asked, watching the two men walking towards Walter's.

'OK,' he said. 'Will you cut my hair tomorrow?'

She turned to look at him. 'Weren't you in about two weeks ago?'

'Yeah, but I want it a bit shorter.'

Finally. 'No problem,' she said. 'I could fit you in around four.'

'OK – and don't say anything to my dad.'

She smiled at him in the darkness. 'You want to surprise him?'

'Yeah.'

James reappeared and got in. He switched on the engine and pulled away. 'Nice evening,' he said.

'Yes. She's good company.'

'Did she tell you who her father was?'

'She did. Imagine.'

He approached the village. Nell looked out at the night sky, tried to place the constellations.

'You were quiet,' James said. 'Not like you.'

'Well, I think Laura made up for me,' Nell replied.

He pulled in outside the salon. Fitz's was still open, the lights casting a yellow glow on the path, a buzz coming from within. 'I'm working tomorrow lunchtime,' James said. 'Drop in.'

'Maybe.' She got out. 'Thanks for the lift,' she said. 'See you, Andy.'

She pulled her key from her bag and opened the door as James drove off. She walked up the stairs and let herself into the salon and through to the little room where she slept. She dropped her bag on the bed and crossed to the window and stood looking out at the street.

She watched a couple walking slowly arm in arm past Lelia's café and she wondered why on earth she'd felt so irritated all evening.

It was possibly the smallest house Denis had ever been in. It had two cramped little bedrooms upstairs and a tiny kitchen and sitting room downstairs, and a bathroom with no bath off the kitchen. The ceilings were low, especially upstairs, and Denis had to duck his head in the doorways. The kitchen had no cabinets, just some open shelving. The only fireplace, in the sitting room, was boarded up.

But it was rural and peaceful, about five miles outside Tralee, with a big garden to the rear that had a little stream running through it, and a small sandy beach less than a mile away. And it was on an elevated site, with wonderful views over the surrounding countryside and Dingle bay.

He'd miss the island, where he'd grown up and married and become a father. He'd miss being surrounded by the sea, and walking into Fitz's on a Friday night and always finding someone to talk to. He'd miss the school, where he taught the children of his former pupils.

But of course there were compensations. Claire would come when she could, and there would be no danger of being seen by anyone who knew her. And, presuming she didn't disown him when he told her, Nell would come too, now and again. And he had his books and his music, and at night he could fall asleep to the music of the stream.

And in the fullness of time, he might even take up golf.

He'd signed a lease for a year, to start at the beginning of August, one week from now. The rent was low and the landlord, three miles across the fields, seemed a decent sort. 'Give me a shout if you've any problems,' he'd said. He hadn't asked questions, hadn't enquired as to why a man in his sixties was looking to rent a house.

And if this was Denis's life, he would be happy with it. It was an honest life, and there would be a share of love in it.

The card caught Andy's eye as he walked back in through the kitchen. He'd just taken another bag of old shoes out to Mr Thompson, who was loading everything into the almost-full skip.

The card sat on the kitchen table, an envelope poking out from under it. *Happy Birthday* was printed on the front, above a picture of a set of golf clubs. Andy didn't think Mr Thompson played golf. He picked up the card and flicked it open and read *Best wishes on your 70th birthday, John.*

It was Mr Thompson's birthday, and he was seventy. Andy had no idea who John was. He looked at the envelope and saw an English stamp. Someone from England had sent a card to Mr Thompson. Andy wondered if anyone on the island knew it was his birthday. Mr Thompson wasn't the kind to go around telling people something like that.

Andy set the card down slowly. It didn't seem right, letting your birthday pass with just one card from someone in England. He didn't think Mr Thompson would want a fuss, but it seemed wrong to do nothing at all.

He'd say it to Nell when he went to get his hair cut this afternoon. Nell usually knew what to do. He heard Mr Thompson approaching and he quickly left the kitchen. When he arrived down with his next load there was no sign of the card, and Mr Thompson was taking juice from the fridge.

'Leave those,' he said to Andy. 'It's time for a break.'

Andy dropped his bundle of coats on a chair

and sat at the table. 'I love *Under Milk Wood*,' he said. 'I love the way it sounds when you read it out loud.' Right from the beginning he'd been captivated by the town of Llareggub and its ridiculous population: blind Captain Tom Cat who dreamt of his dead shipmates, nagging Mrs Ogmore-Pritchard, Mr Willy Nilly the postman, draper Mog Edwards, madly in love with Myfanwy Price and her hot-water-bottled body. He loved that they were all so mad. He loved the way they spoke, the words they used. He'd stood on his bed and recited some of it, making up silly voices for each character, and the words had flowed like a river.

'I'm so glad you enjoyed it,' Mr Thompson said. 'Dylan Thomas was a most gifted poet. You must read more of his works – there's a collection somewhere.'

'My mum wrote poems,' Andy said. 'She used to read them to me when I was small.'

Mr Thompson handed him a glass of juice. 'Did she indeed? How interesting.'

'She had stuff published.' Suddenly Andy wanted to talk about her. 'She wasn't doing it full time or anything, she had a proper job and stuff, but she did it when she was off duty.'

Mr Thompson nodded. 'If it was in her, it needed to come out.'

'Yeah.' Andy cradled his glass but didn't drink. There was silence for a minute or so. 'I wasn't really interested, though,' he went on, 'when she read to me, so she stopped after a while' – and out of nowhere, his eyes filled with tears.

He raised his glass and gulped down the pulpy liquid, blinking furiously, and by the time the juice was gone Mr Thompson was rinsing cups or something at the sink, and making a lot of noise about it.

Andy set his glass down quietly. He lifted the end of his dusty T-shirt and wiped his eyes with it. He picked up the bundle of coats and brought them out to the scullery, and added them to the bag Mr Thompson was filling for a charity shop.

As he passed through the kitchen on his way back upstairs, Mr Thompson continued to clatter, and never once turned around.

Nell tore open the bag of crisps and set it on the counter. 'Dive in.'

James regarded the contents. 'I don't know why you buy crisps. You open them and then do your best to make someone else eat them.'

She popped one into her mouth. 'They're very fattening. The least you could do is help me out. I have to fit into a wedding dress in a few months.'

'And that's your lunch, is it? Very nutritious.'

'You sound like my mother. I had a slice of cake at eleven, so I'm getting all the food groups, sweet and savoury.'

'We're having a shepherd's pie this evening,' he said, 'if you'd like to balance your diet a bit.'

'Oh, thanks. Sevenish?'

'Sevenish.'

A car passed in the street outside. James took a crisp. Nell drank her sparkling water.

'Laura's nice,' Nell said.

'She is.' He polished a glass.

'She seems to be enjoying herself here.'

'She does.'

'You should take her out,' she said – because last night in bed she'd decided that her resentment of Laura and James possibly starting something between them was ridiculous. What objection could she have to James finding someone new? What right had she to object? He deserved to be happy, like she and Tim were. She'd stop this foolishness and encourage him to get involved.

He looked at her with an expression she couldn't define. 'I should take her out?'

'Well,' she said, 'maybe it's time you got back in the game.'

He polished another glass without responding.

'I'm not butting in,' Nell said. 'Well, I am, but I'm just looking out for you. I want you to be happy, like I am.'

'OK.'

'And she's lovely. And the boys are sweet. And Andy would have two new brothers.'

'Steady on,' he said. 'We met yesterday, remember?'

'I know.' She ate crisps. 'But if you wanted to take her out, you should go for it. That's all I'm saying.'

Again that queer look. 'Right,' he said. 'I'll bear that in mind.'

'You're not cross with me?'

'No,' he said. 'I'm not cross with you.'

He was definitely a bit weird, though, for the rest of their conversation, which was mostly about Andy and Walter's current project. Maybe she should have said nothing. Maybe she should learn to mind her own business. Maybe in her next life she'd try that and see how it went.

'Have some more,' she said, pushing the crisps towards him.

'No, thanks,' he said. 'They're all yours.'

'How was Italy?'

'Very enjoyable, if Catherine Whelan hadn't insisted on phoning her daughter practically every half-hour. You'd think nobody had ever had a baby before.'

'Did you check out the places from the film?'

'We did, that beautiful piazza.'

The waiter appeared and refilled her water glass. She waited until he moved off. 'Tim, have you told Nell?'

'Not yet. I've decided to wait until we're back in the house.'

She looked at him disapprovingly. 'You're putting it off.'

'Only for a couple of weeks. What difference will that make?'

'What difference will being in the house make?'

she countered. 'What will it matter to Nell where she is when she hears what you have to tell her?'

Tim sawed through the beautifully pink beef fillet that he always ordered at Bon Appétit. 'I don't know,' he admitted. 'She's not going to be happy, either way. I suppose I just thought I should wait until at least we're back together.'

His mother frowned. 'Back together? Aren't you together now, in the salon?'

'I moved into James's house last weekend,' he told her. 'The other was too cramped for both of us.'

'Oh.' She sipped water. 'So Nell stayed there, and you moved out.'

'That's right.' He added another smear of horse-radish to his plate. 'She's happy with the move.'

'Really?'

'Yes, she's fine about it.'

'Well, fine or not, I still think you need to sit down and have a talk about your future.'

'And we will,' he promised. 'I'll tell her, don't worry.'

Not this weekend, though. He couldn't face it yet. And next weekend was the annual barbecue, always a big deal with the Roone people. And after that there was only a fortnight until they moved back home.

He'd wait, it would be easier then. He finished his beef and they ordered coffee.

★　　★　　★

340

'What? You're not serious.'

'I am,' he said. He looked serious.

'But you don't mean a buzz cut, you just mean nice and short.'

'I do mean a buzz cut,' he insisted. 'Like Beckham.'

'Right . . . and you're quite sure about this?'

'Yeah.'

'And your dad knows nothing.'

'Nah.'

'He won't be mad?'

Andy shrugged. 'It's my hair.'

He had a point. And he was fourteen, not a child any more. She'd have been happier if he'd told James what he was planning, but he hadn't, and there was nothing she could do about that.

She did think that an extreme short cut would look very cute on him – those cheekbones – not that she'd mention cute in the presence of a fourteen-year-old boy.

James would like it, once he got used to it. And even if he didn't, it would grow.

'You're quite sure?' she asked Andy again. 'It'll look very different.'

Andy smiled. 'I know.'

'OK.' She reached for her electric clipper. 'You're the boss.'

'Hello, Moira.'

Nell's mother turned to see Josephine Brown pushing a trolley along the supermarket aisle towards her.

'Lovely weather, isn't it?'

'Beautiful,' Moira agreed. 'How was France?' Josephine and her husband had spent the past fortnight in his cousin's holiday home in Burgundy.

'Fantastic.'

Josephine, originally from Listowel, had moved to Roone two years earlier after getting a teaching job in the island's primary school. She'd lost no time in integrating with the Roone community, taking up with local fisherman Mark Brown a week after her arrival, and marrying him before her first year was out. Josephine had also endeared herself to her teaching colleagues by volunteering at the beginning of her second year to be the staff representative on the school's board of management, a position not generally in demand due to its monthly meetings after the school day had finished.

'I believe,' she said, glancing quickly around, 'that a change is on the cards for us all.'

'A change?'

Josephine smiled. 'Don't worry, mum's the word. My lips are sealed.'

Moira smiled back. 'I have no idea what you're talking about.'

Josephine pulled her trolley aside to allow a woman to pass. 'Oh, come on,' she said. 'I know we were asked to say nothing, but surely I'm allowed to mention it to you.'

'Mention what?'

Josephine laughed. 'All right, have it your own

way, Moira. Look, I'd better get on – Mark is due home for his lunch. I'll be talking to you again.'

She wheeled away and left Moira standing in the household cleaning aisle, wondering what on earth had just happened.

'Andy told me,' she said. 'He spotted a card on your table. Don't be cross with him, he didn't like the thought of you having no kind of celebration. Not that this is much of a celebration.'

She held out the white box she carried. 'Happy birthday,' she said. 'Shop bought, I'm afraid – I didn't have time to bake one, and anyway, I've no oven these days. I did bring candles though, so you can blow them out and make a wish.'

Walter was touched. He took the box and led her into the kitchen, where he insisted on opening a bottle of dessert wine to have with the fresh cream sponge.

'Just a thimbleful,' she said. 'I'm on my way to James's for dinner. I shouldn't be eating cake either, but what the hell. And wait until you see Andy – I cut his hair really, really short. You won't recognise him. I'm dying to hear what James thinks.'

'Goodness, short hair,' Walter said, easing the cork from the bottle with a most genteel pop. 'I look forward to seeing it.'

'I think it's lovely.' She stuck four candles into the cake. 'How's he getting on here?'

'Wonderfully well.' Walter poured the pale golden

liquid into two small crystal glasses. 'He's a good worker – he's almost finished.'

'I'm glad to hear it. Now pass me over that box of matches.'

As birthday parties went it was a small affair, but it was the first anyone had thrown Walter in many years. They drank wine and ate cake – and he wished, as he blew out his candles, that whatever he could sense approaching wouldn't be too hard on them.

For something was coming, of that he had no doubt. No doubt at all.

'Hi.'

James turned. Andy stood at the open patio door.

'*Jesus.*' James set down his wooden spoon and stared at his son's head.

Andy was bald, or as good as. His hair was so short it was hardly there, just a pale shadow on his skull. He looked like a convict, he looked older. His face was thin. His eyes were enormous.

James stared, and searched for words. 'Did Nell do that?' he managed at last. Could she possibly have done that to his son?

Andy's faint smile disappeared. 'Yeah.'

For several seconds neither of them spoke.

'I like it,' Andy said then. 'And so does Nell.'

'Does she.'

Andy stuck his hands into his pockets. 'It's just a buzz cut, it's no big deal.'

It's no big deal. James turned abruptly and began

344

stirring the mince mixture again, unable to trust himself to speak. He heard Andy leaving the room, and cursed under his breath. *Well handled, Baker. Nice parenting. You couldn't find one positive thing to say.*

He dropped the wooden spoon and grabbed his phone and pressed Nell's number.

'Hi there,' she said, sounding happy. 'I'm on my way, just left Walter. Today was—'

James cut in. 'What the hell have you done?'

Silence. 'What? Oh. You mean Andy's haircut.'

'Yes,' he said tightly. 'I mean Andy's haircut.'

'James,' she said quickly, 'he's not a child any more. It was what he wanted, and I did try to—'

He slammed his hand hard on the worktop. 'He's *my* child, he's only fourteen. You had no right.'

'But I think it looks—'

'What you think doesn't matter,' he told her, the anger hot in him. 'It's got nothing to do with you. It wasn't your call.'

More silence. 'I'm sorry I've upset you,' she said quietly.

'Damn right I'm upset. Did you think I was ringing to *thank* you?' The blood pounding in his temples.

There was a long silence. James turned off the heat under the bubbling mince.

'I'm sorry,' she repeated, in a small voice. 'Maybe it's best if I don't come over this evening.'

'Yes,' he said, 'it is.'

'James, I'm really—'

He hung up. He dropped his phone on the worktop and drained the water from the potatoes and pounded them into a pulp. He poured the mince into a casserole dish and topped it with the mashed potato and dotted it with butter before sliding it into the oven.

And all the time the anger blazed hotly through him, and he knew it had nothing to do with Andy's haircut.

Both of them fitted easily into Nell's enormous cast-iron bath. Laura wished she had one as big at home – she could drop in the entire crèche when they got a little overexcited, calm them down with nice warm bubbly water, sing them a few happy songs as they splashed about together.

'I'll be going out for a little while tomorrow,' she told them, scrubbing necks and behind ears, 'but not until night time, and you'll be ready for bed.'

Two faces turned towards her. 'Is Susan coming?'

Susan looked after them on Friday nights, when Laura was performing in Naughton's. They loved Susan because she brought chocolate-covered raisins and always lost at Snakes and Ladders and left them up an hour later than she was supposed to.

'It won't be Susan this time – she's a bit too far away. Nell's mum is coming instead – remember we met her on the first day, when we got here? She was the lady who was cleaning the house.'

They digested this. 'Can she play Snakes an' Ladders?'

'I'm sure she can – and I bet she's great at reading bedtime stories.'

'An' can we stay up late?'

She smiled. 'If you're very good and there's no fighting, she might let you stay up a bit.'

'Yaaay.'

The joys of being five, when pleasures were simple and demands easily met. Different story when you were heading for twenty-six, mother of two and no partner, and the highlight of your week was watching reruns of *The Wire* with a glass of wine for company.

Different when what you really wanted – to meet someone, to have someone – wasn't simply a matter of asking.

Of course, it didn't hurt to ask. It did no harm at all to invite someone to dinner, even if others were coming too. And who knew? Maybe James Baker, with his tragic dark blue eyes, had seen enough last night to want a little more. Tomorrow would tell a lot, when they came face to face again in Nell's uncle's pub.

'Come on,' she said, reaching for a bath towel, 'time for hot chocolate.'

Nell took off her jacket and left it on the back of a chair in the salon. She went into the room where she slept and put the kettle on and made tea, which she drank black because she'd forgotten to get milk. She ate the second half of a banana, a slice of cooked ham and three Mikado biscuits.

She checked her phone, and saw that there were no new messages.

She read her book for twenty minutes before realising that not one word had registered. She switched on the little portable television and sat through three-quarters of a film she didn't understand about secret-service agents and a blonde woman she thought might be a Hungarian spy.

She checked her phone, and saw that there were no new messages.

She wrote a postcard to Katy, the penfriend she'd never met from Donegal. She brushed her teeth and made more tea, forgetting she had no milk. She poured it down the sink, unable to face a second black cup. She washed her face and patted it dry.

She checked her phone, and saw that there were no new messages.

Eventually she took off her clothes and put on her pyjamas and got into bed.

And all the way through, she cried bitterly.

Katy –
I know it's only five days since I last wrote,
but I'm miserable and wanted to tell someone.
Tim moved out to James's house last weekend,
and I know it makes more sense and we both
have more space now but I miss him. And
today James got angry with me because I cut

Andy's hair really short, and we've never fought before and it feels horrible. And now I've run out of space which is just as well.
N xxx

'I meant to tell you, I met Josephine Brown yesterday,' Moira said, 'in the supermarket.'

Her husband sliced the top off his boiled egg. 'Did you?'

Moira spread grapefruit marmalade on her brown toast. 'She wasn't making a whole lot of sense.'

Denis looked up.

'She kept saying there was a change on the way, or something. I didn't know what she was on about.'

Denis reached for the salt cellar.

'Does that make any sense to you?' Moira asked. 'A change, or something – does that mean anything? I thought it might have something to do with school that I was supposed to know about, since she's on the board.'

Denis ate his egg.

'Oh, and it sounded like she'd been asked not to say anything. I can't remember how she put it, but that was what I could gather.' She cut her toast into triangles. 'I was totally confused when she left.'

Denis lifted his cup and drank coffee.

'You don't know what she was on about?'

'No.'

Moira bit into her toast. 'I wonder what on earth she meant by change. What kind of a change could possibly be coming here?'

Her husband dropped his spoon and got to his feet. 'I really have no idea. And now I have to go, I've booked a golf game at ten.'

She looked at him in surprise. 'Ten? You never play that early.'

'The afternoon slots were gone,' he said, taking his crockery to the dishwasher.

'Who are you playing with?'

'Oh, just a few of the other members. You don't know them.'

'I must meet them some time.'

'Yes.'

After he'd left Moira poured herself another cup of coffee and took it out to the front garden. Not so fine this morning, dark clouds gathering on the mainland, headed this way by the look of them. Probably just as well Denis was getting his golf in early today.

She'd thought he might be able to explain whatever Josephine had been on about, but he'd seemed as clueless as Moira. Josephine had got her wires crossed, probably. Picked something up the wrong way, no doubt.

She finished her coffee and went in to put on a wash.

All through lunchtime he sat at the counter in Fitz's, sipping a soda water he didn't want. He waited for her to show up, but she didn't. It was all he could do to hold a civil conversation with Hugh, so thoroughly did he hate himself.

He was a bastard. He'd been vindictive and jealous and he deserved to feel as horrible as he did now. He'd deliberately tried to hurt her, to punish her for not loving him the way he wanted her to. He'd allowed his frustration and misery to take over, and it had found words that were cruel.

What you think doesn't matter – Jesus, had he really said that to her? Serve him right if she never spoke to him again.

But of course that wasn't going to happen because Nell wasn't like that. He would be forgiven – he'd apologise and she'd accept it – and they'd move on, and eventually he might even be able to forgive himself. But right now he felt wretched. He needed to see her, but she wasn't here.

This was impossible. He slipped off his stool. 'I'll be right back,' he said to Hugh, who was in the middle of saying something. He walked out of the pub and up the stairs and into the salon, which was empty.

He crossed the room and tapped on the other door. Footsteps approached, and there she was.

'Oh,' she said, looking at him uncertainly. 'I thought you were Maisie Kiely.' She wore a pale blue top and a faded denim skirt and her white ballerina shoes. Her hair was pulled into a pink sparkly thing. She was unaccountably beautiful to him.

'Nell,' he said quietly, 'I'm very sorry.'

Her eyes filled instantly with tears. 'No, you were right to be mad, I shouldn't—'

'I wasn't right, I had no—'

'It was just that he—'

'I know you were only—'

'No, I'm sorry—'

'Don't *you* be—'

Their words butted into each other, collided and rebounded and floated off into space. He wanted to take her face in his hands and kiss the tears away. He wanted to throw himself at her feet and clutch her silly little shoes and howl out his heartache and loneliness and misery to her.

She pressed a thumb to each of her eyes and smiled. 'Do you know, I think that was our first row, in almost four years? Maybe we were due one.'

He smiled back, although his heart continued to break. 'Come down to the bar and have a Lucozade, show me I'm forgiven.'

'Can't – Maisie Kiely's due any minute. But I'll have one tonight. Tim and I are going to the Clipper for dinner and we'll be in after.'

Tim and I. Would the day come when he could hear those words from her mouth without wanting to smash something?

'See you later then,' he said, and began to turn away – but she caught his arm and pulled him around and gave him a quick, fierce hug. He closed his eyes and hugged her back and breathed her in, couldn't trust himself to speak. Her hair smelt of oranges.

'I'm glad we're friends again,' she murmured into his shoulder. 'I hated fighting with you. I cried buckets.'

'Sorry,' he whispered, drowning in her closeness.

'I was so afraid we'd never make up. I don't know what I'd have done.'

Before he could respond they heard footsteps on the stairs outside. Nell drew back – too soon, too soon – and James dropped his arms as the salon door opened.

'Maisie,' Nell said, moving away from him, and James forced a smile on to his face before turning to make small-talk with Maisie Kiely.

Andy stood in the half-light and looked around. The attic wasn't cleared, not completely. There was still the big old wardrobe in the far corner, and two enormous trunks that reminded him of pirates' treasure chests, which Mr Thompson had told him he could ignore.

But the rest was gone. The folded canvas deck-chairs and rickety wooden tables, the cracked and broken crockery, the tarnished teapots and kettles, the mountains of mildewed coats and jackets and suits, the bundles of sheet music, the piles of magazines and booklets and pamphlets, the baggy-stringed tennis racquets and canvas bags of misshapen shoes, the big wicker baskets of yellowed bed linen, the enormous framed paintings, the stacks of heavy vinyl records, the boxes of books, all gone.

All except one last canvas sack, which held a jumble of ancient, rusting pipes and bathroom fittings. This would be Andy's final visit to the attic.

He crossed the floor slowly, his footsteps loud in the silence. He stood before the wardrobe, whose door was hanging crookedly. When he'd been seven or eight his father had taken him to see *The Lion, the Witch and the Wardrobe* at the cinema, and he'd been mesmerised by the idea of an ordinary piece of furniture being a portal into another world.

The crooked door creaked loudly as he eased it open. The darkness inside was absolute. He stuck in a hand and felt nothing. No clothes, no fur coats. No Narnia here, just an ancient wardrobe.

He stepped inside – and his heart jumped as his head collided with some wire hangers and made them rattle. He pulled the door closed as much as he could. He stood in the blackness – opening and closing his eyes made no difference – and ran his fingertips along the wardrobe's wooden back, and tapped it a few times.

Like anything was going to happen. He stepped out of the wardrobe and sat on one of the chests, not wanting to leave.

In the week that he'd been here, in the three hours he'd spent each morning going up and down

Mr Thompson's stairs, he'd felt something changing in him. He couldn't explain it or control it, but it had felt like a good thing.

And the books he'd borrowed from the attic had had something to do with it. He'd taken Emily Dickinson purely for its smell, but her words had spoken to him, in the same way that *Under Milk Wood* had seemed to climb into his head.

And yesterday Mr Thompson had offered him another book when he was leaving. Andy had never heard of e.e. cummings, and his poems shouldn't have made sense – how could you carry someone else's heart in your heart? – but they did.

Leafing through the old books, breathing in their rich scents, Andy felt something loosening in him, something that had been wound up tightly since Mum had died. He wasn't sure what was happening, but he knew it was something he wanted to happen.

And getting his hair cut, letting Nell take it all away after years of the barest trims, just to keep his father quiet – that was all part of the change that was going on. Without his hair he felt lighter, he felt freer. He liked the way it made him feel.

His father had been mad, like Andy had known he might be. His face when Andy had walked in, as if he'd just been told that Andy had murdered someone. And not a word about it all through dinner, or for the rest of the evening.

But this morning he'd got over it. 'Sorry,' he'd said over breakfast. 'It was just a bit of a shock. I wasn't expecting it. It's a bit shorter than I'd have chosen, but it does suit you.' Which was fair enough.

Mr Thompson had got a bit of a shock too. He'd blinked a bit when he'd seen it, but then he'd called Andy very smart. He'd said well done, and smiled. He was OK.

After a few minutes Andy got off the chest and picked up his last load and left the attic.

'I was passing,' Hugh said. 'I thought there might be a cup of tea going.'

'Of course there is.' His sister stood back to let him in. 'Haven't seen you in a while.'

'No, I've been busy.' He walked ahead of her into the kitchen. 'Is Denis around?'

'No, he's gone off to his golf. He'll be another hour at least.'

'Something smells good,' he said, pulling out a chair.

'I have a quiche in the oven.' She brought the kettle to the sink. 'So, what news have you for me?'

He sat at the table and watched her taking cups from their hooks. 'Not much in the way of news,' he said. 'Business is good, thank God. Other than that, nothing really.'

She scalded the teapot. 'You'll have a scone.'

'I will so.' He rose and got milk from the fridge and brought it to the table. 'You look tired,' he said. 'Are you not sleeping?'

'Me?' She took two scones from a plastic container and put them into the microwave. 'Ah, you know yourself how sleep gets to be a bit of a luxury when you're older.'

'We're not that old.'

She dropped teabags into the pot and poured water over them. 'Is there enough sugar in that bowl?'

'I've given it up,' he said. 'Thought I could stand to lose a few pounds.'

'Will you stop – you're not overweight.'

'I'm not skinny either,' he said. 'Have to keep myself looking good in case Miss Right shows up.'

'Well, that's true,' she said, rummaging in a press. 'I have jam, there's gooseberry jam somewhere, it couldn't be gone already.' Closing the press door, frowning. 'Denis must have put it in the fridge.'

The microwave pinged. Hugh opened the little door and took out the warm scones. 'I don't need jam,' he said. 'Come and sit down.'

'There it is. It'll be too cold now. Why does he do that?' She took the jar of jam from the fridge and sat across from Hugh. 'So,' she said, pushing the butter dish towards him, 'it's looking like the weather is going to break.'

'It is.' He split a scone and spread one half with butter, which began to melt instantly.

She lifted the lid of the pot and stirred the tea. 'Did I put two or three bags in? My head is gone, these days. Here, pass over your cup. I'll know by the way it comes out.'

He watched her pouring. 'I believe you're babysitting tonight.'

'I am – I just hope they behave themselves. I only met them for a minute the day they arrived, but I got the impression they're a bit wild.'

'You'll be grand, you'll be well able.'

'I will of course.'

They drank tea. The clock on the wall ticked out the seconds. A few drops splatted against the window. 'There's the rain now,' Hugh said.

'I'm a bit worried,' Moira said then, picking a scone crumb from the table.

He hadn't been mistaken. The impulse that had told him to visit her had been right. 'What are you worried about?' he asked.

She shook her head slowly. 'That's just it, I don't know. I have . . . a feeling that something's going to happen, something not good.' She took a scone from the plate and split it with her knife. 'Now that sounds really silly, doesn't it? I just hope I'm wrong.'

'It's not silly,' he said. 'I hope you're wrong too.'

He didn't think she was wrong. She had nothing to go on, but her intuition was warning her about something – and Hugh's sixth sense, or whatever you wanted to call it, had been urging him to come and see her. What could it mean? What were the Fates preparing to visit on them?

They drank tea and ate scones, and the rain continued to fall.

★　　★　　★

Nell ran her finger slowly down the short list of main courses. 'I'm going to go for the fried soft-shell crab.'

Tim smiled. 'You always go for that. Every time we come here.'

'That's because I always like it. Anyway, we haven't been here in ages. What are you having?'

'Shellfish pasta.'

'Oh good, I want to try that.'

'Why don't you order it then?'

'Because I mightn't like it.'

He gave her the look she knew well, the one she always got when she said something he considered nonsensical. She didn't care. They were out to dinner in her favourite restaurant, she and James were friends again, and she was wearing a new shell-pink silk top that she'd got for half-price because of a teeny rip in one seam. Let him give her the look all he wanted.

'So you like Andy's hair.'

'I do, now that I'm over the shock. It suits him. I wonder what made him decide to do it.'

'No idea.' She pulled a corner from one of the rolls that sat in the centre of the table. 'James got a shock too when he saw it.'

'I'll bet he did.'

She wouldn't tell him about the angry phone call, or how horrible she'd felt afterwards. He didn't need to hear about that. And she wouldn't mention James's lunchtime visit to the salon the following day, which had been very sweet, and had made her happier all afternoon.

The waiter arrived and took their order. The restaurant was full, waiting staff weaving hurriedly between tables that were occupied by happy-looking holidaymakers. Nell wondered if she and Tim were the only soon-to-be-married couple in the place. Maybe those two in the far corner were engaged – look how she was trailing her hand down his arm as she talked, see how he seemed so interested in whatever she was telling him.

Or maybe he was working up to a proposal. Maybe he was rehearsing it in his head and wasn't actually listening to a word she said. Nell would keep an eye out, see if he produced a ring, or dropped on to one knee.

Tim had popped the question on the beach as the sun had slipped quietly towards the horizon, after one of those perfect September days. They'd been walking with John Silver by the shore, Nell's flip-flops dangling from her hand, the sand still warm under her toes, her shoulders tingling lightly with sunburn.

Tim had put a hand on her arm – 'Nell' – and she'd known by the look on his face what was coming. He'd gone down on one knee, it had all been terribly romantic until John Silver had come galloping back to investigate and almost knocked him over.

They'd gone straight from the beach to her parents to tell them, and from there they'd phoned Tim's mother in Dublin and Hugh in the pub, and after that they'd called at James and Andy's house before going home to bed.

Almost a year ago, eleven months since he'd asked her to spend the rest of her life with him, and she'd said yes. Certain that that was what she wanted, thrilled that he wanted it too. And in less than six months – no, less than five – they were going to bind themselves together forever.

Bind. Sounded like someone was going to slap a pair of handcuffs on them, her right hand to his left. No escape.

'Excuse me.' The waiter placed a glass of white wine in front of her. She smiled her thanks at him.

No escape, indeed. Such melodrama. Whoever said anything about wanting to escape?

Fitz's was packed. Word of the guest performance had spread – along, no doubt, with a description of Laura's physical attractions. Nell elbowed her way to the bar and caught James's eye, their first meeting since he'd visited the salon earlier to make up.

He winked at her. Friends again. 'Where's Tim?'

'Parking. We'll take the usual when you're ready. Is Laura here?'

He pointed towards the far end of the counter and Nell spotted her tenant sitting between two of the local fishermen – and by the look of it, all three were having a good time. Laura, in a short-sleeved low-cut top, was all tousled hair and rosy skin, and the sound of her laughter travelled the length of the bar.

'When is she starting?'

'Any minute – Hugh's just about to announce her.'

As he spoke there was the sound of metal being tapped against glass. People stopped talking and turned to look at Hugh at the end of the room, standing by a bar stool against which a guitar was leaning. He asked them to put their hands together for Laura Dolittle, on holidays from Dublin, who was going to entertain them with a few songs. The applause rang out as Laura rose and crossed the room to him.

'Did I miss anything?'

Nell turned to see Tim peeling off his raincoat. 'Just starting.'

Laura took her seat and began to pluck strings and adjust keys. She wore a pair of white jeans below the blue top, and her feet, as far as Nell could see, were bare. Bare feet in a crowded pub?

'Hey, she's not bad,' Tim whispered, and Nell nudged him in the ribs. James set drinks before them and the performance began.

She sang songs by Adele and Bob Seger and Willie Nelson and Leonard Cohen. In between, she spoke.

'I came here six days ago. I want to stay. I'll accept the minimum wage and crap conditions. Who'll give me a job?'

'We have chickens in the field next door to our house. You have no idea how exciting that is for us – the only chickens we see in Dublin are wrapped in plastic with cooking instructions on the back.'

'Last night I went out to the garden after dark and lay on the grass and looked up at the stars. My God, I'd forgotten that there are so many. Damn those well-lit Dublin streets.'

They loved her. By her third song she had them transfixed. Halfway through the fourth, Nell heard her name being whispered. She turned to see Walter, brushing spots of rain from his peaked cap. 'I shan't stay long,' he murmured, 'but I did promise to come.'

They set him on a stool and Tim got him a glass of shandy. In between songs he leant towards Nell. 'I was thinking,' he said quietly, 'of giving a small dinner party next week. Perhaps you would come.'

'I'd love it.'

Walter hosting a dinner party? Even more unheard-of than his appearance this evening. Her tenant was certainly effecting changes on Roone.

Nell stole a glance at James, leaning against the bar counter, watching Laura as she began to sing 'Famous Blue Raincoat' for the hushed crowd. How could he not fall for her?

And it wasn't until much later, when Nell was lying alone in bed, listening to the muted buzz of the few remaining drinkers, that she realised there'd been no sign of her father in the pub, for the first Friday evening that she could remember.

★   ★   ★

A good night, one of the best she could remember. Chatted up by fishermen with gold rings on their wedding fingers, just a bit of fun that they'd all enjoyed. Her songs going down well, you could feel it – you could see it in their faces. The in-between banter going down well too, lots of laughter, lots of heckling, which she always enjoyed.

Nell and her good-looking fiancé there – and Walter showing up, bless him, when he'd probably much prefer to be at home with a mug of cocoa and a ginger nut. Nell's uncle Hugh, such a sweetheart, presenting her with half a dozen bottles of white and telling her she was welcome back any time.

And best of all, James Baker, offering her a lift home as she was putting her guitar back into its case at the end of the evening, as she was slipping her feet into the sandals she'd thrown off earlier. Not that she'd given him much choice, on her third glass of wine and hoping aloud that the guards weren't out. Of course he offered.

'Leave your car,' he said, 'I'll run you home.' So she did.

And pulling up outside Nell's house, James invited her and the boys to lunch at his house the following day. 'Nothing fancy,' he said, his accent a delicious Dublin-Kerry hybrid, his aftershave pleasingly spicy in the confines of his car. 'Anything the lads don't eat?'

'Plum pudding,' she told him. 'Can't stand it, either of them.'

Wanting to reach across and pull him towards her, the island artist. Wanting to press her open mouth to his and see what happened next.

'Damn,' he said, 'there goes my menu plan. Will we say one o'clock?'

He told her where he lived – 'The first group of houses after you pass the sign for the lighthouse. We're number six' – and gave her his mobile number, which she saved in her phone. Capturing him, or a part of him.

She leant across then, since it looked like he was leaving it up to her, and touched his lips lightly with her own – the contact, brief as it was, sending a lance of desire through her.

'Thanks for the lift,' she said, stepping out into the cool night air. The rain had stopped, leaving behind a salty dampness that wasn't at all unpleasant. 'See you tomorrow,' she said, walking up the path, knowing he was watching as she slipped the key into the lock, as she turned to wave goodbye.

'They were very good,' Moira told her, pulling on her jacket. 'Went off no bother.'

Laura gave her the box of Belgian chocolates she'd bought earlier, and Moira told her there was no need. The usual formalities were observed.

On the doorstep Moira looked around. 'Where's your car?'

'James drove me home,' Laura told her. 'I left mine at the pub. I'll collect it in the morning.'

Moira pulled her keys from her bag. 'James is nice, isn't he?'

'He is.'

'Poor man, losing his wife like that.'

I lost my husband, Laura nearly said. Nobody had asked her about the boys' father, everyone probably thinking he'd done a runner when she'd got pregnant. But maybe now wasn't the time to put Moira right.

After she'd left, Laura tiptoed into the boys' room and looked at their sleeping rosy faces before going back to the kitchen and pouring a final glass of wine, her nightcap after a job well done. She took it out to the patio with the midnight blue cashmere wrap Susan had given her at Christmas and sat looking up at the sky.

Cloudier tonight, the stars mostly hidden. She sipped wine and listened to the distant wash of the sea, the odd car rushing by. And for the first time in years, she felt the stirring of some kind of hope.

One hundred and fifty euro. He'd never had that much money in his life, he'd never had anything near it. The most he'd saved was seventy euro last year when he'd wanted a leather jacket and his dad said he'd pay half, and it had taken Andy seven weeks to save the other half. Now he'd made twice that, more than twice, in one week.

And the mad thing was, he found he didn't really care about the money.

There was a tap at his bedroom door. 'Come in,' he said.

His dad's head appeared. 'I'm just letting you know that I've invited Laura and the two boys here for lunch today, to pay her back for dinner.'

'OK.'

'You won't disappear?'

'No.'

'Thanks. They're coming around one.'

The door closed. Visitors for lunch. Andy couldn't remember the last time they'd had visitors, if you didn't count Uncle Tim and Nell, and Nana Baker once in a blue moon. He thought maybe his father fancied Laura, and he didn't know how he felt about that.

He pushed back the duvet and got out of bed. He switched on his laptop and pulled on his clothes as he waited for it to boot up. He ran a hand over his prickly head, shuffled feet into shoes.

He sat on the bed and opened up a new document. He sat immobile for a few minutes, staring at the blank screen. He placed his fingers on the keys, and took them off again. He closed the document and shut down the laptop.

It was no good. He wasn't in the right place, he couldn't do it here. He left the room and went in search of breakfast.

'How was the babysitting?'

Moira hung her jacket on a hook behind the salon door. 'It was fine, they were no bother.' She sat at the sink. 'Did you know James gave Laura a lift home last night?'

Nell put a towel over her shoulders. 'No, I didn't. She said she had her car with her when I asked her how she was getting home.'

'Well, she left the car here in the village and sat in with James.'

'Oh.' Nell turned on the water and waited for it to get hot. 'There was no sign of Dad last night.'

'He said he wouldn't bother. I think he was a bit tired.'

Nell wetted her hair and added shampoo. 'He's OK, isn't he?'

'Who, your father? Of course he's OK.'

She worked up a lather. 'He's not sick or anything?'

'Not at all. Why would you think that?'

'He's been a bit quiet lately. Haven't you noticed?'

'Ah, he's always quiet.'

Nell rinsed out the shampoo and applied conditioner and combed it through.

'And things are alright with you and Tim?' Moira enquired.

'Yes, of course. Everything's fine.'

And for the rest of the time they spent together, mother and daughter went on keeping things to themselves.

'So it looks like my brother is back in the game, finally.'

Nell picked up her chicken and pesto wrap. 'You mean Laura.'

'Yes, of course I mean Laura. He invited them

368

to lunch today. They arrived as I was leaving. She's a bit full on, isn't she?'

'James is doing lunch for them?'

'Well, sandwiches – and frying cocktail sausages for the kids.'

Nell bit into the wrap. 'Has he said anything to you?'

'About what?'

She made a face as she picked up her mug. 'About the meaning of life. About Laura, of course. Has he said how he feels about her?'

'Nell, men don't have those conversations.' Tim wandered to the window and looked out. 'You really have a bird's eye view up here, don't you? You can keep an eye on everything.'

'Wouldn't it be funny,' she said, 'if James ended up with Laura?'

He looked back at her. 'How funny?'

'Well, I presume she'd move down here, just like you're doing. She keeps going on about how much she loves Roone. So we'd have taken two Dubliners out of the city.'

Tim turned his gaze back to the village street. 'How do you know James wouldn't be the one to move? He's a Dubliner too, don't forget.'

'James? You must be joking. He's more local than the locals. He knows everyone; he's fit in perfectly here.'

'Good for him. And what about Andy? Has he fit in perfectly too?'

'Well, it's different, isn't it? Andy's at a tricky age, still trying to find himself.'

'And you think he'll do it quicker here. You think Roone is the answer for everyone.'

She set down the remains of her lunch. 'I think Andy will be fine, in his own time – and, yes, maybe being on Roone is good for him. I hope so, anyway. You're a bit cranky.'

Tim turned back. 'Sorry, just tired.'

She raised her eyebrows. 'Not sleeping so well in your new digs then?'

'A lot on my mind, that's all. So what time are you finishing up?'

'Last appointment's at five so I'll see you down-stairs around six.'

After he'd left she walked to the window and watched him crossing the street and making his way past the holidaymakers in their brightly coloured rain jackets.

Was he worried about moving to Roone? Surely not. He loved it here. He was probably anxious about job prospects, but by the sound of it he had nothing to be afraid of – hadn't he been promoted just a few months ago?

He was good at what he did, that was obvious. Nobody earned the kind of salary he did without proving their worth. He'd have no trouble getting work, wherever he was.

She picked up her phone and dialled her father's mobile number.

'Hello, love,' he said. 'You all right?'

'I'm fine. Just wondering if we'll see you in Fitz's this evening, since you missed last night.

Tim and I will be there about six, for a drink before dinner.'

A tiny pause. 'Yes,' he said then, 'OK, I'll drop in so.'

'How's the golf?' she asked.

'Grand . . . Look, there's your mother calling me,' he said. 'I'll see you later.'

Gone, less than a minute on the phone. Less than half a minute. As she hung up she heard her two o'clock appointment opening the salon door.

He had to do it. He couldn't wait until the end of the month. He'd find a B&B until he moved into the house. He had to go: it was becoming impossible to stay.

After his wife had gone to the supermarket he took his suitcase down from the attic and filled it with shoes and shirts and trousers and under-clothes. He got his weekend bag from the bottom of the wardrobe and put books and CDs and his passport and cheque book into it.

There were things that would need to be dealt with later – joint bank accounts, insurance policies, all the detritus that went along with running a household as one half of a couple. He'd have to change his address officially from Roone to Tralee, redirect his post, let his solicitor know, and do a myriad other things that hadn't yet occurred to him.

There would be no goodbye party for him in the school, like there had been when Dolores Lennon had retired two years ago. No speech, no present.

There would be shock when people found out. There would be disapproval and maybe revulsion when the knowledge became public that Denis Mulcahy had handed in his notice without telling anyone and run out on his wife and his responsibilities.

The enormity of what he was giving up struck him – his reputation, his friendships, his whole life up to now. He doubted that anyone would understand; he didn't think he'd be awarded any benefit of the doubt. In his absence he'd be tried and found guilty of the most heinous deception. As he was.

A small few might have sympathy, might realise that some things are beyond our control, try as we may to make things different. A few might even have been in his situation, they might empathise privately with his struggle.

He'd come back to Roone from time to time. He'd come back for funerals and because the island was in his blood. Would he be shunned? Would people cross the road when they saw him coming?

He'd tell Moira on Monday morning, after Tim had gone back to Dublin. Monday was Nell's day off, and Moira would need her. He wouldn't have breakfast: he'd tell his wife and then he'd leave.

And on his way to the pier he'd drop a message through Nell's letter-box. He'd try to explain why he was doing what he was doing. He would implore her understanding and forgiveness. He'd tell her how much he loved her, and how he hoped with all his heart that she wouldn't turn against him.

It was the wrong way, it was the coward's way out, but the more he thought about it, the more he knew he couldn't face her. He couldn't do it.

He stowed the suitcase and bag under the desk in the room that Nell used to sleep in. On Sunday night after Moira had gone to bed he'd put them in the car along with his toiletries, and anything that belonged to him from the hallstand. That would have to do for now.

He walked downstairs and put the kettle on, his heart heavy.

She was good company and not unattractive.

Her father was a man whose work James had greatly admired for years.

Since Karen's death he hadn't been on a single date.

He had to stop being in love with Nell.

Lots of reasons to give Laura a chance.

'I was thinking,' she said, 'if the weather picks up I'd like to bring the boys on a picnic tomorrow, to some bit of the island we haven't seen yet. I was thinking Nell and Tim might join us, and yourself and Andy.'

'Sounds good,' he said, wondering how amenable Andy would be to a group picnic. 'Jackson's Lookout is a nice spot.'

Lunch was over. A light drizzle was falling. They were walking back towards the village, James on the afternoon shift at Fitz's, Laura and the boys returning to Nell's house and a DVD until the rain stopped. Laura's arm was linked loosely through his as they walked. The boys ran on ahead, kicking an empty plastic bottle they'd found.

The subject of their respective partners hadn't come up. James thought Nell would probably have told her about Karen. He wondered if she had any contact with the boys' father, or if he was dead too. Most people, he knew, assumed he was either separated or divorced when they discovered he was raising a son alone. As if nobody ever died.

Lunch had been fairly hectic, with the boys and John Silver – who'd taken to each other immediately – requiring roughly equal amounts of monitoring, and James's kitchen bearing the brunt. It didn't bother him. Seldom enough that he had to clean up a mess. Andy might have it done by the time James went home, but he didn't hold out a lot of hope.

At the door to Fitz's Laura kissed his mouth lightly, like she'd done in the car the night before. All around the village by teatime, he thought. James Baker has a woman, finally.

'Thanks for lunch,' she said. 'I do like a man who can cook.'

James grinned. They'd eaten ham and tomato sandwiches. She was fun to be around, he enjoyed her company. That was enough for now.

* * *

'What did you do today?'

'We had sausages an' played with John Silver, an' we watched *Toy Story 3*. Can we go faster?'

Walter gave a light tap to George VI's flank, and the little donkey increased his pace from slow to slightly less slow. 'Sounds like you're having a good holiday,' he remarked, observing Laura as she crossed the field towards them.

'Yeah, 'cept there's no McDonald's here.'

'An' we can't get Nickelodeon on the telly.'

'An' there's no zoo as well.'

'You like the zoo?'

'Yeah, 'specially the snakes.'

'Yeah, an' 'specially the bears too.'

'They love the zoo,' Laura said as she drew close. 'We go nearly every second weekend. Come on, you two, dinner's ready. Say thank you to Mr Thompson.'

'Nell's last tenant works in the zoo,' Walter told her as he lifted the boys down.

'Does he really? Small world. Bet we know him to see.'

He walked with them to the gate that led to the road. 'I was wondering,' he said, 'if the three of you would care to come to dinner some evening this week.'

Laura looked at him in delight. 'Another dinner party? Brilliant – but I hope you don't feel obliged just because I had one.'

'Not at all,' he assured her. 'I've already invited Nell, and I shall ask James and Andy also. How would Wednesday suit?'

'Perfectly. Can I bring a dessert or a salad or anything?'

'Nothing at all, thank you.'

Now that he'd begun to issue his invitations, Walter discovered that he was quite looking forward to the challenge of hosting an evening. So long since he'd done it. Years, if the truth be told.

After Geraldine and Pamela, he'd gone into hibernation – but even when he'd eventually dragged himself out of it he'd never been given to entertaining. His neighbours had respected that, and stopped issuing invitations that might have made him feel under obligation to return.

When Nell had moved in next door she'd fallen into the habit of having him over to dinner at least once a fortnight. 'You're doing me a favour,' she'd tell him. 'I hate to eat alone.' But there was no pressure on Walter to reciprocate. Instead he kept her supplied with eggs and honey and apple juice, and in that way their balance was maintained.

By and large, he was content with the slow, gentle cadence of his life, days spent keeping his little organic enterprise ticking over, or sitting by the fireside with a book in more inclement weather. But he'd found Laura's dinner party the other night unexpectedly enjoyable, and felt the urge to do something similar.

He turned back into the house, weighing up the various merits of sherry trifle and bread and butter pudding.

★　★　★

376

'Nobody knows,' Nell said. 'It's just always been there. One of Roone's little mysteries.'

'Someone must have put it there,' Laura insisted. 'Signs don't just appear out of nowhere, even on Roone.'

Andy looked up briefly from his book. 'That's what I said when she told me.'

Nell spread a tartan blanket on top of the big oilskin sheet James had brought along. 'Things happen here,' she said. 'We can't explain them. This place is called Jackson's Lookout, but nobody knows who Jackson was.'

Laura rubbed sun cream on Ben's face. 'He was probably the one who planted the sign.'

'What does it say?' Ben asked.

'It says it's three thousand miles to the Statue of Liberty, which is in America.'

'Can we go?'

'Certainly, but not today. Keep still, or I'll get this in your eyes.'

The sun had returned. The intensity of recent weeks was gone, but it was warm enough to make Laura's picnic a reality. They arranged themselves on the various rugs and blankets, and peeled tangerines and opened plastic containers of chicken wings and sausages and coleslaw. Nell cut slices of her mother's meat loaf and James tore open a bag of leftovers for John Silver. Tim distributed paper plates.

'This was where Gavin got that bad sunburn,' Nell said. 'He fell asleep.'

Laura stuck a straw into a juice carton and handed it to Seamus. 'Who's Gavin?'

'My last tenant.'

'Is he the one who works in the zoo?'

Nell looked at her in surprise. 'How did you know that?'

'Walter mentioned it.' Laura put sausages on a paper plate and set it between the twins. 'You know he's inviting us all to dinner on Wednesday? Oh, except you, Tim – no offence.'

Tim smiled. 'None taken.'

'*Walter*'s having a dinner party?' James asked.

'Yes – I suspect he feels obliged, after mine. I told him he didn't have to, but he insisted.'

'Who's Walter?' Ben asked.

'Mr Thompson,' Laura told him. 'Walter is the name grown-ups call him.'

The food was eaten, the wine and juice drunk. Laura sang softly, 'Summertime' and 'Shine On Harvest Moon' and 'Summer In Dublin'. Andy read his book, which looked very old. The twins, warned against venturing near the safety fence, contented themselves with covering an uncomplaining John Silver with grass. Tim dozed, hands behind his head. Nell and James played Twenty Questions.

The afternoon passed off pleasantly, not one of the four adults realising that, within a relatively short while, each of their lives would take a very different turn.

★   ★   ★

She released him. 'Don't forget the barbecue next weekend. Be here as soon as you can on Friday.'

He dropped a kiss on her head before turning to his car.

'Call me when you get back,' she said. Back, not home. Home was here for him now, or soon would be.

'Will do.'

As he drove off her father came out of the house. 'Gone a bit chilly,' he said, hands in pockets, looking out to sea.

'It is. Hope it picks up for the barbecue. I'm dying for it.'

He made no response, his gaze still to the horizon. Nell remained silent too. Maybe he was working up to telling her what was wrong with him.

'Nell,' he said finally.

She looked at him. 'Yes?'

He turned to face her. 'I want to say something.'

Here it came. A small trickle of anxiety shivered through her. She waited.

'I just want to say how proud you've made me.' She opened her mouth, but he put up a hand to stop her. 'No, let me – I never tell you how much you mean to me, but you do. You know that, I hope.'

'Dad, what's wrong?' she asked urgently. 'Tell me, please tell me what's wrong. I know there's something.'

'Nothing is wrong,' he said. 'Can't I tell my daughter how I feel about her?'

'Of course you can, but lately you seem . . . I don't know . . . not yourself.'

'Well, now,' he said, smiling gently, 'who else would I be?'

She searched his face, still looking for clues. He'd shown up in Fitz's the night before, he'd had a pint with them, he'd chatted a bit, but he'd been different. And this evening at dinner she'd felt the same.

'Not long now,' he went on, turning back to the sea, 'till your house is yours again.'

'No.'

'And the wedding before you know it. Exciting times ahead.'

'Yes.'

He looked up at the sky. 'Stars coming out already.'

Nell followed his gaze and saw the first faint pinpricks of light. The stars always reminded her of Grandpa Will, who'd known them so well.

'Nell,' her father said then, and she looked at him. 'I'm happy,' he said. 'Really I am.'

She felt a chill and wrapped her cardigan around her. 'Come on,' she said, and he followed her into the house.

He drove through the outskirts of Dublin, wipers flicking, as Nina Simone sang 'Ne Me Quitte Pas' in her wonderful syrupy voice and her awful French accent. He pulled up at traffic lights, their red beam reflected in the wet street, and watched

380

the stream of pedestrians crossing in front of him, umbrellas raised. He drove past noisy pubs and brightly lit cinemas and restaurants filled with diners. He wondered if the rain was on its way across the country to Roone, reversing the journey he'd just taken.

He reached his apartment building and got out, enjoying the feeling of stretching his muscles after almost four hours of inactivity. He let himself in, nodding at the couple who came out of the lift. He recognised their faces but they'd never exchanged more than a hello. He rode to the third floor and opened the door of apartment 3C and walked in.

He stood in the tiny hall, barely room for him to spread his arms. He set down his weekend bag and stepped into the kitchen. He took a beer from the fridge and popped the cap and brought it into the living room.

He sat on the couch and took out his phone. He called Nell.

'Hello?'

'I'm home,' he said.

'No,' she said, louder than before, her clenched hands icy in her lap, 'we've been married for over thirty years. You can't do this to me. You can't destroy what we have. You're not leaving me. I refuse to let you.'

'Moira, I'm sorry,' he repeated. 'I didn't set out to—'

'I won't be disgraced in everyone's eyes,' she said. 'I won't be pitied or laughed at. You're not going, I won't allow it.'

'Moira,' he said again, sitting across from her in his usual place, looking no different – well, maybe paler – hands resting on the table, no tea in the cup she'd set out for him, nothing on his plate. 'Moira, it's happened, and I can't change that.'

'You *can* change it,' she said angrily. 'Nobody's forcing you to go. You can stay here, where you belong. You can forget all this ridiculous talk of leaving your job and moving away, because it's not happening.' She wouldn't mention the woman. She couldn't mention the woman.

He looked down at his hands. His hair was thinning on top, drawing away from his temples. His father had gone exactly the same way, she remembered. Dan Mulcahy, who'd told her at her wedding reception she was as welcome as the flowers in May.

Denis lifted his head. 'I've already left my job,' he said. 'I told you I've got a new one in Tralee. I've packed up my stuff. It's all in the car.'

The thought of him handing in his notice, applying for a new job, going for an interview, all unbeknownst to her, the idea of him filling a suitcase and bringing it out to the car – when she was sleeping, it must have been, or gone shopping for his dinner – sent a fresh sharp rage knifing through her.

'You're not going,' she repeated, 'so you can just take everything in again.'

He got to his feet. 'I'm so sorry,' he said. 'I'll be in touch. There'll be things we have to sort out. If you'd rather I did it through a solicitor I will.'

She looked up at him. 'Did you not hear me?' she asked. 'You're going nowhere.'

He left the room and she heard the front door opening and closing. She sat in front of her cup of cooling tea as he drove away while a politician on the radio talked about fiscal recovery and burning the bondholders. She sat through the weather forecast, which promised a mixed week ahead, and a settled weekend.

And finally, as someone extolled the virtues of a new air freshener, Moira Mulcahy lifted the blue and white jug and threw it across the room with all the force she could muster. The milk flew out in an arc as the jug sailed through the air before colliding with the side of the fridge and shattering into several pieces.

Nell
Poor thing, you sound really miserable. Don't worry about Tim moving out – it'll give him a chance to miss you, and you'll be back home before you know it. And hopefully you and James have made up by now – it can't have been that serious if it was over a haircut. You must have scalped Andy!

Nothing here, same old, same old. Liam

working all hours, hardly see him. Write again
soon, always lovely to hear from you, whatever
the reason.
K xxx

Nell slipped Katy's postcard back into its envelope and turned her attention to the other letter, the one she was afraid to open.

There was no stamp on the white envelope, just *Nell*, in her father's cramped handwriting.

Her father had written to her. He hadn't posted it: he'd dropped it through the letter-box, late last night or early this morning. Whatever was in it was something he didn't want to, or couldn't, say face to face.

This was not good.

She had to open it. She slid a finger under the flap, feeling horribly fearful. She pulled out the folded sheets and saw *My dear Nell* at the top of the first. She leant against the wall and scanned them rapidly, a hand going to press hard against her mouth, a low moan escaping. She went back to the start and began again, blinking away tears as she read the words he'd written.

When she got to the end she folded the sheets. As she tried to shove them back into the envelope she heard her phone ringing upstairs. She stumbled up and raced across the salon.

'Nell—' her mother said, her voice broken.

'I'm coming. I'm on the way.'

She dropped his letter on her bed and splashed

her face with cold water and got her car keys. She left the building and drove to her parents' house, brushing more tears out of the way as she went.

Three missed calls when he came out of the usual Monday-morning meeting, all from Nell. No message on his voicemail. He pressed her number and heard her phone ringing.

'Hang on,' she said, her voice so low he could barely hear it.

Several seconds of silence followed, during which he checked his watch and clicked his briefcase open.

'It's Dad,' she said, in the same small voice.

Dead, heart attack, car crash, raced through Tim's head. He reached for a bundle of folders on the shelf behind his desk and began riffling through them. 'What happened?'

'He's left. He's walked out.'

His hand stilled. 'What? Your father?' It was utterly unexpected.

'He's met someone else.' Her voice cracking, her breathing ragged.

Denis had met someone else? Denis, his future father-in-law, the school principal, that elderly respectable man, had gone off with another woman? Preposterous.

'When did this happen?' he asked, pulling folders from the bundle and adding them to his briefcase.

'This morning.'

'God – I don't know what to say.' Snapping his briefcase shut, checking his watch again. 'Look, love, I have—'

'My mother's in shock. She's hardly said a word.'

'I'm sure she is. Look, I'm really—'

His door opened and his boss's head appeared. Tim nodded, said, *I'll be right there*, with his hand, and the door closed again.

'Tim?'

'I'm really sorry,' he said, getting to his feet and lifting his jacket from the back of his chair, 'I have to go, someone's waiting for me, I'll call you later, right? And –' he pulled on the jacket, searching for inspiration '– call Hugh, OK? Get him to come over. Or James.' James was good in a crisis. 'OK?' He crossed to the door. 'I have to go, sweetheart, OK? I'll call you the minute I can, I promise.'

He hung up and raced out to his boss, who didn't like to keep their clients waiting.

'I think,' Laura said, 'it's too wet for the beach today.'

Two disappointed faces looked up at her from their plates of sausage. 'What'll we do so?'

'Well, we could go to Dingle.' She had an idea there was some kind of water place – Sea World, or Marine World, or something – that would keep them happy for a few hours.

'Do we have to get the ferry there?'

'We sure do, as soon as you finish that breakfast.'

'Yaay.'

'Nell has a boat,' James had said, as he'd driven them home from the picnic, 'just a little rowboat, and she often uses it herself on Monday, her day off, but if it's fine on Tuesday she'd give us a loan. I'm on in the pub at two, but we could take it out in the morning, bring a couple of rods for the boys.'

She loved being part of an 'us' after so long. 'They'd adore it,' she told him, not making it just about him and her, not yet. No kiss as she got out of his car, not with Andy sitting in the back seat. No chance for the two of them to be alone, not with three children between them.

But he'd offered to take them out on Tuesday, and there was still the best part of a week of their holiday left. Who knew what might happen in the best part of a week?

Don't get your hopes up, she told herself. Stop counting those damn chickens, rushing them into a relationship when the man had really given no indication that she meant anything at all to him. Easy to be friendly with someone who was leaving in less than a week.

She'd rushed into love with Aaron, in his bed two weeks after they'd met, engaged after six months, a week before her nineteenth birthday, much to her father's disgust.

'He's a bricklayer – and he doesn't even have a job.'

'He'll get one,' Laura had insisted. 'And I don't care if he doesn't. I love him.'

'You're too young – you don't know what you're doing.'

But she'd known full well what she was doing when she'd moved into Aaron's council flat, when she'd dropped out of her childcare course and got a waitressing job so they'd have more than just his dole cheque coming in. Her father had broken off communication: he hadn't come to their wedding, and she'd been too happy to care. When had he ever shown her a fraction of the love she got from Aaron?

'Yeah, look how that turned out,' she said aloud, topping up her tea from the pot.

'How what turned out?' Ben asked, dipping a sausage into the pool of ketchup on his plate.

'Look how the rain turned out this morning to say hello to us.'

'Rain can't talk,' Seamus said scornfully.

'Oh yes it can. You just have to listen really, really carefully.'

No rushing into anything with James Baker. At the ripe old age of twenty-five she'd actually learnt a thing or two about love. Easy does it this time. One major break was enough for any heart.

James looked up in surprise as Andy walked into the kitchen. 'You're up early.'

'I just woke.'

Not yet nine o'clock, and the job finished at Walter's. James hadn't asked, or been told, how it had gone, or what money had been paid. Knowing Walter, Andy had been well rewarded.

James watched him opening a press and taking down Weetabix. He could hardly remember what Andy had looked like with long hair. Amazing how quickly you got used to something.

'Everything OK?' he asked.

Andy dropped two Weetabix into a bowl and brought it to the table. 'Yeah.'

'This morning I'm painting at O'Sheas',' James told him. 'I don't know if you know them, Frank and Una. I'm doing their sitting room.'

'OK.'

'And I'm working in Fitz's from four to eight. You want to get yourself a pizza for dinner?' Reaching into his back pocket for his wallet.

'It's OK,' Andy said. 'I have money. I'll get it.'

'Right.'

He had money: he could buy his own dinner. He'd got his hair cut without saying anything to James, and now he was feeding himself. He was growing up; he wasn't dependent on his father for everything any more.

His child was becoming an adult, but the chasm between them felt as wide as ever.

'I can't believe it,' Hugh said, for what must surely have been his third time. What did you say – what could you possibly say? – when your sister's thirty-six-year-old marriage collapsed out of the blue?

Except that it wasn't out of the blue. That was the bit he couldn't comprehend.

'He's met someone else,' Nell had wept on the phone. 'He's left her for another woman. Can you come over?'

Denis had met someone else. How could that be? Hugh cradled his cup, which Nell had filled with coffee when he'd arrived. Coffee was the last thing he wanted right now. She'd forgotten, in her distress, that he rarely touched it.

Look at Moira, hunched in her chair and pale as a ghost, hardly a word out of her since Hugh's arrival half an hour earlier. And Nell weeping quietly, a wad of damp kitchen roll clutched in her hand. It was exactly as if someone had died suddenly, and they were both trying to come to terms with the shock of it.

Better if he'd died. The thought came rushing into Hugh's head. He batted it away quickly, but the echo of it stayed. Easier all round if Denis had gone like that. The three of them sat while their coffee cooled, with the cat twining itself around Moira's calves.

Moira felt the whisper of the cat's body as she thought about her wedding day, how perfect it had been. Oh, not the weather, which had been shocking – gale-force winds and rain – but the occasion itself. Her mother's white lace dress, altered to fit her, and the three-tier cake, made by her cousin Angela's friend Lizzie. And the music in the church, a chamber choir from Dingle that a teacher friend of Denis's belonged to, 'Pie Jesu' and 'Ave Maria' and 'How Great Thou Art', all her favourites.

'Do you want me to get you anything? Will I make a fresh pot of coffee?' her brother asked. She looked at him and didn't answer.

Denis taking her hand at the top of the altar, whispering his thanks to her father before promising to be faithful to her for the rest of his life. Father Roche pronouncing them man and wife: 'You may now kiss the bride.' Her new husband kissing her in front of everyone, all their relations and friends looking on, her mother dabbing at her eyes with a cream hanky, her father in his new suit beaming around at everyone.

Congratulations, everyone hugging her and kissing her outside the church, congratulations, the women rubbing their lipstick off her cheek, 'You look beautiful,' they all told her.

'Over here, Mrs Mulcahy,' the photographer said, knowing the new name would bring a smile as she turned to look at him. No more Moira Fitzpatrick: she was Moira Mulcahy now, a married woman. She was a wife.

'Do you need anything at the shop?' Hugh asked, and she shook her head, frowning.

The string quartet in the hotel during the sherry reception, and the band after the meal that began with a waltz and ended with a *céilí*, and that found time in between for a little jazz. And the speeches,

391

her father surprising them all with a Yeats poem that made her mascara run, and the best man, Denis's brother Barry, who died in a house fire three years later, telling a joke that had everyone in stitches, although she couldn't for the life of her remember it now.

And the first dance with her husband, his arm encircling her waist, his hand in hers, his smile as he whirled her around the floor. Everyone looking, the guests all standing by, but all she could see was him.

The cat mewed, and she looked down at it.

He wore a leather jacket. His head was uncovered. Walter supposed it didn't really matter if your hair got wet when you had so little of it.

'Come in,' he said, but Andy stayed where he was.

'I was wondering,' he began, already feeling his face getting hot, 'if it would be OK, if you'd mind if I . . . used your attic, to try and write stuff, I mean, it's just that it's very quiet up there, and I've tried at home but I can't seem to . . .only if you wouldn't mind, I mean, and I'd only stay as long as you said. I have a computer, so I wouldn't need much light, so the dark wouldn't bother me, I mean.'

He stuttered to a stop. There, he'd said what he'd come to say. He waited for Mr Thompson to laugh, or to get annoyed, or to tell him it was out of the question.

★   ★   ★

392

It was totally unexpected. The boy wanted to sit in that dusty space, he wanted to *write* up there? Heavens above. The idea was ludicrous.

Walter recalled Andy's mention of his mother, how his face had crumpled as he'd talked about her reading poetry to him. How difficult it must be, trying to cope with the challenges of adolescence in the wake of a terrible heartbreak. Little wonder he was quiet, not given much to conversation.

But from the day he'd started the attic job, Walter had taken to him. Andy wasn't surly or bored, he was simply sad and lost. He still missed his mother badly, that much was plain. No doubt James, whom Walter respected greatly, was doing what he could, but a lot of grief remained.

And now Andy wanted to sit in Walter's attic and write, presumably to try to put his feelings on to paper – or in this case, into a computer. And even if Walter considered the attic the worst possible surroundings for any kind of creative exercise, Andy evidently disagreed.

It was unorthodox. It was inexplicable, as far as Walter was concerned, but if there was a chance it might help the lad, he was all for it.

'Of course you may use the attic,' he told Andy. 'We shall have to make it a little more comfortable—'

'No,' Andy said quickly. 'I mean, it's fine just the way it is. I have a fold-up chair I can bring. That's all I need.'

A fold-up chair. He wanted to sit in a fold-up chair in Walter's attic. Good grief. But he'd evidently thought it through.

'Come when you please,' he told the lad, 'and if I'm not around, let yourself in through the back door. Perhaps you could leave a note on the kitchen table, so I know that you're up there.'

Andy smiled then, the first time Walter had seen a real smile on his face. It changed him, made him look younger, more vulnerable.

'Thanks very much,' he said. Oblivious, by the look of it, to the rain falling steadily on his bare head. 'Thanks a lot. Can I come this afternoon – say, about two?'

'By all means.'

'Thanks.'

On the point of walking away he stopped. 'Actually,' he said, smile fading, 'there's one more thing. Would you mind not saying it to my father, about me using the attic, I mean? I just . . . would rather keep it to myself for now.'

The question didn't surprise Walter, who'd witnessed the strain between father and son more than once. He saw nothing wrong in honouring the lad's wish for privacy. It wasn't as if he was asking to use the attic for disreputable purposes – on the contrary, Walter was sure James would thoroughly approve of the request. 'I shall say nothing,' he promised.

'Thanks.' Again, the relieved smile.

So easy, Walter thought, as the boy jumped on to

his bike and pedalled off. So easy sometimes to make another person happy. And so nice that it gladdened your own heart too.

James wiped his hands on a rag before pulling his phone from his back pocket. He saw *Nell* on the screen and his heart jumped, as always.

'Good morning.'

'James,' she said – and the single word was enough for him to realise that something was amiss.

'What's up?'

'I shouldn't be ringing you.'

'Why shouldn't you? What's wrong?'

He checked his watch – he could finish this job later, another hour or two in it. Frank and Una would understand. He tucked the phone under his chin and began wrapping his roller in the plastic bag it had arrived in.

A long ragged sigh. 'It's Dad,' she said. 'He's left. He's walked out on my mother.'

James tied the end of the bag. 'Where are you?'

'I'm at Mam's, but—'

'I'll come over,' he said, pouring paint from the roller tray back into the can. 'Do you need me to pick anything up on the way?'

'No, look, if you're busy, you don't have to—'

'I'm not busy,' he said, pressing the lid on to the can with the heel of his hand. 'I'll see you in a few minutes.'

He hung up before she could answer, fishing his

car keys out of his pocket and leaving the room to find Una and explain that he'd been called away.

And it was only as he sat into his car, less than a minute later, that what Nell had said actually registered.

'Holy shit,' he breathed, turning the key in the ignition.

Nell returned to the kitchen. 'I'm going to pick up a few things in the village.'

Her mother didn't look around. Hugh threw her a weak smile.

She needed James. She needed the reassurance of his company, with Tim so far away. Tim, who'd been too busy to talk to her when she'd called him, who still hadn't got back to her more than an hour later. Tim, who was always busy. So she'd called James, who was on his way.

She left the other two in the kitchen and took her basket and went outside to the road to wait for James. He arrived within minutes and she sat into his car and pulled the door closed. 'Thank you for coming,' she said. 'I'm sorry, I shouldn't have dragged you away—'

'Nothing that couldn't be put off,' he said. 'Is someone with your mother?'

'Hugh – he's free till this evening.'

'Right. So where do you need to go?'

'Supermarket. I'll pick up a few things for Mam.'

He made no further comment as he started the engine. She sank back, closing her eyes. He was

396

taking over, not pumping her for details, not expecting anything of her. He was just there, doing what needed to be done. Keeping her eyes closed, she murmured 'Thanks, James.'

She felt the warmth of his hand as he laid it briefly on hers.

Denis put his suitcase on the bed and washed his hands in the tiny en-suite bathroom. The liquid soap had been diluted and wouldn't lather. His face looked grey in the mirror above the sink. He rubbed it with the towel to get some blood back into it.

It was done, the worst was over. Or maybe not the worst if Nell disowned him, if she wanted nothing more to do with him. But he'd done it, he'd left. His life on Roone was in the past. He'd never walk into the school again, never wake up next to Moira.

He thought of his wife's face, the fierce anger in it. Her insistence that he stay, her refusal to countenance his departure. She'd had no warning – but how could he have warned her? How did you warn someone that you were going to leave them?

Maybe he shouldn't have told her about Claire, maybe he should have left her out of it. But he'd wanted to be completely honest: he'd felt his wife deserved that at least.

'You've fallen in *love*?' Moira had repeated, her voice thick with disbelief. 'At *your* age?'

'I'm sorry,' he'd told her, so many times he'd

lost count, because that was all he could say. 'I wish it didn't have to be like this—'

'It doesn't,' she'd said angrily. 'You don't have to leave.'

But he did have to leave, and so he had, and now it was done. He returned to the bedroom and set his case on the floor and lay on the bed, on top of the horrible slippery spread that smelt of rhubarb. Claire was at a hotel, twenty miles or so away from him, celebrating her husband's sixtieth birthday with a family dinner. The thought made him feel sick.

What now? he wondered bleakly. What lay ahead for him now?

'Hi,' he said. 'Sorry I couldn't get back to you sooner, it was mad here all day. How are things?'

'Things,' she said, pushing her fingernail into the banister, 'are much the same as they were this morning. My father is still gone, my mother is still devastated.'

'That's terrible . . . And how are you?'

She bit back a sharp retort. He was doing his best. 'I'm OK.' She ran her nail along the wood, leaving a thin line behind. 'I'm going to move in with Mam until my tenants are gone.'

My tenants, not ours. He'd never wanted them. He'd left it all up to her. He hadn't lifted a finger to help.

'Good idea,' he said. 'Moira will be glad to have you, and you'll have more comfort.'

More comfort. As if she cared about more comfort.

'James called round,' she told him. 'He took me to the supermarket. He came the minute I phoned him.'

'Good. I'm glad he was able to help.' Not acknowledging, maybe not even aware of, the implied criticism.

'I'm taking tomorrow off,' she said. 'I've cancelled my appointments and put a notice on the door. I think I should stay with Mam till she's over the worst.'

'Right.' There was a pause. 'I wish there was something I could do,' he added.

You could surprise me and come down. You could take a few days off from your precious job, just to be here when I need you.

'What's the weather like in Dublin?' she asked.

Just as well he wasn't planning to say anything to Nell for another while. How could she cope with another shock right now?

Not that his news was bad, of course. On the contrary, it was very, very good – and in time, Nell would look on it in the same way. She'd be taken aback initially, he knew that. She'd resist the idea of their plans changing so radically. That was to be expected.

But they loved each other so they wanted what was best for one another and, patently, this was best for him – for both of them, with her becoming his wife. She'd see it that way in time, he was confident.

But he'd wait until they were back home before he told her, like he'd planned all along. You could say that his future father-in-law's abrupt departure had vindicated Tim's decision not to say anything to Nell for the moment.

Not that he'd have wished it to happen for the world, of course not.

'Change of plan for tomorrow,' he said, the noise of the pub coming through behind his voice.

He was going to cancel the boat trip: he was going to say he was too busy, he'd been asked to work in the pub instead, or he'd been offered a painting job. He was going to back out, because she was returning to Dublin in a few days, and what was the point?

'I couldn't get hold of Nell so we won't be going out in her boat, but I've got the offer of another, so will I pick you up at ten?'

He wasn't cancelling, he was just changing plans. He still wanted to see her. He'd made alternative arrangements when he hadn't been able to reach Nell. 'Ten will be fine,' Laura replied. 'What do you need me to bring?'

'Not a thing, unless the boys will want snacks,' he said. 'We'll be out for a couple of hours. I've got lifejackets and rods, and we can get a proper bite to eat afterwards. Wrap up warm. Even at this time of the year, the sea breeze can be chilly.'

'Right.' He'd organised things, sorted everything out – lifejackets and rods and a proper bite to eat afterwards. Laura smiled at the newsreader on television. 'Sounds good.'

'Should be, as long as the weather behaves. See you then.'

After hanging up she turned off the television and filled the bath, adding a glug of the scented oil Susan had given her for the holidays. She refilled her glass with wine and undressed slowly. Lying back in the steaming water, she reminded herself again not to count any chickens.

The eggs weren't even laid yet.

He'd walked out on them; he'd abandoned her mother without the slightest warning. Nell had asked him, the night before he'd left, if something was wrong, she'd begged him to tell her, and he'd insisted everything was fine. He'd lied to her, like he'd been lying to her mother for months. 'I'm happy,' he'd said, as if that made everything alright.

And then the shock of his letter, just a handful of hours later. *I'm so sorry*, he'd written. *I know how much this will hurt you.* He knew, and still he'd done it. He'd turned his back on both of them. *I hope you can understand*, he'd written, *that this is something I had to do.* But she didn't understand, not at all. He was happy, so clearly he wasn't too bothered about hurting them.

She turned over in her old single bed, returned

earlier in Charlie O'Dea's trailer after its short stay in the village. She remembered how excited she'd been the day Charlie had transported it in the other direction, when they'd brought it upstairs and installed it in the little room. She remembered how she'd looked forward to the arrival of her first tenant.

No cloud on her horizon then. How things had changed.

Every time her phone had rung yesterday she'd been afraid to check the caller, in case it was her father. As if she'd talk to him, as if she'd have anything to do with him after this. She never wanted to see him again. None of the calls had come from him, and she was glad.

She flipped her pillow, rested her head against its cool cotton slip. Oh, who was she fooling? Whatever he'd done, he was Dad. He'd taught her how to fish, and he'd driven her to Dingle to meet pals from school during the holidays.

He'd listened to her reciting the poetry she'd learnt by heart for the Junior Cert; he'd loaned her the deposit for her house and then refused to take any repayments. 'What else is that money for?' he'd asked. 'What else would I be doing with it? You'll be getting it after I'm gone – you might as well have some of it now.'

There's no blame to be attached to your mother, he'd written. *She has done nothing wrong. This is all down to me.*

Had he been so unhappy? Had his marriage

meant so little to him that he could up and leave the minute another woman took his fancy?

I've met someone else. I didn't plan it, I wasn't looking for anyone, but it happened, and I can't deny it.

He'd met someone else at sixty-one, after thirty-six years with his wife. How could he dismiss his wedding vows so easily? How could he walk away from his life partner? Was any marriage safe, if one so ostensibly solid could collapse just like that?

An awful new thought occurred to her: he was going to miss her wedding day. He wouldn't be there to walk her up the aisle. How could he, after what he'd just done? But the idea of him not being there on the biggest day of her life caused a renewed wash of despair.

Last night I tried to tell you how much you mean to me. My biggest fear is that you'll turn your back on me now. I beg you not to do that. I'm staying in Kerry, so I won't be far away. What difference did it make how far away he was? If he'd only moved half a mile down the road how could she stay in contact with him? How could she do that to her mother?

She turned her head towards the uncurtained window. She'd taken down the curtains when she was sixteen, wanting to watch the night sky as she lay in bed. Dawn was breaking, the stars winking out, the blackness fading to grey. Another day on Roone, beginning as all the rest had done, as if nothing had happened.

She was wide awake, but there wasn't much

point in getting up until she heard her mother moving about. No point in sitting downstairs alone. When the two of them were up she'd boil the kettle and squeeze oranges and make coffee and toast, and try, for her mother's sake, to keep things as normal as possible.

Word would get out, of course. People would begin to notice that her father wasn't around, they'd ask about him. It would be the talk of Roone, once the news went around. Everyone knew him. He'd lived here all his life, apart from three years at college in Limerick, and two years afterwards at a school in Clare, until a teaching job had come up on Roone. He'd been at the school for well over thirty years, principal for nearly twenty.

Tongues would wag. Conversations would stop when Nell approached, and she'd know they'd been talking about him. The subject would be avoided in the salon, and in time some new scandal would happen and Denis Mulcahy's abrupt disappearance would be set aside. Hopefully.

I'll wait for you to get in touch. I really hope you'll want to. Maybe not immediately, but in time. He was waiting for her to get in touch. She was terribly angry with him, but the thought of not seeing him again was unbearable. She sighed and turned over, and watched the sky changing colour.

★　★　★

404

'Hello.'

'It's me – it's Denis.'

Hugh knew it was Denis. His name had come up when the phone had rung.

'Hugh? Please don't hang up.'

'I'm here,' he said. 'Why are you calling?'

'Look, I know you probably don't want to have anything to do with me now—' He stopped, and Hugh didn't contradict him. He watched a robin hopping across the top of the hedge on the far side of the road.

'Hugh, I'm sorry. I know I didn't put you in the picture before I left—' He broke off again.

'Why did you do it?' Hugh demanded. 'Why did you leave her? Why couldn't you have stayed?'

Silence. The bird spread its wings and took flight, disappearing across the fields.

'I couldn't stay,' Denis said finally. 'My life was empty . . . It's been empty a long time.'

'Empty?' Hugh asked incredulously. 'You have a wife, a daughter, a good job. You call that an empty life? I know plenty who'd trade with you in a minute.'

'I know, but – Hugh, I can't explain, it was just something I had to do. I met someone – but even if I hadn't, I couldn't have gone on living the life I had.'

Hugh had heard enough. 'I have to go,' he said. 'I'd prefer if you didn't call me again.'

'Hugh,' Denis said urgently, 'just look after them, will you?'

'Of course I will,' Hugh replied evenly. '*I* didn't desert them.' He hung up and laid his phone on the passenger seat and started the car again.

Martin Griffin was a retired fisherman who'd sold his working vessel on his retirement and bought himself a little rowboat similar in size to Nell's. It was shabbier – Nell sanded and varnished hers every autumn – and one of its seats was missing, but it served the same purpose, roughly.

Laura insisted on sharing the rowing, which resulted in quite a lot of travelling round in circles, but the boys, dangling their rods in the water, couldn't have cared less, and James wasn't bothered.

'I wish I knew some sea shanties,' she said, laughing, her cheeks flushed from rowing, the breeze whipping her hair. 'All I know is "Row, Row, Row Your Boat" and that's a bit boring.'

She was really very attractive. She'd made it plain she wasn't immune to him. Her children were charming, if a little on the lively side, and she got on well with Andy.

He was still coming up with reasons to get involved. Shame his heart was so far refusing to be diverted from Nell.

Maybe it just needed time. Not all attractions were instant. He'd known from the start that he wanted Karen, but it didn't always happen like that. Maybe he and Laura simply needed to spend more time together. Maybe they needed to grow on each other.

Bit tricky though, when she had three days left on Roone.

'Tell me more about this barbecue,' she said, as James reclaimed control of the oars. 'Nell said the whole island gets involved.'

'It does, or near enough. I've no idea how long it's been going on, but it's always held on the last Friday in July. It takes place on the big beach past the creamery.'

'And Nell says the weather's always good. She says it's never rained on barbecue night, not once since it began.'

'Well, I can only vouch for the past four years, and they've all been fine. But it wouldn't surprise me if that were true.' He began to turn the boat towards the pier. 'Roone is a law unto itself sometimes.'

'Well,' she said, 'I'm looking forward to it.'

'You should bring your guitar – there's always a bit of a singsong.'

He wondered if Nell would come to the barbecue. She hadn't missed one since he'd arrived, and her parents had always shown up, just for an hour or so. He didn't imagine that either Moira or Nell would be in form for it this year.

He'd phoned Nell earlier. Their conversation had been brief.

'Thanks again for coming around yesterday,' she'd said. 'I hope it didn't put you out too much.

I'm leaving the salon closed today,' she'd added. 'Apart from holidays I haven't had a day off in over three years. I figured it was due to me.'

Her voice calm, the sadness evident in it. Her spark gone, for now at any rate.

'What can I do?' James had asked. He wanted to do something. He wanted to help, because she was hurting and he loved her.

'Nothing,' she'd replied. 'We're fine, honestly.'

'Will I pick up some things from the supermarket and drop them around later?'

'No need – Hugh's calling in a while. I'll go out while he's here.'

She didn't need him, she had Hugh. And, of course, she had Tim, except he was two hundred miles away.

'Penny for them,' Laura said, 'or should that be a cent?'

James smiled. 'Just thinking about lunch, since it looks like nobody's catching us any.'

Moira sat alone in the silent kitchen. Nell was upstairs in the shower. Hugh was at work. The day stretched ahead of her, empty as the shell of a hatched egg.

She missed being happy; she was lonesome for it.

'We got three fishes in the sea,' Ben said. 'Seamus got one an' I got one.'

'That's wonderful,' Walter said. 'Will you cook them for your tea?'

'No, they 'scaped again. But James saw them. He said they were huge.'

James had taken them out to sea. Walter digested this information. He'd thought, when James had come to live on Roone, when he'd witnessed the friendship that had sprung up between him and Nell, that perhaps they might be suited. But then Tim had put in an appearance, and that had been that.

Now it looked like James might be moving in a new direction. 'So your fish got away,' he said. 'And then what happened?'

'Then we got sausages an' chips an' I had Coke an' Seamus had Fanta an' then we came back here.'

He would miss them. He'd miss their exuberance and their innocence. He'd miss hearing their high-pitched voices across the stone wall as he worked in his vegetable patch.

'How come honey doesn't have stings?' Seamus asked.

Walter considered. 'Well, I think the bees keep their stings out of the way when they're making it.'

'But what if one fell in by a accident?'

'Oh, I don't think that could happen. The bees would be very careful.'

'Yeah, but if one fell in could they get it out?'

'Yes, I'm sure they could. Bees are very clever.'

'What if a bee fell in?'

'Well, I'm sure its friends would get it out.'

'How does a chicken make a egg?'

Keeping a straight face was becoming more

difficult. 'Er, I'm not sure really. I think that's a chicken secret.'

In due course the donkey ride came to an end, the participants were taken home by their grateful mother and Walter went inside to write his shopping list for the following evening's dinner party.

As he settled at the kitchen table with paper and pen there was a tap at the back door. Without waiting for a response Nell pushed it open. 'Oh Walter, you're here, good. I just wanted a quick word.'

Walter got to his feet and took the kettle off the hob. 'We shall have tea.'

'There's no need,' she said – but she pulled out a chair and sat, and Walter proceeded to fill his copper kettle and light the gas under it.

She watched Walter filling the kettle. She knew it was silly, but the sight of a man pottering around a kitchen on his own always struck her as obscurely sad. She felt the same in Hugh's house. If the feminists could hear her.

'Walter,' she said slowly, as he placed cups and saucers on the table, 'there's something I need to tell you.' She didn't like the idea of him hearing about it from someone else – which he would, sooner or later. 'We need eggs,' she'd told her mother. 'I'll drop around to Walter. I won't be long.'

Moira, sitting at the table with Hugh, had crumbled a scone and made no reply. She was calmer this morning, the anger of the previous day dimmed in her.

'My father has left,' Nell said to Walter. 'He walked out on my mother yesterday morning.' Her lower lip trembled and she dug her nails into her palm. Walter wouldn't know what to do with tears. 'I wanted to tell you before you heard it elsewhere.'

Walter, of course, received the news impeccably. 'I'm terribly sorry, my dear,' he said quietly. 'That must have been extremely upsetting, for both of you.'

'It was, it is – but it's happened and we must deal with it.'

She wouldn't mention the other woman: there was nothing to be gained by it. And there was no need to ask Walter to keep the news to himself because he would never dream of discussing anyone's business with anyone else.

Walter was shocked. Denis Mulcahy had left his wife, out of the blue by the sound of it. The news was difficult to digest, but he struggled to maintain his composure for Nell's sake. He made tea and took apple tart from the cupboard. He made himself busy as she sat at the table, her misery plain to see.

'He's handed in his notice at the school,' she told him. 'He's got another job in Tralee, apparently.'

'My goodness.' Given up his wife, and his job too. What on earth had possessed the man?

Walter had known Denis well – they'd met often over the years at various island events, in the mobile library on Mondays, at Nell's house or simply on the road, both men being keen walkers. And Denis would occasionally call to Walter's to buy produce, although Moira was the more frequent customer from that household.

The men would converse easily when they came face to face. Denis had always struck Walter as an affable fellow, and his marriage had seemed as solid as any other – but who really knew how sound a marriage was except its two participants?

'So I'm back home,' Nell said. 'With Mam, I mean. Just until next door is free again.'

'I see.'

She stirred milk into the tea he poured for her. 'Walter, would you mind awfully if I didn't come to your dinner tomorrow night? I'm really not in form for it.'

'Of course.'

She would be missed, undoubtedly. Laura and James were both good conversationalists, but Walter would miss her – and he suspected Andy might too.

'I'll get back into the swing of things once people know,' she said. 'I mean, once it blows over.'

Walter knew only too well how something like this could cause awkwardness. After Geraldine and Pamela had died, most people of his acquaintance hadn't known how to talk to him. He'd see them turn into shops to avoid him in the village, and he'd known there was no unkindness intended, simply a wish to avoid embarrassment.

And while this was a quite different situation, the general response, he guessed, would be much the same. And Nell would feel it keenly, having to meet people in the hair salon all the time.

'I'll take a dozen eggs,' she said, finishing her tea. 'Sorry I couldn't manage the tart – my appetite has deserted me a bit.'

She was suffering now, but life went on. He knew this better than most. The unthinkable happened, the pain it caused was endured, and in time the darkness faded and days took on some kind of rhythm again. Not the same as before, never the same, but bearable.

He added a bottle of apple juice to the eggs. At the front door he took her hand and pressed it. 'Chin up, my dear,' he said. 'Look after yourself, and your mother.'

'I will,' she said, attempting a smile. 'We'll be fine.'

He stood on the doorstep as she drove off, wondering how long it would take for the news to filter around the island. Not long, if the usual grapevine was working, and he had no reason to think otherwise. Hadn't they all heard about Nell's previous tenant falling into the sea, almost before the poor man had dried himself off?

He returned to the kitchen and resumed his shopping list.

★   ★   ★

413

In the afternoon Moira fed the cat and washed the kitchen floor and made a fish pie. Nell mowed the back lawn and weeded the flower bed nearest to the house. After dinner they sat in front of the television and watched a detective programme and then *News at Ten*. When that was over they made tea and drank it in the kitchen with a plate of chocolate biscuits that Hugh had brought sitting between them.

Denis's name wasn't mentioned, in the scant phrases that passed between them. Tim phoned just after dinner. Hugh phoned during the detective programme. And just as Nell was drying up their cups, at a few minutes past eleven, the doorbell rang.

Moira frowned. 'Who could that be at this hour?'

'I'll go,' Nell said, handing her mother the tea-towel.

'I was passing,' James said, 'on my way home from Fitz's. I hope it's not too late. I saw the light on.'

'This isn't on your way home from Fitz's,' Nell said. 'You live in the opposite direction.'

'Damn,' he said. 'I thought you might have forgotten that.'

He was rewarded with a faint smile. 'Hang on,' she said. She opened the kitchen door and spoke rapidly. He couldn't hear the words. She reappeared and pulled the front door closed behind her. 'Let's sit in the car,' she said, 'unless you're in a rush.'

He wasn't in a rush. He'd called Andy as he was

leaving the pub, when a longing to see Nell had suddenly taken over. He'd told Andy he'd be another while, and Andy hadn't seemed bothered.

He opened the passenger door and she got in. He walked around and sat in beside her. She smelt flowery, as she always did. The nearness of her, in the darkness, soothed his heart.

'So,' he said, 'talk to me.'

She looked through the front windscreen, her face in profile. 'Today was long,' she said. 'It went on forever.'

Silence.

'I'm so angry with him.' She shook her head slowly. 'But I miss him too. Isn't that stupid?'

'Not a bit,' he said. 'I'd be surprised if you didn't.'

'He wants me to get in touch. He said he'll wait for me to call him, but every time my phone rings I'm afraid it's going to be him – and a bit devastated every time it isn't.'

James leant against the driver's door and watched her hands, holding one another loosely in her lap. Who was he trying to kid? He would love her no matter how many Lauras came along, whether she was married to his brother or not. He would love her till the day he died, pathetic fool that he was.

'Mam is so quiet – she barely opened her mouth all day. It's so not like her.' She pushed a strand of hair behind her ear, the movement causing a waft of her scent towards him.

She turned to look at him. 'You have no idea,'

she said, 'how much it means to be able to say all this to someone. I don't know what I'd do without you.'

He made no reply, afraid to trust his idiot tongue.

'Maybe,' she said then, 'we could have some music.'

He turned the key and pressed the button for the radio. J. J. Cale sang 'After Midnight'.

'I love this one,' Nell said.

'Me too.'

'So,' she said, after another minute, 'how was your day?'

'I went out in Martin Griffin's boat this morning,' he said.

She turned to him. 'Martin's boat? On your own?'

'No,' he said, 'with Laura and her kids. I thought the boys might like to go fishing.'

'Oh.' She turned to look out the windscreen again. 'That's nice. But why didn't you take *Jupiter*?'

'I decided you had enough to think about. It wasn't a big deal.'

'James,' she said softly, 'you don't have to ask. You never have to ask.'

'I know.'

Another silence.

'Did the boys catch anything?'

'No, but I told them they nearly did.'

Another faint smile. 'Good.'

J. J. Cale ended and 'Moondance' began. Another winner, as far as James was concerned.

'I love this too,' Nell murmured.

They were right for each other, that was the problem. They were the perfect fit.

At ten o'clock on Wednesday, with her daughter gone off to work and the house to herself, Moira Mulcahy decided it was time to take back control of her life. She searched in the phone book and found Josephine Brown's number.

'Hello?'

'Josephine,' she said, 'it's Moira Mulcahy. I'm ringing to apologise.'

'Apologise?' Josephine's voice rose, both in volume and pitch. 'For what?'

'When we met the other day you must have thought I was terrible, pretending not to know what you were talking about.'

'Er—'

'The thing is,' Moira went on, eyes shut tightly, 'I know you were just talking about him leaving the school, but in fact Denis and I had decided to separate. We'd been planning it for a while, but because it hadn't actually taken place, I felt it better to say nothing when I met you. We thought it best to keep the whole thing private until it was a done deed.'

A stunned silence, and then Josephine said, 'Oh,' in a much lower voice. 'Oh, Moira, I don't know what to say – and there's me putting my two big—'

'Not at all,' Moira cut in briskly. 'You weren't to know. We just felt the time had come to go our separate ways, no big drama, and now he's gone.

We thought it would be better if he left the island altogether. All very amicable, I'm happy to say.'

'I see . . . well . . .'

'So I just thought I'd clear that up with you. I felt bad about leaving you in the dark.'

'Right . . . Thank you, Moira, I appreciate that.'

'Goodbye, Josephine, see you soon.'

She hung up, her palms clammy. In fairness, Josephine was far from the island's biggest gossip, but the school principal's marriage breaking up would be too good, surely, to keep to herself – particularly as Moira had intimated that it was now public knowledge.

After a minute she lifted the phone again and dialled Nell's number.

'I know you're busy,' her mother said. 'I won't keep you long. There's just something you need to know.'

'It's OK, Maisie is under the drier,' Nell said. 'She can't hear a thing.'

A beat passed. 'Mam?'

'I thought you'd better know that I've just rung Josephine Brown,' her mother said. 'I told her your father is gone. I said it had been a mutual decision.'

Nell didn't know which astounded her more, the fact that her mother had gone public or the spin she'd put on it. 'You're not serious.' She glanced at Maisie, but her plastic-capped head was bent over a magazine.

'Nell, I know I've altered the truth.' Her mother sounded perfectly calm. 'Your father left me to cope, and this is the way I've decided to do it. I refuse to be seen as the victim. I'm telling you so you'll be prepared if anyone brings it up. I told her it was nothing dramatic, that we simply felt the time had come to go our separate ways.'

Nothing dramatic, apart from her mother's life being turned on its head with no warning. How could she be so matter-of-fact about it?

'I have no choice, Nell,' her mother went on, in the same even voice. 'Life goes on. We have to carry on.'

Nell made no response.

'Look,' her mother said, 'I'll let you get back. I'll talk to you this evening, all right?'

'OK.'

Nell disconnected and replaced her phone on the shelf. She turned back and smiled at Maisie. 'I think you're done,' she said loudly, bending to switch off the drier.

'Nell,' Hugh said, 'I want to tell you something.'

Nell tore open the crisp packet. 'Nothing bad, please. I don't think I can take any more bad stuff.'

'It's nothing bad.' He poured lime cordial into a glass and topped it up with sparkling water. 'I had a call yesterday,' he said, passing the glass across to her, 'from your father.'

Nell looked mutely at him, a crisp in her hand.

'I wasn't going to mention it,' he said, holding

her gaze, 'but then I thought maybe you'd want to know.'

Her eyes brimmed with tears. She laid down the crisp. 'What did he say?'

'He said he didn't mean to hurt anyone, and he was sorry he'd left the way he had, but he didn't feel he had a choice. He asked me to look after you and Moira.'

'How did he sound?'

Hugh hesitated. 'A bit lost, to be honest.'

'The thing is,' she said, swiping at the tears that spilt over and rolled down her cheeks, 'I miss him. Isn't that weird? He's done this awful thing, but I really miss him.'

'Of course you do. He's your father. Don't be too hard on him, Nell – nobody's perfect.' He pulled paper napkins from a pack behind the counter and handed them to her.

She blew her nose. 'He walked out on us. He left us behind.'

'He didn't leave you, not the way he left your mam. And I'm sure he misses you every bit as much as you miss him.'

She blotted her eyes.

'Nell, he still loves you. That hasn't changed.'

She balled up the tissue and handed it back to him. He dropped it into the wastepaper basket at his feet.

'Thanks,' she said, her eyes red-rimmed. 'I'll think about what you said.'

★　★　★

He wrote to her. Sitting in Mr Thompson's attic, it poured out of him.

I'm living far away from Dublin now, we moved here four years ago. It's a small island called Roone off the west coast, you were here once with Dad. I was too, but I was just a baby and I don't remember. I didn't really want to come, well, I didn't really care. It wasn't leaving Dublin, that didn't bother me. I suppose I just didn't want to be anywhere, because it was just Dad and me, and we forgot how to talk to each other the way we used to when you were there, so I didn't want to go anywhere with him. But actually I like living here now, well, I like the sea and the cliffs, and people are friendly here and say hello and smile when they meet you on the street, even when I'm not really friendly back. To be honest, I feel lonely all the time, but I think I'd be lonely no matter where I was, because I just miss you all the time, I just keep on missing you, so I think it's got nothing to do with Roone. Things went a bit weird with Dad and me after you went, we weren't like we used to be when we were all together in Dublin. We still aren't but I'd like us to be, because I miss him too, which sounds really daft when we're living in the same house. The funny thing is, Tim is getting married to a woman who lives here, so he'll be moving here too. Her name is Nell and she's a hairdresser. She actually lived in Dublin a few years ago, and the other funny thing is she met Tim, he used to go to the place where she worked to get his hair cut, but they didn't get to know each other properly, and then she moved back to live here and she opened up her own hair-dressing place, and then Dad met her when he went for a haircut and they became friends and then Tim met her through Dad. I like her a lot, I think you'd like her too. She's kind, and she doesn't treat me like a kid. I miss you, I really miss you a lot sometimes. I wonder if that will ever get better. I don't want to forget you, but it would be lovely to think about you and not get sad, which probably doesn't make any sense. By the way I'm five foot nine now, in case you're wondering, and I got my hair cut really short last week (by Nell). You might have trouble recognising me if you saw me. I'm sitting in an attic, would you believe? It belongs to an old man who lives on the island too. He was looking for someone to clear it out and I said I'd do it, and then I asked him if I could come up here to write. He sounds dead posh but he's really nice, not stuck up at all, you'd like him too. I don't know why I wanted to write up here, but I did. It's really dusty and I'm sitting on a fold-up chair and my bum is going numb and it's a bit chilly, but I don't care about any of that. It's so quiet, and I can think, and I can write to you. And Mr

Thompson, he's the guy who owns the attic, gave me some poetry books and I really like them. I'm sorry I wasn't more interested when you read your poems to me. When I get a bit better about missing you I'll ask Dad to have a look at them, I'm sure he has them put away somewhere.

It poured out, and he let it. He wrote until his fingers were stiff with cold, until he couldn't find a comfortable position to sit. It poured out, and it left him a little emptier, and a little lighter.

He told her about school, about the maths teacher who all the boys fancied, about the race he'd won at sports day, about the chess club he'd joined last term.

He told her about the beach barbecue that took place each year on Roone. He told her about Mr Thompson's chickens, which scratched at the ground all day and laid big brown eggs, and about the apple tree that bore fruit practically all year round, and the honey Mr Thompson's bees made that helped people to sleep.

He told her about the holy well, where colicky and teething babies were brought to have their tummies or gums rubbed with water. He told her about Maisie Kiely, who read people's tealeaves, but only on Thursdays, and Annie Byrne, who used to be able to predict the weather until her arthritis was cured by eating mushrooms, and the signpost on the cliffs pointing the way to the Statue of Liberty that had been put up by nobody.

He told her about the library that arrived in a lorry every Monday and the boat that Nell owned and the fish he'd caught from it. He told her about Nell's uncle Hugh, with one and a half arms, who owned the pub where Dad worked and always gave Andy a free packet of crisps when he went in.

This was his third afternoon, and he still had lots to tell her, but he could stay only two hours at a time because there was no socket in the attic and his computer's battery lasted just that long. He eased his cramped body from the chair and stretched, and rubbed his cold hands together until they felt a bit warmer. He closed the laptop and brought it downstairs.

Mr Thompson was in the kitchen, scrubbing potatoes with a little brush. He turned and smiled as Andy walked in. 'All done?'

'Yeah, thanks.' Andy took the note he'd left on the table, the one that said, *I'm in the attic – Andy*, and slipped it into his pocket. 'I was wondering,' he said, 'if you'd like me to paint your henhouse.'

Mr Thompson blinked. 'My henhouse?'

'Just to say thanks,' Andy explained, 'for letting me use the attic.'

'Well, that's awfully kind of you, but there's really—'

'Or if there's any other job you'd prefer me to do.' He wondered belatedly if he should be commenting on the state of the henhouse. Maybe

Mr Thompson was perfectly happy with it, despite the paint peeling from practically every part of it.

'Well, that's very kind,' Mr Thompson repeated, 'and the henhouse could certainly do with a fresh coat. I've left it far too long. It's really awfully good of you to offer.'

'I'd like to do it,' Andy told him.

He wanted to do something in return for Mr Thompson helping him to unlock what had been tightly packed away since Mum had gone. He'd thought of the henhouse in bed last night, and the idea had appealed to him.

Arrangements were put in place. The henhouse would be painted on the Saturday, weather permitting. The paint would be purchased by Mr Thompson – Andy's offer to fund the project being firmly dismissed – and James would provide the rest of the materials. Andy hadn't asked his dad, but he knew there wouldn't be a problem.

'See you later,' he said to Mr Thompson, as he was leaving. Three hours or so and he'd be back here with his dad for dinner, and on Saturday he'd be in the garden for several hours, painting the henhouse. It was beginning to feel like he was spending more time around Mr Thompson's place than his own.

Cycling off, he wondered what kind of dinner they'd get. Something posh, anyway.

'I won't be there,' she said. 'I told Walter.'

'Too bad,' James replied.

'Ring me tomorrow,' she said, 'and let me know how it goes.'

She was sorry to be missing the night, if only to lend support to Walter in his unaccustomed role of host. She hoped he wasn't putting himself under too much pressure. She should have baked a cake and dropped it over – she'd had plenty of time yesterday.

Laura would bring the guitar, no doubt, and entertain them all again. She didn't particularly mind missing that. A couple of hours of Laura's singing in Fitz's the other night had been plenty.

'Dad rang Hugh,' she told James.

'Did he?'

'Hugh said he sounded lost.'

'I suppose he would . . . Are you going to phone him?'

'I don't know.' She approached her mother's house. 'I have to go. Thanks for ringing. Enjoy the night.'

She let herself in and hung her umbrella on the hallstand, trying to ignore how terribly bare it looked without her father's bits and pieces. His tweed jacket, his cap, his raincoat, his umbrella.

She took her phone from her bag and found his name. She looked at it for a few seconds.

'Nell? Is that you?'

She slipped her phone back and opened the kitchen door.

★   ★   ★

426

Walter's temporary neighbours were the first to arrive, a few minutes past seven.

'Don't you look smart,' Laura said, looking extremely smart herself in a deep red dress, her feet in little gold pumps, hair pulled into a white ribbon, gold studs in her ears. The twins, hair combed, faces washed, presented their host with two original works of art.

'That's George,' Ben said, 'an' that's me on his back.'

'This is all the chickens,' Seamus said, 'an' that's the bees.'

The drawings were much praised and stuck with Sellotape on to Walter's fridge door. Laura presented him with a bottle of wine, a jar of mint humbugs and a big bunch of montbretia – 'I know they're everywhere here, but I couldn't resist them.'

'I don't want to go home,' she confided, as Walter filled a vase with water. 'I'm really not looking forward to it.'

'But of course,' he said, arranging the flowers, 'you'll be back.' Because he was quite sure of this, in the way he was often sure of things that had no logical certainty but that invariably came to pass.

'We will,' she agreed, 'as soon and as often as we can. You'll have to start doing B&B.'

James and Andy turned up just then, bearing a bottle of port and a box of fudge, and were ushered along with the other guests into the drawing room.

Walter, in his grey suit, immaculate white shirt and bottle green bow tie, offered little glasses of sherry to the adults and tumblers of apple juice to the minors. China dishes of cashew nuts and big green olives were produced; the former were devoured by the twins, who left the latter untouched for the older guests.

They sat on Walter's antique furniture in the drawing room, which was rather chilly despite the turf fire burning in the beautiful marble fireplace. The little boys, armed with drawing pads and crayons, took over the padded bench seat set into the bay window. Their mother sat between James and Walter on the larger of the two couches. Andy occupied the other, and looked mostly into the fire.

'Nell is late,' Laura remarked, taking an olive. 'I hope nothing's wrong.'

'I'm afraid Nell won't be joining us this evening,' Walter replied. 'She had some family occasion to attend to.'

'Oh, that's a pity. I haven't seen her since our picnic. She'll be at the barbecue on Friday, won't she?'

'I dare say.'

In due course they were ushered into the much warmer kitchen. 'I considered the dining room for our meal,' Walter explained, 'but I felt it might be a little formal.'

They assured him that the kitchen was fine, and gathered around the pine table, where they were presented with an enormous fish pie, beautifully seasoned with fresh herbs, and a medley of perfectly steamed vegetables.

'Rather simple fare,' Walter said apologetically, as he distributed plates – to be reassured, once again, by his guests. The twins pushed their chunks of fish and broccoli florets aside, but otherwise no complaints were heard. Andy, unsurprisingly, asked for seconds.

Conversation flowed. The artwork of the younger guests was removed from the fridge and passed around the table and much praised. James was persuaded to sketch a hen on a sheet from Ben's drawing pad – and immediately had to repeat the exercise in Seamus's. Laura promised to compose a hen-themed song at the earliest opportunity.

The main course was followed by an accomplished bread-and-butter pudding – 'Mother insisted I learn how to cook at least one dessert properly' – and a jug of pouring custard.

When the youngest guests had demolished the remains of the custard, coffee was made and the fudge opened. Laura, prevailed upon to sing, offered a rendition of 'Danny Boy', after which Walter blushingly produced a tin whistle and played a trio of hornpipes, much to the twins' fascination.

'What can you two sing?' James asked – and after serious consultation they launched into an enthusiastic, if not perfectly tuneful, version of 'Old MacDonald', who, it would appear, had had a very well-stocked farm indeed.

Andy declined to perform, and wasn't pushed. James, after much protestation, impressed them all with a dramatic recitation of 'The Owl and the Pussycat'.

All things considered, Walter reflected, rinsing the last teaspoon at a quarter to one in the morning, not a bad evening. His guests seemed to enjoy themselves, and the preparations had caused him far less anxiety than he'd envisaged.

And it had been nice to appreciate the elegance of the drawing room once again – so long since he'd sat in there in the evenings. Now that its bookshelves had been refilled, thanks to Andy's efforts, Walter had determined to resurrect the room his parents had been so fond of.

Yes, he must have more dinner parties.

'Hey, sweetheart,' he said. 'It's not too late, is it?'

Nell checked the digital readout on her clock radio. Eleven fifteen. 'It's pretty late,' she said. 'I'm in bed.'

'Sorry, sorry,' he said. 'I would have rung earlier but I was at a business dinner, last-minute thing, had to stand in for Eoin, couldn't get out of it.'

'Who's Eoin?'

'Eoin O'Connor, my boss. I've often mentioned him.'

'Oh yes . . . You sound a bit tipsy.'

'Me? No, I had a couple of glasses of wine, and a drop of port after, but I'm grand.'

'So,' she said, lying back against the pillow.

'So,' he repeated, 'how are things?'

She lay in the darkness, her eyes closed. 'Things are . . . difficult,' she said. 'Mam actually rang someone today and told them Dad was gone. She made it sound like it had been a mutual decision.'

Silence. She opened her eyes. 'Hello?'

'Hi . . . Sorry, I dropped my watch,' he said. 'I'm shattered. It's been a long week so far, and I've another new client meeting in the morning.'

She said nothing.

'Nell,' he said.

'I'm still here.'

'Are you cross with me?'

'Of course not.'

Another short silence.

'I miss my father,' she said then. 'I want to ring him, but I can't bring myself.'

'That's a tough one,' he said. 'You'll have to decide what's best. How's your mother doing?'

Nell closed her eyes again. 'She's OK. Look,' she said, 'you should get to bed.'

'OK . . . I'll give you a shout tomorrow. Love you.'

'Good night.' She hung up and turned over and tried to sleep.

And Moira Mulcahy, climbing into bed at twenty past eleven, having spent most of the day wondering when the repercussions from her phone call to Josephine would begin, and the past few hours putting a brave face on it for her daughter, who was battling with her own heartache, abandoned herself finally to the release of hot, bitter tears.

'Can I borrow some paintbrushes on Saturday?'

James looked up from his scrambled egg, surprised. 'What are you painting?'

'Mr Thompson's henhouse. I offered.'

'You offered to paint his henhouse? He's not paying you?'

'No, he's just buying the paint.'

James smiled. 'What's brought this on?'

Andy shrugged. 'No reason. It just looked a bit . . . wrecked. Can I have the brushes?'

'Sure, as long as you rinse them well afterwards.'

'I will. Thanks.'

'And you'll need to rub down the walls beforehand, get the old stuff off. I'll give you a brush for that.'

'OK.'

James had sometimes wondered if he should insist on knowing exactly how and where Andy spent his time during the holidays. He was often missing from the house when James got back from wherever he'd been, and rarely offered an explanation when he did show up.

But this was Roone, probably the safest place in Ireland. And Andy had never been in trouble: there had been no reports of him getting into any kind of mischief. And now here he was helping Walter,

432

simply doing a good turn for a neighbour by the sound of it. Maybe he was finally settling in to life on Roone, finding his own place on it. Maybe things were coming right for him, like Nell had always said they would.

James finished his scrambled egg and brought his plate to the sink. On his way out of the kitchen he dropped a hand briefly on his son's shoulder. 'Have a good day. See you later.'

'See you,' Andy replied.

Katy –
Me again, more bad news. You'll stop opening my envelopes. On Monday Dad walked out on Mam. No warning, he just left. He's met someone else, would you believe? He's given up his job, moved completely away. I can't bring myself to phone him yet. Such a shock. I've moved back home to be with Mam, we're coping as best we can. You never know what's around the corner. I hope you're having a happier time than me right now.
N xxx

'So,' she said, pouring water on to coffee grounds, 'how was last night?'

James leant against the windowsill, arms folded. 'Good. We had a very good fish pie.'

'Ah, bless him. And dessert?'

'Bread-and-butter pudding.'

'Damn, I love that.'

'And custard. And I recited a poem.'

'Which one?'

'"The Owl and the Pussycat".'

He watched her laughing. She seemed OK. He'd taken a chance that she had no lunch plans and bought two salad rolls at Lelia's. They ate them in the little room off the salon. He remembered painting it in June, a week or so before she'd moved in. Now it was vacant again, the bed moved back to her parents' house, the bits and pieces she'd assembled returned to their various owners. The shelves were bare, awaiting the hairdressing supplies she had yet to bring back.

She handed James a mug. Their hands touched briefly as he took it. He told her about his conversation with Andy earlier.

'That's wonderful,' she said. 'Such a kind thing to do for Walter. I always knew there was no need to worry about Andy.'

James smiled. 'So how are you?' he asked.

She looked down into her coffee mug. 'Alright,' she said finally. 'Lonely. Angry with him still, but less so. Trying to understand why he did it.' She looked up and met his gaze. 'James, do you think I should ring him?'

'Yes,' James said simply.

She drank more coffee. James patted the window-sill, the only place left to sit. 'Come and eat your lunch,' he ordered, and she walked over. 'How's Moira?'

She lifted the top half of her roll and inspected

its contents. 'She puts up a brave front, but I heard her crying last night after she went to bed.'

'To be expected.'

'I suppose so.' She picked out slices of cucumber and handed them to him. He'd forgotten to tell Lelia no cucumber; he knew Nell didn't like it. He knew so much about her. He added the slices to his own roll.

'Mam rang one of the teachers yesterday,' she said. 'She told them she and Dad had decided to split up, made out it was mutual. The teacher already knew about Dad leaving the school so maybe Mam thought she was the logical person to tell.'

'Good for her,' James said. 'It'll come out, and then blow over, like everything.'

'Hope so. Nobody's said anything to me yet, but maybe they know and don't want to bring it up.'

'Possibly.'

No need to tell her that Denis Mulcahy's sudden departure was already common knowledge, had been the main topic of conversation in the pub before he'd left for Walter's dinner party. Not in front of Hugh, of course – Moira's brother being considered, presumably, too close to the whole affair – but a few had asked James what he knew, aware of his friendship with Nell.

His claim of ignorance was probably not believed, which didn't unduly bother him. They'd have something else to talk about in a week.

'James,' Nell said then, looking across at him.

He waited. Her eyes were bitter-chocolate brown. Her nose was dusted with tiny dark freckles. Her expression was solemn.

'Yes?' he prompted.

'Nothing, sorry, it's nothing.' She picked up her roll and began to eat. Silence fell again between them. James watched the comings and goings on the street below and wondered what she'd been about to say, what had put such a serious expression on her face. For the first time he sensed a slight discomfort, a minute tension between them.

'Looking good for tomorrow night,' he said eventually, just for something to put into the silence.

'Yes – the weather always obliges for the barbecue, doesn't it?' She brushed crumbs from her lap, let them fall on to the floor. Half of her roll was still uneaten.

'Will you come?' he asked. She loved the annual beach barbecue, loved the sociability of it. And of course he wanted her there.

'Maybe,' she replied. 'I'll wait and see how Mam is. She was going to brave the supermarket this afternoon.'

James imagined Moira walking into the shop, knowing everyone who worked there, and probably quite a few of the customers too. Unaware of whether they'd heard about her situation, waiting to see how they greeted her, how they looked at her. What they said or didn't say. Some ordeal, all on her own – but from what little he knew about her, Nell's mother struck him as a strong woman.

He recalled their recent conversation, Moira asking him if he'd noticed anything amiss between Nell and Tim. Little realising that her own relationship was in such straits. Little guessing how James felt about her daughter.

Nell got to her feet, wrapping the remains of her roll in her paper napkin. 'Better make a move. I have someone coming at half one. You stay here and finish, though.'

She went through to the salon and James heard her moving about as he ate the roll Lelia had made for him. He looked out the window and wondered again what it was she had started to say.

They knew. They all knew, but everyone talked about something else.

'Isn't it great the weather's picking up again?' Catherine Jones said. 'Just in time for the barbecue.'

'I love your skirt,' Jessie Moran said, 'and have you done something different with your hair?'

'That milk is dated tomorrow,' Helen O'Doherty said, at the checkout. 'Hang on and I'll get you one with a longer date.'

It was as if Denis had never existed. He'd been wiped away, like a solved sum on a blackboard. He'd been rubbed out like a misspelling.

'Nell has moved back in with me,' Moira said, loud enough for the others to hear, 'now that Denis is gone. Only until her own house is free again, of course, but it's lovely to have her back all the same.'

And, for some reason, not one of them had anything to say to that.

'I was passing,' Nell said. 'I just thought I'd drop in and see how you're doing.' They were still her tenants: she couldn't just ignore them.

'Perfect timing,' Laura told her. 'I'm just about to feed my two monkeys.'

'Oh, I don't want to disturb—'

'You're disturbing nothing, I'm eating later. Come on in, I'm dying for a chat.' She led the way into the kitchen.

The twins sat at the table.

'Hi,' Nell said.

'We went to Mr Thompson's,' Ben told her. 'We gave him pitchers an' he stuck them on he's fridge. I did George an' Seamus did chickens.'

Nell smiled. 'They sound wonderful.'

'I'm going out with Nell to the garden,' Laura told them, spooning scrambled egg from a saucepan on to two slices of buttered toast. 'Will you be good and not make a mess?'

Not make a mess. The kitchen was, if anything, worse than when Nell had seen it on their first day. The worktop was completely hidden under cereal boxes and brown-paper bags and tumbled heaps of fruit. Dishes were piled in the sink and on the draining-board. A dribble of something orange ran down along the cooker to the floor. The fridge door was smeared all over with fingerprints – and was that Grandpa Will's mirror sitting on top?

Her mother had been right, urging Nell to store it safely in the attic. Not much she could do about it now, except hope to God it survived till Saturday.

'Come on,' Laura said, opening the back door. She held a wine bottle and two glasses, one of which was half full. 'I'd just poured one for myself.'

She'd just poured one for herself the last time Nell had dropped by too. Something told Nell that she just poured one several times a day.

'I'm not staying long,' Nell said. 'Mam will have dinner waiting.'

'You're going to your parents for dinner? That's nice.'

She didn't know. James hadn't told her, or Walter. Of course they hadn't.

'Actually,' Nell said slowly, 'my father has left, and I've moved back home to be with Mam.' She might as well know, off to Dublin in two more days. What did it matter?

Laura paused in the act of filling the glasses. 'He left? You mean he walked out?'

'Yes, on Monday. That's why I wasn't at Walter's last night.'

'God, that's shocking.' Laura slid a glass across the table. 'How's your mother? How are you?'

Nell sipped the wine, ice cold and sharp. 'We're OK. You just go on, don't you? Life goes on.'

'It certainly does,' Laura replied.

A beat passed. Nell caught a drop of moisture as it slid down the glass. The day was grey, but dry and mild. From the kitchen someone said, 'I am *not*.'

'So tell me,' Laura said then, 'about Andy's mother.'

Nell was relieved at the change of topic. 'She died four years ago. Cancer.'

Laura nodded. She sipped wine and laid down her glass.

'My husband died too,' she said, 'just before the boys were born. Bad, bad time.' Her smile, for once, lacking warmth.

Nell felt instantly ashamed of her slight resentment of her tenant. The woman had done nothing wrong, except come on holidays and set her cap at James, who was free to have a relationship with anyone he chose. Nell had no claim on him, none at all.

'He had depression,' Laura went on. 'It killed him in the end. Suicide.'

Nell was horrified. 'My God, how did you cope?'

'I coped because I had to,' Laura answered. 'The boys were my reason for going on. I couldn't give up, like I wanted to, because they were depending on me.'

Look at her, sitting there drinking wine, talking about her life falling apart. Look how bubbly she'd been since they'd arrived on Roone, how full of enthusiasm for the island and its inhabitants.

'So you raised the boys on your own.'

'No, thank goodness – I had Susan, my wicked stepmother. She was brilliant, still is. She babysits every Friday when I'm on at the pub.' Laura swirled the wine in her glass. 'She thinks it's inevitable that I'll meet a new man there eventually.'

'And haven't you?' Surely she attracted them, with her figure and her charm.

Laura shrugged. 'Well, I meet them, of course, but half of them don't interest me, and as soon as I mention the boys the other half run a mile.'

'That's too bad.'

'Maybe,' she went on, smiling at Nell, 'I've just been looking in the wrong pub.'

Nell made no response. She was talking about James.

Laura didn't seem to notice her lack of enthusiasm. 'He's coming here this evening, actually, on his way home. My suggestion, I have to admit. The two will be tucked up in bed, so we'll finally have some time to ourselves.'

He'd said nothing at lunch. Maybe Laura hadn't issued her invitation by then. Not that it was any of Nell's business.

'I've got candles,' Laura said, 'and some late-night CDs. I'll set the scene and see what happens.' She grinned. 'Hope you don't mind your house being used for purposes of seduction.'

Nell managed an answering smile. 'No.'

'Those two are suspiciously quiet.' Laura rose to look in the window. 'I can't tell if James is interested, though. He's not easy to work out. I'll just have to see how it goes.'

Candles, CDs, boys in bed – and Laura, no

doubt, in something low cut. It all sounded so calculating. It was *James* they were talking about, who'd dropped everything a few days ago when Nell had needed him. James, who'd made her chicken soup when she'd had a sore throat a few months back, who'd helped her turn the house upside down looking for a lost bracelet, her parents' engagement present to her.

James wasn't someone to charm into bed with a few candles. James was her rock. She couldn't imagine life without him, and she hated the thought of him being manipulated.

She drained her glass, struggling not to show her feelings. 'Well, I'd better be off. Dinner will be waiting. Thanks for that.'

'Aren't you going to wish me luck?' Laura asked, as they walked around the side of the house.

They were both consenting adults. For all Nell knew, James wanted it as much as Laura. He'd agreed to call round late at night: he must at least be open to the possibility of something happening between them, with the boys out of the way.

'Have a good evening,' Nell said. 'I hope it goes well.'

So stiff it sounded, but again Laura gave no sign that she'd noticed anything amiss. She stood on the doorstep and waved cheerily as Nell drove off.

What difference would it make if anything happened tonight? Laura would be gone in two days. She and James had been thrown together for a couple of weeks, that was all. He'd forget her in another week. Her life was in Dublin.

But Tim's life was in Dublin, or it had been up to this. He and Nell had met on Roone; they'd been introduced when he'd come down on holidays. They'd met briefly, they'd spent a couple of evenings in each other's company, and then he'd gone back to Dublin.

And then he'd come back to Roone, and now they were getting married.

And maybe it would be the same for James, and Nell would be happy for him if it made him happy, of course she would. Laura loved Roone – she kept telling them all how much she loved it. She'd fit right in as James's wife.

James's wife. For some reason, the phrase caused a twist inside her. She turned into her parents' driveway – her *mother's* driveway – and pulled up behind Moira's car, and tried to put the whole thing out of her head.

'I've been wondering what this would be like,' she whispered, leaning across to put her mouth on his, bringing his hands up to cup her breasts as she undid his shirt buttons one by one before reaching lower to undo his jeans.

'Why don't I slip into something more comfortable?' she said softly, turning from the waist to allow him to slide down the zip of her dress, getting to her feet as she pushed the straps from her shoulders, letting the dress swish silently to the floor. Slowly, tantalisingly, removing her under-wear, hips swaying to the music, her eyes on his face.

'Come on,' she whispered, pulling him to his feet. She pushed his shirt down from his shoulders and pressed her naked body into him—

'*Muuuum!*'

The sound came out of nowhere. Laura stiffened.

'*Muuuum!*'

In one swift movement she bent down, retrieved her dress and pulled it on. 'Don't go away,' she whispered, holding it closed as she made her way silently, barefoot, from the room.

James stood in the candlelight, her perfume on his hands, the taste of her mouth still in his. He looked down at the couch, where he and Nell had often sat after one of her dinners, talking quietly as Andy watched television.

He pictured Nell's kitchen, where he'd some-times call round for coffee on Mondays, Andy at school and Nell on her day off, and him with a free morning.

He was in Nell's house. He couldn't do this. He didn't want to do this. He pulled on his shirt and closed it, buttoned his jeans, pushed a hand through his hair, slipped his feet back into shoes. At the door he met Laura.

'I'm sorry,' he said.

She looked at him, her face charmingly flushed, her dress still undone, the top falling open to reveal most of her breasts. 'He's gone back to sleep,' she murmured. 'It was just a bad dream.' She reached for him, but James stepped away.

'I'm sorry,' he repeated, 'I just can't do this. I'm really sorry.'

Silence. He saw the disappointment in her face, and cursed himself for letting it get as far as it had. He'd known full well what to expect this evening and he'd gone along with it, trying to convince himself that it made sense.

'Fair enough,' she said. 'At least we gave it a go.' She pulled her dress together and led him to the door.

'I'll see you tomorrow night at the barbecue,' he said. 'I can collect you and the boys if you want.'

'We'll be fine, thanks,' she told him, smiling faintly. 'We'll make our own way there.'

He drove home in despair. Talk about making a mess of things. He should move away from Roone, he should sell up and take Andy and go, but life without Nell was simply unthinkable.

The trouble was, life with her was pretty unbearable too.

The phone call Denis had been waiting for came at last on Friday morning. He saw her name on the display and grabbed his phone.

'Nell,' he said, closing his eyes and seeing her face.

His voice, even though she'd been expecting it, threw her. He was there, at the other end of the line, talking to her.

'Are you there?' he asked, when the silence lengthened.

'Yes, I'm here.' She didn't know how to have this conversation.

'Thank you for ringing,' he said, and when she made no response to that, he added, 'Nell, I'm sorry.'

She stood at the window of the room beside the salon, watching the scatter of people on the street. Her first customer was due in a few minutes. She'd hang up when she saw her coming.

'I don't know what to say to you,' she said eventually. 'I don't know why I rang. You really hurt me – you hurt both of us.'

She heard his long indrawn breath. 'I'll never forgive myself for that,' he said quietly. 'I couldn't see how to avoid it.'

'You could have told me,' she said. 'That would have been a start. You could at least have said it to my face.'

'No,' he said, 'I couldn't. I know I should have, but I wasn't brave enough, Nell. I just couldn't do it.'

She watched a man crossing the road, pushing open his umbrella as the rain began to fall. 'Where are you?' she asked.

'I'm in a B&B,' he told her, 'in Tralee. I've got a job in a school here.'

She knew about the school, but she said nothing. He was living in a B&B.

'I'll be moving into a rented house next week,' he added.

446

She clenched her free hand into a fist. 'With her?'

'No,' he said quickly. 'I'll be living alone. Look, can we meet up? I'd really love to see you and have a proper talk.'

She saw her customer approaching. 'Maybe,' she said. 'I have to go. I'll ring you again.'

She hung up quickly. Too soon to meet him. Much too soon.

Denis folded his phone closed and returned it to the bedside locker. He lay back in the single bed and put his hands behind his head and replayed their short conversation.

She'd phoned him; she'd talked to him. That was a cause for rejoicing. She wasn't ready to meet him, but he'd wait. 'I'll ring you again,' she'd said.

On Monday he was moving into the house. Claire would come when she could. Nell was going to ring him again. And in September he would begin his new job.

He swung his legs out of bed, hungry suddenly for a rasher and sausage breakfast.

'Want some help?' Andy asked, setting his laptop on the table.

Mr Thompson looked up. 'Very kind. They're for the barbecue – I shall be heading down there in an hour or so.'

Andy sat opposite and took a potato from the pile and wrapped it in tinfoil.

'I take it you'll be going?' Mr Thompson asked.

Andy shrugged, adding the potato to the other wrapped ones in the wooden crate. 'Maybe, for a while.' Part of him wanted to go, but he didn't fancy hanging around with his dad all evening, and he didn't know people his own age well enough to mix with them. His own fault. He reached for another potato.

They worked in silence for a few minutes.

'I'm writing to my mum,' Andy said then, keeping his eyes on the job in hand. 'In the attic, I mean. I'm telling her about my life.'

'Excellent,' Mr Thompson replied.

'I'd like to try writing a poem,' Andy said.

'In that case, you should.'

'I got the idea from the books you lent me.'

'Ah.'

'I don't know how to, though.'

Mr Thompson wrapped another potato. 'I should think the poem will write itself,' he said, 'when it's ready.'

It shouldn't have made sense, but it did.

'Keep the books,' Mr Thompson added, 'if you would like to, that is.'

Andy smiled. 'I would. Thanks.'

They finished their task. Andy got to his feet. 'Want me to put the box in your car?'

'No need,' Mr Thompson told him. 'Many thanks for your help.'

'See you later then.'

He cycled all the way home, his laptop on his

back. The house was empty, his father on duty in Fitz's till five when the bar would shut, like it always did on the day of the barbecue. No point in staying open when everyone, or practically everyone, was down on the beach.

In the kitchen he drank a cup of juice standing at the sink, John Silver butting against his legs. 'Want to go walking?' he asked, and the dog's tail wagged vigorously. Andy put down his empty cup. 'Come on then. Let's see what's happening out there.'

They left the house and turned for the sea, John Silver bounding ahead. Andy pulled a stick from the hedge and flung it towards the dog, who snatched it up and raced back to drop it at Andy's feet.

Andy grabbed the stick and broke into a run, John Silver galloping along beside him, barking. Andy ran faster, his feet pounding on the road, his arms pumping. He ran as fast as he could, feeling everything bursting with life inside him, everything bubbling through him, his whole being filling with happiness—

He slowed to a jog and then stopped altogether, bending forwards to plant his palms on his thighs, catching his breath, his face hot and damp with sweat.

Happiness?

John Silver pushed his nose into the stick Andy still held. Andy laughed and flung it as far as he was able, and the dog raced off in pursuit.

Yes, maybe happiness. Maybe, finally, the beginning of happiness.

As expected, the sun shone on the late afternoon and early evening of Roone's annual beach barbecue, which was held on the largest of the island's beaches. A posse of locals manned the half-dozen or so barbecue pits that had been dug and lined by another group earlier in the day.

They turned sausages and burgers and steaks and fish, all of which had been donated from various sources among the local populace, along with bowls of salads, trays of cakes, bags of rolls and boxes of crisps. Crates of soft drinks, boxes of wine bottles and barrels of beer were brought to a specially erected tent, and distributed throughout the affair by some of the older residents, who kept a careful eye on the ages of the various drinkers.

As ever, the event was attended by the vast majority of islanders, along with those fortunate tourists whose holiday happened to include the last Friday in July. From late afternoon, when the festivities began to get under way, the beach began to fill with people, and by twilight it was thronged.

The tantalising scent of barbecuing meat and fish drifted through the crowd as the sun sank towards the horizon. A couple of fiddles started up with a few lively tunes, a space was cleared as men grabbed women and claimed a dance.

Children chased each other along the sand; teenage girls made a great show of ignoring teenage boys; older women sat on deck-chairs, narrowing their eyes at husbands who had migrated with their friends towards the drinks tent.

As the sun disappeared and the moon came up, James Baker got two bottles of beer from the tent and walked along the beach, searching through the crowd until he found Hugh Fitzpatrick. He lowered himself on to the sand next to him and passed him a bottle.

'Where's your Andy?' Hugh asked, accepting it.

'He came for a while but he's gone home. I'll be off myself after this one. No sign of Nell and Moira,' he added.

'They thought they'd give it a miss this year.' Hugh swigged from his bottle.

'Bad business with Denis,' James said, his head buzzing softly from the four beers he'd already had.

'It is. Tim is down, is he?'

James had forgotten about Tim. 'I suppose he is – I haven't met him yet.'

They sat in companionable silence, watching the couples dancing in the soft glow from the barbecue pits, the music switched some time ago from jigs to waltzes.

No sign either of Laura Dolittle, much to the secret disappointment of several of the locals from Fitz's, who'd looked forward to another glimpse of that magnificent bosom.

And Walter Thompson, much-loved market gardener, beekeeper and chicken farmer, who had missed just two Roone barbecues in all his seventy years, was also nowhere to be seen.

Laura kicked off her shoes and tucked her bare feet under her. Nell's couch wasn't luxurious, but it was very welcome after the day of cycling and swimming they'd had. Cycling to the far side of the island, swimming at the little pebble beach they'd found at the foot of some cliffs, deliberately avoiding the big sandy beach on this side where she knew the barbecue was to take place.

She hadn't wanted to come face to face with him again; no need to subject herself to that.

Not that she was heartbroken, far from it. James's sudden change of heart last night had been disappointing, certainly. It would have been lovely to have someone's arms around her, to experience a bit of physical intimacy with someone she quite fancied. But she wasn't in love with James, much as she would have liked to be.

And clearly he didn't love her either. Whatever James was looking for, he hadn't found it in Laura. Meeting him again today wouldn't have been traumatic, but it would have felt a bit awkward for both of them. Why go through that when she didn't need to?

She would probably have had a good time at the barbecue, and the boys would have loved it, but such was life. There'd be other barbecues – and hopefully a more successful outcome the next time she thought love might happen.

Shame that her last night on Roone was such a quiet one, though. Sitting in Nell's house all on her own, the boys fast asleep. So lonely being a lone parent, so hard to meet someone new when all your friends were married, or in steady relationships.

What she'd said to Nell had been true – she *had* been chatted up in Naughton's, plenty of times, but nobody had come close to breaking her heart. Susan told her she was far too fussy, but having been truly in love once, Laura wasn't about to settle for anything less.

The only other outing she had most weeks was on Wednesday, when she and the boys had dinner at her father's house, on her stepmother's insistence. 'The boys have to get to know their granddad,' Susan said, and Laura didn't have the heart to point out that their granddad didn't seem very interested in getting to know the boys. He rarely addressed them directly at dinner – Laura suspected he didn't know one from the other – and never looked for any further interaction with them during the week.

When they were younger, Laura had been inclined to leave it at the weekly visit – what was the point of pushing in where they were so clearly not wanted? But as the years went on, her father's lack of interest in his grandsons began to breed rebellion within her. He was a household name, for God's sake – why shouldn't the boys bask in his reflected glory?

So she'd started bringing them to art galleries and pointing out his paintings, showing them his picture in magazines, trying to instil in them some pride in his achievements. And already the artistic gene was manifesting itself: Ben's teacher, who had no idea of his connection with Luke, had enthused more than once about his drawing. Seamus was showing little flair so far, but he might yet.

Laura had long since decided that she'd been dealt a bum hand as far as parents were concerned. Her father so distant and her mother, the highly strung opera singer, handing Laura over to a succession of nannies until the age of twelve, at which point she'd absconded abruptly to Australia with Trudi, her voice coach, and Laura had been packed off to boarding-school.

Surprisingly – or maybe not – she'd adapted very well to life in an institution. Surrounded by girls of her own age, bound by rules and routine from morning to night, she'd flourished, made lots of friends and worked hard. Holidays had been lonely, left to her own devices by her father as she generally was, until she'd learnt to wangle invitations from her friends' families, who were usually very happy to have the famous artist's daughter under their roofs for a few weeks.

And she hadn't turned out badly at the end of it, had she? Despite falling in love with someone who'd chosen death instead of her, despite bringing up two children pretty much on her own, most people who met her would probably say she was doing all right. She had a business that paid the bills, just about, and most of the time she was happy.

The boys made her happy – and she was good at making the best of things, she'd had plenty of practice. But of course she was lonely too. Happy and lonely in just about equal measure – and maybe that was as good as it got for anyone.

She shifted on the couch. Not the most comfortable, that was for sure. Something hard was digging into her rear end – a spring? She slid her hand under the cushion to investigate, and pulled out a thick paperback book.

The Wrong Mr Dunstable, she read, and underneath, an *Inspector Trimble Mystery*. The cover illustration was a black and white sketch of a front door with the number three on it. She opened the book and saw *Gavin Connolly* written in the top corner of the first page in green ink. She leant across to set the book on the coffee-table and a bookmark slid out. *Dublin Zoo* she read, above a picture of a lion.

Nell's previous tenant, the zookeeper. It must be his. She could bring it back to Dublin, do her good deed. Drop it into the zoo next time she and the boys visited.

She thought about going back to Dublin. Back

home, back to reality. Crèche starting up again on Monday, same nine-to-three routine, same 'Old MacDonald Had A Farm' umpteen times with God knew how many animals, and then 'Ten Green Bottles' when they got bored with the farm. Same bottoms needing to be cleaned, same bottles and teethers and soothers. But it was what she'd chosen, and on the whole she enjoyed it.

She pushed the bookmark back into the book and stretched her arms above her head. Early start in the morning: no packing done and they had to be ready to leave by eleven. She'd better have a stab at cleaning the place too – couldn't leave a pigsty behind them.

She wondered if Nell's mother would be the one to see them off, take back the keys and return Laura's deposit, or if Nell would have found someone else, after what had happened. Poor Moira, her husband walking out after so many years. Hardly another woman, at his age.

She finished her wine and left the glass on the coffee-table as she slipped her shoes back on and went from the room.

As the credits rolled Tim got to his feet. 'I'll be off so.'

Nell rose and followed him to the door.

'See you tomorrow, Tim,' Moira said, remaining in her armchair. 'Thanks again for the flowers.'

'No problem.'

Outside the front door he turned to Nell. 'Will

we go out to dinner tomorrow night, with Moira, I mean? I could book somewhere in Dingle.'

'That'd be nice. I'll ask her.'

'The flowers were my mother's idea, by the way,' he said. 'She was sorry to hear.'

'That's nice of her.' Colette had never met Nell's father, and maybe never would now. Nell stood on tiptoe to kiss him. 'Hi to James and Andy, hope they enjoyed the barbecue.'

He pressed her to him briefly. 'Missed you. Call you in the morning.'

Back in the sitting room the television was switched off and her mother had closed her eyes. Nell stood looking down at her for a few seconds. She seemed so small, sitting there. 'Mam?'

Her mother stirred, opened her eyes. 'Mm?'

'Are you sure you're OK to do the changeover tomorrow? It's not too late to get someone else. I could make a few calls in the morning.'

'I'll do it, I've already said.' She got to her feet, taking her book and glasses from the arm of her chair. 'Who would you get anyway, at this late stage?'

'I'm sure I could find someone.'

'Well, there's no need. I'm making tea – will you have a cup?'

'I'll come out with you.'

The smell of the salmon the three of them had eaten earlier still hung in the air of the kitchen. Nell filled the kettle and plugged it in.

'I thought I'd bring them a bit of that fruit cake I made yesterday,' Moira said.

'Who?'

'Your new tenants.'

'Oh, right . . . That'd be nice.'

With everything that had happened she'd forgotten that new people were moving in tomorrow. She hadn't thought beyond Laura's departure.

'I wonder how the barbecue went.' Moira took down two cups. 'At least they had the weather.'

'This is the first one I've missed,' Nell said.

'You'll have lots more.' Her mother looked at her. 'Are you alright? I thought you were a bit quiet this evening.'

Nell didn't answer straight away. She dropped two teabags into the teapot, searching for the right words, the right question.

'Scald it first,' Moira said, and Nell lifted out the teabags.

'Mam,' she said, her hand on the kettle, waiting for it to boil, 'does everyone have doubts?'

'Doubts? How do you mean?'

'Before they get married.' She turned to look at her mother. 'Do people wonder if they're doing the right thing? Is that normal?'

It was out. It had been said. What she hadn't even formulated in her own head, in her own heart, what she'd been afraid to put into words, was out in the open.

'Well,' her mother said, 'I'm no expert, God knows. All I can tell you is I had no doubts when I married your father, and look where that went.' She took the teapot from Nell and scalded it.

'There are no guarantees, love, in any marriage. But I would say that if you're not fully convinced he's right for you, then don't go ahead with it. When you're both committed, you've some hope of making it work. If one of you isn't . . .' She trailed off, cradling the warmed pot.

The kettle bubbled and clicked off. Moira replaced the teabags and filled the pot. Nell got milk from the fridge.

'You want a biscuit?' Moira asked, setting the pot on its trivet.

'No thanks.'

They took their seats. The cat leapt lightly on to Moira's lap and she pushed it off. It sat on the floor, unconcerned, and began to wash its face.

When the tea was brewed Moira filled their cups. 'This is a hard time for you,' she said. 'Maybe do nothing for the moment, see how things go when you're back in your own house with Tim.'

'Sorry, Mam,' Nell said, adding milk to her cup. 'As if you don't have enough on your plate.'

'Don't be daft,' her mother said quickly. 'There's always time for you, you know that. I'm glad you felt you could say it to me.'

Her mother had never been demonstrative. There had always been a better chance of a hug from Dad. And love wasn't something that was mentioned much, by either of them. But growing up, Nell had never been in any doubt that both her parents loved her.

Maybe her father hadn't loved her mother,

though – or not enough to stay with her. Maybe he'd have left even if he hadn't met someone else. Or they might have started out in love, and then, somewhere along the way, he had changed.

Was that what was happening to her? Was she falling out of love with Tim? The thought was horrible. It was the last thing she wanted to happen. Look how happy they'd been. Remember how delighted she'd felt when he'd proposed. Look at the life she'd seen for them, Mr and Mrs Baker living happily ever after on Roone.

Maybe there was no happy-ever-after. Maybe that was something dreamt up by a few filmmakers in Hollywood and pounced on by everyone else because it sounded so good. Happy ever after, surrounded by love till the end of your days. Who wouldn't want that?

She drank her tea and forced herself to think about her new tenants, three of them arriving tomorrow from Mayo. Three adults; a man and two women. So long since they'd made the booking – way back in March, was it? Or April. They'd been the first, anyway. She remembered rushing downstairs from the salon to tell James when she'd got their email.

So full of plans she'd been then. Booking the hotel and the photographer, trying on the dress, poring over holiday brochures to find the perfect honeymoon, trying to decide on cake recipes.

She hadn't baked a cake in ages – or not one she was considering for her wedding. She hadn't looked at the dress since the day she'd brought it home; it was still sitting in its box in her attic. She hadn't done anything about a bridesmaid's dress since she and Helen had gone looking in May, and Helen was coming home again in a couple of weeks – no, less – to try on some more.

The start of August on Monday. Less than five months to her wedding day. She drank her tea, telling herself that things would sort themselves out, that everything would be fine, that she'd look back on this time and wonder what she'd been so worried about.

She got to her feet. 'I'm just going outside for a minute.'

The evening was clear, the air pure and cool. She walked to the gate and leant against it, looking up at the sky. Searching for Sagittarius among the stars, as she'd done so often with Grandpa Will. Sometimes she saw him clearly, drawing back his bow, but tonight for some reason she couldn't pick him out.

She gave up and stood listening to the music that travelled faintly up from the beach. The barbecue, still in full swing. She imagined Laura and James there, dancing with the other couples while the little boys played on the sand, or maybe dozed on a blanket at this stage.

And Walter would be there. He never missed it, always brought a big box of potatoes, wrapped in foil and ready to be tossed on to the glowing charcoal. Although by now he had probably gone home to bed.

Tim would probably be in bed too, or maybe he was still up, talking to Andy, who didn't normally stay too long at the barbecue. Shy around the other teenagers, although he went to school with most of them. Poor Andy.

After a minute she turned, shivering slightly, and made her way back into the house.

LETTING THE HOUSE: THE THIRD TWO WEEKS

LETTING THE HOUSE:
THE THIRD TWO WEEKS

Lelia Doherty, proprietor of one of Roone's three cafés, checked her watch as she refilled a basket with fruit scones. Twenty past ten. Walter must have slept it out. Not a bit like him: normally you could set your clock by his deliveries.

If he didn't get here in the next ten minutes the salads wouldn't be ready in time for lunch, to go with the cold meats and cheeses in her deli section. She was also down to three jars of honey, which wasn't nearly enough for a Saturday. And she hadn't a single bottle of apple juice, which disappeared off the shelves as soon as she put it out. Where was he?

For the second time in five minutes she lifted the receiver from the phone behind the counter and dialled his number and waited. Still no answer. As she hung up the café door opened and Paul and Dorothy Herbert walked in. 'I can't get hold of Walter,' she told them. 'He's always here by ten and there's no sign of him. And he's not answering his phone.'

'He probably overslept after the barbecue,' Paul said.

'Was he there?' Dorothy asked. 'I didn't see him.'

'He must have been,' Lelia said. 'He never misses it.' But come to think of it, she hadn't spotted him either.

'Want me to call round?' Paul asked. Walter's house was less than a five-minute drive from the village.

'Would you mind? It's not a bit like him.'

'He'll be fine,' Dorothy said, taking a seat. 'Probably forgot to set his alarm.'

'That'll be it,' Lelia agreed. 'Tea, is it, Dorothy?'

'Please – and a fruit scone, love.'

He's fine, Lelia told herself, as she placed the scone in the microwave to warm it up, the way Dorothy liked it. He's just slept it out, there's nothing wrong.

'Nell told me what happened,' Laura said. 'I'm very sorry.'

Moira looked much the same. A little tired maybe, shadows under her eyes that Laura didn't remember, but that was surely to be expected.

'Thank you,' she replied – a little stiffly, Laura thought. Preferred not to discuss her business with strangers, perhaps. And no comment about Aaron: Nell must have kept that to herself.

Laura showed her the book. 'I found this last night – it had slipped down the back of the couch.

I think it belongs to the man who was here before me.' She opened it. 'Gavin Connolly?'

'That's right. We'll send it back to him, I'm sure Nell has his address.'

'Or I could deliver it, if you like. He works in the zoo, doesn't he?'

'He does – but would that be out of your way?'

'Not at all, we often go there.'

'Well, if you're sure it's no bother, that would be very good of you.'

'No problem at all.'

The formalities were observed, the keys returned, the deposit handed back.

'Oh,' Laura said, tapping on the kitchen window for the boys, 'would you ever give a message to Walter for us? We called round earlier to say goodbye but there was no answer. He must have gone out somewhere.'

'He'll be in the village. He makes morning deliveries.'

'That'll be it so. Would you ever say thanks for all the donkey rides, and letting the boys collect the eggs and everything? They were charmed, never had anything like that before. We were so lucky to have him next door. Will you pass on that message?'

'Certainly.'

'And tell him we'll see him in December. We're planning to gatecrash Nell's wedding. We'd love to be here for it, if nobody minded.'

Moira smiled. 'I'm sure you'd be most welcome.'

'Thanks so much. Come on, you two,' Laura said, as the twins entered, 'time to go. Say thank you and goodbye to Mrs Mulcahy.'

'We saw a cat,' they told Nell's mother.

'Yeah. He was grey, but he runned off.'

Thanks were given, goodbyes exchanged. The boys were bundled into the back seat of the car, finding room somehow in the jumble of luggage. Laura strapped them in and turned to Moira. 'We've really enjoyed it, thanks again. See you in December, hopefully. I'll drop Nell an email.'

As the house with the red door disappeared from her rear-view mirror, Laura glanced back at the boys. 'Are you sorry to be leaving?'

'Yeah. We left out cake for the cat.'

'Did you now? I was wondering where that had got to.'

'Yeah, but he didn't eat it.'

'I don't think cats really like cake. I have a surprise when you get back home,' she told them.

'What?'

'Guess where we're going tomorrow.'

'Where?'

'The zoo.'

'Yaaay.'

Better return his book right away, while it was in her head. If she put it aside somewhere at home, it could be months before she thought of it again. And you never knew, they might get a few free passes out of it.

They drove through the village, past Nell's hair

salon, where they'd gone for cuts they didn't need. Past Fitz's bar, where James Baker worked. Past the supermarket, with the assistant who hadn't wanted to be bothered by a small boy who only had fifty cents to spend. She kept an eye out for Walter, but there was no sign of him.

They came to the pier, where a line of cars was waiting for the approaching ferry. Laura took her place in the queue, wondering when they'd be back.

Not if, when.

Mr Thompson's car was in its usual spot, around by the side of the house, but there was no sign of him in the field. He wasn't digging in his vegetable patch or attending to his beehives. He wasn't in the hen run. Andy dropped his bag of painting paraphernalia on the path and pushed open the scullery door.

'Hello? Mr Thompson?'

No response. He walked through the scullery and into the kitchen. On the table was the wooden crate, full of the tinfoil-covered potatoes they'd prepared the day before.

For the barbecue. A worm of anxiety slithered through him.

He went out to the hall. 'Mr Thompson? It's Andy. I've come to paint the henhouse.' He walked as he called, peering around the drawing-room and dining-room doors, finding nobody.

He stood at the bottom of the stairs, listening

to the silence. Fearful of going up, but knowing he had to. He mounted them slowly, his body tingling with apprehension.

'Mr Thompson? Are you there?'

And on the landing, he found him.

Less than a minute later, Paul Herbert entered the house the same way as Andy. All the locals used Walter's back door. 'Hello?' he called, walking swiftly through the kitchen and out to the hall, where he heard a sound he couldn't immediately identify coming from the top of the stairs.

'*Walter –*'

He bounded up and discovered a teenage boy kneeling by Walter's inert form, sobbing loudly. The boy looked up at Paul, his face contorted, his breath coming in gasps. He looked familiar, but Paul couldn't place him.

'I was coming to paint his henhouse,' the boy cried, tears streaming unchecked down his face. 'I just wanted to—' He broke off, his sobs increasing, his shoulders heaving.

Paul crossed the landing and dropped to his knees and pressed his fingers briefly to the ice-cold skin at the side of Walter's neck. He made a swift sign of the cross. 'Come on,' he said quietly, half lifting the weeping boy to his feet. 'Come on downstairs, come on, lad.'

James's son, he realised. His long hair was gone, but it was definitely him.

In the kitchen he pulled out a chair for the boy,

who continued to weep brokenly, his head in his hands. Paul rang his wife and told her quietly what had happened. 'Ring Dr Jack, and the Reverend,' he said, 'and try to get hold of James Baker, his boy is here. He found Walter, he's very upset.'

He hung up and took the crate of potatoes to the draining-board. He returned upstairs and covered the body with a blanket from the nearest bedroom, and said a silent prayer.

Back in the kitchen he plugged in the kettle. If in doubt, make tea. He pulled out a chair and sat, resting his hand on the boy's still heaving shoulder.

'Hugh,' James said. 'What can I do for you?'

'I'm ringing about Andy,' Hugh told him, his voice calm but the words rushing out. 'He's alright, but you need to get over to Walter's house.'

James stood up abruptly, his knees bumping against the table leg, the jolt sending his coffee cup flying. 'What's happened? Is he hurt?'

'He's OK, James, but he . . . found Walter. Walter is dead, James, and Andy was the one who found him.'

'*Jesus*—' James hung up and grabbed his car keys from their hook. He drove the mile and a quarter to Walter's house as fast as he dared, his heart in his mouth, cursing when he had to slow for a delivery van outside the supermarket.

He parked crookedly behind the three other cars outside the house and rushed the back way into Walter's kitchen. Andy raised his head as he came in, and James's heart constricted at the sight of his pain. He walked over, ignoring Dr Jack and Paul Herbert who stood by the sink, and he took his son into his arms and held him tightly.

'I'm here . . . I'm here . . . You're OK, you're OK now.'

And Andy leant into him and cried, 'Why did she have to *go*? Why did she have to *die* like that? It wasn't *fair*.'

'No, son,' James whispered, hanging on tightly, Andy's scalp prickly against his cheek, 'you're right there. It wasn't fair. It wasn't one bit fair.'

The news of the sudden death of Walter Thompson spread like lightning along the roads and lanes of Roone. Nell Mulcahy heard it from her half-eleven customer, who'd got it from Lelia, standing on the street outside her café, still in her apron.

By noon it was the only topic of conversation. The path outside Lelia's was crowded with huddles of people, shaking their heads and talking in low voices, stopping passers-by to inform them, or ask for further news.

'Never a bad word to say about anyone.'

'And manners, such beautiful manners. Remember his mother? A real lady.'

'What happened to him, though? Does anyone know?'

'Heart, I suppose.'

'He wasn't that old, was he? He was hardly seventy.'

472

'Was he at the barbecue? I didn't see him.'

'Poor old creature, he had it tough.'

Fitz's counter was full of farmers and fishermen who'd grown up with Walter, or whose fathers had. They sat mostly in silence, an occasional murmured comment passed among them. Everyone had known Walter; everyone had had dealings with him of one sort or another.

'Grand potatoes.'

'Oh, the finest. Balls of flour.'

'And the honey.'

'He'll be missed.'

'He will.'

And ironically, Moira Mulcahy, making beds and mopping floors not a hundred yards from where Walter's body lay, was one of the last to hear.

'I thought she'd never go,' Marian said. 'I was gasping for a cuppa.'

'Dried grape,' Vernon said. 'Seven letters, *a* is the fifth.'

Sultana, Imelda thought, scalding the teapot. Or currant. She never remembered what the difference was.

'Oh, put that thing away, would you,' Marian said, 'and make yourself useful. Cut a few slices off that bit of cake she brought us.'

Vernon folded the newspaper. 'There's no knife.'

Marian rolled her eyes to heaven. 'Have a look around, open drawers.'

'There's one over there, on the bread board,' Imelda told him.

'Thanks.' He divided the wedge of fruit cake into thick slices.

'Will you look at those doorsteps?' Marian said. 'You'll have to cut them into fingers. That cake is probably as rich as anything.'

Imelda dropped three teabags into the pot.

'Vernon, find a cloth and wipe up those crumbs.' Marian arranged the cake on a plate. 'You're very quiet,' she added. 'Are you sorry you came?'

'Not a bit,' Imelda replied, bringing the tea to the table. 'Did anyone see cups?'

But a search of the kitchen presses revealed only mugs. 'I hate tea out of a mug,' Marian said. 'Horrible clumsy things. Here, pass it over, if I have no choice.'

The cake was good, rich and dark and moist. 'You should ask for the recipe, Imelda,' Vernon said.

'What about me?' Marian demanded. 'Imelda isn't the only one in the family capable of producing a fruit cake.'

'You only do scones,' her husband pointed out mildly. 'Imelda makes the Christmas cake, that's why I said it to her.'

'I'm as well able to make a cake as Imelda. I've just got other things to do, that's all. You've no trouble eating my scones, have you?'

'I never said a word against them.'

'Well then.'

Stop it, stop it, Imelda begged them silently. Just stop talking. Drink your tea and eat your cake and say nothing.

Not half a day gone, and already she was wishing for the two weeks to be over. She should never have come. She should never have let Marian talk her into it.

'It'll do you good,' Marian had said. 'A change of scene. I won't take no for an answer. Our treat, of course. We'd be paying anyway, it makes no difference to the price if a third person comes.'

And because it was easier to say yes to Marian, Imelda had said yes, and here she was, stuck in this little house for two whole weeks with her sister and brother-in-law, who thought they were doing her a favour by taking her along.

'It's the least we can do,' Marian had said, 'after you being so good to Dad' – and Imelda had to acknowledge the truth of that. It *was* the least they could do, since Marian had never lifted a finger to help her when their father was alive.

But she meant well, Imelda knew that. There was no badness in Marian, she just didn't think. It had probably never crossed her mind to take Dad for a week now and again, or even a weekend, and give Imelda a break. The only time Dad had gone to Marian and Vernon's house was for Christmas dinner, and of course Imelda always went too, and brought the cake with her.

Poor Dad hadn't had it easy. His wife had died young, leaving him with two small daughters to raise – and just when he should have been putting his feet up, his daughters reared, his responsibilities ended, he'd been diagnosed with osteoarthritis and was crippled with pain for the last several years of his life. Was it any wonder he'd been cranky? Wouldn't anyone have been?

'I don't know how you put up with him,' Marian would say, after one of her weekly visits, during which she and Dad would have spent most of the hour snapping at each other. 'You should be canonised,' she'd tell Imelda.

But Imelda was no saint. He was her father, and she was single. She'd never moved out of home; after Marian had married it was just Imelda and Dad. How could she have left him on his own? And why wouldn't she look after him, when he'd looked after her and Marian for years? Who else did he have, only her?

And it wasn't as if men were flocking around, trying to steal her away. Nobody had ever shown much interest in Imelda O'Brien, so shy, so unremarkable. So different from her sister.

When their father had died just under a year ago, Marian had taken over and arranged the funeral. Imelda didn't mind – if the truth be told she was relieved. Marian was a born organiser, and it had made perfect sense.

Imelda had prepared ham and cheese sandwiches in the kitchen and listened to her sister talking on the phone to the undertaker, fielding the neighbours who called with apple tarts, making a shopping list for Vernon – 'Mind you don't get that cheap whiskey. I'm not having anyone saying the O'Briens cut corners.'

It had been Marian's idea, Imelda was sure, to invite her to join them on their annual fortnight away. Not that Vernon would have objected: he and Imelda had always got on. It just wouldn't have occurred to him to include her.

'You're free to come and go as you please now,' Marian had said. 'You should take advantage of that. But you can't go on holidays on your own., you'd be miserable. We'd love to have you along, we really would. I'm not just saying that.'

Every year Marian and Vernon took a house for a couple of weeks somewhere in Ireland, just the two of them. They hadn't had children, and Imelda had never enquired about that. It was none of her business.

Imelda hadn't had a holiday in years. She'd gone away lots of times with friends when she was younger, before the friends had all got married. Wales and Jersey and the Isle of Man, and a few city breaks too, Paris, Rome, Barcelona, Berlin.

But even if she'd still had a single friend, Imelda wouldn't have felt right leaving Dad on his own after he'd got sick. They'd have had to organise a full-time carer unless Marian and Vernon had taken him in, which probably wouldn't have happened.

And now, when she could go wherever she wanted, there was nobody left for Imelda to ring up and persuade to come away for a few days.

But going on holidays wasn't a priority – and going with Vernon and Marian certainly wouldn't have been Imelda's choice. She'd have been perfectly happy to stay at home. Since Dad's death she'd stripped the wallpaper in all the rooms and given a lot of the old furniture to Vincent de Paul, much to Marian's disapproval. She'd put her own stamp on the house she'd grown up in, and it was finally beginning to feel like hers.

But staying at home was out, for this year at least. Not that Imelda had any intention of letting this become a tradition – if she had to go away on her own from now on, she would. She'd book a walking holiday or something, join a group somewhere. Was there anything more pathetic than tagging along with your sister and her husband?

'A hot drop?' Vernon was offering the teapot.

Imelda shook her head. 'I think I might unpack.'

'We'll have dinner out later,' Marian announced. 'If it stays dry we could walk back to the village – it can't be more than half a mile.'

'Lovely.'

Two weeks, that was all she had to do. Thirteen days, if you didn't count today.

His dad made him hot chocolate and floated marshmallows in it. The last time he'd done that, Andy had been about seven, and he'd been sick with something – chicken pox, maybe. He didn't think he was that keen on marshmallows any more,

478

but his dad must have got them specially so he said nothing.

He hadn't known anyone could cry that much. Once he'd started he couldn't stop. He'd cried all the way home in his dad's car. He'd cried in the sitting room, hunched on the couch, wiping his face every so often with his sleeve, his dad sitting silently beside him.

He'd still been crying when his dad had left at two to go to work at the pub.

'I can phone Hugh,' he'd said, 'he can find someone else,' but Andy had said no, so he'd gone. And shortly after he'd left Tim had shown up, probably having been asked by his dad to go and keep an eye on him.

Thankfully, Tim hadn't felt the need to sit beside him. He'd read the paper in the kitchen while Andy had moved to his room and gone on crying as silently as he could. Tim had appeared just once, with a pizza he'd taken from the freezer. Andy hadn't even thought about food, but once he'd started to eat he'd found he was starving.

And now it was much later, and his dad was back from work, and Andy had finally managed to stop crying and had come out to the sitting room again. He felt empty, as if someone had scooped his insides away. He cradled the mug of hot chocolate that his dad had made him, complete with marshmallows.

It was just the two of them. Tim had disappeared again.

'It was a massive heart attack,' his dad told him. 'It would have happened very quickly. He wouldn't have known a thing.'

Andy nodded, the thought of Mr Thompson lying alone all night on the landing bringing another lump to his throat. 'I'd still like to paint the henhouse,' he said.

His father nodded. 'Go ahead then, if you want to.'

Andy drank his hot chocolate, which was surprisingly comforting. 'I have something to tell you,' he said then.

His father didn't interrupt while Andy told him about writing to Mum in the attic.

'I wanted to tell her stuff, about my life. I wanted her to know. And the attic . . . I dunno, it was peaceful up there. It just made it easy to do it.'

'OK.'

Andy drank more hot chocolate. He sucked a marshmallow into his mouth. It was deliciously sweet and gooey. 'I was going to tell you,' he said. 'I wasn't deliberately doing it in secret. Well, I was, but it's just . . . I didn't really know . . .'

'That's fine,' his dad said.

Andy's face, around his eyes especially, felt tight. 'I think I was the last person to see him,' he said then. 'Mr Thompson, I mean. I was in the attic yesterday, and when I came down he was . . . wrapping potatoes for the barbecue, and I—' He pressed a hand to his face.

'It's all right, pet,' James said.

Andy took a tissue from the box on the coffee-table and blew his nose. 'I liked him,' he said, bottom lip trembling. 'He was . . . kind.'

'He was.'

'I like Roone too,' he said. 'I'm glad we came to live here.'

His dad smiled. 'Good. I was hoping you were.'

Silence fell. Andy poked at the remaining marshmallow, shoved it under the creamy liquid with his finger. It reappeared, like a spongy pink island in a chocolate sea. 'What'll happen now?' he asked. 'To Mr Thompson's place, I mean.'

'I don't know,' his father replied. 'I suppose he's got some family somewhere.'

'What about the hens, though? Who'll collect the eggs, and feed them and stuff? And the donkey?'

'There's talk of a few of his neighbours looking after the place for the moment,' his father told him. 'They'll probably make out a rota.'

'I'd like to help.'

'That'd be good. I'll ask around tomorrow, see who to talk to.'

'Thanks.' Silence fell again. He finished his hot chocolate and set his mug on the coffee-table. 'Dad.'

'Yes.'

'Do you have Mum's poems? I mean, did you keep them?'

His father looked at him. 'I did.'

'Maybe I could read them some time.'

'Sure. Want me to get them now?'

'No . . .' He was suddenly exhausted. 'I think I'll go to bed,' he said. 'Maybe tomorrow.'

James watched his child leaving the room. Face still blotched, eyes swollen, looking heartbreakingly young and sad. But talking. For the first time since Karen's death, he was talking to his father about her. Telling James he was writing to her, asking to see her poems.

James thought of Walter, felt a pang of sorrow for that gentle man, gone from them for good. His death somehow unlocking something in Andy – or maybe the unlocking had already started up in the attic. Maybe Walter's death had pushed open a door that had already been ajar. Maybe Walter himself had found a way to prise it open.

His phone beeped with a text message. He saw that it was from Nell.

Hope you and Andy are OK. At Walter's house, terribly lonesome. See you tomorrow XX

He looked at the screen for several seconds. Then he got up and left the room.

The drawing room, where Walter had been laid out, was full of people. Chairs had been brought in from the kitchen and dining room and arranged in a ragged semi-circle that began behind the door and ended just before the bay window, splitting to accommodate the two couches. People without a seat leant against any available wall space, or perched on arm rests, or retreated to the hall. Every so often, a chair would be vacated by one mourner and claimed shortly afterwards by another.

Walter lay in his coffin in the centre of the semi-circle, wearing his best grey suit. His hair had been neatly combed, his features waxen and still. A small bunch of wildflowers had been placed in his clasped hands.

Islanders talked in quiet tones, cups of tea came and went, plates of sandwiches and apple tart and barm brack were passed around. The island tradition was to keep the body at home until the day of the burial, with family members, or in this case friends and neighbours, keeping it company. Day or night, Walter would not be alone until he was taken from the house on Monday and laid to rest in the Church of Ireland cemetery, some three miles away.

Nell sat on a kitchen chair facing the door, between Tim and her mother, still trying to comprehend what had happened. Walter, dead. Walter, gone. No more chats over the stone wall, no more cups of tea in his kitchen. No more Walter coming to dinner with a basket of eggs or a jar of honey.

Impossible to take it in, impossible.

Her mother's arm was linked in Nell's, her thumb stroking Nell's forearm absently. 'They seem nice,' she said, her voice low enough that

Nell had to bend her head slightly to hear it. 'The new people.'

'Oh.' Nell regarded a small dark stain on her camel-coloured shoes. She couldn't have cared less about her new tenants.

'The sister is quiet, the single one, I mean. The other one, Marian, did practically all of the talking. I'd say the husband doesn't get much of a say.'

'Mm.'

Paul and Dorothy Herbert edged their way into the room and moved towards the coffin. They stood there for several seconds. Dorothy placed a hand lightly on Walter's, her lips moving silently, before they made their way to the recently vacated window seat, nodding at those they passed on the way.

Paul had gone to Walter's house; he'd discovered Andy and Walter. 'Poor Andy was very upset,' Lelia had told Nell. 'Can you imagine, a boy of his age having to cope with that? And after him losing his mother as well.'

Nell turned to Tim. 'You go,' she whispered. 'Mam and I will probably stay another while.' He'd hardly known Walter, even though they'd lived next door to one another for over a year. Tim had never, as far as she could remember, been inside Walter's house until this evening.

'You sure?' he murmured. 'I could stay, I don't mind.'

'There's no need,' she told him. 'You should go and get something to eat.' Their planned meal out

484

had been aborted, of course. She didn't feel at all hungry, but Tim probably did. 'I'll give you a ring in the morning, when I'm up.'

'OK.' He pressed her hand, whispered goodbye to Moira and was gone. Glad to get away, no doubt, the other islanders virtual strangers to him. Gone back to James's for something to eat.

James should be here. Tim was the wrong brother for Walter's wake. James knew everyone in this room, and he and Walter had enjoyed each other's company. Nell remembered how delighted Walter had been with the small painting James had done of the hens last year. It hung on the wall, halfway up the stairs.

She hadn't seen James all day: he hadn't been in the pub when she'd looked in at lunchtime. She'd sat at the counter for twenty minutes, too stunned to eat, and sipped the brandy that Hugh had poured for her. She'd tried calling James when she'd heard Andy had found Walter, but his phone had been switched off.

She'd tried again on her way home, having closed the salon half an hour early, nobody wanting a haircut, and still there had been no answer. She'd called Tim, who told her James was working in the pub till eight. She hadn't even thought of checking the pub again, so distracted she'd been.

And in the hours since then, as she'd picked at a sandwich she didn't want in her mother's house, as she'd changed into her grey skirt and black top and walked the half-mile with Moira and Tim to Walter's, as she'd stood by the coffin, wiping her eyes, and sat beside it afterwards, not wanting to leave him, there'd been no word from James, no sign of him.

She took her phone out of her bag and typed quickly

Hope you and Andy are OK. At Walter's house, terribly lonesome. See you tomorrow XX

She would have liked him there. He should have been there.

Imelda didn't bother with a raincoat, or even an umbrella. She knew the rain was coming. As soon as she'd woken and looked out, some time before seven, she'd known they were in for a day of showers, but as she finished a blessedly solitary breakfast of yogurt with honey – delicious honey, a brand new jar of it sitting in one of the presses, *lavender* handwritten in beautiful copperplate on the label – a feeling of such inexplicable reckless-ness had come over her that she'd dropped her bowl into the sink and walked straight out through the hall, not even glancing at the hallstand as she'd opened the red front door and stepped into the morning.

She was an escapee, heading off to find an adven-ture. Who brought an umbrella on an adventure?

And for a while, as she half walked, half ran along the deserted Sunday-morning road – noting the pile of cars parked all higgledy-piggledy outside the big old house next to theirs, wondering how many people could possibly live there – it looked like she might get away with it. The clouds were low, but the rain held off as she hurried past curtained windows and silent houses, walking in the opposite direction to the village, keeping the sea to her left.

There was no rush, of course. She could stay out all day if she wanted to, even if she'd left the house without a penny. Marian would probably have something to say when she got home, but Marian never stayed annoyed for long. No, something else propelled Imelda forward, some giddiness, some bubbling excitement – oh, she didn't know what it was that sent her scurrying along like a mischievous child. If anyone saw her, if any of her friends from Westport could see quiet, sensible Imelda O'Brien rushing down the road so early on a Sunday morning, they'd think she'd taken leave of her senses.

She came to a crossroads and slowed, panting slightly from her exertions. No signpost, no indication as to where any of the roads led, except that the turn to her left must follow the coast, so she took it. Almost immediately the road began to climb quite steeply, but Imelda kept going. She passed a field of neatly laid out haystacks, another of black and white cows, a third filled with nothing but trees, not a leaf stirring in the cool, still air.

After another fifteen minutes or so she saw a narrow downward-sloping track leading off the road in the general direction of the sea, bordered on both sides by a line of trees. Parked just beyond it was a small dark blue car, pulled well into the side.

She regarded the track doubtfully. What if it was someone's private land? What if it led into a field of cattle, with maybe a bull in the middle of them? But again there was no sign, and no gate either – and she was in the mood to take a chance.

She turned and began walking along the track, slithering a little when the downward slope became more pronounced, ducking under the occasional overhanging branch. The further down she travelled, the louder the sea sounded. After a short while the track veered to the right, and so did Imelda.

The ground underfoot began to change, the packed earth giving way to small grey stones, rounded and slippery. The further she went, the more they increased in number, making the going gradually more precarious. She put her arms out for balance as she crunched her way over them, increasingly uncertain as to the wisdom of having chosen this unpredictable route.

Imagine if she stumbled and twisted an ankle, and kept slithering downwards for however far the track went. That would be the end of her glittering ballet career, over practically before it had begun. Would anyone discover her if she did herself an injury here and became unable to move? Was she very foolish to be heading down this deserted track all on her own? Perhaps the owner of the dark blue car was about, but so far there was no sign of him or her.

No: she'd come this far, she'd keep going. And just as she'd made the decision, as she rounded another slight bend, the track opened out abruptly and became a little curved strip of pebbly beach running off to her right, behind which cliffs rose sharply and dramatically.

'Oh—' Imelda caught her breath at the sight of the sea spread out so suddenly before her. She stumbled towards it, her shoes sinking into the pebbles – but before she'd taken half a dozen steps something caused her to stop dead, her heart jumping.

A man sat on a towel, not three yards away to her left.

'Hello,' he said. 'I hope I didn't give you a fright.'

He wore a pair of dark trousers. The sleeves of his white shirt were rolled to the elbows. One of his forearms appeared to be missing.

Her cheeks were flushed. Her hair was all over the place. She wore a biscuit-coloured top and brown trousers, and she had a sturdy figure. She had appeared suddenly from the lane – although he'd heard her approach, of course – and her face had transformed at the sight of the sea.

'Oh—' she breathed, and headed towards it,

almost falling in her eagerness. Like a child, no inhibitions. And then she spotted him, and her mouth dropped open.

'Hello,' he said. 'I hope I didn't give you a fright,' although it was quite obvious that he had.

He didn't look dangerous. He didn't look as if he had any plans to attack her. Still, there wasn't anyone else on the beach, maybe nobody for miles around.

'I wasn't expecting to meet anyone,' she said. 'At this hour, I mean.' That must be his car, at the top of the lane.

'It's early,' he agreed. 'I didn't think I'd meet anyone either.'

He looked tired. His face was pale, his chin dotted with stubble. No, he wasn't dangerous. Imelda scanned the narrow pebbly strip. She could see why it might not appeal to most people. No long sandy beach, no waves. No direct sunshine ever, probably, with the cliffs blocking it out.

But the peace was wonderful, the soft *lap lap* of the water on the pebbles so calming. She'd sit here all day and read a book, no problem.

'You're on holidays?' the man asked.

'Yes, since yesterday.'

'Ah.'

'Are you from here?' she asked him.

'I am, born and bred.' He nodded, looking out to sea. 'All my life.'

She imagined growing up here, spending your

whole life on this small stretch of land in the middle of the sea. After less than a day, she realised that she was taken with the island. Lying in bed last night after the steaks they'd eaten in the only place they could find open – a local death, they'd been told, businesses closed as a mark of respect – Imelda had realised she was glad she'd come.

Roone was different. It felt different from any place she'd been before. She didn't fully understand the appeal it had for her, but she knew she liked being here.

She wondered if it would be a bit forward to sit down. He might want the place to himself, as he'd had it before she arrived. He might be wishing she'd leave. But she didn't want to leave, she liked it here – and they couldn't very well sit at either end of the beach and pretend the other wasn't there, now that they'd struck up a bit of a conversation. Tricky.

'Why don't you sit down?' he asked.

Imelda felt the colour rising in her face. Still blushing at fifty-three, when everyone else seemed to grow out of it at eighteen. She crunched across the pebbles and lowered herself to the ground as gracefully as she could, hearing Mrs Shine's voice in her head, urging her to 'Keep your chin *up*, Imelda, back *straight*, chest *forward*. You are a *swan*.'

Swan my foot. With a great effort, she avoided slithering on her backside as it made contact with the pebbles.

★　★　★

She held herself well, back very straight, arms clasped loosely around her bent knees. Her voice was deep for a woman's. He smelt soap when she sat, or maybe it was shampoo. A fresh smell anyway, not cloying.

He offered her some of his towel but she said no, thank you, she was fine. He thought she wasn't a woman overly concerned with her appearance. Her face was lightly freckled, her eyes yellowy brown, like butterscotch. She didn't appear to be wearing makeup, but you could never be sure.

He thought she was around his own age, and she wore no rings. She was shy: he had to coax information from her. She lived in Westport, she told him, she'd come here with her sister and brother-in-law. No, she'd never been to the island before. She worked part-time as a dental assistant in a large clinic.

She glanced at his deformed arm once or twice but didn't comment. She asked him little about himself, and Hugh volunteered less. He made no mention of Walter; he didn't tell her that he'd spent the night sitting up with the island's finest gentleman.

He didn't explain that he'd felt the urge to visit the beach for a while on his way home, tired and dishevelled as he was. He must look a fright, and his teeth needed brushing. He hoped his breath didn't smell too stale.

He told her what there was to see on the island:

492

the lighthouse, the holy well, the viewing point, the caves. He recommended the cliff walk. He didn't mention the pub – it might have looked as if he was touting for business.

She was nice. He enjoyed their chat.

He was nice. He asked questions – not in a nosy way though – and he seemed interested in her answers. His arm might have been caused by thalidomide, which would make him around her own age. So lucky she and Marian had been, thalidomide all the go when their mother had been expecting them.

He had a sad smile. Something had made him sad. She wondered if he had a job, or if his disability got in the way. She wondered if he was married, if he had children. She couldn't ask: it wasn't a question for someone you'd just met. It didn't matter anyway. She'd be gone home in a couple of weeks.

Thirteen days, if you counted today.

The rain came, as he'd been expecting since leaving Walter's house, shortly after dawn. He held his umbrella over both of them, but they still got wet.

He didn't mind. She didn't seem bothered either.

Nell went to early Mass with her mother, who knew well that Nell rarely went any more but who held her peace as they walked the quarter-mile to the church. Funny, Nell thought, how Walter's death had completely overshadowed her father's departure. Not one of the locals they'd spoken to at Walter's had shown a sign of the awkwardness Nell had seen among her customers in the salon over the past couple of days. It was as if they'd completely forgotten what had happened. Maybe they had.

Her father. He'd have to be told. He might see it in the death notices in today's papers, but she couldn't be sure. She couldn't let him miss Walter's funeral – they'd known each other well.

She waited until they were walking home from Mass. 'I'd better drop over to say hello to the new people,' she said.

'Yes, you should.'

'And I'll ring Dad and tell him about Walter.'

A tiny pause. 'I suppose you should. I'm going to make a brack to bring over to the house later. Will you do your lemon cake?'

And that was it.

Marian came into the sitting room. 'Look what I found.'

Vernon lowered his book. 'What is it?'

She held out her hand. 'It's cake, it looks like coffee cake. Do you know where I found it?'

'In a cake tin?'

Marian clicked her tongue. 'Of *course* not in a cake tin – what would be wrong with that? I found it in the garden, lying on the grass by the shed.

God knows how long it's been there. It's a wonder we're not overrun with—'

Her expression changed. She peered at the chunk of cake, and then shrieked and dropped it on the sitting-room carpet. 'Ants crawling all over it! Vernon, get the Hoover, quick! God, they're on my hand – disgusting!'

The Hoover was employed, the cake and ants dealt with. Vernon made tea to settle her, and decided against producing the remaining piece of the other cake, the one that hadn't been sitting in the grass.

He was pleased enough with the holiday house. To be sure it was basic enough, no en-suite like they had at home, no bidet, which Marian had insisted on installing after she'd come across one in the Gordons' house some years ago. Not that Vernon had ever used the bidet. He wasn't entirely sure how it worked, and he wasn't about to ask. But the house was clean and comfortable, and he had no serious fault to find with it. And it was well situated, just a short stroll from the village and close to plenty of beaches. And a nice few sights to see, when they took the notion. Marian liked her sights.

'Where could Imelda be gone?' Marian asked, for what must have been the tenth time since they'd got up that morning. 'She'll be drenched in this rain without a coat.'

'She'll shelter,' Vernon said again. 'She's enough sense to shelter.'

'She should have had enough sense to take a coat.'

Vernon had always liked Imelda. He might have gone for Imelda if Marian hadn't been around, he might have had a chance to notice Imelda more. But Marian had taken him over – and to be fair, he hadn't objected: he'd been well pleased with her.

'You'll have to go out and look for her if she's not back soon,' Marian said. 'God knows who might be living here, preying on women on their own. You could get all sorts of strange characters, driven mad with the isolation.'

With difficulty Vernon kept a straight face. 'Ah, I wouldn't think there's any danger here. It seems a nice quiet spot.'

'It's the quiet places you find them. Is there none of that cake left from yesterday?'

As Vernon was putting it on to a plate they heard the front door opening.

'There she is, at last,' Marian said. 'That you, Imelda?'

'Yes.'

'She wasn't attacked then,' Vernon said lightly, and Marian gave him a look he knew well.

The kitchen door opened and Imelda appeared. 'Hello.'

'Look at you – you're *drenched*,' Marian said.

'Ah, no, just a bit damp.'

She looked drenched to Vernon. Her hair was flat with moisture. Her beige top clung to her. She took the hand towel from the back of a chair and began rubbing her head briskly with it. 'Is there tea in the pot? I could murder a cup.'

'You're not changing out of those clothes?' Marian asked. 'You'll catch your death.'

'I will. I'll just have a quick cuppa first, if it's there.'

Vernon got another mug and filled it. 'Did you find anywhere nice?'

'I did, actually – a lovely little beach, about half an hour's walk from here.'

Marian took a piece of fruit cake. 'A beach? In this weather?'

'Well, it was dry when I got there.' She threw the towel on to the draining-board and sat at the table and picked up the milk jug.

'Your hair is sticking up all over the place,' Marian told her.

Imelda smiled as she raised her mug. 'What harm?'

She seemed in good form this morning – and she looked well, despite the hair. The walk had put colour in her cheeks. Vernon was glad they'd brought her along. The change of scene was obviously agreeing with her.

'That's a lovely cake, isn't it?' she said. 'I must get the recipe.'

Just then the doorbell rang.

'Lord, who could that be now?' Marian asked. 'Vernon, see who it is.'

The brown-haired young woman on the doorstep held up an umbrella. 'Hello,' she said. 'I hope this isn't a bad time. I just called to say welcome – I'm the house owner, Nell Mulcahy. You met my mother yesterday.'

Vernon introduced himself and led her into the kitchen, where Marian offered tea, which she declined, telling them she'd just had some.

'I'm sorry I didn't get to meet you all yesterday,' she said, perching on the edge of a chair, pushing her hair back from her face, 'but we had a sudden death here – the man next door, in fact, my neighbour.' Her smile dimmed as she pressed her lips together. 'So we were all a bit shaken up, as you can imagine.'

They murmured their sympathies, and after a minute or so of more stilted conversation she left, promising to look in again in a few days, and reminding them that they had her mobile phone number if anything arose.

Vernon walked her back to the front door. 'If there's anything we can do to help,' he said, 'you will let us know, won't you?'

She looked at him gratefully. 'You're so kind . . . but everyone is rallying around. That's the beauty of living here, it's like a big family.' She turned to look at the house next door, her smile fading again. 'Walter didn't have a family of his own. He lived alone, but everyone knew him. He was . . . very popular.'

Her eyes filled with tears. Vernon pulled his handkerchief from his trouser pocket and offered it, but she waved it away, all apologies, and walked quickly towards her car, brushing at her face, not bothering to unfurl her umbrella.

As she drove off Vernon closed the red front door gently. Thank God Marian hadn't mentioned the ants.

'Hi,' the blonde woman in the blue dress said. 'I'm looking for Gavin Connolly. I was told I'd find him in the African savannah.'

'You've found him.'

She was pretty and lightly tanned, and the neckline of her dress revealed interesting curves. The two small boys with her had twin heads of red hair. They reminded Gavin of the freckly children that used to be photographed sitting on donkeys for Irish postcards.

'I have your book.' The woman rummaged in the green bag that was slung over her shoulder.

'My book?'

'From Roone.' She pulled it out. 'I found it down the sofa. We stayed in the same house.'

Gavin peered at the book he'd already replaced, and finished reading, more than a week ago. 'Thanks a lot. I hope this wasn't out of your way.'

'Not at all – we live just down the road in Collins Court.'

There was a scatter of tiny dark freckles on her nose. Her hair, piled on her head, looked as if it was just about to fall down.

'I'm Laura,' she said.

* * *

He found Nell standing by the wire mesh of the hen run, staring at the hens which were wandering about, pecking nonchalantly at the ground. She wore a blue raincoat he hadn't seen before. She held a basket of pale brown eggs.

'Tim said I'd find you here.'

She turned and gave him a bleak smile. 'There you are. How's Andy?'

'He's OK. He's inside with Tim and your mother. He wanted to come.'

'Poor thing.'

They were silent, watching the activity within the hen run. The rain that had been falling since early morning had lightened to a soft mist. James felt it settling on his head.

'How was the barbecue?' she asked eventually.

'Fine. The usual.'

'I hope Laura enjoyed it. I should have gone, just to say goodbye.'

'She wasn't there,' he told her.

She glanced at him. 'Oh. I assumed she'd be going with you.'

James didn't reply. A large brown hen made a sudden sideways lunge at a smaller white one, causing a flurry of squawking and a flapping of feathers, over as soon as it had started.

'Daft,' James said. 'No sense.'

'Are you meeting her again?'

He turned and regarded her mildly. 'Why do you ask?'

She flushed, looked away. 'Sorry. None of my

business.' She twined her fingers through the mesh. 'Forget it.'

James watched her for a few seconds. 'Andy's going to paint the henhouse,' he told her then.

'The henhouse?' She frowned at it. 'Why?'

'He'd offered to do it. That's why he called round yesterday. He says he still wants to.'

'Oh . . .'

He wanted to tell her about the conversation he and Andy had had the previous night, but she was in no mood to hear it. He squeezed her shoulder. 'Come on in,' he said softly, 'you'll dissolve.'

Her lashes were beaded with rain, or maybe tears. 'I'll be in in a minute,' she said, turning back to the hens.

'Did you know that chimpanzees build nests?' Gavin asked. 'In trees, just like birds.'

The twins regarded the enclosure.

'I don't see no nest.'

'Me too.'

'They don't do it here because they don't need to, but in the wild, that's what they do. And another thing: if you smile at a chimpanzee and show your teeth, it'll think you're scared.'

'Why?'

'Because that's what *they* do. They show their teeth when they're frightened.'

They watched a chimp scampering across the grass. Ben grimaced, displaying a row of tiny teeth. 'Like this?'

'Yes, but he wasn't looking.'

'What's he's name?' Seamus asked.

'Ginger. He's two.'

'We're five.'

'Yeah, but we're nearly six.'

'An' our mum is twenty-five.'

'And once again,' their mum said, 'she's very sorry she told you that.'

She didn't seem sorry. She looked younger than twenty-five. They talked about the island as they walked from one enclosure to another.

'I fell in the sea. I was getting out of a boat and I missed my footing.'

'Good Lord. I sang in Fitz's pub. And I told Nell I'm going to sing at her wedding.'

'You're a singer?'

'Amateur – but we loved Roone. I'm just looking for an excuse to go back.'

'I'm opening a zoo there,' he said. 'That was the plan anyway, on my last night. After several beers.'

'Oh, brilliant idea. We'll come and visit.'

'Fine.'

'And I presume you met Walter next door, complete with donkey.'

'Oh, yes, we had some interesting conversations. And sometimes Walter joined us.'

He liked to hear her laugh. She was easy to talk to. Her eyes were green. There was a small gap between her front teeth. Her smile came often, dimpling her left cheek. There was no mention of a partner. She wasn't wearing a ring.

Pity they hadn't been on Roone at the same time.

'This was great,' she said, as he walked with them to the gates. 'Thanks so much. I sing in Naughton's on Friday nights, at the back of the Four Courts. You must drop in some time.'

He'd never heard of Naughton's. He lived miles from the Four Courts. It would take two buses and at least an hour to get there. 'Will do,' he said.

'Nell,' he said. 'This is a nice—'

'I'm afraid I have bad news,' she said. 'I don't know whether you saw it in the paper.'

He hadn't bought one yet, too busy packing his things and moving into the house. The keys had been handed over this morning, a day before he'd expected them.

He sat on the bed he had yet to spend a night in. 'What is it?'

She told him. He bowed his head, closed his eyes. 'Ah, God,' he said. 'Walter.'

The seconds passed. She didn't speak.

'The funeral?' he asked eventually.

'Tomorrow, eleven o'clock from the house.'

'Right,' he said. 'Right. Thank you, love. Thank you for telling me.'

There was a pause. 'Will you come?' she asked.

'Yes,' he said quickly. 'I'll be there.'

'OK. See you then.'

Her voice disappeared. Denis dropped his phone on the bed and put his head into his hands.

Walter Thompson, suddenly gone. Walter, whom he'd known all his life. Eight or nine years between them, too much of a gap to be close growing up, but nothing at all as adults. Walter tipping his hat to Denis on the road, stopping to congratulate him on his new baby daughter, when it must have reminded him so cruelly of his own awful tragedy, just a few years previously. Walter waving from his vegetable garden any time Denis walked past, calling to Nell with a bottle of wine the day she'd become his neighbour, staying to help her hang curtains. Walter coming down the steps of the mobile library every Monday, clutching his bundle of books. Walter visiting the Church of Ireland cemetery each week without fail, standing by the headstone of his wife and child, head bent, hat pressed to his chest.

Walter, whom he might never have seen again but who at least should still be alive so that the possibility existed.

Walter being brought to the cemetery tomorrow, accompanied on his final journey by probably the whole island. And Denis would be there, whatever reception awaited him, whatever stares and nudges his presence would provoke.

After a long time he got to his feet and lifted his suitcase on to the bed, and began to unzip it.

'You OK?' Tim asked.

The question sent a jolt of irritation through her. Of course she wasn't OK. Walter was dead and her father was gone. But none of it was Tim's fault. She mustn't take it out on him. 'Not really,' she said. 'Sorry, I know I haven't been much company this weekend.'

He reached for her hand. 'Don't be daft.'

She turned away from him and watched as a small green car flashed by, sending a spray of water from its tyres. Shame about the weather – rain nearly the whole day. Her new tenants weren't having much luck so far. She remembered Seamus and Ben cycling with Laura in the sunshine, Gavin getting badly sunburnt.

'He's coming to the funeral tomorrow,' she said.

'Who?'

'My father.'

'Your *father* is coming here? Did he ring you?'

'No, I rang him.'

'When?'

Another twinge of annoyance. What did it matter when she'd rung? 'At Walter's, when I was out collecting the eggs.'

'You never said.'

She sighed. 'Well, I'm saying now.'

'Have I done something?' he asked. 'Are you annoyed with me?'

'No.' She turned back to him. 'I'm not annoyed. I'm just . . . fed up, and sad, and . . . lonely. It's not always about you.' In less than five months, if they got that far, he was taking her for better or worse. Let him have a bit of the worse now, see how he coped.

'Drive carefully,' she said. 'See you next weekend. I'll be in better form then.' She opened the car door and let herself out. She walked into the house, not looking back to wave goodbye. No kiss, no wave.

'So tomorrow,' Marian said, 'if the weather is still bad, I vote we get the ferry to Dingle for lunch. We could do the holy well on the way.'

Imelda went on chopping carrots.

'What do you think?'

'Hmm? Oh, fine, yes, that sounds fine.'

They heard the front door opening and closing softly.

'He's back at last,' Marian said. 'Vernon!'

The kitchen door opened. 'Hello, ladies. All well here?'

'What kept you? I thought you were just going to the village and back. You must have been gone an hour.'

'I dropped in for a drink,' he said, sitting and easing off his wet shoes. 'Nice little pub. The owner is an uncle of our landlady. I got a drink on the house.'

'Well for some,' Marian said, sweeping chopped onions into the pan, 'and us stuck here slaving over your dinner.'

He threw Imelda a guilty smile. 'Oh dear – I'll be happy to bring you both back there later.'

'In that rain? No, thanks. We'll see what's on telly.'

Imelda would have liked to go for a drink. She didn't often get the opportunity in Westport, her friends more interested in dinner parties than pubs. She would have liked a gin and tonic or two, the chance to be in the company of happy holiday-makers for a few hours.

But Marian wasn't interested in going out, which meant Vernon wouldn't be going anywhere either, and Imelda had never had the courage to walk into a pub on her own.

She wouldn't have minded going for a drink with the man from the beach this morning. Hugh, his name was. They'd only got as far as first names. Imelda and Hugh.

She'd have said yes if he'd asked; she'd have hugged it to herself all the way home. She was sorry she'd turned down the lift he'd offered: he might have asked her out if she'd let him drive her back. But shyness had overtaken her, and she'd told him she didn't mind the rain, not at all – she loved walking in it.

He'd wanted her to take his umbrella but she'd laughed and said she was wet enough already, it wouldn't make any difference. She should have taken it: she'd have had a reason to see him again. Stupid. She never thought things through.

They hadn't shaken hands on parting. Imelda had lifted hers in a wave as she'd moved off. It might have embarrassed him, shaking hands. He'd have had to use his left.

'Imelda, have you those carrots?'

'Nearly,' she said, chopping.

★　★　★

She was staying in Nell's house. 'My wife and her sister,' the man had said this afternoon, eager for a chat. 'We arrived yesterday from Westport, staying for a fortnight.' He hadn't mentioned the women's names, but it had to be her.

He'd never met anyone called Imelda before. He'd look out for her on the street, although she'd hardly be looking out for him. Backing away when he'd offered her the lift home, saying she liked the rain. What else had he expected?

Imelda. Her smile was warm, and she was here for a fortnight. He'd keep an eye out for her all the same.

Driving back to Dublin, a hard knot inside him caused his speedometer to tip slightly above the limit for most of the journey. He drove with his face set, hooting at drivers who slowed him down, ignoring the toll booth operator's greeting as he tossed coins at her, gunning the accelerator impatiently while the barrier was being raised.

He trekked across the country every Friday without fail, drove for almost four hours after a week of work, so tired sometimes he had to have both front windows fully open just to keep awake. And for what? To sleep in his brother's tiny spare room in a bed that gave him backache, and to see Nell whenever she could spare the time.

It's not all about you. Her remark repeated itself at intervals in his head, enraging him further. It bloody well *was* all about him, or it should be, when the weekend was all they had and he made such an effort to spend it with her.

And fair enough, this had been a lousy weekend, with Walter dying and her father doing a runner, but, Christ, none of that was *his* fault, was it? And hadn't he sat dutifully in Walter's house for more than two hours on Saturday night, doing his best to talk to people he hardly knew, with Nell not giving a damn that he'd booked a restaurant in Dingle for dinner, not bothering to tell him they weren't going until he'd turned up to collect her and her mother?

'We're going to Walter's,' she'd said. 'You'll come, won't you?' Expecting him not to mind, even though he hadn't eaten since lunchtime. And hardly acknowledging the flowers he'd brought on Friday for her mother – which, fair enough, were no great shakes, from the forecourt of the garage outside Dingle, but bloody hell, he'd *brought* them, hadn't he? Wasn't it the thought that was supposed to count?

'You should bring flowers,' his mother had told him, 'spend some time with Moira, show Nell that you're the caring sort,' and he'd done all that, and in return Nell had as good as ignored him all weekend, practically shoved him back on the road to Dublin as if she couldn't wait to get rid of him.

He sped through the outskirts of the city, accelerating at orange lights, narrowly avoiding a cyclist on an unlit bicycle at one intersection. Serve the fool right if he'd run him over.

He made his way through the city streets, the lights and bustle and pulse of them reaching out to him, as always. When he finally parked and switched the engine off, his hands were stiff from being clamped on the wheel, his calf muscles aching as if he'd run a marathon.

He'd tell her his news, ridiculous to be holding it from her. It was *good* news, and she had a right to know, as his future wife. He'd tell her next weekend, face to face. She'd be in better form by then: she'd said so herself.

He took his jacket from the passenger seat and pulled out his phone and saw *one missed call*.

He switched it off. The mood he was in, better not risk talking to her tonight.

Nell
Your father walked out – I can't believe it, you poor thing. I wish there was some way I could help, other than scribbling on a silly postcard. My thoughts are with you, if that's any comfort – and I hope Tim is being suitably supportive of you and your mum. Won't be long till you're back in your own house, which might help too. Look after yourself, Nell – or make sure Tim does.

My news is that Liam and I have split up. To be honest, I was trying to feel something I didn't, no hearts broken. I think he felt the same.
K xxx

Nell slipped Katy's postcard back into its envelope. Another relationship ended, not that she had approved of Katy going back to a man she'd caught cheating on her. At least she didn't have that worry with Tim.

She climbed the stairs to the salon. No work today, no reason to come here, but she wanted to be by herself for a while. She needed to sit quietly and think, and this was as good a place as any.

She walked through the salon and into the little room she'd lived in for a few weeks, till things had started to go wrong. Till Tim had moved out and gone to James's house. That had been the start of it, discovering that he wasn't prepared to put up with a bit of discomfort to be with her. Telling herself it didn't matter when it did.

Things had been alright between them up to then, hadn't they? She sat on the windowsill and tried to cast her mind back, but it was hard to pinpoint when her anxieties had begun. Surely they'd been fine up to the time they'd moved out of her – their – house. Well, as fine as they could be, with Tim gone all week.

Maybe that was all that was wrong. Maybe the problem was that he simply wasn't around enough, that they weren't spending enough time together. Could that be it? Would she look back after they were married and wonder why she'd been so worried? Would she laugh at the idea of all this tossing and turning things over in her head, all this agonising about her future? She hoped so.

She turned her head to look out the window. The village street was quiet, not yet nine o'clock on a drizzly Monday morning. Lelia's was closed, the blinds drawn for Walter. Nothing much open till after the funeral, when normal life would have to resume on Roone without him.

She thought of the funeral, thought of meeting her father again. Her mother hadn't asked if she'd phoned him. She dreaded the encounter, so soon after his departure. Too soon to know what to say, face to face.

Maybe she'd go out in *Jupiter* when it was all over. She hadn't been out in two weeks. She could call round to James's and get John Silver – she hadn't seen him in a while either. Maybe James would come, if he wasn't working, or Andy.

She took her phone from her pocket and tried Tim for the second time that morning – he'd surely be at work by now – but his phone went straight to voicemail again. 'It's me,' she said. 'Hope you got back OK. The funeral this morning – I'm dreading it. Give me a call later if you get a chance.'

They hadn't had much time to themselves at the weekend. Next time would be better. They'd go out to dinner, just the two of them, have a proper chat. Maybe take a hotel room for the night in Dingle, why not? Reconnect, in every way.

And then the following weekend they'd be at home, and everything would be fine. She slipped her phone back into her pocket and turned to look out at the street again.

As she emerged with her newspaper from the shop at the petrol station – the only place that seemed to be open this morning – Imelda became aware, as she pushed open her umbrella, of something approaching from the other end of the street. She glanced around – and stopped dead.

Coming towards her, not fifty yards away, was a funeral procession. At its head a coffin was being borne on men's shoulders, and in its wake a mass of people stretched back as far as she could see, taking up the width of the road as they walked slowly and silently past the closed shops.

She took a step backwards as the procession drew nearer. She made the sign of the cross as the coffin was carried past, remembering their land-lady's incipient tears as she told them about her neighbour's death – and there was Nell walking behind the coffin, linking arms with her mother, a man on their far side holding an umbrella over them.

A man whose right arm ended at his elbow, his jacket sleeve folded back on itself. Imelda stood and watched him walking slowly with the others, no more than ten feet from her. He looked straight ahead, no glance in her direction.

It took at least ten minutes for the crowd to pass, eerie in its complete silence, the only sound the steady fall of hundreds of pairs of shoes on the wet ground. Imelda turned to watch the last of the mourners as they disappeared round a bend. Surely most of the island's population must have been there.

She stood unmoving until all sound of their measured progress had completely faded. Then she turned and walked up the street, passing the shuttered windows of Fitz's bar on her right.

'So how are you?' he asked.

He looked thinner, which was silly. You couldn't look thinner in a week. He wore a shirt Nell hadn't seen before, white with navy stripes so thin they could have been drawn on with a biro. He'd cut himself shaving, a tiny dot of dried blood just below his bottom lip.

'I'm OK,' she told him, although that wasn't at all what she'd planned to say the first time they met. Lying in bed on the nights following his departure, she'd rehearsed her angry words to him. She'd been all set to demand an explanation, to tell him how shattered her mother had been, to force him to see how badly he'd hurt them both.

But that was before Walter's death had turned everything the wrong way around, causing her to come face to face with her father long before she'd thought it would happen – only to discover that her anger with him had vanished somewhere along the way.

Maybe Walter had had something to do with it. Maybe his death had reminded her how little time any of them might have, and how sad it would be to waste any of it in being angry. Maybe that was why she felt no bitterness towards her father now.

They stood together as the mourners trooped from the cemetery. She hadn't spotted him until the funeral was almost over, as Walter was being lowered carefully into the ground, as the grave-diggers were preparing to throw the symbolic handfuls of earth on top of the coffin. Unable to watch, Nell had looked away – and there he'd been, standing some distance apart from the rest of the crowd. Their eyes had met for an instant before someone had moved and blocked her view of him.

He and her mother had come face to face briefly, after the minister had given the final blessing and everyone had begun to make their way to the gates. Denis had approached them then, and Moira had nodded stiffly at him before turning to Nell. 'I'll see you back at Walter's,' she'd said, and off she'd gone with Hugh, who'd lifted a hand briefly to Denis but said nothing. Nell caught a few curious glances as people passed. A few saluted her father, and he murmured a greeting in return.

They stood waiting for people to empty out of the cemetery. Her father held his big black umbrella over both of them.

'So how are you?' he asked, when most of the crowd had gone.

'I'm OK. How are you?'

'I'm alright.'

'Are you still in the B&B?'

'No – I moved into the house yesterday.'

'How is it?'

'It's not too bad,' he said, giving a half-smile that left his face quickly.

'And you got another job.'

'I did, in Tralee.'

The rain pattered on to his umbrella. It occurred to her that he didn't look happy, not in the least.

'Are you with the other woman?' she asked quietly, dreading his answer but wanting to know.

'No,' he said quickly. 'I mean, I'm living alone, but we meet now and again.'

She could hear the grave-diggers behind her, shovelling earth into Walter's grave. She heard the clods hitting the coffin with a dull thud. 'Is she married?'

He hesitated. Nell regretted the question – what did it matter, after all? 'Forget it,' she said.

'Nell,' he said, 'it's not straightforward.'

She turned her face up, looked at the gulls wheeling in the sky. 'But you're not coming back,' she said.

'No, love,' he answered. 'I'm not coming back.'

'Hi,' she said, walking into the kitchen from the patio. 'Are you home alone?'

Andy flipped his laptop closed. 'Yeah. Dad's gone to work.'

Nell bent to stroke John Silver.

'You want tea, or coffee?'

'No, thanks – had my fill at Walter's.' She looked up at him. 'How're you doing, lovey?'

'OK.'

'I like your hair,' she said. 'Whoever cut it did a fine job.'

He smiled. 'Even my dad likes it now.'

'He'd better.' She took a seat opposite him. 'He tells me you're going to paint the henhouse.'

'I promised him,' he answered, smile gone, a faint colour rising in his face.

'I think that's a real good thing to do,' she said. 'No less than I'd expect from you.' She got to her feet again. 'Now that the rain's stopped, I'm taking *Jupiter* out for an hour with this fellow – want to join us?'

'Yeah,' he said. 'OK.'

The three of them set off. He was fourteen, and already he'd had two close encounters with death. He was taller than her by several inches, but he was still little more than a child. The least she could do was make sure he had a bit of fun. They could both do with it.

'Race you to the pier,' she said, breaking into a run.

Nell,

Guess who – your favourite tenant and her two sons. They're fast asleep so I'm sending off a few quick emails. Sorry we never got to say goodbye, didn't fancy the barbecue after all, the boys were worn out from all the cycling and swimming we did on Friday, trying to squeeze as much in as we could before heading back to dirty old Dublin.

Hope all's well on Roone, thanks so much for the use of your lovely house, we had the best two weeks. Hope you're bearing up, after what happened. Give my love to Walter, we called round on Saturday morning to say goodbye but there was no sign of him. Tell him we'll be back for more honey when my jar runs out – the boys can't get enough of it on their toast.

Presume your mum told you I found Gavin's book. We called to the zoo yesterday and met him. You never said he was the image of Sean Penn – well, with a few more freckles, of course – and so nice. Insisted on giving us a guided tour, took us everywhere, the lads were tickled pink. I told him about singing in Naughton's on Friday night – he says he'll come. Watch this space.

Give James a hug. Poor old James.

Laura x

'It's me,' he said.

'I know it's you. Your name came up.' Pause. 'That was a joke.'

'I know . . . So how did today go?'

'Sad,' she said, 'much as expected. Dad came and I talked to him.'

'How was that?'

'Sad too. He looks . . . a bit lost. But at least we spoke.'

'Yes . . . And afterwards? You went back to Walter's?'

'For an hour or so. This afternoon Andy and I went out in *Jupiter*. We fished. Andy caught a bicycle wheel.'

He laughed softly. 'A good day's work.'

'How's your day going?'

'The usual.' Another pause. 'Where are you?'

'In my room.'

'In bed?'

'No . . . I'm on the internet. I got an email from Laura. She doesn't know about Walter. I'd better tell her.'

'I suppose . . . Well, I'll let you get back to it. Talk tomorrow.'

'OK.'

After she'd hung up, she realised she'd forgotten to suggest booking a hotel room for next Saturday night. But maybe that wasn't such a good idea. Maybe she'd feel bad leaving her mother on her own when she didn't have to.

Then again, her mother would be on her own in less than a fortnight, when Nell and Tim reclaimed the house and moved back in. Would she feel Nell's father's absence more acutely then, when she was living by herself for the first time since it had happened?

And did Nell and Tim really need a hotel room, now that the six weeks were practically over? No, she'd forget that idea. They'd go out to dinner, just the two of them. That would do.

She began a reply to Laura, but halfway through her first sentence she stopped and deleted it. She was too weary, the words weren't coming out right. She switched off her computer and began to undress.

Watch this space, Laura had said, when she was talking about Gavin. Poor old James, she'd said. She hadn't gone to the barbecue with him, the day after he'd been due to call round to her on his way home from work. Nell remembered all Laura's plans – candles, music, the boys in bed. What had happened? Looked like Nell would never know, with James giving nothing away.

But it didn't sound like there were any plans for them to meet up again. Maybe it was for the best. Maybe Gavin was more Laura's type. Wouldn't it be funny if they got together, her two lots of tenants? Who said love stories didn't begin on Roone, in Nell Mulcahy's house?

She reached under the pillow for her pyjamas.

It felt strange, being there when Mr Thompson wasn't, when there was no chance of him walking out from the house with a glass of apple juice, like Andy knew he would have done if he was still around. Or maybe he'd have brought out a new book for Andy to borrow, and they'd have talked about it.

He still had the three books he'd already been

lent. He knew it was alright to keep them, because Mr Thompson had told him he could, the last time they'd spoken, but since Saturday Andy hadn't been able to go near them. He would, though. He knew now that things got easier in time.

He dipped his brush into the paint, trying to remember his father's instructions. Don't overload your brush; start at the top and work your way down; paint with the grain of the wood. Keep an eye out for drips; catch them before they can dry. He'd never painted anything before, and he didn't imagine he was very good, but once he got going, he found he quite enjoyed the rhythm of it.

The hens had eyed him without much interest when he'd arrived, keeping their distance as he'd unfolded the plastic sheet his father had given him, but wandering closer once he paid them no attention. He'd had a quick look into the henhouse before beginning to paint, but there were no eggs to be seen. Someone must have collected them already.

As he completed the second wall of the building, a little over an hour after he'd begun, a phrase popped all at once into his head. He heard it as clearly as if someone had uttered it into his ear.

Many moons ago, or thereabouts, you went away.

He stopped, straightened up. He repeated it aloud, his voice startling in the silence. A hen skittered away from him. He laid down his paintbrush and wiped his hands on his father's overalls and took his phone from his rucksack, which sat on the ground some distance away. He opened up a text box and typed the words.

He read them over. He set the phone on top of his rucksack and stood immobile for a few seconds before returning to his painting. Less than a minute later he dropped his brush for the second time and lifted his phone, and again typed a short burst.

By the time he finished painting, another hour or so later, his phone was covered with white daubs. He packed up his bits and pieces, folded the sheet and stored everything in his rucksack.

He regarded the newly painted henhouse, but his mind was somewhere else altogether. His mind was remembering Mr Thompson telling him that a poem would write itself when it was ready.

Marian pushed open the supermarket door and stepped inside. The woman behind the counter looked up from her magazine.

'Brightening up today,' Marian said, propping her umbrella by the bundle of wire baskets. 'I'm looking for something for a corn.'

'Round that corner, top shelf, right behind the beans.'

'I'm crippled,' Marian went on, making her way around the aisle. 'The side of my small toe. Tiny little thing, but the pain out of it.'

'I get them on my soles. And a verruca once, I'll never forget it.'

Marian re-emerged. 'An uncle of mine had gout. His big toe swelled up like an elephant's. He was never right after it.' She approached the counter with her packet of corn plasters.

'You should see my grandmother's bunions,' the shop assistant said. 'She can't get a shoe to fit her.'

'There's no bunions in my family, but there's ingrown toenails,' Marian said. 'My father was a martyr to them all his life.'

'And athlete's foot, that's another thing.'

'Oh God, that's desperate. I saw an ad for that once – I was nearly sick over the magazine.'

There was a small, satisfied pause.

'Where you staying?' the assistant asked.

'Nell Mulcahy's house.'

'Oh yes, I know Nell. She has the hair salon, you probably know that.'

'No, I didn't.'

The woman rang up the corn plasters on the till. 'She's good, and not too dear. Two forty-four, that'll be.'

Marian counted out the money. 'I might get a wash and set while I'm here so.'

'You should, when you're on your holidays. Especially if the rain comes back.' She gave Marian her change. 'You'll be in again.'

'I will, I'm sure. Good luck now.'

'What kept you?' Vernon asked, as she climbed into the car.

'She was an awful talker, going on about her

523

corns and her grandmother's bunions. I couldn't get away.'

Just outside the village they followed the sign for the island's main sandy beach, less than half a mile away. Vernon parked and began to unload the boot.

'Wouldn't you think Imelda would have come with us instead of going off on her own like that? Can you manage?'

'I can,' he replied, tottering under the weight of the two baskets, which between them contained Nell Mulcahy's tartan rug, a large bottle of sparkling water and two mugs, Marian's book and three magazines, a tube of factor-thirty sun cream, their swimsuits and Marian's rubber hat, Vernon's newspaper and sudoku book, two towels, a packet of hand wipes, two tinfoil-wrapped ham and tomato sandwiches on granary bread, Nell's flask, filled with milky tea, and the remains of Moira Mulcahy's fruit cake, cut into fingers.

They began their short trek down the lane that led to the beach.

Lovely again today, after all the rain yesterday. If they even got every second day fine, Imelda would be happy. All you could expect really, with an Irish summer.

She walked rapidly past fields that today looked very green and fresh. She waved at a flock of sheep, and they stared back at her. She smiled at other walkers, tourists mostly by the look of them, and they returned her smile. Everyone happy, everyone enjoying being on holidays.

She wore her favourite green top. She thought green suited her, or this shade at least. She'd washed her hair in the shower after breakfast and blow-dried it carefully. She'd waited until she was away from the house before putting on lipstick. Not wanting Marian to question it, afraid her face would give her away.

She felt her heart skipping a beat every time she remembered where she was going. Ridiculous, at fifty-three, to be still hoping – and this was someone she'd met for half an hour on a beach, who didn't even live in her locality, who lived miles away. Everything about it was wrong. Talk about wishful thinking.

She imagined Marian's reaction if she discovered that her sister was off chasing a man she barely knew. She pictured Marian's face if she heard that. Marian wouldn't mince her words – she never did. She'd have plenty to say.

Imelda reached the lane and saw no sign of his car. As she negotiated the sloping path, the sound of the sea grew louder. She smelt the brine in the air, she thought she felt spray on her skin. Not rain, surely, no sign of rain in the sky.

He probably wouldn't be here. In all likelihood he wouldn't. He hardly spent his day sitting on a beach, and his car wasn't there. She reached the final bend and stopped, her heart thumping. She took her little mirror from her pocket and checked her face. Lord above – but it would have to do.

She turned on to the beach and scanned the narrow length of it. At the far end she saw two children skimming stones into the water, watched by a couple sitting on a blanket behind them. Nobody else.

She lowered herself on to the stones, hugging her knees. She'd sit awhile. She liked it here even if he didn't show. She listened to the soft lapping of the water on the stones, the rattle as they dragged away, the children's high-pitched voices, the screech of gulls as they wheeled in the sky. She should have brought her togs – ages since she'd been for a swim.

She sat for well over an hour, until she had to leave if she wanted to be in time to meet Marian and Vernon for a drink before dinner.

He didn't come. There was no sign of him.

'You missed it,' Marian said. 'We had a lovely swim, didn't we?'

'Well, more of a doggy paddle in my case,' Vernon said, steering the car out of Nell's driveway. 'I couldn't keep up with this mermaid here.'

'Listen to him, and me barely able to do two lengths in the pool at home without collapsing. But it's a lovely beach, and the water was really clean, wasn't it?'

'It certainly was.'

'Oh, and do you know what I was told in the

shop?' Marian went on, turning in her seat to look at Imelda. 'Our landlady is the local hairdresser. I had to say we'd go to her, and I really don't need a cut, or even a trim.'

'I'll go,' Imelda said. 'I'll get a wash and blow-dry or something. I'd like that.'

'Would you? Are you sure you wouldn't mind?'

Imelda smiled. 'I'm sure.' She was on holidays, and she was determined to enjoy it. She wasn't going to moon over a man she'd met for half an hour, however much they'd hit it off. 'We must look out for her salon,' she said as they approached the village.

'Here's the pub anyway,' Vernon said, pointing. 'And look, isn't that a hair salon, right next door?'

'Won't feel it now,' Hugh said, setting a grapefruit juice in front of her, 'till you're back home again.'

'No, not long. Hope Mam will be OK on her own when I go.'

'She will, of course.' He wiped the counter in front of her. 'How did you find your father yesterday?'

She shook the glass and the ice cubes rattled. 'He was quiet. He's got a new job in a school in Tralee, don't know if you knew that. He's renting a house. On his own.'

'Is that so.' Hugh dropped the empty bottle into the bin behind him. 'Speaking of renting, I met the man who's staying in your house. He called in here on Sunday.'

'Vernon,' she said. 'He's here with his wife and sister-in-law.'

'So he told me.' He straightened a stack of beer-mats. 'You've met the women, I suppose.'

'Just for a few minutes. They seem nice.'

'You won't feel it,' he said again. 'Things'll be back to normal soon.'

She looked up at him. 'Will they?'

Just then the pub door opened, and two women walked in.

Nell turned. 'Hello,' she said. 'We were just talking about you.'

Imelda felt the blood rushing to her face. The sight of him behind the counter, so unexpected. Looking as surprised to see her as she was to see him.

'No Vernon?' Nell was asking.

'He's parking,' Marian replied. 'He'll be in in a minute.'

'My uncle Hugh,' Nell said, 'and this is Marian, and her sister Imelda.'

He raised his good arm in greeting to them. 'Welcome to Roone,' he said. Letting on not to have met her before. She dared to look directly at him, and discovered him to be looking right back.

'What'll it be?' he was asking. 'Nell's treat, least she can do.'

They laughed. Imelda was glad of the joke, giving her a chance to regain her composure.

'A white wine, please,' Marian said, 'seeing as how we're on holidays.'

'And yourself?' Holding her gaze, looking, it felt, right inside her head.

'Gin and tonic,' she said. 'Lemon, no ice. Thank you.'

Her hair was a show, whipped up by the breeze on her way back from the pebble beach, all her blow-drying wasted. She hadn't bothered to comb it out when she'd got back to the house, the possibility of a chance meeting not occurring to her. Typical.

Her cheeks felt hot. Her green top was too warm for the pub, her back damp already. Her lipstick was probably all worn off by now too.

He placed the drinks in front of them. 'Happy holidays, ladies.'

His smile was lovely. His eyes were brown and warm. 'Have a seat,' he said, 'if you don't mind the stools.'

Imelda knew that Marian would have preferred to sit at a table – to tell the truth, she didn't care for bar stools herself – but they clambered up beside Nell, just as Vernon appeared.

They stayed almost an hour, long enough to order, and pay for, a second round. Nell excused herself after twenty minutes or so, telling them she was due at her mother's for dinner. Hugh left them to attend to customers now and again, but always returned to their section of the counter immediately afterwards.

His disability didn't seem to bother him. He opened bottles, measured spirits and pulled pints effortlessly. Every so often Imelda caught him glancing her way. Thankfully, neither Vernon nor Marian seemed to notice.

The second gin and tonic floated around pleasantly in her head. She listened to Hugh and Vernon discussing an upcoming hurling quarter-final match. His accent was hard to pin down, not quite Kerry, the vowels more rounded, and Nell spoke in just the same way. Not an accent she'd heard anywhere else.

Roone, she felt, was unique in many ways. She was so glad she'd come.

'Imelda,' Marian said.

She turned. The three of them were looking at her.

'Sorry, what was that?' She thought she caught a smile out of the corner of her eye. She felt an urge to wink at him, and resisted it with great difficulty.

'I said, are you ready? My tongue is hanging out for something to eat.'

She climbed down from the stool as gracefully as she could manage, an image of Mrs Shine's face flashing again for a second into her head. Shoulders *back*, chest *out*.

'We'll see you again,' he was saying, his glance taking them all in.

'To be sure,' Vernon replied.

Imelda smiled at him. He smiled back.

'Enjoy your dinner,' he said.

To her, only to her.

★　　★　　★

530

It was finished. There was no more to do. After the hours spent typing in Mr Thompson's attic, after all the words he'd written to her, the right ones had come along at last. Here was what he really wanted to say. He pressed *save* and called the file 'Mum's poem'. He scrolled to the top and read it slowly from the beginning.

Many moons ago
Or thereabouts
You went away.
Are you OK?
Or is your hair a little grey
Or thereabouts?
And by the way
I think about you every day
Or thereabouts.
Do you remember too?
Do you get blue?
All these years between
What have you done?
Where have you been?
I don't even know
Your whereabouts.
And did I say
I think about you every day
Or thereabouts?

Finished. What did they call it in America? Closure.

And was it only a coincidence, he wondered, that it had come to him, that the perfect words had come to him all in a gush, while he'd been working in Mr Thompson's garden?

He shut down the laptop and went out to see if his dad needed help with the dinner. He must learn how to cook stuff properly. He hardly knew anything.

Nell
I can't believe it. Walter, lovely old Walter? I'm in shock. I'm so, so sorry. That gorgeous kind gentleman. I must confess I shed a little tear when I read your email, and offered up a prayer, not that Walter needs it. So sad. Who's going to look after the chickens, and that sweet little donkey? Who's going to tend the bees? I suppose someone will take it all over.

I'll tell Gavin when — sorry, if — he turns up at Naughton's on Friday. I don't know how I'll tell the boys, or if I should say anything. He was so nice to them.

Such a tragedy. I do hope you're OK, Nell, I know how fond of him you were. Make sure that fiancé of yours looks after you. Tell him he'll have me to answer to if he doesn't.
Laura xx

The salon door opened as Nell was just about to begin her last cut of the day, on Molly Garvin's grey head. 'Excuse me a sec,' she said, dropping her scissors on the ledge beneath the mirror and walking across.

'Hi there,' she said. 'Nothing's wrong, I hope?'

'Nothing at all,' Imelda replied. 'I just wanted to make an appointment. I thought you might give me a bit of colour and a trim. Whenever you have time.'

'No problem at all.' Nell flicked to the next page of her appointments book. 'I could take you tomorrow at twelve.'

Imelda hesitated. 'Maybe a bit later; we might be going out to lunch. What about three or four?'

'I have half three.'

'Perfect.'

Nell wrote *Imelda* under *3.30*. 'And you want a trim and a colour.'

'Yes, I thought you could brighten it up a bit. I'll leave it to you.'

Nell studied her hair. 'A chestnut rinse, I think, would be lovely. Give it a great shine too, and not all that dramatic a change, colour-wise.'

Imelda smiled. 'Sounds great.'

After she'd gone Nell returned to Molly and picked up her scissors. 'That was one of my tenants. I told you I was letting my house out for a few weeks, didn't I, to help pay for my wedding?'

'Oh, you did, I think, dear,' Molly said vaguely.

'She's here with her sister, and the sister's husband. They just arrived on Saturday, for two weeks.'

'Is that right?'

'The sister would talk for Ireland, but that lady is much quieter.'

'Really?'

It didn't matter what you said to Molly. You could divulge your deepest secrets or the juiciest gossip, safe in the knowledge that it was completely forgotten by the time Molly got to the bottom of the stairs.

Imelda walked past the door of Fitz's, still closed at half past eleven in the morning. He probably opened at twelve. She'd go in tomorrow, after Nell had cut and coloured her hair. She'd take her courage in both hands and push open the door and walk in. It would be late enough for the lunch-time crowds to have gone home and early enough for the night-time drinkers not to have arrived. It should be quiet. He shouldn't be busy.

She'd sit up at the counter and order a Diet Coke – not an alcoholic drink when she was on her own: that might put him off. She'd do her best to be good company, not to show any sign of nervousness, not to look as if she was trying too hard. She'd smile, but not too much. She'd listen when he spoke; she'd be interested in what he had to say.

She'd be open to meeting up again. If he suggested anything she'd accept. She walked on, picturing herself sitting on a high stool in her chestnut rinse.

'How did you find Nell and her mother?'

His mother had come straight to lunch from the

hairdresser's. Her hair, cut in a neat short bob, gleamed softly in the muted restaurant lighting, every strand lying exactly where it should. In sixty-four years she had never coloured it, and it was only in the last few months that he'd noticed the first scatter of pale grey among the dark brown.

'They weren't too bad on Friday,' he told her. 'I had dinner with them at Moira's, and we just sat in for the night. Neither of them felt like going to the barbecue, which was fine by me.'

'Oh, pity, though,' his mother said. 'It might have done them good.'

Tim shook salt on to his potato gratin. 'Well, anyway, the next day her neighbour dropped dead – or rather, he died on Friday night but wasn't discovered until Saturday.' He decided not to tell her that Andy had made the discovery. Nothing to be gained by passing on that particular piece of information.

'How awful. You must have known him.'

'I did, a bit. Nice man, widower, lived on his own. Nell said he was just gone seventy.'

'Dear.' Colette laid her knife and fork side by side on her plate. 'That's too bad, coming so soon after Denis walking out.'

'Yeah – not the best of weekends.' Tim chased the last petit pois around his plate. 'I'm going to tell her, by the way. Next weekend.'

His mother frowned. 'Tim, are you sure that's wise?'

'Hang on – you're the one who told me I should.'

'I know, but she has a lot on her plate at the moment. Maybe you should wait, like you were saying, until you're both back in the house.'

'I've made up my mind,' he said. 'I've let it go too long. I need to tell her, see how she takes it.'

'Well, if you're sure.' His mother took a sip of water. 'I really hope she'll see it from your point of view. But what if she doesn't?'

'She will,' he said, with far more confidence than he felt.

'Now then,' James said, clinking his glass of mineral water against hers, 'here's to happier times.'

'God, I'll drink to that.' Nell split open the packet of crisps he'd just given her. 'One of my tenants came in earlier, made an appointment for tomorrow.'

'What's she like?'

'Nice, the quieter one of the two sisters. Not married, I gather.'

'I hope,' he said, 'you're not planning to match me up with her.'

Nell smiled. 'She's probably a little mature for you.' She pretended to consider. 'She might be nice for Hugh, though.'

'Stop it now,' he warned. 'Let people make up their own minds.'

She ate a crisp. 'I heard from Laura,' she said. 'She met Gavin – remember him?'

The mention of Laura's name didn't provoke any reaction that Nell could see. 'Chap that fell in the sea,' James said.

'Yes, him. Did I tell you she found a book he'd left behind?'

'You didn't.'

'Well, she delivered it to the zoo and met him.'

'Good for her. I suppose you have them married off too.'

'Well,' she said, 'stranger things have happened.' She took another crisp from the bag but didn't eat it. 'You two didn't have a row, did you?'

'What two?'

'You and Laura.'

'Not at all.'

No hint of anything left unsaid, no sign of unhappiness or regret on his face. His heart was unscathed, it would appear.

Good.

'There's a donkey in the field next door,' Marian said. 'Gave me the shock of my life when I turned around from the clothes line and saw him standing there, staring over at me.'

'Must have belonged to the man who died,' Vernon remarked. 'Wonder what'll become of him now. "Run after tea for a small remainder", five letters.'

'Give over,' Marian said, refilling her mug from the teapot. 'You know I can't do those things.'

'"Trace",' Imelda offered, and Vernon wrote it in, while Marian stuck a toast finger into her boiled egg and ignored them until it was time to clear up the breakfast dishes and get ready to visit the prehistoric remains. Followed, if the weather held, by a picnic lunch at the lookout point Nell had told them about.

'You want toast?' James asked, slotting a slice of bread into the toaster.

'No thanks.' Andy took his empty cereal bowl and dropped it into the sink. 'If you leave the dishes I'll wash them when I get back.'

This was a recent development, offering to do the washing-up without being asked. It was accompanied by offering to help prepare the dinner. James was enjoying his new and improved son.

'Great,' he said, although he was free himself that morning, with plenty of time for washing up. 'So you're off to Mr Thompson's.'

'Yeah, me this morning and Hugh this afternoon.'

'Good.'

Andy had been put on the rota of people who were tending Walter's place each day until more permanent arrangements could be made. They fed the hens and watered the donkey, collected the eggs, checked that nothing was amiss in the house. An honesty box had been put in place by the back door so that Walter's former customers who wished to do so could continue to avail themselves of his eggs and produce.

A retired postal worker from the village, himself a keen gardener, had offered to keep things going in the vegetable garden for the time being. A beekeeper from the far side of the island was going to take over the two hives. Bit by bit, Walter's loose ends were being tidied up.

After Andy had left, James finished his toast and walked out to the patio. The day was fine, but the forecast was for more rain spreading from the east, travelling from the mainland across the sea to Roone. Before breakfast James had set out his painting paraphernalia, and now he took a photo from the patio table and studied it.

Walter's smiling face looked out at him. James had taken the picture two days before Walter's death, at the dinner party he had hosted on Wednesday night.

He was sitting at the kitchen table, Laura on his right side and Andy on his left. In front of him was a blue and white willow-pattern bowl that held the remains of his bread-and-butter pudding. He wore a white shirt and dark green bow tie; his cheeks were lightly flushed, his hair was a little tousled. He looked happy.

James taped the photo to the side of the stepladder, just below the new canvas. He squeezed a blob of yellow ochre on to his palette, dipped his brush into white spirit and proceeded to cover the canvas with an ochre wash.

'I've taken up ballet,' Imelda said. 'Imagine, at my age. Marian thinks I'm daft, and I'm no good at it, but I love it. I always dreamt of being a dancer. I'm the oldest in the class by a mile – all the others are in their late teens or early twenties – but it doesn't bother me.'

She was lovely, once she relaxed and forgot to be shy.

'I took it up last year,' she said, 'after my father died. I'd been taking care of him up to then, and working as well, so I didn't really have much spare time. I didn't mind. I was happy to look after him, poor thing.'

Her manner was gentle, her voice soft. She had a habit of pressing a finger into her cheek as she spoke.

'My ballet teacher, Mrs Shine, is seventy-two and holds herself as straight as a ruler. She used to be a dancer – she lived in Paris for years. She's tiny, barely five foot, and moves like a cat. I love to watch her hands when she talks.'

She had beautiful porcelain skin, the kind that flushed easily. She wore no makeup apart from a slick of beige-pink lipstick. A mesh of lines travelled out from the corners of her eyes when she smiled.

'We've been to the lookout point for lunch,' she said. 'That view is marvellous. Vernon took lots of photos, but I wonder if they'll do it justice— Oh, thank you, no sugar, yes, just a little milk, that's perfect.'

She wore a pale blue dress that gathered at the waist and fell to just below her knee, and cream sandals. Her toenails had been painted pink.

'I have to confess I was in two minds about this

holiday,' she said, flushing a little as she caught Nell's eye in the mirror. 'I was very touched to be asked, of course – I just wasn't at all sure we'd cope with living under the same roof for two weeks. But so far it's been lovely. We're all getting on very well.'

Her hips were wide, her figure solid rather than heavy. Her posture was good, perhaps thanks to Mrs Shine. Her mid-brown hair didn't look as if it had ever been coloured.

'I've taken a few walks,' she said. 'Marian isn't really a walker, she's prone to corns, so I've gone alone. I found a lovely little pebbly beach the other morning, a bit tricky to get to but worth the effort. I could have stayed longer, but the rain came.'

. . . 'Oh, I do like what you've done,' she said. 'You've shaped it very nicely, and there's such a lovely shine from it now. I just hope I'll be able to make it look like this at home when I wash it.'

. . . 'Thank you so much,' she said, pressing a five-euro note into Nell's hand. 'No doubt we'll see you around while we're here. Do call in for a cuppa any time you're passing.'

She closed the salon door quietly and Nell listened to her footsteps going down the stairs. Not married, definitely.

Perfect for Hugh, if only he knew it.

He wasn't there. By the time Imelda realised that a different man stood behind the counter, she was already halfway to the bar, and couldn't very well turn around and leave.

'Hello,' he said. Younger, darker. Good cheekbones, blue eyes. 'What can I get you?'

'I'm looking for –' she couldn't say Hugh '– I was to meet someone here, my sister, but maybe I got the time wrong.'

'She might be a bit late,' he said. 'You could wait a while.'

Imelda looked uncertainly about. 'Well . . .' She couldn't stay. All the optimism and anticipation she'd felt as she'd come down from the salon was seeping away from her now. 'I'll probably meet her on the way – I mean, on her way. Thank you,' she added, turning for the door.

Silly idea, running after him. Just as well he hadn't been there.

She left the pub and walked quickly out of the village and back towards Nell's house, the breeze from the sea lifting her new haircut, the scent from the colour Nell had used – or maybe from the conditioner she'd put in afterwards – wafting across her face every so often.

By the time she could see the house her feet were aching, the cream sandals not really suitable for walking, but they looked better with the dress than her others. Listen to her, dressing up for nothing at all.

She passed the house next door, where the man had died. The little grey donkey stood in the neighbouring field, his head coming over the wooden fence that bordered the road. He looked at Imelda as she approached. She crossed the grassy verge and lifted a hand to stroke his long nose. 'Hello,' she murmured. 'You must be lonely.' He stood silently, accepting her caress. 'You must miss your owner.'

She became aware of someone in the field coming towards her. She looked up.

'I was afraid you were trying to kidnap him,' he said, as he drew near. 'I had to stop you.'

He wore a grey shirt, rolled to the elbows, and a pair of blue jeans. He carried a basket of eggs. Imelda felt her insides dissolve at the sight of him.

'Here,' he said, lifting an egg from the basket and offering it to her. 'I'll give you this if you promise to leave the donkey.'

Imelda laughed. Her face felt as if it was on fire. She took the egg, which felt warm and had a small downy feather stuck to it. 'Thank you,' she said, her heart hammering. 'I suppose it will have to do instead.'

'Your hair is nice,' he said. 'Have you been to Nell?'

The compliment warmed her through. 'Yes.' She wouldn't mention calling into the bar afterwards. 'You've a day off,' she said instead.

'No, I'm on duty this evening,' he told her. 'I'm just helping out here – a few of us are keeping things ticking over until it gets sorted.'

She thought of the funeral, of the island population coming together to bury one of its own. She

liked the idea of living in such a close-knit community, where people looked out for one another, and
came together in times of grief.

'I might take a run over to that little beach in
the morning,' he went on, 'if the weather's any
way decent.'

Was he inviting her to join him? Imelda had
no idea. But her hair was newly cut and she
had only eight full days left on the island, and
if she couldn't take a chance at fifty-three she
never would.

'I liked it there,' she said, the blood flying around
her body. 'I was thinking of going back some time
myself.'

He smiled. 'I'll keep you a place so,' he said.
'Front row.'

You could call it a date, if you were looking to
put a name on it. Or if it wasn't a date, it was the
closest she'd come to one in a very long time.

It would do her fine.

'It's me.'

'Hi, you,' she said.

'What are you up to?'

'Just washed up after dinner. There's a film on
TV in a while. You?'

'Just finishing up at work.'

'Tim, it's nearly eight.'

'I know . . . How's Moira?'

'She's alright.'

Pause.

'Imelda came into the salon today, one of the people in our house.'

'Yeah?'

'Oh, and Andy painted Walter's henhouse.'

'He painted the henhouse? When?'

'Tuesday, I think. He'd already promised Walter.'

'Yeah, but the man is dead.'

Another pause.

'Sorry,' he said. 'It just seems a bit weird, that's all.'

'. . . So, any plans for this evening?'

'Nope, dinner and a few beers when I get home, that's about it.'

'I thought we might go to the Clipper on Saturday night,' she said. 'Just the two of us.'

'That'd be nice. Will you book it?'

'I will.'

'Thanks, love . . . I'll see you tomorrow anyway.'

'Bye.'

Hugh poured too many pints, or not enough. He gave someone gin instead of vodka. He undercharged, or forgot to charge at all, or gave the wrong change. He stared into space, humming, as customers waved ten-euro notes at him.

'You're miles away,' he heard all evening.

He wasn't miles away. He was half a mile down the road.

'How's the house?' she asked.

'It's grand,' he told her. 'It has what I need.'

'Is it out the country, or are you in the town?'

'It's about twelve miles from Tralee, very quiet. The owner is my nearest neighbour, about three miles across the fields.'

'And you don't mind being that isolated?'

'Not really.'

She didn't like the thought of him living alone in the middle of nowhere, eating his meals by himself, going for solitary walks and coming back to an empty house. And, much as she resented the existence of the woman who'd taken him away from them, it was some odd consolation that at least he had her, now and again.

'How are things with you?' he asked. 'You alright?'

'I'm sad after Walter,' she told him. And I miss you, she added silently.

'You'll have Tim tomorrow night,' he said. 'That'll be good.'

Nell gathered the hem of her T-shirt between her fingers. 'Dad,' she said.

'Yes, love?'

'I'm feeling a bit unsure,' she said.

'About Tim?'

'Yes.'

She heard his breath, pictured him pursing his lips as he considered what to say.

'Nell,' he said after a long pause, 'I could never regret my marriage because it brought you, but . . . I can see now that I did your mother a disservice. I should have left her free to meet someone

546

better, someone who deserved her more than I did.'

Nell digested this in silence. 'You mean,' she said then, 'you didn't love her?'

Another long interval. She wondered if she should have asked him such an intimate question.

'Not the way she deserved,' he replied at last. 'You have to be true to yourself, my dear. Look into your heart and see what it tells you.'

Her eyes filled with tears. She blinked hard. 'You're right.'

Tim, who'd held her in the night, who'd lain beside her on countless nights, who'd whispered all the things she'd wanted to hear. Who'd given her a beautiful diamond ring and asked her to spend the rest of her life with him.

'Don't do anything in haste,' her father said. 'Think about it carefully. And talk it over with your mother. She's very wise.'

Nell scrubbed a sleeve across her face. 'I've kind of spoken with her already . . . She's said much the same as you're saying.'

'Just be sure,' he said. 'You need to be so sure.'

Nell watched a little spider travelling along the floor by the skirting-board. Hurrying to wherever it was going. She heard her mother's voice calling up the stairs.

'I have to go,' she said. 'I'll call you tomorrow. Take care.'

'Look after yourself, love,' he said. 'Be good to yourself.'

She hung up, blew her nose and wiped her eyes and left the room.

Marian stared. 'You're never going out in this. You'll be soaked.'

Imelda belted her raincoat. 'I just had a look outside. It sounds a lot heavier than it is. The walks here are so nice and I want to take full advantage while I have the chance.'

'You'll ruin your new hair.'

'Not at all, I'll bring my brolly. I'll be fine.'

She didn't like walking with an umbrella, didn't like not being able to swing her arms, but she had no intention of turning up at the beach with her hair hanging around her head in wet ropes.

'You didn't even have breakfast.'

'I did – I had yogurt.'

She'd been too keyed up to manage more than a few mouthfuls. Pity about her, she'd have a big lunch to make up.

'I'll be off so,' she said. 'I'll see you when I get back. Head out if you want, if it clears. Leave the key under the stone.'

'It hasn't a hope of clearing before lunchtime. Ring Vernon if you want him to come and get you,' Marian said. 'Make sure you do now, it's no trouble.'

'Thanks.'

She hadn't a notion of ringing Vernon. If the heavens opened on the way to the beach, if she was in imminent danger of being swept out to sea, she wouldn't ring Vernon.

548

It wasn't too bad, she decided, making her way along the now familiar road. It was heavyish, but not a total downpour. And it had to lighten up soon – hadn't she heard it raining for most of the night, when she was unable to sleep with thoughts of this morning? It couldn't keep going like this for much longer.

But in the twenty-five minutes or so it took her to reach the turn for the beach, the rain continued to fall steadily, dripping from the hedges on either side of her, pooling in muddy puddles wherever the road dipped. Despite her umbrella, Imelda's raincoat was soon patched with damp, and her grey trousers clung unpleasantly to her calves when the wind pushed them from behind. Her hair was still dry, just about.

She rounded the last bend, and there was the lane ahead of her. His car was nowhere in sight.

She stopped. Of course his car wasn't there. It was raining. It was pelting down. He'd said if the weather was decent, and nobody in his or her right mind could call this weather decent.

She made to turn around, and stopped again. She'd got this far; she'd go down to the beach anyway. Shame to come all the way and not spend a few minutes there at least. She'd have a long hot bath when she got home and a cup of tea, and maybe go back to bed for a few hours, try to catch up on the sleep she'd missed during the night.

She made her way down the lane, water plopping in big drops from the overhanging branches on to her umbrella. She needed her head examined, traipsing around in this weather. Serve her right if she got a cold out of it, if she spent the second week of their holidays coughing and sneezing. Her socks were wet, she could feel it. Oh, what had possessed her?

She slithered on the wet stones, barely managing to keep her balance and hang on to the umbrella. If anyone saw her. If Mrs Shine saw her, looking more like a goose than a swan.

She reached the end of the lane and walked as steadily as she could on to the beach.

'You took your time,' he said.

She stared at him. He stood about a foot from the water's edge, under the same big black umbrella he'd had the first time she'd met him there.

She said the first thing that came into her head: 'Where's your car?'

'At home, with a flat tyre.'

Imelda burst out laughing, pure delight fizzing through her. He'd walked to the beach to meet her in the pouring rain. He was as mad as she was.

'I fail to see the joke,' he said, grinning back at her. 'Look at the cut of you,' he said, his eyes crinkling with merriment.

Nell's phone rang as she was walking downstairs. She looked at the screen and saw *Helen*.

'Hi,' she said. 'Great timing. I'm just on my way to lunch.'

'I won't keep you,' her cousin replied. 'I'm calling to remind you that I'll be over next week to try on all the bridesmaid's dresses you've picked out.'

Nell stopped at the bottom of the stairs and sat. 'Helen, I'm not sure—' She broke off, unable to get to the end of the sentence.

'Not sure of what? Can't decide on dresses? That's why I'm coming over. I thought if I arrived on Saturday we'd have Sunday and Monday – presume places are open on Sunday, are they?'

'Some would be, in the afternoon . . .' Nell rubbed her face, thinking quickly. 'Look, I don't know how to say this but, well, things are a bit . . .' She trailed off again.

'What? Nell, what's up? Is there something wrong?'

'I don't know . . . I'm in a bit of a heap, to be honest.' She took a deep breath. 'Helen, I'm not sure that I'm doing the right thing.'

'Oh, Lord . . . Well, look, I'm coming anyway because my ticket's booked. I'm flying into Kerry airport around noon, and I know you'll be at work but I thought maybe your dad could collect me.'

Nell closed her eyes. Don't go into all that now, don't hit her with two bombshells. 'Text me your details,' she said, 'and you'll be picked up.'

'Nell, don't fret,' Helen said. 'We'll have a chat and you can tell me everything. If you knew how many of my friends had pre-wedding jitters – it happens all the time.'

'Maybe.'

'And your house is let, isn't it? That can't be helping.'

'No, it's not.'

'Look, don't worry,' Helen said. 'You have plenty of time till December to sort everything out.'

'You're right.'

After she'd hung up Nell sat on the stairs, feeling somewhat comforted. Pre-wedding jitters, it happened all the time.

Eventually she got up and went out to get a roll from Lelia.

He left it until after ten to go to Naughton's. He took off his blue shirt and put on a green one. A minute later he changed into a T-shirt. It would probably be warm in the pub. He took off the T-shirt and sprayed deodorant under his arms and pulled it on again.

It *was* warm in the pub. It was hot. Gavin pushed his way to the bar and asked for a bottle of cider and a glass of ice. He took his drink and walked the length of the long, narrow room – and there was Laura at the end, sitting on a high stool in front of a red-brick wall, singing 'It's Not Easy Being Green'.

Her voice was sweet and brave. It reminded him of Joni Mitchell. He stood at the periphery of the assembled crowd and watched her.

She wore a short-sleeved white top and jeans, her hair tumbling on to her shoulders. In between songs she laughed and joked with the customers, some of whom called up requests. Occasionally she drank from a pint glass of water that stood on a low table beside her stool.

Gavin couldn't tell if she knew he was there. At one stage he thought she smiled at him, but he wasn't sure until she said, at the end of a song, 'Break time – back in ten.' She laid her guitar across the stool and made her way directly towards him.

'You came.' She fanned herself with her fingers. 'Boy, it's hot.' Her cheeks were pink. A few strands of damp hair clung to the sides of her face.

'Can I get you a drink?' he asked – but just then one of the barmen appeared and handed her a glass of white wine.

'Thanks, Paul.' She winked at Gavin. 'I have him well trained.'

'You're very good,' he told her. 'Your voice is great.'

'I know,' she said, and laughed. She lifted her glass and laid it against each of her cheeks in turn. 'Phew, it's hot. Listen,' she went on, her smile fading, 'I have to tell you about Walter.'

Gavin was shocked and saddened. Roone had often strayed into his thoughts since coming home, the island and its inhabitants seeming to have lodged somewhere within him, and Walter's features were still clear in his mind. He remembered the poor man's look of horror when he'd caught sight of Gavin's yogurt-covered face. He wondered who was looking after the little donkey.

'Sorry,' Laura said, 'I didn't mean to put a damper on your Friday night, but I thought I should mention it.'

'No, that's fine . . . Who's got your kids tonight?'

'Susan, my stepmother and best pal. I promised her I'd be home at midnight.'

'Like Cinderella,' he said.

'Exactly like Cinderella, apart from the glass slipper and the ugly sisters and the fairy godmother. I *do* have the stepmother, but like I said, she's not at all wicked.'

He was intrigued by her. She was unexpected, like a present that had arrived out of the blue. She'd been to Roone, arriving on the day he'd left. They'd probably passed each other on the way. They'd stayed in the same house. He'd left a book behind and she'd found it, and then she'd found him.

He wondered whether to take the chance. What the hell? All she could say was no.

'How about dinner some time?' he asked.

She grinned. 'How about tomorrow night?'

They were fine. He loved her and she loved him. He'd chosen her over all the women he could have had in Dublin. Doubts were natural, everyone had them. Look at him, tilting his head towards her mother as she spoke to him, in that adorable way he had. Her mother loved him; both her parents did.

And the way they'd met, the serendipitous way

they'd come together on Roone, all the blips of Fate that had led up to it. Karen's death, leading to James's move to the island, which had resulted in him and Nell becoming friends, drawn as she'd been to the lost soul he was then, wanting to help him and Andy.

And her and Tim knowing each other slightly already, having encountered one another in Dublin, so that when they'd come face to face again on Roone she'd looked at Tim, frowning, and said, 'Don't I remember you?' at the exact same moment as he'd said, 'I know your face.'

They were destined for each other. They had to be. All those stepping stones that had led them towards one another couldn't be wrong.

When they moved back into the house next weekend she'd take her dress down from the attic and try it on again, first chance she got. She'd go to Dingle on Monday morning and do the rounds of the boutiques, and pick out dresses for Helen to try on when she came. She might go to Listowel too, some good boutiques there.

And she must get back to trying out cake recipes. She fancied a really rich chocolate one, maybe with a liqueur in it. Or ginger, that would be different, chocolate and ginger. And poppy seeds, she loved them. She could make up her own recipe, experiment with flavours.

'I've booked a table at the Clipper for tomorrow night,' she told him, as he was leaving for James's. 'Seven o'clock.'

'Great . . . I have some news,' he said. 'I'll tell you then.'

They stood beside his car, the day's rain finished at last. She searched his face, but it gave nothing away.

'What kind of news?'

'Good news. You'll just have to wait and see.'

She leant into his chest. 'You're such a tease.'

She felt the ripple of his laughter. 'I am, aren't I?' He ran his fingers lightly up her spine. 'A week,' he said, 'and we'll be home again.'

'I know.'

'Was it worth it?' he asked. 'Moving out for six weeks.'

'Of course,' she answered lightly. 'I've bought the dress, the reception's half paid for, I've put the deposit on the honeymoon, and there's enough left over for Helen's outfit and a new bed. The rest, I'm afraid, is up to you.'

'No problem.' He dropped a kiss on her head. 'I'll let you get to sleep and see you for lunch.'

After he'd driven off she went inside. Her mother was making tea. 'He seems in good form,' Moira said.

'He is,' Nell replied. 'We're going out to dinner tomorrow night. Do you mind?'

'Of course I don't mind.'

'You could ask Hugh over, if he's not working.'

'Nell,' her mother said, dropping teabags into the pot, 'I'm not incapable of being on my own.'

'I know, sorry.'

'This is the way it is now. I have to get used to it.'

'Do you miss him?' The question was out before Nell could stop it.

Her mother looked at her. 'What a question,' she said calmly. 'Of course I do.'

Don't get your hopes up. He knows you're here on holidays: he's not thinking long term.

Imelda lay in bed listening to the faint sound of the television from the sitting room. Vernon liked it so loud; he should get his hearing tested. Amazing it didn't bother Marian; maybe her ears needed checking too. Funny the things you discovered about people when you lived with them.

Imelda wasn't much of a one for television. She liked period dramas, but forgot more often than not to check the schedule so she usually missed more episodes than she saw. It didn't bother her; she'd always preferred a book.

Hugh liked reading too. 'Detective stories,' he'd told her. 'The body in the library. Sherlock Holmes, Hercule Poirot. And biographies, I like those. I'm reading one on Leonardo da Vinci right now.'

He described the mobile library, which Imelda found charming. A lorry of books arriving every Monday, crossing the sea for the readers of Roone.

Hugh had been to Rome in his twenties. 'I remember the Trevi Fountain,' he'd said, and Imelda recalled how transfixed she'd been at her first sight of it, how she'd stood gazing at Neptune in his shell chariot as tourists all around her were tossing coins and taking photos.

He was fifty-one, two years younger than her. His mother had died when he was in his twenties, and he'd stayed in the family home with his father until the sea had claimed Will Fitzpatrick, fifteen years ago.

He'd never been married. He had no children. She wondered if he'd ever fallen in love.

He'd walked back with her to Nell's house. They'd both been wet through, after half an hour of walking and talking on the beach. A few cars had hooted as they'd driven past. A couple had slowed, but Hugh had waved them on. Imelda thought they must be wondering what the local publican was doing out walking in the rain with an unknown woman.

'We might have a bit of lunch some day,' he'd said, as Nell's house had come into view, 'if you'd like. I could juggle my time off to suit you.'

A bit of lunch. He'd juggle his time off to suit her. She'd said Monday, three days away, so she wouldn't look too keen – and as soon as she'd said it, she wished she'd said tomorrow. Two days of not seeing him, out of the seven they had left.

'But I'll probably see you before that,' he'd said. 'You might drop into the bar again,' and she'd agreed that they probably would.

'Tell you what,' he'd said, 'I'll bring a picnic to the beach on Monday, if the day is good. Otherwise we could have something in the village.'

As they approached the house she dreaded Marian or Vernon happening to look out. Imelda would say they'd met by chance, she'd make nothing of it. But Marian would still want all the details; she'd start quizzing Imelda about him, and Imelda couldn't bear that.

Much to her relief, they were spared. Nobody emerged from the house, no curtain twitched. They arranged to meet at the beach at one on Monday, or if the day was wet, in Lelia's. He didn't ask for Imelda's phone number, and she didn't offer it.

'Well,' he said, 'it was nice meeting you again. And it was a good job we got the sun, or we'd both be soaked by now.'

Imelda laughed, her raincoat damp and heavy, her shoes sodden, her trousers saturated. Her hair, despite her best efforts, stuck to her head.

'See you soon,' he said, moving off. 'I'm on duty the next two afternoons and evenings, if you're passing.'

Marian, of course, had had plenty to say when Imelda walked in.

'*Look* at the state of you, why didn't you ring? Vernon would have gone, only we hadn't a clue which way. I should have sent him out anyway – he'd probably have found you. You'll be lucky if you don't get pneumonia.'

Imelda had let her fuss for a few minutes, and then she'd escaped to run a bath. She'd peeled off her wet clothes and got in, replaying their conversation in her head as the rain had continued to slap against the window.

After lunch they took the ferry to the mainland and drove up the Dingle peninsula to Tralee, where Imelda and Marian deposited Vernon in a café with a crossword while they explored the boutiques. Marian tried on, and rejected, two navy blouses and a pair of black trousers. Imelda bought a cream skirt and a top the colour of toffee that she thought toned in nicely with her new hair colour.

They had dinner in a small family-run restaurant – Marian's duck was tough, the custard on her apple tart not warm enough – before making their way back to Roone as the daylight was beginning to fade. Imelda, weary from her lack of sleep the night before, took herself off to bed while the other two opted for the sitting room and television, with Vernon being allowed a small whiskey after his alcohol-free day.

Don't get your hopes up, Imelda told herself, lying in the single bed nearest to the window in Nell Mulcahy's spare room. Pretending that her hopes hadn't already floated sky-high.

Nell pushed open the pub door and made her way to the counter. At just after six there was a small buzz, locals dropping in after work, tourists beginning their evening out with a drink before dinner.

A woman sat on Nell's usual corner stool, talking to Hugh who was behind the bar. She turned at

Nell's approach, and flushed slightly as she recognised her.

'Hi,' Nell said, glancing around. 'Are the others here?'

'No,' Imelda told her. 'I'm on my way home from a walk, and I felt thirsty.'

'What'll it be?' Hugh asked.

'Fizzy water,' she told him, pulling up a nearby stool. 'Tim's taking me out to dinner, so I'm not staying. Just a flying visit.'

Interesting that Imelda had come into the bar on her own. Nell wouldn't have thought she'd have the confidence. But here she was, half a glass of red wine sitting in front of her, chatting away to Hugh.

'You're getting married,' Imelda said. 'Your uncle told me. Congratulations.'

Nell remembered James warning her against matchmaking, but here they were, not needing anyone's help at all. Or maybe Nell was jumping to conclusions. Maybe there was nothing in it. Imelda might simply be quenching her thirst, like she'd said.

With wine.

'Lemon?' Hugh asked. 'Ice?'

He knew she liked lots of ice and no lemon. He'd poured fizzy water for her hundreds of times. Was he *nervous*? Could he possibly be ill at ease because Nell had happened on him and Imelda?

No – she mustn't let her imagination run away with her, as it was fond of doing. She drank her water, made small-talk, and attached no significance at all to the fact that Hugh topped up Imelda's glass without being asked, and that Imelda was looking particularly smart this evening, in a cream skirt and a top the colour of toffee that went perfectly with her chestnut rinse.

Laura pushed her fork into a scallop. 'Two nights out in a row. I'll be arrested.'

'You were working last night,' Gavin replied, 'so it doesn't count.' His beef was tough. He was sorry he hadn't ordered the scallops.

'Here,' she said, 'you have to try these, they're divine.' She tumbled two on to his plate. 'Do you love anyone enough to give them your last two scallops?'

He emptied the wine bottle into her glass. 'They're not your last two, you've got loads left.'

'Do you want me to take them back?'

He speared them both with his fork and stuffed them into his mouth. 'Too late,' he mumbled.

Her laugh rang through the little restaurant. 'That's like something the boys would do.'

She was gorgeous. She wore a green dress, whose neckline made it very difficult for him to keep his eyes on her face, and earrings with green stones that looked like real emeralds. He was smitten, and slightly drunk.

'I wonder if Nell will let me sing at her wedding,' she said, picking up her glass. 'I hope she took me seriously because I meant it. God, this wine is going down far too easily. Just as well I've got no crèche tomorrow.'

He swallowed his scallops. 'When's she getting married?'

'End of December.'

He thought of the island in the dead of winter. The rain lashing in from the Atlantic, the wind howling around the chimneys at night. The sea crashing on to rocks, boiling with foam. The roaring fires, the hot ports, the chat in Fitzpatrick's. 'Can I come too?' he asked.

'Why not? The more the merrier. Nell never actually invited me, so technically I'd be gate-crashing too. Anyway, I thought you were opening a zoo.'

'Might take a while.' He caught the eye of the wine waiter and signalled for another bottle. 'We could hang around outside the church looking hopeful,' he said.

'Bugger that – we'd freeze to death. We'll just arrive in all our finery and get them a really big present, and they'll be too embarrassed to turn us away.'

'I could bring them an elephant,' he said. 'I'm sure the zoo wouldn't even notice – they've got four.'

She smiled at Gavin. 'I'm glad you forgot your book.'

Gavin smiled back. 'Me too.'

'Come on then,' she said. 'You've kept me waiting long enough. What are we toasting?'

Tim clinked his glass lightly against hers. 'You're looking at the new partner in O'Connor Staunton Computing Solutions. From September it's going to be O'Connor Staunton Baker.'

Nell's mouth dropped open. 'What?'

He took a sip. He smiled. 'They've offered me a partnership. I've said yes. Effective from next month.'

She lowered her glass. 'Tim, that's . . . wonderful. A partnership, wow. That's great. You must be thrilled.'

'I am. It's pretty good going after just three years, don't you think?'

'It is. It's marvellous. And they don't mind you'll be relocating to the other side of the country? Will you be opening another branch over here, is that it?' Watching his face intently.

'Well,' he said, 'that's the thing. That's the only thing about it really. I won't be able to leave Dublin just yet.'

She frowned, tightening her grip on the stem of her glass. 'You won't . . .'

'Nell,' he said, reaching for her hand, 'sweetheart, please try and see the big picture. This is a fantastic plus for me, a partner at thirty-five—'

'I get that,' she said. 'Really, I do. But you have to stay in Dublin? You won't be moving down here?'

'I won't be able to straight away, no. Obviously I can't accept a partnership and then disappear across the country. You must see that.'

She tried to collect her thoughts, but they spun and bumped around in her head and wouldn't be made sense of. 'Hang on,' she said, 'let me get this straight. You're staying in Dublin after the wedding. I'll still be living here on my own, like I am now.'

His expression was half puzzled, half amused. 'Of course you won't,' he said. 'That would be crazy. You'll come to Dublin and live in the apartment with me. Or we could sell it and get a house if you prefer – we'll be able to afford it, easily. And it won't be forever, it might be as little as five years – it'll depend on what direction we decide to go with the business. And you can come back here as often as you like, that'll be up to you. You could get part-time work and have three or four days a week free – or you could set up your own hairdressing business, work from home or go to other people's houses, and that way you could organise your own holidays . . . say, one week in every six off, or something . . .'

She watched the words coming out of his mouth, but she stopped listening as soon as it became clear to her that he had it all mapped out, that whatever she said would make no difference to his plans. He had decided on their future without asking if it was what she wanted too.

He had accepted a partnership, knowing it would tie him to Dublin for several years, knowing how much she'd pined for Roone when she'd been working in the Dublin salon.

He'd thought it would be alright, that she'd pack up and move back with him, because he didn't know her at all, he had no idea. She looked at his face, at his mouth opening and closing, at the eyes she'd gazed into over so many candlelit tables. She looked down at his hand, still holding hers. She loved his hands, the broad fingers, the neatly filed nails.

She looked at the man she was not, after all, going to spend the rest of her life with, and she waited for him to finish speaking.

Imelda was what their aunt Evelyn would call 'nicely'. She kept wanting to giggle, even though nobody was saying anything in the least bit funny.

'Imelda, would you pass the salt?' Vernon asked.

Imelda snorted, and turned it into a cough. Marian looked at her curiously. 'Are you alright? I bet you're coming down with a cold after that ducking you got yesterday.'

Hilarious. Imelda lifted her water glass. 'I'm fine, just a bit thirsty.' Thirsty, with at least half a bottle of wine inside her. She should have stopped him – wine always went straight to her head – but she hadn't.

It was just so nice, sitting there chatting to him. He was so easy to talk to. He was the easiest person to talk to she'd ever met. She could have stayed there all evening, but Marian had warned her to be back for dinner at half six.

She'd walked out from the village with Nell.

Nell was lovely, and so lucky to be getting married. When they reached her mother's house, Nell had offered to drive Imelda the rest of the way – Lord, had it been obvious that she was a bit tiddly? – but Imelda had opted to walk, anxious to clear her head as much as she could before she got back.

She loved the island; she was so glad they'd come here. 'I love the island,' she said, and hiccuped gently.

Marian frowned. 'Imelda, have you by any chance been drinking?'

No point in denying it. 'I have,' Imelda confessed. 'I got thirsty when I was out walking so I dropped in for a glass of wine.'

'You went into a pub on your own?'

'I did. It's not unheard of,' she said mildly, 'for a woman to go for a drink.'

'Well, I know that, but—'

'And while I was there,' Imelda went on, 'Nell came in and insisted on standing me a second glass, and I couldn't very well refuse her.'

A little white lie that hurt nobody. You'd hardly even call it a lie. Nell would definitely have offered her a drink, she was sure, if Hugh hadn't topped up her glass first.

'Well, that's good, anyway,' Marian said, 'that you weren't sitting there on your own.'

'Oh, no,' Imelda said, stifling another giggle with difficulty. 'I wasn't on my own.'

★   ★   ★

'I'm going back to Dublin.'

James, thinking about the offer that had come his way earlier in the day – a painting job on a new house, inside and out, the works, on the far side of the island – turned to his brother at the patio door. 'Did you say something?'

'I'm going back to Dublin,' Tim repeated evenly.

'What – now?'

'Yes, now.' The words coming out too carefully, the anger simmering just below them. He turned and disappeared into the house.

James set down his beer can and got to his feet. He followed Tim through the kitchen, down the corridor and into the spare room. Tim was zipping his laptop case closed.

'Tim,' James said mildly, 'it's a quarter to ten.'

'Good – I'll make the last ferry.' Tim took his overnight bag from the floor and tossed it on to the bed. He yanked clothes from the narrow wardrobe, causing hangers to rattle, and shoved them into the bag.

'Go easy,' James said quietly. 'Andy's next door.'

Tim brushed past him, came back with a handful of toiletries and stuffed them into the bag's side pocket.

'Will you tell me what's going on?' James asked.

Tim zipped his bag closed, lifted the strap on to his shoulder.

'Look,' James said, 'don't go like this. I'm assuming you and Nell have had some kind of a falling out—'

Tim stood before him, his face white. 'We're finished.'

'What?'

'She finished with me. Wedding's off.'

'*What?*'

'I've been offered a partnership,' Tim said, 'at work. I told her this evening, and that was it.'

'Hang on, why would she—'

'Ask her,' Tim said, pushing past him again, 'since you're such good pals.'

James followed him down the corridor. 'What's that supposed to—'

'See you in Dublin some time,' Tim said, opening the front door. 'Thanks for putting me up.' He stalked to his car and flung his bag into the boot. 'No offence, but I'll be *bloody* glad not to see that spare room again.'

He got into the car and drove off, gravel spraying from under his wheels.

'What was that about?'

James turned. Andy stood at the front door in boxers and a T-shirt.

'Sorry about that – hope he didn't wake you.'

'I wasn't asleep. Where's he gone?'

'Back to Dublin.'

'He sounded mad,' Andy said.

'Yeah,' James said, turning to watch his brother's car disappearing in the direction of the ferry, 'he did.'

They'd had a row. She'd called it off. Tim was gone. James refused to let his mind move on from there. They'd make it up. They'd be back together by next weekend, when their house would become theirs again. It wasn't over. It was just a row.

'See you in the morning,' Andy said, turning away.

'Good night.' James returned to the patio, the daylight almost completely gone, and finished his beer.

'Here, you could do with this.'

Nell looked at the plate of food her mother had just placed in front of her. She wondered where it had come from, this notion that you fed a person when things went wrong. As if the full Irish would make it all better.

I can't marry you. I can't live the life you want me to live.

She picked up her fork and poked it into the fried egg, and the orange yolk oozed out. Runny yolk, firm white, just the way she liked it.

'Thanks, Mam.'

'Don't play with it,' her mother said. 'Eat it.'

She'd loved him. He'd been the first man she'd been truly in love with. The love had been there at the start. She remembered the thrill of his first kiss at the gate of her house, the first time he'd walked her home from Fitz's. The first night they'd spent together, after a dinner she'd cooked for him. Lying in his arms, afraid to fall asleep in case she was dreaming.

Can't you see? she'd asked. *Can't you understand how important this is to me?*

But he hadn't seen. He hadn't understood at all. Somewhere along the way he'd changed into someone she didn't recognise – or was she the one who had changed? Oh, she didn't know, she hadn't the smallest idea.

All night she'd sat up in bed, knowing sleep was impossible. Trying, and failing, to distract her thoughts. Giving up on her book after half a page. Writing a postcard to Katy, tearing it up. Katy had had enough bad-news postcards; she'd stop answering them if Nell sent any more. Reading and rereading crossword clues that made no sense.

It's not going to work, she'd said. *We want different things.*

His face across the table. Their dinners, uneaten. Their waiter coming over to ask if everything was alright, Tim asking him quietly for the bill. Not a word out of him in the car on the way back to Roone, no goodbye when he'd dropped her at her mother's house.

I don't want to hurt you, she'd said. *That's the last thing I want.*

But of course she'd hurt him. And the worst of it all was that she couldn't turn to the one person she wanted to talk to because he was his brother. What could she say to James? How could she involve him without putting him in an impossible position?

What had Tim said when he'd got back? What had he told James? What was he doing now?

'What are you doing after Mass?' her mother asked. 'Any plans? Because if you haven't, I thought we could go for a drive. Get the ferry across, have lunch out somewhere.'

Look at her, trying her best to help Nell when she had more than enough troubles of her own. Frying sausages for Nell, planning ways to distract her.

I'm sorry, she'd said. *I just can't do it. I'm so sorry.*

'Sorry,' Nell said. 'You need this like a hole in the head.'

Her mother stirred milk into her tea. 'I'm your mother. It's my job to look after you. Try this new marmalade, cranberry orange. It's lovely.'

And because she was trying so hard, Nell took the jar of marmalade and spread it on toast she didn't want.

It's over. I'm so sorry.

'Look at that rain,' Marian said, stirring her tea. 'Makes you want to go back to bed. I don't know why we bothered coming. Next year I'm going to Spain.'

Imelda added milk to her muesli. 'Aren't you having breakfast?'

Marian shook her head. 'Couldn't look at it. I'm not a bit hungry this morning.'

'That's not like you.'

Imelda was hungry. Imelda was starving. She'd

572

chopped a banana into her yogurt and honey, and it still hadn't been nearly enough. After the muesli she was planning a slice or two of toast.

'My stomach is upset,' Marian said. 'I might skip Mass and go back to bed for a while.'

'Do, if you feel like it.' Little enough to occupy yourself on a rainy day on Roone, unless you were a walker who didn't mind getting wet. 'It might pick up this afternoon, and we could drive to the cliffs, get a breath of fresh air.'

'That'd be nice.'

Vernon came into the kitchen, buttoning his cuffs.

'I'll let you and Imelda off to Mass,' Marian told him. 'I don't feel that good. I'm going back to bed for a while.'

He looked at her. 'Do you want me to stay with you? You wouldn't mind going on your own, would you, Imelda?'

'No, no, you go with Imelda, I just want to lie down for a while. Bring back a couple of oranges – I might have one later.'

'Will I put on the heat in the bedroom?' Imelda asked.

'No, I'll fill the hot-water bottle.'

In due course she was packed off to bed. Imelda washed up while Vernon ate his breakfast.

'Pity about the weather,' he said, spreading honey on a brown scone. 'I thought today was going to be nice.'

'It might clear up.'

Imelda didn't mind the rain so much. The more that fell today, the less likelihood there was of another wet day tomorrow. The more chance of her and Hugh Fitzpatrick sitting on the pebble beach, eating the picnic lunch he'd promised to provide.

Of course, the alternative would be fine too. She had no objection to having lunch with him in a café in the village, for all the locals to see. The rain wouldn't bother her in the least, if that was what it dictated should happen.

But already the beach, the place where she'd first laid eyes on him, had come to be important to her.

No word from Nell, and now it was half past three. He was on duty at Fitz's in half an hour, with little chance to talk if she phoned.

He couldn't be the one to call. As Tim's brother, he might be the last person she wanted to talk to right now.

He'd driven past her mother's home at eleven, on his way back from talking with the owners of the house he'd been asked to paint, but there'd been no sign of her. He'd worked on his portrait of Walter since then, thinking she might turn up, but she hadn't. And now it was time to clean himself up for work.

After Tim had left, James had pieced things together in his head. That his brother had been made a partner after just three years was impressive, certainly – but it meant, of course, that Tim would be remaining in the company, at least for the foreseeable future. And that presumably meant staying on in Dublin.

What had Tim thought? That the situation with Nell would remain unchanged after they were married, that he'd continue to commute to Roone every weekend? Or had he imagined that Nell would drop everything, give up her life here and move to Dublin to be with him?

Yes, James decided, that was what Tim would have seen happening. He'd have expected Nell to fall in with his plans, regardless of the implications for her. Tim had always been driven, had pursued his objectives with a single-mindedness that had brought him to where he was now – but consideration for others would never have been a priority.

James badly wanted to talk to her. He wanted to see her, to console her if she needed it, but as Tim's brother he felt bound to hold back, to wait until she came to him. They'd talk eventually. They had to.

And then what, though? Would she expect James to act as the go-between, to talk to Tim on her behalf, to effect some kind of reconciliation? If such a person were needed, surely James would be the obvious choice, being close to both of them.

He couldn't do it. He couldn't be the one to bring them back together. She couldn't ask him to do that.

He wiped his hands on a rag and went to have a shower.

'Tim and I aren't getting married,' she said. 'He's been made a partner in the company he works for, so he can't leave Dublin. He wants me to move to Dublin after we're married, but I can't do that. So the wedding is off.

'I know you're probably shocked to hear it. I was shocked when he told me about the partnership last night. I couldn't believe he was presenting this thing to me as a done deal, that he hadn't even thought to consider if I'd be willing to go and live in Dublin.

'The thing is, though, I'd been having doubts before all this. I wasn't sure any more that we were right for each other. I don't know how it happened, or when exactly I began to feel like that, but I knew something had changed between us.

'I was hoping that when we moved back into the house things would sort themselves out, but I can see now that was wrong. It shouldn't have mattered where we lived – that shouldn't have made a difference to how we felt about one another. The house wouldn't have helped at all.

'And last night, when I couldn't sleep and I was thinking it all out in my head, I saw that if I still loved Tim, I would have been prepared to move to Dublin. I would have been willing to leave Roone because being with him would have been the most important thing.

'So it's finished. I told him I couldn't go ahead with the wedding, and of course he argued with me and tried to persuade me to think about it, but I knew all the thinking in the world wouldn't help. I knew that we had come to the end of whatever we'd had.

'I'm sorry that I've upset him. I wouldn't have hurt him for the world. He'll always be Tim, who made me happier than I'd ever been. But I think if he truly loved me, he wouldn't have acted the way he did. He would have thought more about what was important to me. I'd have mattered more to him, if he loved me.

'It's good to talk to you. It was always good to talk to you. You were always such a good listener, and you never told me to grow up and have sense, which I'm sure you were tempted to do, lots of times. I like that I feel I can still talk to you, that you're still listening.

'And it would be wonderful,' she said, 'if you could still talk to me.'

She turned away from Walter's grave, as the rain dripped from the overhanging trees on to her bare head, and she made her way back to the road.

His mother poured gravy over his roast lamb. 'Will you have a small bit of spinach?'

'No, thanks.'

Tim's head throbbed, a combination of lack of sleep and the bottle of wine he'd drunk when he'd got back to Dublin at just after two in the morning.

Downed in less than an hour, trying to blot out his last conversation with Nell. It hadn't worked, of course. All it had done was to wake him up at six with a raging thirst and a headache.

His mother's house wasn't helping. The kitchen was uncomfortably stuffy, windows tightly closed against the rain. Not that it was much better when they were open, traffic fumes floating in from the busy road outside. He thought of the fresh island air, the wonderful briny tang on the breeze that came off the sea.

'You and Nell will make it up, of course,' his mother said. 'This is a setback, that's all. You'll find a compromise.'

His mother had been to the island a few times. She'd seen it before Tim had. She'd gone down a few weeks after James and Andy had moved in and stayed with them for a weekend. 'It's beautiful,' she'd told Tim when she got back. 'You must go and see it. The scenery is just lovely, and everyone smiles at you on the street.'

But another year and a half had passed before Tim had made it to the island. He'd brought Amy, his girlfriend of four months, and on their first day they'd visited the local pub at lunchtime because James was working there, and he'd introduced them to the girl who had cut his hair.

It was his own fault, springing the idea on Nell like that. He shouldn't have blurted it out. He should have worked up to the notion of her living in Dublin. He should have insisted she came up

578

to the city every now and again instead of him always going to Roone. Make Saturday her day off instead of Monday.

They could have gone to the theatre, or to an art exhibition, or to the bloody zoo, if that was what she wanted. There was so much choice in Dublin, so much to see and do. He could have brought her out to meet his friends again, let her get to know them. Instead he'd messed up.

He pushed his plate away. 'Sorry,' he said. 'I thought I was hungry, but my appetite is gone.'

'Tim, you have to eat something.'

But he didn't have to eat something. He didn't have to do anything except go to work and pay his bills, and think about what a fool he'd been.

'I'll take it home with me and heat it up later,' he told his mother. Easier to put it in his bin than argue with her. He watched her covering the plate with tinfoil and tried to remember if he had any Panadol in the apartment.

He'd get a couple of rolls from Lelia. No, he'd get some cooked chicken, and a bottle of wine, and some salads. And maybe a couple of rolls too, in case she didn't like chicken.

The forecast was for a wet start, clearing from the west by midday. The gods were smiling on him, pulling the rain away in time for a picnic.

She's leaving on Saturday, he told himself. In five days she'll be taking the ferry off the island

and going back to Mayo. Back to her job, back to a life that didn't have a one-armed man in it.

Let him have now, though. Let him at least have five days, or however many she chose to spend with him, for however long. Let them eat lunch together tomorrow, let him make her laugh again. Let her talk to him about the dental clinic, or her house, or her ballet, or anything that would give him pictures when she was gone, when he was remembering the time they'd had.

Peaches: he'd bring peaches for dessert. Or maybe strawberries. He bet she liked strawberries.

By teatime it was official. The off-colour feeling that Marian had had in the morning had worsened steadily into a full-blown migraine attack.

'She hasn't been sleeping as well here as at home,' Vernon said. 'She finds it too quiet. She thinks that might have triggered it, or the bit of cheese she had yesterday at lunch. There's nothing we can do but wait for it to pass.'

'Can I go in to her?' Imelda asked. 'Is she awake?'

'She is, so go on in.'

Imelda opened the bedroom door quietly and slipped inside. The room was dim, the daylight muted by the drawn curtains. The scent of Marian's lily-of-the-valley talc hung in the air. Imelda made her way to the bedside.

'Marian,' she whispered.

A low moan.

'I just wanted to come and see you for a minute.'

580

Imelda sat carefully on the edge of the bed and felt for Marian's hand and held it between her own. 'Poor you.'

She sat without talking for a while, stroking the back of her sister's hand. A single car passed by on the road outside. In the sitting room Vernon coughed. The television was silent this evening.

'Will I get a wet cloth?' Imelda whispered. 'Would that help at all?'

'No . . . just sit with me.'

Imelda remembered Marian's migraines from when they were both teenagers. The whole house hushed, the only sound the gentle ripple of the water as their father squeezed out cloths and laid them on his daughter's hot forehead in the darkness. Over the years the episodes had become infrequent, but no less intense.

It could have been the change in routine here, the different sleep patterns. It could have been the thin slice of cheese in Marian's lunchtime sandwich, the half-cup of coffee she'd drunk after dinner last evening. It could have been any number of things, impossible to tell.

'Sorry,' Marian whispered. 'Nuisance.'

'Don't be silly.'

She'd be weak in the morning. With any luck the headache would have lifted, but the echo of it would linger, sapping her energy. She'd probably want to stay in bed, at least for some of the day.

'There's soup – I could heat it up,' Imelda whispered, after another few minutes.

'Couldn't look at it.'

Vernon would be here; Imelda could leave at midday. Even if she wasn't back to her old self by then, Marian wouldn't need the two of them looking after her.

'Could you drink tea?'

'No . . . Maybe in a while.'

'Or a bit of orange?'

'No.'

The minutes ticked by. Imelda held her sister's hand. The evening moved on into night.

As Andy crossed the field with his basket of eggs, his shoes wet from the dew, his attention was caught by a sound from the neighbouring house. He turned to see a man coming out the front door with a suitcase. The man walked to the car that was parked in the driveway and stowed the suitcase in its boot. He went back inside, leaving the boot open.

A suitcase? But this was only Monday – weren't Nell's tenants supposed to stay till the weekend? In less than a minute the man reappeared with two smaller suitcases. He added them to the boot and slammed it closed and vanished again.

Andy left the eggs by Mr Thompson's back door, beside the honesty box. He walked around the side of the house and retrieved his bicycle, which was propped against the front wall.

As he cycled past Nell's house the man emerged again, his arm about the shoulders of a woman who leant against him. They crossed to the car and he held open the passenger door while she got in.

They must have had to leave early. Or maybe Andy had got it wrong, and they were supposed to go home today. He presumed Nell knew all about it. By the time he got to the end of the road he'd put them from his mind.

Vernon walked back into the house. 'Imelda? You ready?'

She came out of the kitchen holding an envelope. 'All done,' she said. 'Just let me get my bag.' She headed towards her bedroom.

Vernon opened the sitting-room door and gave a last look around. Nothing left behind, no books forgotten, no glasses lying on the coffee-table. Shame they'd had to cut short the holiday, but there'd really been no other option, Marian as limp as a wet rag this morning, wanting her own bed, her own things around her.

He didn't think Imelda would mind too much. Glad to get home probably, only here because Marian had insisted. Out walking in the rain every day, how could anyone enjoy that? And rain again today, although looking like it might clear; the forecast had been hopeful.

To tell the truth, Vernon was happy enough to be going home too. Holidays were all very well, but to be stuck on a little island in bad weather was more like an endurance test, as far as he was concerned. He'd give Cormac a call when he got home, see if he wanted a round of golf this afternoon, if Marian was well enough for him to leave her.

Imelda would be around, of course. She'd stay with Marian if he asked her. You could always depend on Imelda.

'Right.' She stood in the hall. 'I'm ready.'

Vernon locked the house and Imelda added the keys to her envelope, and sealed it. They drove into the village and he pulled up outside Nell's hairdressing salon.

'Want me to do it?'

'Not at all.'

Imelda got out of the back seat and slipped the envelope through the letter-box of the blue salon door.

She heard the little clink as it hit the floor inside. The salon still closed, at nearly eleven o'clock. Nell must open later on Mondays. As long as she got it in time, as long as Hugh got word before he left for the beach.

But maybe Nell wasn't going to open at all. Maybe Monday was her day off. He mightn't get it until tomorrow. He mightn't know that Imelda had had to go home.

She couldn't bear the thought of him waiting for her. Watching the time passing, the realisation dawning that she wasn't coming. She should have posted it through the door of the pub, should have put his name on it instead of Nell's. Too late now, nothing to be done.

She climbed back into the car, her heart like a stone in her chest. As they approached the ferry a large white van drove off, *County Kerry Mobile Library* in dark blue lettering along its side.

And as they crossed the sea the last of the rain petered out, and a shaft of sunlight broke through.

When she'd rowed out far enough Nell stowed the oars and spread her raincoat along the length of the still-damp wooden seat and stretched out on it, knees bent, head resting on a folded towel. The rain that had been falling earlier had cleared, the white sky patched now with blue, the sun coming and going as it moved across.

The boat swayed gently in the placid water. She listened to the *plunk* of the little wavelets as they bumped against the side. The sun, whenever it appeared, fell warmly on her face. Nice to have it back again, after all the rain they'd endured over the past few days.

After a few minutes she sat up and took her phone from her bag. She opened her contacts list and found James's name. She looked at it. *JB*, she'd called him.

'Makes me sound like an ice-cream company,' he'd complained, when she'd shown him. 'Fancy a JB cone? Or an oil baron. Who shot JB?'

'Kristin.'

'Who?'

'Kristin. She was his cousin, or Sue Ellen's sister, or something.'

'She shot JR. Who shot JB?'

'Was JB shot too? I hadn't heard.'

'Oh, yes. And it wasn't Kristin – she was across town. Cast-iron alibi.'

'Let me guess – shooting JR.'

'Precisely.'

Their conversations made no sense to anyone but themselves. Their thoughts often collided, running on parallel lines. She hadn't seen him since Wednesday, when he'd appeared unannounced in the salon with lunch for her, and this was Monday. They never went nearly five days without one of them getting in contact.

She'd been preoccupied. She'd been sad about Walter and her father, anxious and confused about Tim. But she'd always gone to James in the past when she'd been feeling bad, knowing that just being around him would help her to feel better.

He must have been busy too, not to have rung or called round since Wednesday. She wondered if Tim had told him what had happened. Surely he'd have confided in his brother? Even if he hadn't, he must have gone back to Dublin earlier than normal on Sunday. She couldn't see him wanting to hang around Roone.

James must have known something was up. And still no word from him.

Maybe he knew about the break-up and was angry with her – maybe he resented her finishing with his brother. The thought was awful. She remembered how bad she'd felt when she and James had fallen out over Andy's haircut.

Maybe he was waiting for her to get in touch. Maybe he felt she'd prefer to be alone, which was silly.

Or maybe he simply didn't care. Maybe he was tired of being the one she always turned to when she was in trouble.

She replaced her phone and lay back, closing her eyes against the rays of the sun and trying not to think about anything.

As usual, the beach was quiet. A man stood at the water's edge, holding by the hand a toddler in shorts and T-shirt, who squealed each time a little wave ran over its podgy bare feet. Two swimmers, gender uncertain, breast-stroked sedately side by side in the water, travelling parallel with the shore.

A disabled man crunched across the pebbles, nodding to the man with the child. He held a basket in his hand, and there was a blanket tucked under his shortened arm. He passed a pair of towels and scattered paraphernalia – bag, book, newspaper – and chose a spot further on.

He spread out the blanket and lowered himself on to it. He opened the basket and took out a bottle of red wine, which he set on the blanket, presumably to allow the sun to warm it.

He sat and watched the antics of the toddler. The two swimmers – one male, one female, sixties or seventies – emerged from the sea and began to dry themselves before manoeuvring their clothes back on.

The minutes passed. The older couple gathered their things and made their way cautiously across the pebbles, the woman's hand gripping her companion's arm, and disappeared up the lane. A few minutes later the man with the child scooped him up, causing him to break immediately into loud, indignant wails. They left the scene, the child's cries floating back to the beach's only remaining occupant.

Shortly afterwards a new group arrived. A couple in their forties, an older woman, a young girl with a baby in her arms. They assembled themselves some distance from the disabled man, spreading rugs and towels, unfurling a beach umbrella, opening a canvas chair.

The young woman took off her jeans and T-shirt to reveal a red swimsuit. She lifted the baby into her arms and took it down to the sea and stood knee deep in the water, looking out towards the horizon.

A few minutes later the disabled man replaced the bottle in his basket and bundled up his blanket and left the beach, nodding at the others as he passed.

Nell –
I do hope this finds you well, and not too sad. I thought it might cheer you up to hear

that Gavin turned up at Naughton's on Friday and invited me out to dinner, and we ended up going out the following night – and Nell, I do believe I'm a bit smitten. He's just the nicest man, didn't you think? We laugh all the time, he's such good company. I wanted to bring him home and throw him on to the bed and fling myself on top of him, but you'll be glad to hear I exercised terrific restraint and contented myself with a bloody good kiss at the Luas stop instead. He'll be back.

Now, remember I asked if you'd like me to sing at your wedding? Well, I was half joking at the time, but the more I think about it the more I really would like to. Obviously I'm not looking for payment, just an invite to the rest of the wedding – and I'm afraid it would have to include the boys, and maybe Gavin too, if he's still on the scene by then. Look how cheeky I am – but I've found a bit of cheek usually gets you what you want.

So there you have it. When you can spare the time from all your wedding preparations drop me a line back – and hug that hunky fiancé for me.
L xx
PS Walter is in my head a lot, I feel really sad when I think of him. Gavin was very sorry to hear.

James drove home from the other side of the island for lunch. He passed the pier and checked automatically for *Jupiter*, but it wasn't moored in its usual spot.

He looked out to sea and saw a yellow dot, far out in the harbour. Half a nautical mile from him, and she might as well have been on another planet.

He drove on.

Nell unlocked the salon door and let herself in. Ten to nine: time for a coffee before the first of her customers was due. She bent to retrieve the post, a single envelope this morning. She read *Nell* in unfamiliar writing on the front, and felt the weight of something inside. She brought it upstairs to the salon and slit it open – and out tumbled two keys on a ring, and another, folded, envelope.

She unfolded the envelope and saw *Hugh*. She checked the first envelope again and found a sheet of paper.

> *Dear Nell,*
> *You'll be surprised to get this. We've had to leave early, I'm afraid – my sister Marian had a bad migraine attack yesterday, and while she's over the worst of it now, she's not really in the form to stay on, so we've packed up and gone home. I was sorry to leave, I really enjoyed our stay, and I know the other two did as well, up to this. I don't feel too bad, knowing you're paid for the two weeks, but still it's a shame.*
> *All the best with your wedding, and maybe*

we'll make it back to Roone in the future.
Sincerely,
Imelda O'Brien
PS I wonder if you'd mind passing on the
enclosed to your uncle? Many thanks.

Her tenants were gone. The house was free again, five days early. She could move back today if she wanted, sleep in her own bed again tonight.

She put the keys into her bag. She brought Hugh's letter downstairs and posted it through his letter-box. She hadn't seen him since Saturday, when she'd called into the pub before going out to dinner with Tim, and found Imelda sitting at the bar, talking to him.

She wondered what was in the letter, and then decided she was too tired and sad to be curious. If James were there he'd tell her to mind her own business, and he'd be right.

She mounted the stairs again and checked her appointments diary. Just one booking for the afternoon, and hopefully Doris Keane wouldn't mind being moved to tomorrow. She couldn't face the prospect of the whole day at work, people asking her about the wedding, about the cake and the dress and the honeymoon.

She'd switch Doris, and if anyone phoned or called in looking for a cut this afternoon she'd tell them she had a dental appointment. She'd close the salon at noon and go to her house and just sit there for a while. She needed its familiarity

– she needed the comfort of it around her right now.

She closed the book and listened to her first customer's footsteps on the stairs. Coffee would have to wait.

Monday
Dear Hugh,
If I had your phone number I would have rung you, but as I don't I have to write. I'll drop this into Nell's and hopefully you'll get it this morning.

We're leaving, I'm afraid. Marian had a bad migraine last night and this morning all she wants to do is go home. I have no choice but to go with her and Vernon. She's still quite weak and I can't desert her.

I'm truly sorry. I was so looking forward to seeing you again. You are a good and genuine man, and it was lovely to cross paths with you, even if it was only for a short time.
Take care of yourself.
Yours sincerely
Imelda (O'Brien)

Hugh read it through twice. She'd left Roone. She'd gone back to Westport, her holiday cut short through circumstances beyond her control. She was truly sorry, she'd been so looking forward to seeing him again.

She'd dropped the letter into Nell's salon – not

realising, he supposed, that Nell didn't work on Mondays. She would have wanted him to get it before he left for the beach. She wouldn't have wanted him sitting there waiting for her, she wasn't like that.

But she'd included no address, no phone number, nothing for him to use if he wanted to get in touch with her again. It wasn't as if Westport was the other side of the globe: they could have stayed in contact easily, if she'd wanted.

She'd felt sorry for him. She'd befriended him because it was easy to be nice to someone you knew you were going to be leaving behind in a week or so. She might have been flattered at the thought that he was interested.

He folded up the letter and returned it to its envelope, and dropped it in the bin behind the bar counter.

Imelda flicked a duster over her mother's collection of glass animals on the side table. She didn't care for them in the least, the squirrels and hedgehogs, the foxes and owls, but Daddy had been fond of them, and she hadn't had the heart to let them go to Oxfam with his clothes and shoes.

She ran the Hoover over the carpet that didn't need it – she'd done it the day before they'd left for Roone – but what else was she to do, with no work till next week and Vernon happy to fuss over Marian, who was pretty much back to her old self anyway? What else was there to do but clean her already clean house before heading out to trail around the shops until it was time to come home and prepare another solitary dinner?

Ridiculous how lonely she'd been last night, sitting down to her meal for one, fighting back the tears as she'd peeled her single potato, enduring the piercing sadness of what might have been, if they'd been able to spend a little more time together.

Twenty-five to eleven. He wouldn't be open yet, but he might be there, restocking shelves, cleaning glasses, doing whatever needed to be done before his customers appeared. Already forgetting the woman who'd stayed in his niece's house, and who in all likelihood he'd never lay eyes on again.

She hoped he'd got her note yesterday. She'd never know if he'd gone to the beach, expecting to find her there. The not knowing was the worst thing.

She should have put her address on the note, should at least have given him the opportunity to get in touch again. But the waiting and hoping she would have had to endure then, the thought of nothing happening maybe, all of this had stopped her.

If she were still on the island she'd probably be out walking now, if the day was any way fine. It was cool and dry in Westport, probably not much different on Roone. Perfect walking weather.

Or if yesterday had gone well, she might be

meeting up with him again. They might take the ferry across to the mainland and go to lunch somewhere different, or if he was working she could sit up at the counter like she'd done before. She wouldn't care.

She unplugged the Hoover and rewound the flex. She returned it to its cubbyhole under the stairs. Twenty to eleven.

She stood in the hall, an idea unfurling and taking slow shape inside her head.

As he drove out of the village on his way back to work, he saw Moira Mulcahy walking along the side of the road with a shopping bag. He pulled over and leant across to open the passenger door. 'Moira – can I give you a lift?'

She turned her head and, as always, he was struck by her similarity to Nell. 'James, that's kind.' She got in, settling her bag on her lap, and he drove off.

'I've got a painting job on, over by the lighthouse,' he told her. 'I'm on my way back there now.'

'Is that the new house the son of the Cassidys built?'

'That's right.'

'I believe it's lovely.'

'It is, very nice.'

They approached her house and he pulled up outside. Nell's yellow Beetle was parked in the driveway, behind her mother's.

Moira made no move to get out. 'I won't keep

you,' she said, 'but I presume you know about Nell and Tim.'

'I do,' he replied. 'It's too bad.'

'Yes, but better it happened now, I suppose. Was Tim very upset?'

'He didn't say much, but I could gather he was.' James hesitated. 'How's Nell?'

Moira shook her head slowly. 'She's miserable about everything. She's putting a brave face on it but . . .' She turned to him. 'You might give her a call, James, when you get a chance. I know how fond she is of you, I'm sure she'd appreciate it.'

'I will,' he promised. *I know how fond she is of you.*

Moira opened the door and got out. 'Thanks for the lift, dear. See you soon.'

He waited until she'd gone inside before pulling out his phone and dialling Nell's number. *The number you are trying to reach is unavailable,* he was told. *Please try again later.* He drove off, passing the scatter of houses in between until he got to Nell's.

Little realising, as he drove past, that she was inside.

The fridge was still full. There was more than half a bottle of whiskey in one of the kitchen presses. They'd clearly left in a bit of a hurry. Nell walked into the sitting room and saw three fat candles on the mantelpiece, and remembered Laura's plans to seduce James.

She wandered wearily through the house, waiting for it to reclaim her. Less than six weeks ago she'd been so full of plans, delighted with her big idea to raise money for the wedding, looking forward to her first tenant moving in, wondering what he'd be like, what he'd make of the house.

She remembered moving into the little room off the salon, trying to make it as nice as she could before Tim got down from Dublin. Flowers on the windowsill, his favourite wine on the shelf, a quiche her mother had made for his dinner.

'Have it here, in this house,' Moira had said to Nell, but Nell had wanted to eat dinner with Tim in the little room, to feel that they were still in their own space, just the two of them.

How could everything have changed so utterly in a few short weeks? Walter gone, her parents living apart, Tim out of her life – and James, by the look of it, edging away too. How could it all have come to this?

She returned to the kitchen and took the bottle of whiskey from the press. She never drank it, apart from an occasional hot one in winter if the weather was particularly cruel, but one or two glasses might take the edge off her misery.

She brought the bottle and a glass into the sitting room. She found matches in the drawer under the television and lit Laura's candles and placed them on the coffee-table. Might as well go the whole hog, if she was planning to wallow.

She opened the window to air the room – for

all she knew, it could have been closed for the last five and a half weeks. She had to have open windows, had to let the sea air in. She checked that her phone was turned off. She sat on the couch and poured whiskey into the glass and brought it to her lips.

The first swallow burnt her throat and made her splutter. The second, a more cautious sip, went down slightly easier. Maybe she should have put water into it. Maybe she shouldn't be sitting alone in her house drinking neat whiskey in the middle of the afternoon. If her mother could see her . . .

But she was tired of being good, of always trying to do the right thing and make everyone happy. Today she was going to think only of herself – at least for the afternoon – and do exactly what she wanted.

By the second glass her cheeks felt warm and there was a gentle and not unpleasant buzzing in her head. She sat on the couch and sipped, and thought about redecorating. Nobody else to please now, no other taste to consider. Duck egg blue in this room, or lavender. A soft yellow in the kitchen, warmer than the cream Tim had preferred.

She wondered if she would ever get married, or if she'd live out her days alone, the object of vague pity among the islanders. 'Poor Nell,' they'd whisper. 'She nearly got married once, but it fell through. Such a shame.'

She lifted the bottle for the third time, knocking it against the glass as she poured. Her eyes were getting so heavy. Too many sleepless nights in the last few weeks. Too many tears, and not nearly enough hugs and kisses.

She set the empty glass on the table – had she finished that last one already? – and stretched out on the couch. Sleep was what she needed, sleep would help.

Within minutes she was unconscious. Time passed. The three candles flickered softly in the little breeze that came in through the open window. The net curtain fluttered, touching the wavering flame of the closest candle.

A quarter past five. James debated stopping at Fitz's for a pint before heading home. He felt like one after seven hours of painting, broken only by a quick sandwich at home. He'd put his head into the pub anyway, see if Hugh needed him later on.

He turned on to the coast road, where Nell and Moira's houses were. He'd tried calling Nell twice more during the afternoon, but her phone remained turned off. He'd call round to Moira's this evening, just drop in like he'd done before, the time Denis had walked out.

He smelt the smoke before he saw it. He scanned houses as he passed, searching for the source – and then he saw it, pouring from Nell's cottage.

Nell's cottage. The tenants.

He slammed on the brakes and got out – registering, as he ran towards the house, the smoke billowing from the sitting-room window, the open front door, through which a woman was struggling to drag something out—

Not something, somebody. He covered the last few yards.

Not somebody – Nell.

Nell. His heart froze as he realised it was Nell on the ground, being pulled by the arms.

Jesus Christ, it was *Nell*.

The woman turned as he reached her, her face smeared with black – 'Oh, thank God, I just found her, I can't—'

James crouched and gathered Nell's inert body into his arms. He took her to the front of the garden, away from the burning house.

'Nell,' he said urgently, laying her gently on the grass, 'Nell,' pressing his fingers to her faint pulse, his ear to her mouth, 'Nell,' all he could say was her name, 'Nell,' willing her to wake up, 'Nell,' his heart about to fly from his chest, 'Nell,' the world had shrunk to the patch of grass where he cradled her, 'Nell,' wiping the smears from her face, 'Nell,' was all he could say, 'Nell, Nell, Nell . . .'

And the jump his heart gave when her eyes fluttered open after an eternity, when she coughed and gasped and wheezed as more cars drew up, as people ran towards them—

'She's all right,' James said, holding her, 'she's OK.' Not wanting to let her go, stroking her hair, telling her, 'You're OK, it's me, it's James, I'm here, I've got you,' until Dr Jack arrived and took over.

He found her hand and hung on tightly as the doctor laid her flat on the grass and placed a mask over her face and held a stethoscope to her chest. He watched the colour returning slowly to her face, oblivious to the neighbours who were rushing to do what they could about the burning building behind him, which he'd completely forgotten about.

It wasn't until much later, after Nell had been taken by ambulance to a hospital in Dingle, after James had made his way home and told Andy what had happened, after they'd reheated the remains of last night's shepherd's pie, after James had phoned Nell's mother, who told him Nell was going to be fine, they were just keeping her in for observation – it wasn't until then that Andy said, holding a tea-towel while James lifted plates from steaming water, that he'd written a poem for Mum, if James wanted to read it some time.

James looked at him. 'You've written a poem?'

'Yeah.'

'I would,' James said. 'Like to read it, I mean.'

'Now?'

'Yeah.'

The poem was simple and true and very beautiful. James read it through slowly three times as Andy dried cutlery and clunked it back into the drawer.

'It's perfect.'

Andy turned, dropping the tea-towel on the empty draining-board.

'It's perfect,' James repeated. It was all he could do to keep from breaking down. His eyes burnt with tears he refused to allow. He cleared his throat.

'I'm proud of you,' he said simply. 'Mum would have been proud too.'

Andy smiled, folding his arms. Probably so his father wouldn't try anything as embarrassing as hugging him.

And that was all, but it was enough.

After Andy eventually went to bed James showered the smoke off himself and changed into clean jeans and a T-shirt. He opened the beer he'd been planning to drink five hours earlier and sat on his darkening patio. He reread his son's poem and thought about all he had to be grateful for.

Her mother looked searchingly at her as she lowered her blue bag to the floor. 'I brought you clean clothes. How're you feeling?'

'Fine. My throat's a bit scratchy, that's all. They're going to do another chest X-ray before they let me go, but they say it's just a precaution.'

Her mother shook her head. 'I still can't understand it.'

'I told you, the tenants went home early because Marian—'

'I know all that, but what on earth were you doing in your house in the middle of the day?'

'I took the afternoon off, I only had one appointment and I changed it. I just wanted to . . . spend some time in the house.'

'And how did Imelda come to be back here, after only leaving the day before?'

Nell remembered seeing her tenant sitting at the counter in Fitz's, her and Hugh talking and smiling at one another. 'I don't know . . . Where did she stay last night?'

'They booked her into the hotel. Lelia phoned to tell me.'

'Oh, good. I must call around to see her when I get home, and I must catch Henry and get him to send me the bill.'

'You'll do no such thing – I'm putting you straight to bed. You can ring them on the way.'

Nell smiled. 'I'm fine, Mam.'

'Still, we're taking no chances. Oh, and I rang the insurance company first thing. They're sending someone tomorrow to have a look.'

'Thanks.'

The fire had badly damaged the house. Despite the efforts of the islanders the sitting room and kitchen were pretty much gutted by the time the fire brigade arrived. The bedrooms, though intact, were smoke-damaged and subsequently drenched with water in an effort to contain the flames.

Some time before she'd drifted off to sleep, Nell had remembered the beautiful sea-green dress, sitting in its box in the attic. She had grieved for it, and everything it had stood for. All over, her dreams literally gone up in smoke.

'What can I do?' her mother asked. 'What do you need?'

'I'd kill for a decent coffee,' Nell told her. It wasn't true at all – she could easily wait until she got home in a few hours. But her mother wanted a mission, and a trip to the nearest coffee shop would do.

Left alone, she replayed the events of the day before, as far as she could remember them. She saw herself sitting on the couch, full of self-pity, filling up with whiskey in the hope that it would make everything go away. What had she been thinking? Since when had alcohol ever solved anything? And whiskey, of all things.

She recalled lighting the candles Laura had left. She remembered opening the sitting-room window. These actions, harmless in themselves, had combined to set her house on fire. She shuddered, imagining what might have happened next, if it hadn't been for Imelda's mysterious return.

'She was trying to get you out of the house when James arrived,' her mother had told her. 'Apparently she'd climbed in the window.'

It was hard to imagine Imelda climbing through a window. What an absurd series of events, all things considered. Nell remembered someone calling her name, over and over, and struggling to open her eyes and seeing James. She remembered her chest hurting when she coughed, which she didn't seem able to stop doing, and then Dr Jack putting a mask over her face, which had helped, and James holding her hand.

She recalled being bundled into the back of

an ambulance, lots of people running around and shouting, and the horrible, terrifying smell of burning, the air thick with black flecks. She remembered her mother arriving, her mother stumbling up the ambulance steps, crying. She remembered seeing Imelda, whose face and clothes were streaked with black and who Nell couldn't place for a while, because she wasn't supposed to be there, she was supposed to be back in Mayo. But there she was, looking at Nell in concern.

She remembered trying to find James as the ambulance doors closed, searching for his face in the crowd but there were too many people. She remembered her mother's questions in the ambulance, and her head pounding from the smoke and the whiskey, and the bustle in the hospital as they'd hurried her to X-ray—

There was a tap at the door. 'Come in,' she called, feeling the scratch in her throat.

He held flowers, a bunch of montbretia, a little bit of Roone for her bedside. He looked exhausted, his eyes shadowed, his face pale and unshaven. He crossed the room and lowered himself heavily into the chair her mother had sat in. He set the flowers on the bed.

'Thank you,' Nell said – seeing all at once what had been there all along, plain as day all of a sudden, but what had passed her by, what she'd refused to acknowledge, week after week, month after month.

She'd said yes to the wrong brother, simply because the right one hadn't asked.

James reached for her hand, lying on the sheet. 'If you ever pull a stunt like that again,' he said wearily, fishing a rather rumpled bag of pink and white marshmallows from the pocket of his jacket and placing them in the hand he held, 'we're finished.'

Nell looked into his blue eyes, bloodshot from lack of sleep.

James Baker, who loved Roone as much as she did, whom she couldn't imagine living without. James Baker, who'd brought marshmallows because her throat might be sore.

How could she have been so completely blind?

Imelda lay in her hotel bath, surrounded by bubbles, her hair tucked into a plastic shower cap. Unable to stop smiling.

Poor Marian. Such a lot to take in during a single phone call.

'You're back on *Roone*? Imelda, what on *earth* possessed you? . . . The house was on *fire*? Bless us and save us! . . . You climbed in a *window*? . . . Who was inside? . . . Lord Almighty! . . . You're staying *where*? . . . Vernon! Come here, *quickly*!'

And they'd all been so nice, all the villagers who'd gathered at Nell's ruined house, offering her a bed for the night, someone driving her to the hotel when she'd told them thank you, but she'd be staying a few days, and was there anywhere she could book into?

And the lovely proprietor – 'Please call me Henry' – taking her clothes to be dry-cleaned, telling her it was all around the island, how she'd saved Nell, bringing her a glass of brandy without being asked, wondering if she'd like her dinner upstairs.

And a tap at her door a little later, as she'd been drying her hair. Thinking it was the dinner coming, she hadn't bothered to tidy herself before opening the door.

'I thought it must be you,' he'd said, the sight of him such a surprise and so welcome after the drama of the day that Imelda had made a right fool of herself by bursting into tears. His concern, his embarrassment, as she'd wept into his handkerchief, as she'd assured him not to mind her, she was just a bit . . . overcome by everything. A right holy show she must have looked, her hair still half wet, her face blotchy, not a scrap of lipstick on as he'd led her to a chair and sat her down, and waited in another chair until she'd composed herself.

And the first thing she'd asked, stupidly, was if he'd got her note in time yesterday, and his hesitation that told her he hadn't, and she'd buried her face again, sobbing that she was so sorry, she'd thought Nell would deliver it in time—

And he'd knelt by her chair and put a hand on her shoulder and told her it didn't matter, it didn't matter at all. He'd thought she'd had a good reason, and didn't he like the beach anyway, and what harm had been done, really?

And thankfully, when she'd finally been in a fit state to have a conversation he hadn't questioned her return to the island, because that would have mortified her beyond reason. Instead he'd invited her out to dinner the following evening – 'I have to say thank you for saving my niece's life' – and he was calling for her in half an hour.

And they still had three days left.

She imagined how horrified poor Mrs Shine would have been to see her scrambling in through Nell's sitting-room window, dignity forgotten as she'd hitched up her skirt, showing her underwear in all likelihood, thank God that nice man hadn't come along until afterwards. His face familiar, but she couldn't place him. Very fond of Nell, clearly.

And thank God Nell was going to be alright. Such a lovely phone call Imelda had had from her that afternoon as she'd been out walking, full of thanks for what Imelda had done, inviting her to lunch tomorrow in Lelia's. So nice, everyone was being.

She lay back in the water and marvelled at how things had turned out. She'd acted on impulse, maybe for the first time in her life, and it had been exactly the right thing to do.

Fifty-three years of age. Taken her long enough.

DECEMBER:
THE WEDDING

The day was bitterly cold, which hadn't deterred a large proportion of the island's population from cramming into the little church. It might have been any Sunday Mass gathering – albeit a particularly well-turned-out-for one – if it wasn't for the pew ends, decorated with sprays of holly and trailing ivy, and the hats worn by several of the ladies.

Lelia Doherty's was black, with a shimmering green peacock feather that had already almost blinded her neighbour, Maisie Kiely, twice. Moira Mulcahy's was red, with a velvet trim. Laura Dolittle's was purple to match her mascara, with a wide brim so she could kiss Gavin Connolly pretty much unobserved whenever she got the urge (which came upon her frequently).

At the top of the church a man stood, known to every person there. He wore a new grey suit with a pale blue tie and a nervous, but terribly happy, smile.

To pass the time as they waited for the bride the congregation fiddled with cameras and commented on their neighbours' outfits. The organist played something unobtrusive. Two little red-headed boys in identical brown jackets and beige trousers were heard to ask several times if they could go home yet. Their mother distracted them with jelly babies and cartons of apricot juice and colouring books of zoo animals.

Eventually the organist, on receipt of a discreet signal, increased her volume and switched to the Bridal March. There was a rustle in the pews as everyone stood and turned to face the church porch, and a collective sigh as the pink-faced bride appeared.

She wore a dress and matching coat of pale blue, and she carried a simple bouquet of cream flowers. She was followed by a matron of honour in navy wool blend and a bridesmaid in dove grey silk, hair pinned up with silver clips.

'I'm far too old to go decking myself out in something bright,' the matron of honour had declared some weeks previously, 'especially in the middle of winter.'

'You're not old, dear,' her husband had murmured. 'You'll never be old to me.'

'Oh really, you talk the greatest rubbish some-times.' But of course she had lapped it up, as he'd known she would.

Cameras flashed, necks craned, women fished for tissues as the trio reached the altar, as the groom stepped towards his bride, as the music faded and the ceremony began.

★   ★   ★

'I don't mind telling you,' the matron of honour said afterwards, holding out her sherry glass for a refill, 'when she told me she was getting married you could have knocked me down with a feather.'

'I know what you mean,' Maisie Kiely replied. 'It took us all a bit by surprise here too.' She wondered how much longer they were going to be left waiting for the meal. Nothing since her boiled egg at half eight this morning and now it was past two. A miracle she hadn't fainted with the hunger.

'Still,' the matron of honour went on, 'I have to say they seem to be well suited.'

Maisie turned to regard the newlyweds, chatting across the hotel bar with the bridesmaid. 'They're made for each other,' she said.

'Every wedding should have one set of gate-crashers,' Laura said. 'I felt it my duty, especially as we'd already arranged to be on the island for Christmas.' It was December the twenty first.

'And it would appear,' James said, pulling at the knot in his tie, 'that you are now a party of four.'

'We sure are.' Laura turned to regard Gavin, sitting at a nearby table with a twin on either side. 'And if he hadn't stayed in Nell's house we'd probably never have met. Funny old world, isn't it?'

James rolled up his tie and stuffed it into his pocket. 'It certainly is,' he replied, smiling.

★　★　★

The bell finally sounded to summon the wedding guests to the dining room, and places were taken at the various tables. The menu was uncomplicated: soup or prawn cocktail, beef or salmon, apple tart or sherry trifle. There being no best man or father of the bride in attendance, the only speech afterwards came from the groom. Like the food, it was simple.

'I never thought this day would come,' he told the hushed room. 'I still can't believe it – and I'm sure half of you can't either.' A ripple of self-conscious laughter followed.

'And I know,' he went on, 'that it all happened very fast. I was afraid she might change her mind if I gave her longer to think about it.' More laughter, and a renewed pinkness in the bride's cheeks.

He waited until the room was quiet again.

'Of course, the truth is that I knew from day one what I wanted – and, by some miracle, she felt the same. And we decided we'd both waited long enough.' He lifted his glass with his left hand and raised it to the room. 'I give you my beautiful Imelda.'

The guests stood and echoed, 'Imelda.' And as they drank her health, Hugh Fitzpatrick bent and placed a gentle kiss on his new wife's lips.

'Are bridesmaids allowed to dance with common folk?'

Nell turned and smiled. 'Not strictly speaking, but I think I could make an exception.'

James took her in his arms and they began to move around the crowded floor. 'So,' he said.

'So,' she said.

'You look wonderful.'

She tucked a wisp of shiny hair back behind its clip. 'You old charmer.'

He imagined how hard it must have been for her, walking up the aisle as a bridesmaid. He'd watched her smiling, and wondered if she was thinking of the wedding that had never happened. 'What's it like in the new house?' he asked.

'Good. Different, but good.'

Built on the site of her old one, which had had to be knocked down in the end. She'd finally moved in the week before, having stayed with her mother up to that. John Silver had moved with her, happy to be back in familiar surroundings after his long absence.

'Am I imagining things,' she asked, 'or does Andy have a bit of a crush on Jean Doherty?'

'Think so. Lelia's warned me to keep an eye on him anyway.'

James sensed the eyes of some of the islanders on them as they danced. Everyone wondering about them, together so much since Nell's engagement had been called off in August. Nothing concrete for anyone to go on, but he knew everyone wondered all the same.

'Let's take it easy,' Nell had said, 'just because.'

And because James could hear Tim's name in that, and because he'd already waited so long for her, he'd done as she'd asked, and they were taking it easy.

'Maybe you and Andy will come to dinner,' she said, 'after Christmas, when you're back from Dublin.'

It would take some time. Because of Tim, because of Andy. But because both of them knew it was just a matter of time, because of that certainty, they could wait.

'That'd be nice,' he said as the music came to an end, as he let her go with great difficulty.

As he emerged from the office he saw a woman gathering up books that were strewn across the path.

'Here—' He bent and retrieved the last two, both of which, he noticed, had been written by the same author.

As she took them from him he smelt lemons. 'Thanks so much,' she said, her accent soft northern. 'A man bumped into me and knocked them out of my hand. He must have been in a wild hurry to get somewhere because he never stopped.'

The fringe of her straight black hair was thick and blunt. The rest fell to skim her shoulders. She wore a burgundy wool dress under an open cream coat and soft black boots. She was tall, almost his own height. There was a purple gleam in her hair that was echoed by a smudge of colour above her eyes, which were grey.

'Which way are you going?' he asked.

She used her elbow to gesture. 'Just as far as the library on the next block.' She clasped the pile of books, half a dozen or so, to her chest. Her nails were oval and unpainted.

'In that case, I can take them,' he said. 'I'm going that way.'

'Ach, no, they're really not that heavy—' but she didn't resist as he reached and took the pile of books from her. 'Well, if you don't mind, that would be lovely. Thanks again.'

They began to walk. A few people hurried past them – on their way, he guessed, to Grafton Street or Stephen's Green, just a few blocks away. Three shopping days before Christmas, the city pulsed with even more life than usual.

'I'm guessing you're a fan of . . .' He glanced down and named the author.

She laughed as they approached the intersection. 'Actually I'm not, not in the least. I'm in a book club with five others. We try to find different books written by the same author. We think it's more interesting than everyone reading the same book.'

'And they've given you the job,' he said, 'of doing the library runs.'

'Not at all – we rotate. We're fierce democratic.'

The lights changed and they crossed the road with the other pedestrians.

'You're from the north,' he said.

'Donegal.'

'Going home for Christmas?'

617

'I am, surely. Day after tomorrow.'

They approached the library. The restaurant where he was meeting his mother for lunch was two doors beyond it. He shifted his armload of books and put out his hand.

'Tim Baker,' he said, because he was tired of being alone.

An expression he couldn't define flashed across her face as she shook his hand.

'Katy,' she replied. 'Katy O'Donnell. Very nice to meet you.'